How to...

Firewalls

24 seven™

Matthew Strebe
Charles Perkins

NETWORK PRESS®
SYBEX

San Francisco   Paris   Düsseldorf   Soest   London

Associate Publisher: Guy Hart-Davis
Contracts and Licensing Manager: Kristine O'Callaghan
Acquisitions & Developmental Editor: Maureen Adams
Editor: Malka Geffen
Technical Editors: Ariel Silverstone, Eric Ray
Book Designer: Bill Gibson
Graphic Illustrators: Tony Jonick, Jerry Williams
Electronic Publishing Specialists: Grey Magauran, Nila Nichols
Project Team Leader: Lisa Reardon
Proofreaders: Richard Ganis, Elaine Lewinnek, Camera Obscura
Indexer: Ted Laux
Cover Designer: Ingalls + Associates
Cover Illustrator/Photographer: Ingalls + Associates

SYBEX, Network Press, and the Network Press logo are registered trademarks of SYBEX Inc.

24seven and the 24seven logo are trademarks of SYBEX Inc.

Screen reproductions produced with Collage Complete.
Collage Complete is a trademark of Inner Media Inc.

TRADEMARKS: SYBEX has attempted throughout this book to distinguish proprietary trademarks from descriptive terms by following the capitalization style used by the manufacturer.

The author and publisher have made their best efforts to prepare this book, and the content is based upon final release software whenever possible. Portions of the manuscript may be based upon pre-release versions supplied by software manufacturer(s). The author and the publisher make no representation or warranties of any kind with regard to the completeness or accuracy of the contents herein and accept no liability of any kind including but not limited to performance, merchantability, fitness for any particular purpose, or any losses or damages of any kind caused or alleged to be caused directly or indirectly from this book.

Library of Congress Card Number: 99-65211
ISBN: 0-7821-2529-8

Manufactured in the United States of America

10 9 8 7 6 5 4 3 2 1

Acknowledgements

I'd like to thank my co-author, Charles Perkins, for stepping up to help on what was to have been a solo project when I realized how horribly wrong I'd been about how long this project should take. Without his help, you'd be reading these words at least two months in the future.

I'd like to thank the people at Sybex for putting this book together, especially Malka Geffen for remaining enthusiastic for months longer than expected, Maureen Adams for putting up with my technical difficulties, Guy Hart-Davis for the informative discussion of the various sizes of wine vessels, and Rodnay Zaks for writing my first technical book. Also thanks to Ariel Silverstone and Eric Ray for making sure everything passed the smell test. Also thanks to the unsung heroes at Sybex: Kristine O'Callaghan, Senoria Bilbo-Brown, Richard Ganis, Grey Magauran, Nila Nichols, and Lisa Reardon. Thanks also to my customers for providing the experience upon which this book is based.

–Matthew Strebe

I'd like to thank everyone at Sybex for the hard work they've put into this book, especially Guy Hart-Davis, Maureen Adams, Malka Geffen, and Lisa Reardon. I'd also like to thank my family for their constant support: Charles & Georgia, Donna & Cliff, Cathy & Jeff, Becky & Mike, and Joe.

–Charles Perkins

Contents at a Glance

Table of Contents

Introduction

Firewalls are among the newest developments in Internet technology. Developed from rudimentary security systems that major computer vendors like Compaq and IBM developed to secure their own networks in the mid eighties, these network sentinels have developed in lock-step with the burgeoning threat of information warfare. The most interesting and innovative developments, like Network Address Translation and multi-layer security filtering, are so new that books just two years old are already obsolete—as I expect this edition will be in two years' time.

The security problems of the past could be solved with simple packet filters and dial-back modem banks. The security problems of the future will require rifling through and validating every byte of an Internet message, requiring encrypted certification of a Web site's true identity before connecting, and then encrypting nearly everything that travels between. Fortunately, as technology and the technological society it mirrors progress, these measures will become simple and invisible. As vendors make operating systems more hardened against attack, the World Wide Web will secretly grow more secure for people who will freely surf the Web as they please, hampered only by the occasionally warning that a site is not accredited or that a message contains suspicious content. This is as it should be.

The security problems of today are most effectively solved with firewalls and virtual private tunnels. Peripheral security utilities like intrusion detectors and security scanners do their part to alarm and alert, but firewalls will remain the foundation of Internet security until their functionality is built into the very protocols upon which the Internet operates and until every Internet-connected computer contains the equivalent of a firewall. Even then, centralized management of Internet policy may make firewalls a permanent addition to corporate networking.

About This Book

This book was written to accomplish one goal: to teach network administrators what they need to know to understand the Internet security threat, the technologies used to prevent it, and the products that exist to help them. It's the book I wish I'd had when I couldn't find a common language between various vendors to compare firewall literature and books heavy on theory to the marketing blurbs I read on Web sites, and when I needed help matching a specific customer's requirements to a specific firewall product.

This book will help you answer questions like these:

- What's the difference between packet filtering and stateful inspection, and why is it important?

- What's the difference between using Network Address Translation and a proxy server to hide clients?
- How much can I expect to budget for a firewall?
- Which firewall is right for my company?

This book was written primarily for active network administrators with the assumption that they understand the use and configuration of TCP/IP, and that they are used to working with Windows NT, Novell NetWare, or UNIX (although very little operating system specific information is presented).

If you're not a network administrator, but you know you need a firewall, this book can still help you find one—a number of Plug-and-Play firewall devices exist that are both secure and easy to use and configure. If you fall into this later category, you may find your eyes glazing over during some of the more technical discussions early in the book. Feel free to skip over anything you don't understand and come back to it later if you need.

How This Book is Organized

This book is divided into four parts that consist of 19 chapters and one appendix. You should read through Parts I and II in order from beginning to end, but you can read the remainder of the book in any order.

Part I: The Internet

Chapters 1–5 cover information you should understand before we delve into firewall technology, like the Internet and the basic functions if firewalls, hackers, encryption, and a detailed explanation of the inner workings of TCP/IP.

Part II: Firewall Technology

Chapters 6–10 cover the five major technologies upon which most firewalls are based: packet filtering, Network Address Translation, authentication, and tunneling. It also details those measures you should take with any firewall to make sure it's securely configured.

Part III: Operating System Support for Firewalling

Chapters 11 and 12 discuss what you can do with major operating systems to secure the services you provide. This is especially important for public servers.

Part IV: Commercial Firewalls

Chapters 13–16 are the really unique part of this book—they provide an overview of a large portion of the commercially available firewall solutions. You can use these chapters to compare various firewalls and find the right fit for your organization.

Part V: Additional Security Resources

Chapters 17–19 cover additional tools you can use to secure your network beyond firewalling, as well as a description of the various attacks hackers use to compromise firewalls.

Where to Go From Here

Security is not a static thing, it's a continually evolving process. You can't just plug in a firewall and expect it to solve your security problem forever. Attacks change, methods become obsolete, and so do firewalls. To obtain true security, you have to maintain constant vigilance. The easiest way I've found to do that is by getting on some of the mailing lists provided by organizations listed in Appendix A and by visiting their Web sites.

The Web site for this book is available at www.24sevenbooks.com, where I'll post new links to important security information on a regular basis. Think of it as your Web portal to the world of security.

Part 1

The Internet

Topics Covered:

- How the Internet works
- How firewalls work
- Who hacks
- Hacker's motivations
- TCP/IP fundamentals
- TCP/IP higher level protocols
- How hackers exploit weaknesses in TCP/IP
- How encryption works
- How encryption provides security over the Internet
- How encryption provides a mechanism to prove user identity

1

Understanding Firewalls

Nations without controlled borders cannot ensure the security and safety of their citizens, nor can they prevent piracy and theft. Networks without controlled access cannot ensure the security or privacy of stored data, nor can they keep network resources from being exploited by hackers.

The communication efficiency provided by the Internet has caused a rush to attach private networks directly to it. Direct Internet connections make it easy for hackers to exploit private network resources. Prior to the Internet, the only widely available way for a hacker to connect from home to a private network was direct dialing with modems and the public telephony network. Remote access security was a relatively small issue.

When you connect your private network to the Internet, you are actually connecting your network directly to every other network attached to the Internet directly. There's no inherent central point of security control.

Firewalls are used to create security checkpoints at the boundaries of private networks. By providing the routing function between the private network and the Internet, firewalls inspect all communications passing between the two networks and either pass or drop the communications depending on how they match the programmed policy rules. If your firewall is properly configured and contains no serious exploitable bugs, your network will be as free from risk as possible.

There are literally hundreds of firewall products available, and there are different theories from different security experts on how firewalls should be used to secure your network. This chapter will explore the operation of a generic firewall in detail, outline the important features you need in a firewall, and discuss how firewalls should be deployed in networks of any size. The remainder of Part 1 covers the concepts introduced in this chapter in more detail. Part 2 covers advanced firewall concepts in detail. Part 3 of the book compares popular products, including their installation and basic configuration.

Firewall Components

Firewalls keep your Internet connection as secure as possible by inspecting and then approving or rejecting each connection attempt made between your internal network and external networks like the Internet. Strong firewalls protect your network at all software layers—from the data link layer up through the application layer.

Firewalls sit on the borders of your network—at those gateways that provide access to other networks. For that reason, firewalls are considered border security. The concept of border security is important—without it, every host on your network would have to perform the functions of a firewall themselves, needlessly consuming compute resources and increasing the amount of time required to connect, authenticate, and encrypt data in local area, high speed networks. Firewalls allow you to centralize all external security services in machines that are optimized for and dedicated to the task.

By their nature, firewalls create bottlenecks between the internal and external networks because all traffic transiting between the internal network and the external must pass through a single point of control. This is a small price to pay for security. Since external leased-line connections are relatively slow compared to the speed of modern computers, the latency caused by firewalls can be completely transparent.

Firewalls primarily function using three fundamental methods:

Packet Filtering   Rejects TCP/IP packets from unauthorized hosts and rejects connection attempts to unauthorized services.

Network Address Translation (NAT)   Translates the IP addresses of internal hosts to hide them from outside monitoring. NAT is also called IP masquerading.

Proxy Services   Makes high-level application connections on behalf of internal hosts to completely break the network layer connection between internal and external hosts.

Most firewalls also perform two other important security services:

Encrypted Authentication   Allows users on the public network to prove their identity to the firewall in order to gain access to the private network from external locations.

Encrypted Tunnels Establishes a secure connection between two private networks over a public medium like the Internet. This allows physically separated networks to use the Internet rather than leased-line connections to communicate. Tunneling is also called Virtual Private Networking (VPN).

Nearly all firewalls use these basic methods to provide a security service. There are literally hundreds of firewall products on the market now, all vying for your security dollar. Most are very strong products that vary only in superficial details. The remainder of this section covers the five primary functions that most firewalls support.

You can use devices or servers that perform only one of the above functions; for instance, you could have a router that performs packet filtering, and then a proxy server in a separate machine. This way, the packet filter must either pass traffic through to the proxy server, or the proxy server must sit outside your network without the protection of packet filtering. Both are more dangerous than using a single firewall product that performs all the security functions in one place.

Packet Filters

The first Internet firewalls were just packet filters. Filters compare network protocols (such as IP) and transport protocol packets (such as TCP) to a database of rules and forward only those packets that conform to the criteria specified in the database of rules. Filters can either be implemented in routers or in the TCP/IP stacks of servers (see Figure 1.1).

Figure 1.1 Filtered Internet connections block undesired traffic.

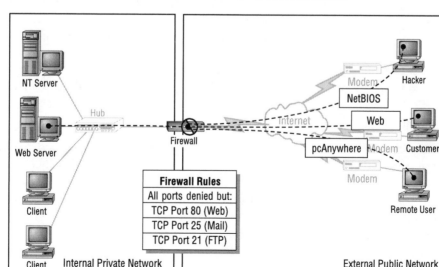

Filters implemented inside routers prevent suspicious traffic from reaching the destination network, whereas TCP/IP filter modules in servers merely prevent that specific machine from responding to suspicious traffic. The traffic still reaches the network and could target any machine on it. Routing filters protect all the machines on the destination network from suspicious traffic. For that reason, filtering in the TCP/IP stacks of servers (such as that provided by Windows NT) should only be used in addition to routed filtering, not instead of it. Filters typically follow these rules:

- Dropping inbound connection attempts but allowing outbound connection attempts to pass.
- Eliminating TCP packets bound for ports that shouldn't be available to the Internet (such as the NetBIOS session port) but allowing packets that should (such as SMTP) to pass. Most filters can specify exactly which server a specific sort of traffic should go to—for instance, SMTP traffic on port 25 should only go to the IP address of a mail server.
- Restricting inbound access to certain IP ranges.

WARNING Simple packet filters or routers with a packet filtering function that requires opening ports above 1023 for return channels are not effective security devices. These packet filters do not prevent internal users or Trojan horses from setting up a service on a client station in the port range above 1024 and simply listening for connection attempts from the outside. Firewalls (stateful inspection filters and security proxies) only open channels for servers that have been invited back in by a connection attempt from inside the security perimeter—choose them rather than simple packet filters that can't maintain the state of a connection.

Sophisticated filters use proprietary algorithms to examine the states of all connections that flow through them, looking for the telltale signs of hacking, such as source routing, ICMP redirection, and IP spoofing. Connections that exhibit these characteristics are dropped.

Internal clients are generally allowed to create connections to outside hosts, and external hosts are usually prevented from initiating connection attempts. When an internal host decides to initiate a TCP connection, it sends a TCP message to the IP address and port number of the public server (for example, `www.microsoft.com:80` to connect to Microsoft's Web site). In the connection initiation message, it tells the remote server what its IP address is and which port it is listening for a response on (for example, `localhost: 2050`).

WARNING Older FTP clients and servers may only work correctly if the remote server is allowed to establish the data channel on TCP port 20, which violates the general rule that all inbound connection attempts are dropped. More recent FTP implementations support passive connection, which allows the client to establish the command channel (21) and the data channel (20). Modern stateful inspection firewalls will allow the client to establish its back channel. It usually isn't worth compromising security to support older FTP software.

The external server sends data back by transmitting it to the port given by the internal client. Since your firewall inspects all the traffic exchanged between both hosts, it knows that the connection was initiated by an internal host attached to its internal interface, what that host's IP address is, and what port that host expects to receive return traffic on. The firewall then remembers to allow the host addressed in the connection message to return traffic to the internal host's IP address only at the port specified.

When the hosts involved in the connection close down the TCP connection, the firewall removes the entry in its state table (its connection memory) that allows the remote host to return traffic to the internal host.

Filtering does not completely solve the Internet security problem. First, the IP addresses of computers inside the filter are present in outbound traffic, which makes it somewhat easy to determine the type and number of Internet hosts inside a filter, and to target attacks against those addresses. Filtering does not hide the identity of hosts inside the filter.

Filters cannot check all the fragments of an IP message based on higher-level protocols like TCP headers because the header exists only in the first fragment. Subsequent fragments have no header information and can only be compared to IP level rules, which are usually relaxed to allow some traffic through the filter. This allows bugs in the destination IP stacks of computers on the network to be exploited, and could allow communications with a Trojan horse installed inside the network.

Operating System Filtering

You might not be aware that most versions of UNIX and Windows NT Server include packet filtering in the TCP/IP protocol interface. You can use this filtering in addition to a strong firewall to control access to individual servers; you can also use this filtering to provide an additional measure of internal security without the cost of firewalls inside your organization. Just as filtering alone is not sufficient to protect your network entirely, your operating system's internal filtering is not sufficient to create a completely secure environment.

Do not rely upon your operating system's built-in filtering alone to protect your network. You should use your operating system's filtering functions inside your network to establish filters to pass only those protocols you explicitly intend to serve. This prevents software from working in ways you don't expect and keeps Trojan horses from functioning even if they manage to get installed.

Basic OS filtering allows you to define acceptance criteria for each network adapter in your computer for incoming connections based on:

- IP protocol number
- TCP port number
- UDP port number

The filtering usually does not apply to outbound connections (those originating on your server), and is defined separately for each adapter in your system.

NOTE   Windows 2000 supports outbound filtering; Windows NT 4 does not.

A typical server sets up services to listen on the following ports. These ports must be open through your filter for these services to work correctly.

Simple TCP/IP services usually listen on the following ports:

Port	TCP/IP Service
7	Echo
9	Discard
13	Daytime
17	Quote of the Day
19	Character Generator

Internet Servers usually listen on the following ports:

Port	Server
21	File Transfer Protocol (FTP)
23	Telnet
70	Gopher
80	World Wide Web (HTTP)
119	Net News (NNTP)

File Servers usually listen on the following ports:

Port	Service
53	Domain Name Service (DNS service, if installed).
135	RPC Locator Service (Windows NT only).
137	NetBIOS Name Service (WINS servers only).
139	NetBIOS Session Service (Windows network and SMB/CIFS servers only).
515	LPR is used by the TCP/IP print service, if installed.
530	Remote Procedure Call (RPC connections are used by the Windows NT WinLogon service as well as many other high-level network applications).

Mail Servers are usually configured to listen on the following ports:

Port	Mail Server
25	Simple Mail Transfer Protocol (Mail server to server exchanges).
110	Post Office Protocol version 3 (Server to client mail exchanges).
143	Internet Mail Access Protocol (Client access to mail server).

If you install other service software, you must make sure your server's filter is set up to listen on the ports required by the service—otherwise the service will not work. Find out from the software manufacturer what ports are required for that service. This does not apply to border firewalls, which should only be configured to pass a service if you intend to provide that service to the public.

Disallow all protocols and addresses by default, then explicitly allow services and hosts you wish to support. Disallow all connection attempts to hosts inside your network. By allowing any inbound connections, you allow hackers to establish connections to Trojan horses or exploit bugs in service software. Filter out and do not respond to ICMP redirect and echo (ping) messages. Drop all packets that are TCP source routed. Source routing is rarely used for legitimate purposes. Drop all external routing protocol (RIP, OSPF) updates bound for internal routers. No one outside your network should be transmitting RIP updates. Consider disallowing fragments beyond number zero, since this functionality is largely obsolete and often exploited. Place public service hosts like Web servers and SMTP servers outside your packet filters rather than opening holes through your packet filters. Do not rely upon packet filtering alone to protect your network.

Using IP Masquerades

Network Address Translation (NAT), also known as IP masquerading, solves the problem of hiding internal hosts. NAT is actually a fundamental proxy: A single host makes requests on behalf of all internal hosts, thus hiding their identity from the public network. Windows NT does not provide this function—you must use a third-party firewall if you want IP masquerading. Linux and many other UNIX operating systems do provide this function as part of the operating system distribution.

NOTE   Windows 2000 supports Network Address Translation; Windows NT 4 does not.

NAT hides internal IP addresses by converting all internal host addresses to the address of the firewall. The firewall then retransmits the data payload of the internal host from its own address using the TCP port number to keep track of which connections on the public side map to which hosts on the private side. To the Internet, all the traffic on your network appears to be coming from one extremely busy computer.

NAT effectively hides all TCP/IP-level information about your internal hosts from prying eyes on the Internet. Address translation also allows you to use any IP address range you want on your internal network even if those addresses are already in use elsewhere on the Internet. This means you don't have to register a large block from InterNIC or reassign network numbers from those you simply plugged in before you connected your network to the Internet.

WARNING   Although you can use any block of IP addresses behind a firewall with NAT, be aware that you may encounter strange problems accessing Internet hosts that have the same public IP address as a computer inside your network. For that reason, use the reserved 10.0.0.0 network (or one of the other reserved networks) inside your firewall to avoid these problems.

Finally, NAT allows you to multiplex a single IP address across an entire network. Many small companies rely upon the services of an upstream Internet service provider that may be reluctant to provide large blocks of addresses because their own range is relatively restricted. You may want to share a single dial-up or cable modem address without telling your ISP. These options are all possible using IP masquerades.

On the down side, NAT is implemented only at the TCP/IP level. Again, this means that information hidden in the data payload of TCP/IP traffic could be transmitted to a higher-level service and used to exploit weaknesses in higher-level traffic or to communicate with a Trojan horse. You'll still have to use a higher-level service like a proxy to prevent higher-level service security breaches.

Proxies

NAT solves many of the problems associated with direct Internet connections, but it still doesn't completely restrict the flow of datagrams through your firewall. It's possible for someone with a network monitor to watch traffic coming out of your firewall and determine that the firewall is translating addresses for other machines. It is then possible for a hacker to hijack TCP connections or to spoof connections back through the firewall.

Application-level proxies prevent this. Application-level proxies allow you to completely disconnect the flow of network-level protocols through your firewall and restrict traffic only to higher-level protocols like HTTP, FTP, and SMTP.

Proxies stand in for outbound connection attempts to servers and then make the request to the actual target server on behalf of the client. When the server returns data, the proxy transmits that data to the client. Proxies essentially perform a benign man-in-the-middle attack, and they're a good example of how any router between you and another end system could potentially perform any sort of processing without your permission.

Application proxies (like Microsoft Proxy Server) are unlike Network Address Translators and filters in that the Internet client application is (usually) set up to talk to the proxy. For instance, you tell Internet Explorer the address of your Web proxy, and Internet Explorer sends all Web requests to that server rather than resolving the IP address and establishing a connection directly.

> **NOTE**   Without a filter or IP masquerade, there's nothing to prevent users from bypassing the application proxy by simply disabling the proxy settings in the Web browser.

Application proxies don't have to run on firewalls; any server can perform the role of a proxy either inside or outside your network. Without a firewall, you still don't have any real security, so you need both. At least some sort of packet filter must be in place to protect the proxy server from network layer denial-of-service attacks (like the infamous "ping of death"). And, if the proxy doesn't run on the firewall, you'll have to open a channel through your firewall one way or another. Ideally, your firewall should perform the proxy function. This keeps packets from the public side from being forwarded through your firewall.

Some firewall proxies are more sophisticated than others. Because they have the functionality of an IP filter and masquerade, they can simply block outbound connection attempts (on port 80 in the case of HTTP) to remote hosts rather than having the client software configured to address the proxy service specifically. The firewall proxy then connects to the remote server and requests data on behalf of the blocked client. The retrieved data is returned to the requesting client using the firewall's NAT functionality to look just like the actual remote server. Proxies that operate in this manner are said to be transparent.

Security proxies are even capable of performing application-level filtering for specific content. For instance, some firewall HTTP proxies look for tags in HTML pages that refer to Java or ActiveX embedded applets and then strip out that content from them. This prevents the applet from executing on your client computers and eliminates the risk that a user will accidentally download a Trojan horse. This sort of filtering is extremely important because filtering, proxying, and masquerading can't prevent your network from being compromised if your users are lured into downloading a Trojan horse embedded in an ActiveX applet.

You may have noticed that as we climb through the networking layers, the security services have gotten more specific. For instance, filtering is specific to IP and then to TCP and UDP. Applications that use IP with other protocols like Banyan Vines must use special high-cost or unusually robust firewalls.

Proxies are extremely specific because they can only work for a specific application. For instance, you must have a proxy software module for HTTP, another proxy module for FTP, and another module for Telnet. As these protocols evolve (HTTP is particularly fast moving), the proxy module for that protocol will have to be updated.

Many protocols exist that are either proprietary or rare enough that no security proxies exist. Proxies don't exist for proprietary application protocols like Lotus Notes, so those protocols must either be sent through a Network Layer filter or proxied by a generic TCP proxy that regenerates the packet but simply transfers the payload. SOCKS is a specific form of generic proxy, which are sometimes called circuit-level gateways. Although generic proxying cannot prevent attacks from the content of a protocol, it is still more secure than filtered routing because the Network Layer packets are completely regenerated and thus scrubbed of malformations that might not be detected by the firewall.

Whenever possible, use proxy servers for all application protocols. Consider disallowing services for which you do not have proxy servers. Use high-level proxies capable of stripping executable content like ActiveX and Java from Web pages.

Encrypted Tunnels

Encrypted tunnels (also called Virtual Private Networks or VPNs) allow you to securely connect two physically separated networks over the Internet without exposing your data to monitors. Encrypted tunnels on their own could be subject to redirection attempts, spoofed connection initiation, and all manner of hacking indignity while the tunnel is being established. But when implemented as an integral part of a firewall, the firewall authentication and security services can be used to prevent exploitation while the tunnel is being established.

Once established, the tunnels are impervious to exploitation so long as the encryption remains secure. And, since firewalls sit at the Internet borders, they exist at the perfect terminal points for each end of the tunnel. Essentially, your private networks can pass traffic as if they were two subnets in the same domain.

Encrypted tunnels also allow users to address remote internal hosts directly by their hidden IP addresses. IP masquerades and packet filters would prevent this if the connection attempt came directly from the Internet.

> **TIP**   The Point-to-Point Tunneling Protocol for Windows NT provides an encrypted tunnel using the security services of the Remote Access Server. Most distributions of Linux include support for encrypted tunnels.

Use leased lines rather than encrypted tunnels whenever practical. Use encrypted tunnels for all communications over the Internet between organizational units if leased lines are not available or are cost prohibitive. Never communicate between organizational units over the Internet without using some form of encryption. Unencrypted packet headers contain valuable nuggets of information about the structure of your internal network.

Encrypted Authentication

Encrypted authentication allows external users on the Internet to prove to a firewall that they are authorized users and thereby authorized to open a connection through the firewall to the internal network. The encrypted authentication might use any number of secure authentication protocols. Once the connection is established, it may or may not be encrypted depending upon the firewall product in use and whether additional software has been installed on the client to support tunneling.

Using encryption authentication is convenient because it occurs at the transport level between a client software package and the firewall. Once the connection is open, all normal application software and operating system logon software will run without hindrance—so you don't have to use special software packages that support your specific firewall.

Unfortunately, encrypted authentication reduces the security of your firewall. By its nature, it causes the following problems:

- The firewall must respond on some port because it listens for connection attempts. This can show hackers that the firewall exists.
- The connection could be redirected using ICMP after establishment, especially if it's not encrypted.

- A hacker who monitored the establishment might be able to spoof the address of the authorized client to gain access inside the network without redirecting any existing connections.

- A stolen laptop computer with the appropriate keys could be used to gain access to the network.

- Work-at-home employees could become a target for breaking and entering because their computers are able to access the private network.

- The authentication procedure could be buggy or less than completely secure, thus allowing anyone on the Internet to open holes through the firewall.

All of these risks are not so likely to actually occur. Administrators of medium- to low-risk environments should not feel uncomfortable using encrypted authentication as long as the connection is encrypted for the duration.

NOTE   Linux comes with a form of encrypted authentication called IP Chains, which is much like an encrypted tunnel but without the encryption. Windows NT uses encrypted authentication by default, but it is weak and not appropriate for use on the Internet.

Effective Border Security

To maintain the absolute minimum level of effective Internet security, you must control your border security using firewalls that perform all three of the basic firewall functions (packet filtering, Network Address Translation, and high-level service proxy). Your firewalls must also be dedicated primarily to the performance of firewall functions; avoid the temptation to run other services such as mail, Web, or other public services on the firewall unless the service software comes from the firewall software vendor. Even in this case, be aware that you are increasing your risk because a bug in any of the high-level services running on your firewall might be exploited to bypass the firewall completely.

Minimize the services running on the firewalls. This reduces the complexity of the software running on the machine, thereby reducing the probability that a bug in the operating system or security software will allow a security breach. In the case of Windows NT, none of the services in the service control panel are needed for a computer running only as a firewall. Turn off all services that the server will allow you to shut off and set them to start manually. In the case of Linux, install only those packages necessary for the operation of the firewall, or select the "firewall" installation option if the distribution has one. Normally, you won't have to deal with this because the firewall software installation program will shut down all unnecessary services for you. If it doesn't, look elsewhere for firewall software.

It's always tempting to pile services like HTTP, FTP, Telnet, Gopher, and mail onto the same machine you use as an Internet router and firewall because it's cheaper and because that machine probably has a lot of spare compute time and disk space. Unfortunately, few operating systems are both secure enough and bug-free enough to guarantee that services won't interfere with each other or that a service won't crash the firewall. It's also quite probable that a high-level service running on the firewall, even if it doesn't affect other security services, could provide a way to circumvent the security services of the firewall. And lastly, as I mentioned earlier in this chapter, many services contain logon banners or automatically generated error pages that identify the firewall product you are using. This could be dangerous if hackers have found a weakness in your specific firewall.

You must also enforce a single point of control in your firewall policy. If you have more than one firewall in your company (perhaps one firewall attaching each remote office to the Internet), you need to make absolutely certain they are all configured the same way.

> **WARNING**   A lapse on any of your firewalls can compromise your entire network, especially if you use secure tunneling or private leased lines to connect offices. Hackers can be relied upon to use the path of least resistance.

Comparing Firewall Functionality

There is a common misconception among network administrators that a firewall has to be based on the same operating system as the network file servers—UNIX firewalls for UNIX-based networks and NT firewalls for Windows NT-based networks. In fact, there's no functional reason why the operating system used by a firewall should be the same as that used by the network, since (and only in very special circumstances) you'll never run any other software on the firewall computer.

All firewalls filter TCP/IP traffic, and in most cases you'll set them up once and leave them to do their job with minor tweaks as security policies and work habits change in the organization. Some firewalls run proprietary operating systems that aren't related to UNIX or Windows NT; they are just as appropriate on any network.

The second most important factor in choosing a firewall operating system (after security, of course) is familiarity—the administrator should be familiar with the user interface and know how to configure the firewall correctly. Most Windows NT-based firewalls are far easier to set up than UNIX-based firewalls, but many UNIX-based firewalls are catching up by using Java-based graphical interfaces that run remotely on the administrator's PC.

Some firewall vendors claim that their products are superior to firewalls based on Windows NT or standard versions of UNIX because the products are based on a "hardened" implementation of the TCP/IP protocol stack or a theoretically more secure operating system. They also claim that bugs in Windows NT or UNIX releases can be exploited to get past the firewall software of their competitors. While this may be true, those vendors can't prove that similar bugs don't exist in their own software. In fact, there's no practical way to prove that complex code is bug free, and firewall vendors are no more likely to get it absolutely right than are large vendors like Microsoft or Sun.

One major advantage of using a widely available operating system as the foundation of a firewall is that the code is put through its paces by millions of users. Bugs are more likely to be found and corrected, and patches are available far sooner and with greater regularity than is true for proprietary products provided by smaller vendors who usually don't have the programming resources to throw at problems as they arise.

Most firewall products that are based on a standard operating system don't rely on the standard TCP/IP stack or higher-level services that ship with the operating system; they implement their own TCP/IP stack so that they can have absolute control over its operation. The base operating system serves only as a platform for the firewall software, providing functions like booting, multitasking, and user interface.

Firewall products vary in the following ways:

Security   Some firewall products are fundamentally flawed because they rely too heavily on the host operating system, because they contain bugs that can be exploited, or because there is a flaw in the authentication protocol used for remote authentication.

Interface   Some firewalls are very difficult to configure because you must administer them via Telnet or an attached console and learn some cryptic command line interface. Others use very intuitive graphical interfaces that make configuration easy and obvious.

Enterprise Functionality   Some firewalls are fortresses unto themselves, while others use a centrally maintained security policy that is replicated among all firewalls in the enterprise.

Security Features   Many firewalls offer important security features such as virtual private networking and encrypted authentication to allow remote office networking with a high degree of security.

Service Features   Some firewalls include services such as FTP, Telnet, HTTP, and so forth so that you don't have to dedicate a machine to those functions. These features can be convenient, but they're often somewhat obsolete in functionality and can reduce the security of the firewall if they aren't properly implemented. Also, many services reveal a copyright that tells hackers exactly which firewall product you are using and allows them to target any weaknesses it may have.

Your primary criterion for firewalls should be security. The next most important feature is ease of use for you—you must be able to correctly configure a firewall for it to work correctly. Flashy features, performance, and services galore are tertiary to these primary requirements.

Problems Firewalls Can't Solve

No network attached to the Internet can be made completely secure. Firewalls are extremely effective, they will keep the hacking masses at bay, but there are so many different ways to exploit network connections that no method is entirely secure. Many administrators mistakenly assume that once their firewall is online and shown to be effective, their security problem is gone. That's simply not the case.

For example, let's say that the only thing you allow through your firewall is e-mail. An employee gets a message from a branch office asking him to e-mail a CAD file to them. So the employee looks at the From address, verifies that it's correct, clicks reply, attaches the file, and unknowingly sends the CAD file to the hackers that forged the e-mail request because the Reply-to address isn't the same as the From address. Your firewall can't realistically do anything about this type of exploitation because many typical users have different From and Reply-to addresses for very valid reasons, like they send mail from multiple e-mail addresses but only want to receive mail at one.

There is another serious threat to the security of your network: hidden border crossing. Modems provide the ability for any user on your network to dial out to their own Internet service provider and completely circumvent your firewall. Modems are cheap and they come in most computers sold these days. All modern client operating systems come with the software required for setting up modems to connect to a dial-up Internet service provider. And it's a good bet that most of your computer-savvy employees have their own dial-up networking accounts they could use from work.

Most users don't understand that all IP connections are a security risk. Modem PPP connections to the Internet are bi-directional just like leased lines. And there's a good chance that their client has file sharing turned on, so their computer can be exploited directly from the Internet.

> **WARNING**   It's quite common for businesses with firewalls to allow unrestricted file and print sharing among peers because it's an easy and efficient way for users to transfer files. If one of those users is dialed into the Net, it's also an easy and efficient way for hackers to transfer your files.

Why would a user choose a dial-up modem connection when they have a faster and secure Internet connection? Reasons include:

- Your firewall doesn't pass Internet Relay Chat and they want to talk to their friends.
- So they can use NetPhone to talk to their mother for free.
- So they can work from home using pcAnywhere.
- Because AOL uses a port your firewall doesn't pass and they want to check their personal e-mail.
- Because you filter FTP and they want to download a file.
- Because your network is configured to block pornography sites.

Users dial out so they can circumvent your security policy without your knowledge. To control border security, you must control all the border crossings; it must be impossible to establish a new border crossing without your permission. Exceptions to this rule endanger the security of your entire network.

Reduce the number of connections to the Internet to the minimum number possible: one per campus. Many large organizations allow only a single link to the Internet at headquarters and then route all remote offices to that point using the same frame relay lines used to connect internal networks.

Don't allow dial-up connections to the Internet. Remove modems and all other uncontrolled network access devices. Disable free COM ports in the BIOS settings of client computers and password protect the BIOS to prevent users from overriding your security settings.

Don't allow unrestricted file sharing. Use file sharing with user-based authentication or, at the very least, passwords. Don't install file and print sharing on client computers unless absolutely necessary. Encourage users to store all files on network file servers, and create server pools of resources like CD-ROMs or modems that can be centrally controlled.

Configure internal client computers with IP addresses in the 10 domain, which is not routed by most Internet routers. Use an IP masquerade to translate these internal addresses to routable external addresses. This may prevent hackers from exploiting modem connections into your network beyond the computer that established the connection.

Border Security Options

Once you've got your firewall running on the border between your private network and the Internet, you're going to run into a problem. How do you provide the public services your customers need while securing your internal network from attack? There is more than one answer to this question, and which one is right depends entirely upon your security posture and the level of service you need to provide.

Methods used by companies to protect their networks range from the simple to the complex, the risky to the very secure. These methods (in order of security risk from highest to lowest) are:

1. Filtered packet services

2. Single firewall with internal public servers

3. Single firewall with external public servers

4. Dual firewalls or multihomed firewalls

5. Enterprise firewalls

6. Disconnection

The following sections discuss each method in detail, along with relative risks and issues.

Filtered Packet Services

Most Internet Service Providers provide packet filtering as a value-added service for leased-line customers. For a small monthly charge (generally about $100), your ISP will probably set up their own firewall to filter traffic into and out of your network. Some ISPs also offer proxy servers and IP masquerades, but you may still be at risk from security attacks by other customers served by that ISP. Remember that all hackers have an ISP somewhere along the line. Figure 1.2 illustrates how filtered packet services work.

Figure 1.2   Filtered packet service

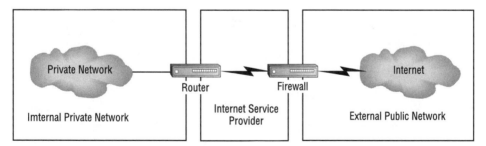

There are a number of problems with filtered firewall services:

- Packet filters can be exploited more easily than complete firewalls.

- Your security is in the hands of a third party. Their motivations may not always coincide with yours, especially if a legal dispute arises between your company and theirs.

- The responsibility for reliability isn't controllable.

- There's no provision for alarming and alerting.

- Configuration is a difficult and error-prone administrative hassle. Reconfiguration is also a pain in the neck if the ISP doesn't have a strong customer support ethic.
- You are probably vulnerable to the ISP's other subscribers, who are usually inside the same firewall.

ISP provided packet filters have the following advantage:

- No up-front capital expenditure is required.

Even if the firewall service provided by an ISP were complete, it's still never a good idea to put the security of your network in the hands of another organization. You don't know anything about your ISP's employees, and you don't know what measures your ISP might take if for some reason a dispute arose between your company and theirs. Add to that the simple fact that most people who can hack do so at least occasionally, and that many good hackers work for the people who can get them closest to the action.

Locally control and administer all security services for your network. Don't put responsibility for the security of your network in the hands of an external organization. Don't rely solely on packet filters for security protection from the Internet.

The Single-Firewall Approach

The simplest complete border security solution is that of the single firewall. With one firewall and one connection to the Internet, you have a single point of management and control. Figure 1.3 shows a single firewall border security solution.

Figure 1.3   A single firewall with public servers exposed to the Internet.

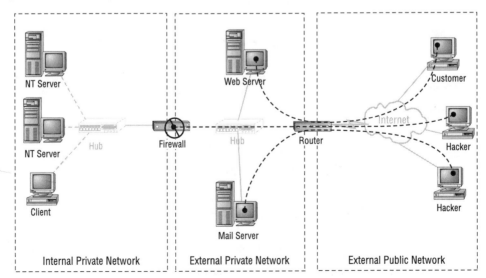

You have a problem if you intend to provide public services like a Web or FTP site, or if you want to operate a mail server. You must either open a connection through your firewall to an internal host, or you must expose your public server to the Internet without the protection of a firewall. Both methods are risky.

The problem with putting public servers, like mail servers, outside your firewall is that they are at risk for unrestricted hacking. You can set these computers up so that they don't contain much useful information, but hacking attempts could easily cause denial of service if your servers are crashed, or at least cause embarrassment if hackers modify your Web pages. Figure 1.4 shows public servers inside the firewall.

Figure 1.4   A single firewall with public servers protected but allowing external traffic in through the firewall.

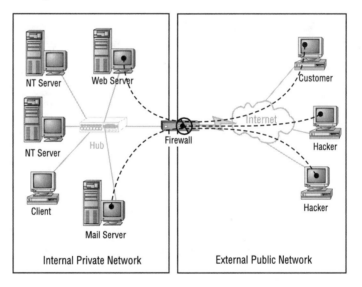

The problem with opening a path through your firewall for externally sourced connection attempts is that inappropriate packets could potentially make their way onto your internal network if they look like packets that conform to the rules used by your packet filter. It also means that a hacker who manages to exploit a bug in high-level service software might gain control of a computer inside your network—a very dangerous situation. For this reason, most organizations put public servers outside their firewalls and simply do not allow any external connections in through the firewall.

Dual Firewalls and Virtual Dual Firewalls

You can reduce the risk of having exposed public servers with two firewalls and two levels of firewall protection. Basically, you put the first firewall at your Internet connection and secure your Web servers behind it. It provides strong security, but allows connection attempts from the Internet for the services you want to provide.

Between that network and your internal network, you place a second firewall with a stronger security policy that simply does not allow external connection attempts and hides the identity of internal clients. Figure 1.5 shows a network with two firewalls providing two levels of security.

Figure 1.5   Two firewalls acting in concert to completely protect a network.

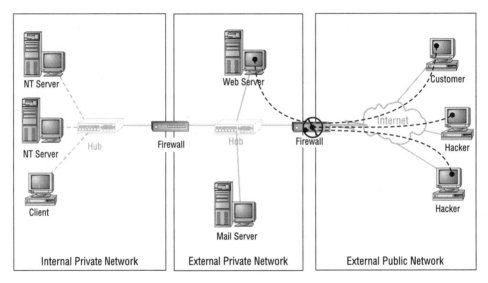

Most modern firewall products allow the use of dual virtual firewalls by providing different security policies for each attached interface in the firewall. With three interfaces—external network, internal network, and public server network; you can customize your security policy to block connection attempts to your internal network but pass certain protocols to your public server. This allows you the functionality of two firewalls using a single product. This is sometimes referred to as a *demilitarized zone* or *trihomed firewalls*. Figure 1.6 shows a trihomed firewall with different security settings for each network.

Figure 1.6   A trihomed firewall provides different security for different needs.

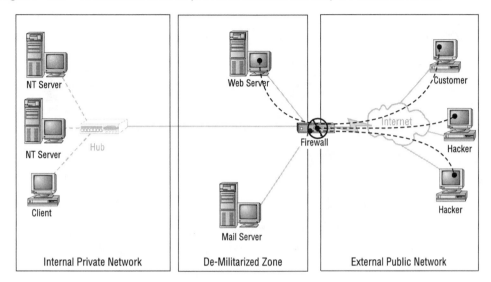

Enterprise Firewalls

Enterprise firewalls are those products that share a single, centralized firewall policy among multiple firewalls. Enterprise firewalls allow you to retain central control of security policy without having to worry about whether or not the policy is correctly implemented on each of the firewalls in your organization. The firewall policy is usually defined on a security workstation, and then replicated to each firewall in your organization using some means of secure authentication. Figure 1.7 shows an enterprise with multiple firewalls, one at each Internet connection.

> **TIP**   Dual firewalls (or trihomed firewalls that provide different security settings for each adapter) are the best bet. Keep in mind that both firewalls don't have to be of the same type. The front firewall can be a simple packet filter, but the back firewall should be a strong enterprise-quality firewall that provides the utmost in security.

Figure 1.7 Multiple firewalls in an enterprise.

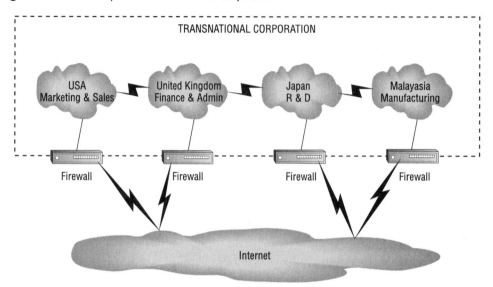

Disconnection

The most secure way to provide service on the Internet and access for internal users is not to connect your internal network to the Internet at all, but to have a separate network used only for Internet-related services. Figure 1.8 shows a network that is disconnected from the Internet.

This method is absolutely impenetrable from the Internet because no connection exists between the internal and the external networks. The public-access servers for Web, FTP, and mail are located on a small network segment that is attached to the Internet along with a few clients. The client stations contain e-mail, news, and Web browsers but no sensitive information. Employees travel to the external clients to check their e-mail, browse the Web, or perform any other Internet-related task.

This model has three very important benefits:

- The private network is absolutely secure. Data can't flow freely between the external and internal networks. You may consider putting a high-capacity removable media drive on one of the clients to facilitate large file transfers when necessary—but this can be a security problem!

- It's free. It doesn't require esoteric software or sophisticated hardware, and you can use outdated computers for the client stations.

- It provides a natural disincentive for employees to waste time surfing the Web randomly or downloading content that could cause legal liability problems.

Figure 1.8   The disconnected security model provides the most protection from Internet intrusion.

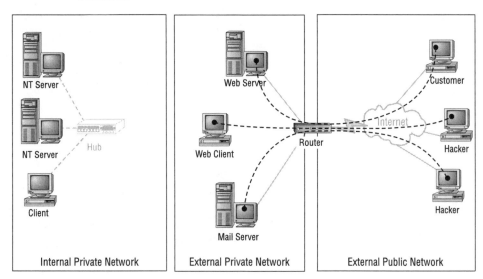

And of course, there is one very important detractor: Employees hate it. They have to travel to access stations, which are typically located in one central area. Transferring files becomes problematic. It can cause a work bottleneck if there aren't enough access stations. Many employees simply won't use it, which reduces the efficiency of e-mail and other such important business tools.

In a nutshell, disconnection is the most secure and the least efficient way to connect your employees to the Internet.

> **WARNING**   The disconnected security model provides the most incentive for employees to blow off your security policy and dial up the Internet with their modem. Make sure your security policy prevents that and that your users understand why you've chosen this model.

Don't attach your network to public networks if it can possibly be avoided. Use the disconnected network model to provide Internet access to your users rather than to your network. Use a Web and FTP hosting service rather than computers on your own network to provide your customers with information about your company. This puts the Web hosting agency at risk rather than your own network and allows you to provide no public services.

Firewall Options

A customer of mine relies on a filtered packet service from their Internet Service Provider for security. Since the client runs a very small startup business and is strapped for cash, I didn't put up too much resistance to this initially.

As part of my services for them, I made periodic light hacking attempts against their server to make sure no easily exploitable methods could be used to gain access. After having verified the service a number of times, one scan showed that the service had suddenly failed, exposing the NetBIOS session ports of their NT server to the Internet. I mapped a drive connection right to their server over the Internet!

A panic call to their ISP verified that for some reason the filter had been turned off. The ISP could not explain why or how this had happened and did not know how long the filter had been down. They simply turned the filter service back on and apologized.

My client decided that they needed to administer security themselves since the ISP could not be trusted to maintain their filtering.

To keep costs as low as possible, I suggested using a Linux-based firewall product or perhaps Linux alone. My client was not comfortable with the user interface however, and decided to go with a Windows NT-based firewall solution. We acquired a machine running Windows NT Workstation and installed Checkpoint Firewall-1. Although Firewall-1 is a more expensive solution, its interface is very intuitive. I was able to train the client to administer policy without the help of a consultant, which serves to lower the total cost of ownership. They now have a reliable and secure connection to the Internet.

Hackers

Hackers are the reason you need a firewall. An in-depth defense against any adversary requires an in-depth understanding of that adversary, so this chapter will attempt to describe hackers, their motivations, and their methods.

I am a hacker. The term "hacker" originally meant someone who understood computers deeply, but as computers became popular, the media used hacker to refer to those who committed computer crimes, and so the population at large learned the term in the context of the computer criminal. This bothered us ethical hackers, so we began calling malicious hackers "crackers" in order to differentiate them from us. So far, it hasn't worked very well—most people outside the computer security world don't understand the difference. After much contemplation, we have decided to use the term hackers to refer to anyone who would break into your computer systems because we're not differentiating their motivations. It doesn't matter to us whether the hacker is malicious, joy-riding, a law enforcement agent, one of your own employees, an ethical hacker you've paid to attempt to break into your network, or even myself. This book is about keeping everyone out. We use the term hacker because it encompasses all these motivations, not just those of the malicious cracker.

Hacker Species

Learning to hack takes an enormous amount of time, as do acts of hacking. Because of the time hacking takes, there are only two serious types of hackers: the underemployed, and those hackers being paid by someone to hack. The word "hacker" conjures up images of skinny teenage boys aglow in the phosphorescence of their monitors. Indeed, this group makes up the largest portion of the teeming millions of hackers, but they are far from the most serious threat.

Hackers fall quite specifically into these categories, in increasing threat order:

- Security Experts
- Students
- Underemployed Adults
- Criminal Hackers
- Corporate Spies
- Disgruntled Employees

Security Experts

Most security experts (ourselves included) are capable of hacking, but decline from doing so for moral or economic reasons. Computer security experts have found that there's more money in preventing hacking than in perpetrating it, so they spend their time keeping up with the hacking community and current techniques to become more effective in the fight against it. A number of larger Internet service companies employ ethical hackers to test their security systems and those of their large customers. Hundreds of former hackers now consult independently as security experts to medium sized businesses. These experts often are the first to find new hacking exploits, and they often write software to test or exacerbate a condition. However, practicing hackers can exploit this software just as they can exploit any other software.

I've placed security experts as being the lowest threat because if they became a threat, they would by definition immediately become criminal hackers. The problem with security experts is the same as with any trusted and powerful (in this specific context) individual— what do you do when they turn on you? In those rare cases where a security expert goes to the dark side of the force, the damage is far reaching and can be so vast that it's difficult to determine exactly what happened. The rarity of this event, not the possible consequences, is what makes security experts a low threat. Even a security expert who is exceptionally ethical can be pissed off—I myself have on occasion contemplated perpetrating unethical hacks against companies with inordinately long telephone support hold times.

Reality Check: Ethical Hackers

In rare cases, the dividing line between a hacker and a security expert is so blurred that they can only be distinguished by their activities. This is the case with groups like the L0pht, where a cadre of expert hackers have converted into security experts operating a for-profit business. They have, to all appearances, ceased illegal activities, but they write software that is useful both for security administration and hacking; their sympathies lie firmly with the hacking community.

Reality Check: Ethical Hackers *(continued)*

These security experts understand more about hacking than any academic study could ever provide. Their ethos is that the only secure environment is one well tested for security failure. They come under constant fire from those who don't understand that the people who find a problem and publicize it aren't encouraging hacking—they're preventing it.

These security experts and hackers in general have had the effect of boosting the Internet's immunity to attack. Imagine what would happen if nobody hacked: Firewalls would be unnecessary, encryption would be unnecessary, and the Internet would be a simpler place. The first criminal hacker to come along would have free and unencumbered access to everything.

Student Hackers

Student hackers are currently enrolled in some scholastic endeavor—junior high, high school, or college. I call them student hackers because their societal position is student, not because they study hacking. Their parents support them, and if they have a job it's only part time. They are usually enrolled in whatever computer-related courses are available if only to have access to the computer lab. These hackers may use their own computers, or (especially at colleges) they may use the greater resources of the school to perpetrate their hacks.

Student hackers are joy-riding through cyberspace looking for targets of opportunity and concerned mostly with impressing their peers and not getting caught. They usually are not motivated to harm you, and in most instances, you'll never know they were there unless you have some alarming software or a firewall that logs attacks. These hackers constitute about 90% of the total hacking activity on the Internet.

If you considered the hacking community as an economic endeavor, these hackers are the consumers. They use the tools produced by others, stand in awe of the hacking feats of others, and generally produce a fan base to which more serious student hackers and underemployed adult hackers play. Any serious attempt at security will keep these hackers at bay.

Student hackers hack primarily to get free stuff: software and music mostly. They pirate software amongst themselves, make MP3 compressed audio tracks from CDs of their favorite music, and trade the serial numbers needed to unlock the full functionality of demo software that can be downloaded from the Internet.

Reality Check: Hacker Terminology

If you want to find hackers on the Internet, you need to know the unique words to search for their community Web pages. Hackers have adopted the convention of replacing the plural "s" with a "z," specifically for the purpose of making it easy to use a search engine to find their sites. They also use jargon to refer to the various commodities of their trade:

- **warez**   Software packages
- **mp3z**   Music, from the MPEG-3 encoding scheme used for compression
- **serialz**   Serial numbers and unlock codes
- **hackz**   Hacking techniques
- **crackz**   Patches that will remove the license checks from software packages

Do a Web search using these terms to see what you come up with.

Underemployed Adult Hackers

Underemployed adults are former student hackers who have either dropped out of school or who have failed to achieve full-time employment and family commitments for some other reason. They usually hold "pay the rent" jobs. Their first love is probably hacking, and they are quite good at it. Many of the tools student hackers use are created by these adult hackers.

Adult hackers are not outright criminals in that they do not intend to harm others. However, the majority of them are software and content pirates, and they often create the "crackz" applied by other hackers to unlock commercial software. This group also writes the majority of the software viruses.

Adult hackers hack for notoriety in the hacking community—they want to impress their peers with exploits and information they've obtained, and to make a statement of defiance against the government or business. These hackers hack for the technical challenge. This group constitutes only about a tenth of the hacking community, but they are the sources for the vast majority of the software written specifically for hackers.

A new and important segment of underemployed adults has recently emerged from the former Warsaw Pact nations. Because of the high quality of education in those countries and the current economic conditions, hundreds of thousands of bright and otherwise professional people hack. Sometimes they have an axe to grind, but most often they are simply looking for something that will make or save them money, like pirated software.

Professors, computer scientists, and engineers from those countries have turned their hopes to the Internet looking for employment or whatever else they can find. Students graduate from college, but for lack of employment never graduate from hacking. For similar economic reasons, and because of technological penetration into their society, Israel, India, and Pakistan have recently become hotbeds of hacking activity.

The global nature of the Internet means that literally anyone anywhere has access to your Internet connection machines. In the old days, it took at least money or talent to reach out and hack someone. These days, there's no difference between hacking a computer in your neighborhood and one on the other side of the world. The problem is that in many countries, hacking is not a crime because intellectual property is not strongly protected by law. If you're being hacked from outside your country, you won't be able to bring the perpetrator to justice even if you found out who it was unless they also committed some major crime like grand theft of something besides intellectual property.

Criminal Hackers

Criminal hackers hack for revenge or to perpetrate theft. This category doesn't bespeak a level of skill so much as an ethical standard. Criminal hackers are the ones you hear about in the paper—those who have compromised Internet servers to steal credit card numbers, performed wire transfers from banks, or hacked the Internet banking mechanism of a bank to steal money.

These hackers are as socially deformed as any real criminal—they are out to get what they can from whomever they can regardless of the cost to the victim. Criminal hackers are exceedingly rare because the intelligence required to hack usually also provides ample opportunity for the individual to find some socially acceptable means of support.

Spies

Actual corporate spies are also rare because it's extremely costly and legally very risky to employ these tactics against competing companies. Who does have the time, money, and interest to use these tactics? Believe it or not, these attacks are usually engaged against high technology businesses by foreign governments. Many high technology businesses are young and naive about security, making them ripe for the picking by the experienced intelligence agencies of foreign governments. These agencies already have budgets for spying, and taking on a few medium sized businesses to extract technology that would give their own corporations an edge is commonplace.

Nearly all high-level military spy cases involve individuals who have incredible access to information, but as public servants don't make much money. This is a recipe for disaster. Low pay and wide access is probably the worst security breach you could have if you think your competition might actually take active measures to acquire information about your systems.

For some, loyalty is bought, and it goes to the highest bidder. Would someone at your company who makes ten dollars an hour think twice about selling their account name and password for a hundred thousand dollars? Money is a powerful motivator, especially to those with crushing debt problems. Many spies are also recruited from the ranks of the socially inept using love, sex, or the promise thereof. Think about the people who work with you—would every one of them be immune to the charms of someone who wanted access?

Remember that these sorts of attacks are not generally perpetrated by your domestic competition, but by the governments of foreign competitors. Domestic competitors prefer the time honored (and legal) method of simply hiring away those individuals in your company who created the information your network stores. There's very little that can be done about this sort of security breach, unless you already have employment agreements in place that stipulate non-competition when employees leave the company.

Disgruntled Employees

Disgruntled employees are the most dangerous security problem of all. An employee with an axe to grind has both the means and the motive to do serious damage to your network. These sorts of attacks are difficult to detect before they happen, but some sort of behavioral warning generally precipitates them.

Overreacting to an employee who is simply blowing off steam by denigrating management or coworkers is a good way to create a disgruntled employee, however. So be cautious about the measures you take to prevent damage from a disgruntled employee.

Also remember that outsourced network service companies may have policies that make them hard to replace if you decide you no longer wish to retain their services, and that disgruntled small companies tend to behave a lot like disgruntled employees. There's very little that can be done about attacks that come from people with an intimate knowledge of your network, so you should either choose your service providers wisely and exercise a lot of oversight, or require the escort of a trusted employee at all times.

Unfortunately, there's very little you can do about a disgruntled employee's ability to damage your network. Attacks range from the complex (a network administrator who spends time reading other people's e-mail) to the simple (a frustrated clerk who takes a fire-axe to your database server).

Vectors Of Attack

There are only three ways for a hacker to access your network:

- By using a computer on your network directly
- By connecting over the Internet
- By dialing in via a RAS or remote control server

There are no other possible vectors. This small number of possible vectors defines the boundaries of the security problem quite well, and as the following sections show, make it possible to contain them even further.

Direct Intrusion

Hackers are notoriously nonchalant, and have on numerous occasions simply walked into a business, sat down at a local terminal or network client, and began setting the stage for further remote penetration.

In large companies, there's no way to know everyone by sight, so an unfamiliar worker in the IS department isn't uncommon or suspicious at all. In companies that don't have ID badges or security guards, there isn't anybody to check credentials, so penetration is relatively easy. And even in small companies, it's easy to put on a pair of coveralls and pretend to be with a telephone or network wiring company, or even the spouse of a fictitious employee. With a simple excuse like telephone problems in the area, access to the server room is granted (oddly, these are nearly always co-located with telephone equipment). If left unattended, a hacker can simply create a new administrative user account. A small external modem can be attached and configured to answer in less than a minute, often without rebooting your server.

Other possible but more rare possibilities include intruding over a wireless link or tapping some wide area network to which your network is directly attached, like an X.25 link or a frame relay connection.

Solving the direct intrusion problem is easy: Employ strong physical security at your premises and treat any cable or connection that leaves the building as a public medium. This means you should put firewalls between your WAN links and your internal network, or behind wireless links. By employing your firewalls to monitor any connections that leave the building, you are able to eliminate direct intrusion as a vector.

The final direct intrusion problem is that of a hacker who works for your company. This problem is far more difficult to solve than border security, because the perpetrator has a valid account on your network and knowledge of the information it contains. Solving the disgruntled employee/spy problem requires such stringent security measures that your network may become difficult to use for legitimate employees. Many companies find that it's simply not worth the bother and allow the threat to go unchecked.

There is a better way to deal with this remote possibility: strong auditing. Unlike permission based restriction to resources, an audit approach allows wide access to information on the network, and also tracks everything employees do. This doesn't prevent theft or loss of information, but it does show exactly how it occurred and from which account the attack was perpetrated. Because you know the perpetrator directly, you will be able to bring criminal charges against them.

It's most effective to let all employees know that the IT department audits everything that comes and goes in the network for the purpose of security. This prevents problems from starting, since hacking attempts would be a dead giveaway.

Dial-up

Dial-up hacking via modems used to be the only sort of hacking that existed, but it has quickly fallen to second place after Internet intrusions. Hacking over the Internet is simply easier and more interesting for hackers.

This doesn't mean that the dial-up vector has gone away—hackers with a specific target will employ any available means to gain access.

Although the dial-up problem usually means exploiting a modem attached to a RAS server, it also includes the possibilty of dialing into an individual computer with a modem set to answer for the purpose of allowing remote access or remote control for the client. Many organizations allow employees to remotely access their computers from home using this method.

Containing the dial-up problem is conceptually easy: Put your RAS servers outside your firewall, and force legitimate users to authenticate with your firewall to gain access to resources inside. Allow no device to answer a telephone line inside your firewall. This eliminates dial-up as a vector by forcing it to work like any other Internet connection.

Internet

Internet intrusion is the most available, most easily exploited, and most problematic vector of intrusion into your network. This vector is the primary topic of this book. If you follow the advice in this section, the Internet will be the only true vector into your network.

You already know that the Internet vector is solved using firewalls. There's no point in belaboring the topic here since the remainder of this book is about solving the Internet intrusion vector.

Hacking Techniques

Hacking attacks progress in a series of stages, using various tools and techniques. A hacking attack consists of the following stages:

Target Selection   A hacker identifies a specific computer to attack. To pass this stage, some vector of attack must be available, so the machine must have either advertised its presence or have been found through some search activity.

Target Identification   The hacker determines the characteristics of the target before actually engaging it. They may achieve this through publicly available information published about the target, or by probing the target using non-attack methods to glean information from it.

Attack Method Selection   The hacker selects one or more specific attacks to use against the target based on the information gathered in the previous stage.

Attack Progression   The hacker proceeds with the actual attack or series of attacks.

The hacker will attempt to find out more about your network through each successive attack, so the stages above actually feed back into the process as more information is gathered from failed attacks. The stages of attack can be broken down further into the following areas:

- Eavesdropping and snooping
- Denial-of-service
- Impersonation
- Man-in-the-middle
- Hijacking

Once you evaluate your network infrastructure and find weaknesses that a hacker can exploit, you can take measures to shore up your network's defenses.

Eavesdropping and Snooping

The first and easiest things a hacker can do to gain information about your network is simply to listen, and then to ask your network computers information about themselves. The hacker may not even contact your computers directly but instead communicate with other computers that provide services your computers rely on (Domain Name Service computers on the Internet, for example.) Networked computers will volunteer a remarkable amount of information about themselves and how they are configured, especially if they are left in their default configurations as supplied by operating system vendors.

Hackers will attempt to exploit any data or network service that is exposed to them. Common hacking practices include (but are by no means limited to) the following activities:

- Password capture
- Traffic analysis
- Network address scanning
- Port scanning
- Finger, Whois, NSLookup, and DNS range grabbing
- SNMP data gathering

Password Capture

Most hacking activities place the hacker at some risk of being detected. One activity that does not pose this threat is eavesdropping on the local networking medium for logon information.

Many networking protocols do not encrypt passwords, allowing any computer on the path between the client and the server to "overhear" the username and password. Not all encrypted logon procedures are safe from eavesdropping either, because (if the logon procedure is naïve) a hacker can record the username and encrypted password to send to the server later in a "replay attack."

Eavesdropping requires software that will listen to all of the communications that flow over a network medium, such as Ethernet, rather than just listening to communications that are sent specifically to the hacker's computer. An eavesdropping hacker must also have access to a computer that is situated on a network link with network traffic flowing over it (such as a campus Ethernet or a computer in the server room of an Internet Service Provider). The more data that flows over the link, the more likely the hacker will capture passwords sent in the clear, i.e. in unencrypted form.

Physical location will not restrict the eavesdropping ability of a hacker who has penetrated other computers on the network. The hacker can install software on those computers that will allow them to snoop as well. The hacker may be typing at a computer in New York while a compromised computer in San Francisco records everything that goes over that remote network for the hacker's later perusal. A determined network intruder may even physically intrude on an otherwise secure LAN and connect a snooping device to the network cable. Casual hackers more interested in network joy-riding or in finding a place to store their pirated software will seldom exhibit this level of effort (or brave this degree of risk), but other network intruders who might target your network for financial gain could easily do so if you don't take precautions.

Network eavesdropping is a technique hackers can use regardless of the technology used to implement the network. An IPX wide area network is just as vulnerable to someone eavesdropping on network connections as is the Internet or an Intranet that uses TCP/IP.

Snooping Windows passwords over the Internet is surprisingly easy. Microsoft has built in a password Challenge/Response authentication mechanism into Internet Explorer to make secure Intranets easy to build. This mechanism allows a Web server to challenge a client for that client's password. The client will respond with the account name of the logged-on user and that user's one-way encrypted password. The password can be decrypted by comparing it to a list of pre-computed decrypted English words, or through a brute-force keyspace comparison (á la NT Crack, from L0pht Heavy Industries). At this point, a hacker has your account name and password, but you would have had to go to the hacker's Web site to compromise it.

That, too, is surprisingly easy to force. If your boss sent you an e-mail with a link to a Web site embedded in it and a note saying, "Check these guys out—they may be competition. What do you think?" Would you click the link? Voila—you're compromised. Forging e-mail is so easy, it's child's play. A hacker can make his e-mail look like it's coming from anyone.

E-Mail from Heaven

It's particularly easy to forge Internet e-mail. Try this:

Telnet to a mail server by opening a command prompt and typing **telnet mailserver 25**. Use the mail server configured in your e-mail program if you don't know of another one.

Type the following at the telnet prompts, pressing return after each listed line. You won't see text until you press return, and when you type the body text you won't see anything until you press a period by itself and hit enter. Replace the text "YOU@YOURSERVER.COM" with your own e-mail address.

```
MAIL FROM: <GOD@HEAVEN.ORG>
RCPT TO: <YOU@YOURSERVER.COM>
DATA
To: <YOU@YOURSERVER.COM>
From: <GOD@HEAVEN.ORG>
```

E-Mail from Heaven *(continued)*

Subject: Concerning your recent activities

Date: Mon, 1 Jan 2000 00:00:01

In case you were wondering, forging e-mail is unethical.

.

QUIT

Now that you know how easy it is, you should take forged e-mail warnings very seriously.

Network Traffic Analysis

Passwords aren't the only things a determined hacker will listen for while eavesdropping on network traffic. Quite a bit of information about your network can be determined just from the nature of the traffic in and out of your network (or within your network if the hacker has compromised a computer within your security). Some things a hacker will look for include:

- The IP addresses of the source and destination computers of network traffic.

- The locations of gateways and routers.

- The amount of traffic originating from, being sent to, or flowing through computers identified by the hacker.

- Particular kinds of network traffic going to or from a computer that might identify the computer's function (DNS requests to one computer, or FTP responses from another, for example).

- Network service availability broadcasts (such as NetBIOS browse list updates) that (from an external to a private network) indicate a network security hole or that (within a network) indicate targets for further attack.

The application proxy or Network Address Translation features of a firewall are the best tools for keeping traffic analysis from revealing too much about your network. The firewall will make all of the Internet (or other public network) traffic appear to come from one computer. A hacker from outside will not be able to determine the true extent of your network behind the firewall. You must also configure your firewall not to pass service availability broadcasts beyond your network boundary.

Network Address Scanning

Hackers with a little more time and energy often use a technique called network address scanning. The hacker will specify a beginning and ending address to scan, and then the hacker's computer program will attempt to establish a connection to a computer on each of those network addresses in turn. If a computer answers from any one of those addresses then the hacker has found another target.

All network technologies that specify an address of one kind or another for each computer on the network are vulnerable to this kind of attack. TCP/IP is the network technology most often scanned by hackers, and tools to scan TCP/IP are widely available. Other technologies such as NWLink, X.25, and FDDI are equally susceptible if the hacker is willing to find or create the tools necessary to perform the scan.

The best way to foil this kind of attack is to watch for it. A network administrator that determines that this kind of attack is in progress can take steps to halt it, including configuring gateways or routers to discard network traffic from the offending host(s).

You need to configure gateways, packet filters, and routers to log connection requests to hosts that do not exist on your network. Periodically examine log data for network address scanning, and (if the logging software supports it) configure a network alert that will signal if a scan is in progress.

Port Scanning

Once a hacker has identified a target computer, the hacker will attempt to determine what operating system it is running and what services it is providing to network clients. On a TCP/IP based network (such as the Internet), services are provided on numbered connections called *sockets*. The sockets that a computer responds to often identifies the operating system and supported services of the target computer.

There are a number of tools available on the Internet that a hacker can use to determine which sockets are responding to network connection requests. These tools try each port in turn and report to the hacker which ports refuse connections and which do not. The hacker can then concentrate on ports corresponding to services that are often left unsecured or that have security problems.

Port scanning can reveal what operating system your computer is running because each OS has a different set of default services. For example, by scanning the TCP ports between 0 and 150, a hacker can discern Windows hosts (by the presence of port 139 in the scan list), NT hosts (by the presence of port 135 in the list), and various UNIX hosts (simply by the presence of TCP/IP services like port 23 (Telnet)), which NT and Windows do not install by default. This information tells the hacker which tools to use to further compromise your network.

The defense for port scanning is the same as for network address scanning—watch for connection attempts to unsupported ports and then deny access to the computers doing the scanning. The Web site for this book contains a downloadable copy of Suck Server, which you can use to easily monitor hacking attempts on your server. Periodically examine log data for port scanning, and (if the logging software supports it) configure a network alert that will signal if a scan is in progress.

Finger, Whois, NSLookup, and DNS Zone Transfer

There are a number of network services that hackers will use to gather information if the ports used by those services are enabled on your Internet host. The Finger and Whois services are hacker favorites because they supply the account name and personal contact information for users of network computers. These are useful services for people who need to contact members of your organization or who need to find an e-mail address for a network user, but hackers will take usernames returned by these services and then attemp to break into those accounts by trying commonly used passwords.

> **NOTE** By default, Windows NT does not support Finger or Whois. If you support UNIX computers in your network, however, you should either disable these services or curtail the information they return. You can install software for Windows NT that provides these services, but you probably shouldn't.

Few network users will miss the Finger and Whois services, but the same cannot be said for the DNS service. The DNS service is required by Internet client software to convert human-friendly Internet names such as `www.microsoft.com` into computer-friendly IP addresses such as 10.1.1.2. Without the DNS service, many Internet client tools such as Web browsers, FTP clients, and Telnet clients will not work as the users expect.

Windows NT Server does support the DNS service. Most networks that support the use of Internet tools within the network (instead of just the use of Internet tools to connect to services on the Internet) will include support for DNS. A smaller network can rely on an external DNS server to provide Internet name service translation for its clients, but a large IP network or an IP network behind a firewall is difficult to manage without a DNS server of its own.

Hackers can use a DNS service to discover the structure of your network. Since DNS records the IP addresses and Internet names of all of the servers on your network, a hacker can attain a list of the most important computers in your network. The NSLookup tool is a standard Internet program for interrogating DNS servers, and a hacker can craft a program based on the NSLookup that would even make the hacker's computer appear to be a peer DNS server that needs information. Your task is to configure security in a way that allows clients from within to access the DNS server and get the information they need, but also prevents computers from outside your network security from getting that information.

The security problem is compounded by the fact that DNS is a hierarchical service. If one DNS server does not have the answer to a query, it will ask the next server up or down the DNS tree. This means that in a traditionally configured network, a DNS service within your firewall will need to be able to communicate with DNS servers outside the firewall. DNS servers are also configured to transfer blocks of Internet name and address data using a feature called Zone Transfer. In addition, many Web sites will not respond to Internet requests from client computers that don't have DNS reverse mappings, so the Internet servers that run those sites must be able to connect to your DNS server (via their DNS server or the DNS server up the tree from yours) to verify that the DNS reverse mapping exists.

A firewall can solve these problems by handling name translation inside your network. If your network requirements mandate that computers external to your network must be able to resolve IP addresses for computers inside your firewall or vice versa (if you use a software package that does not support use of a proxy server, for example), you should configure your firewall to disallow connections to your DNS server for all external computers except that of the DNS server up the tree from yours. You should also disable zone transfers for all DNS servers except those within your security domain. Chapter 10 covers specific policies you should enable in your firewalls based on your level of risk.

SNMP Data Gathering

The Simple Network Management Protocol (SNMP) is an essential tool for managing large TCP/IP networks. SNMP allows the administrator to remotely query the status of and control the operation of network devices that support SNMP. Unfortunately, hackers can also use SNMP to gather data about a network or (as described in the next section) interfere with the operation of the network.

Again, a firewall solves the problem. There's little reason why any computer outside your network should be able to use SNMP, so simply block SNMP messages through your firewalls. Chapter 10 will show you exactly what services you should block with your firewall.

Denial of Service

The next easiest attack on your network is to disable some aspect of it or even bring the entire network down. The hacker may be merely interested in inconveniencing your organization, or the hacker may have a more sinister purpose. In any case, you should remember that it is much easier for one computer to impersonate another computer (see the next section on impersonation) if that other computer is disabled.

There are a number of methods a hacker can use to disable a computer or a service provided by a computer. Most of these methods affect computers using TCP/IP because TCP/IP is the most widely used internetwork protocol and because the most pressing hacker threat is from the Internet. Methods hackers can use to disable computers or computer services include:

- Ping of Death
- SYN (Synchronize Connection Establishments) Attacks and ICMP (Internet Control Message Protocol) flooding
- Service Specific Attacks
- DNS Redirection
- Route redirection: RIP (Router Information Protocol), BGP (Border Gateway Protocol), and ICMP
- SNMP reconfiguration

Ping of Death

Perhaps the most ominous sounding of Network Layer attacks is the aptly named Ping of Death. A specially constructed ICMP packet that violates the construction rules can cause the recipient computer to crash if that computer's networking software does not check for invalid ICMP packets.

The only solution for computers outside your gateway (or the gateway computer itself) to resist the Ping of Death is to use a version of the operating system that is not susceptible to the Ping of Death. You can shield computers inside your network by not passing Ping packets through your firewall.

SYN Attacks and ICMP Flooding

Another way hackers disable the networking capability of computers is by overloading the network protocol software of the target computer with connection attempts or information requests. The initial IP packet of a TCP connection attempt is simple and easy to generate (a distinguishing characteristic of these packets is that they have the SYN bit set). Responding to a connection attempt takes more compute time and memory space than does generating the packet because the receiving computer must record information about the new connection and allocate memory for connection data. An attacker can send one SYN packet after another to a target computer, and that target computer will then be unable to process other connection attempts from legitimate users because all of its available time and memory will be spent processing SYN requests.

A similar network protocol attack is ICMP flooding, in which the hacker sends a constant stream of ICMP echo requests to the target computer. The target computer then spends most of its time responding to the echo requests instead of processing legitimate network traffic.

Keep your firewall and operating system software updated to prevent against these attacks. You should configure your firewalls or servers to log instances of extremely frequent SYN connection attempts or abnormally high volume of ICMP traffic in order to protect operating systems outside your firewall that may be vulnerable to these attacks.

Service Specific Attacks

Hackers are usually not interested in crashing your computer. The hacker may instead be more interested in shutting down one of the services supported by your network-connected computer (perhaps in order to impersonate that service, as described in the next section on impersonation).

Although any service provided by your computer may be the target of a service-specific attack, there are four services that hackers are particularly attracted to because they are either fundamental components of a TCP/IP network or are fundamental components of Windows networking. The four services are RPC, NetBIOS, DNS, and WINS. Other services, such as Chargen or Time, do not provide a sufficiently rich environment for a hacker to have any real chance of using the service to break into or take down your computer.

Network clients connect to specific ports for each network service, and each service expects the network client to send the data to the service in a specific format. The DNS service, for example, expects that data sent to the DNS port from the client is formatted in a different manner than for WINS requests, and DNS will not be able to respond properly to WINS requests sent to it.

This is much like real world services such as the Department of Motor Vehicles and the Social Security Administration, each of which needs different information from you in order to perform their services, and each of which has different forms for you to fill out. You could send a form requesting a duplicate social security card to the DMV, but you would neither get a social security card nor a driver's license in return. You must send the right form to the right service.

While the repercussions of sending misleading or incorrect information to government institutions can be severe for the perpetrator, it will have negligible effects on the operation of the government service. However, sending incorrect or nonsense messages to network services can crash the service and is difficult to track back to the hacker, especially if the hacker is using obfuscatory techniques such as source routing or has suborned another computer into being a relay for hacker activity.

Many implementations of DNS, RPC, and WINS are particularly vulnerable to receiving random information at their ports. Some implementations of DNS also crash if they receive a DNS response without having first sent a DNS request. You can protect against unsolicited DNS responses by only allowing authorized external hosts to communicate with your DNS server.

The NetBIOS service of Windows and Windows NT is vulnerable to an Out of Band attack sent to the NetBIOS ports. NetBIOS ports should not be accessible to computers outside your network at all, so the best solution to this problem (after installing the latest version of the operating system software) is not to bind NetBIOS to network adapters that can be reached from outside your network.

DNS Cache Pollution

An additional DNS service attack that deserves special mention is DNS cache pollution. A hacker can observe a computer that provides DNS services (using techniques described in the previous section on eavesdropping and snooping) and determine the sequence used by the computer to provide query IDs for recursive DNS queries. The hacker can then forge a response to the next DNS query that contains invalid information or information that will redirect Internet traffic to a computer the hacker has already suborned. (The hacker may have to perform a denial-of-service attack on the DNS server being queried in order for the substitution to be accepted by the querying, targeted DNS server.)

This sort of attack can cause client computers that rely on the DNS server to not be able to resolve Internet names into valid IP addresses. That alone can cause problems on a TCP/IP network. More dangerous, however, is when a hacker populates the DNS server with valid IP addresses that are different from the correct IP addresses, especially if the hacker controls the computers at those addresses. A DNS cache pollution attack can therefore be the beginning of an impersonation attack on computers in your network.

Route Redirection (RIP, BGP, ICMP)

A hacker can cause a great deal of havoc in your network if the hacker can get control of your network's routers. Routers direct the flow of information within your network as well as in and out of it from information stored in their routing tables. By making changes to those routing tables a hacker can isolate parts of your network and direct network traffic out of your network.

Routers must adapt to network conditions in order to maintain network functionality in the face of slowdowns or failures in network links. The routers in your network will exchange information about routing conditions, accept routing updates from network administrative programs, and communicate with routers outside your network if you allow them to. These routing updates are transmitted using a routing protocol, usually RIP, OSPF, or BGP.

RIP has no authentication capability. If a hacker can communicate with a router that uses RIP to update its network information, then the hacker can easily reconfigure the router to deny service to computers in your network or redirect the network traffic from computers in your network. OSPF provides more security than RIP does, and BGP is fairly secure about who it will communicate with in order to update routing tables.

Another way a hacker can get your computers to send data to the wrong address is to send ICMP redirect packets to the computer. An ICMP redirect packet instructs the computer that an IP packet is being sent to the wrong router and that there is another route to the destination address that is either more efficient, faster, or that avoids a network problem. It is difficult to forge ICMP packets, however, because they must appear to come from the router closest to the originating computer.

SNMP Reconfiguration

Many network devices, including Windows NT Server computers (if you install the SNMP service for them) can be managed remotely using SNMP. In addition to data snooping, a hacker can use SNMP to reconfigure your network to deny service to network computers or even to route data out of your network depending on the SNMP features of the device the hacker gains control of.

Impersonation

Impersonation is the next step for a hacker to take if the hacker still doesn't have access to your network computers. The goal of a hacker is to penetrate your network security and get at the information or resources on the computers in your network.

Merely snooping on your network traffic may give the hacker enough information to log on to your network. If that does not work, the hacker may reduce the functionality of your network via a denial-of-service attack, causing computers on your network to reveal enough information to allow the hacker to break in. The hacker might also pursue a denial-of-service attack just to inconvenience users of your network.

By impersonating another computer that the computers on your network trust, the hacker's computer may be able to trick your computers into revealing enough information for the hacker to get through your network security. Alternatively, by impersonating another computer, the hacker's computer may be able to trick one of your computers into executing a command that weakens your security enough to let the hacker in. The tactics a hacker may use depend on the computer or service that the hacker may attempt to impersonate, as follows:

- Source Routed Attacks
- DHCP, WINS, and DNS Service Impersonation
- Password Playback, Server Impersonation, and Password Capture

Source Routed Attacks

The TCP/IP protocol suite includes a little-used option for specifying the exact route a packet should take as it crosses a TCP/IP-based network (such as the Internet). This option is called source routing, and it allows a hacker to send data from one computer and make it look like it comes from another (usually more trusted) computer. Source routing is a useful tool for diagnosing network failures and circumventing network problems, but it is too easily exploited by hackers and so you should not use it in your TCP/IP network. Configure your firewalls to drop all source-routed TCP/IP packets from the Internet.

The hacker can use source routing to impersonate an already connected user and inject additional information into an otherwise benign communication between a server and the authorized client computer. For example, a hacker might detect that an administrator has logged on to a server from a client computer. If that administrator is at a command prompt, the hacker could inject a packet into the communications stream that appears to come from the administrator and that tells the server to execute the change password command—thereby locking the administrator account and letting the hacker in.

The hacker also might use source routing to impersonate a trusted external DNS server and send DNS updates to your DNS server. This redirects all of the network clients that rely on the DNS server to translate Internet names into IP addresses so that the client computers go instead to a hostile server under the control of the hacker. The hacker could then use the hostile server to capture passwords, as described below in the section on password playback, server impersonation, and password capture.

DHCP, WINS, and DNS Service Impersonation

Another tactic a hacker can use to penetrate your network is to impersonate a service that your client computers get configuration information from at boot time. Network clients can be set up to get their configuration (including the location of the default gateway, DNS, and WINS servers) from a DHCP server, so a hacker who can impersonate a DHCP server can redirect your network clients to talk to almost any hostile host. By impersonating a WINS server, the hacker can return invalid or hostile IP addresses for NetBIOS computer names. By impersonating a DNS server, the hacker can return invalid or hostile IP addresses for Internet names as well.

In order for a hacker to impersonate a DHCP, WINS, or DNS server, the hacker must get control of one computer within your network and then initiate a denial-of-service attack against the legitimate DHCP, WINS, or DNS target computer. Once the target computer goes down, the computer controlled by the hacker can begin satisfying DHCP, WINS, or DNS requests in its place. This is just one way that a hacker can use one compromised computer in your network to penetrate your network security further and gain control of other computers in your network.

A DHCP, WINS, or DNS impersonation attack on your network relies on other attack methods to succeed. The hacker must first gather information about your network in order to identify targets, and then cause a denial of service on the service being impersonated. After that succeeds, the hacker must either gain control of at least one computer in your network that will be used to take the place of the server being impersonated. Alternatively, the hacker may redirect network traffic to an external computer that can take the place of the server being impersonated. The defensive measures you put in place to stop denial-of-service attacks and to restrict information about your network will help prevent an impersonation attack as well. You should also watch your network traffic for DHCP, WINS, or DNS services being hosted by unauthorized computers in your network, and you should take swift action to shut down any unauthorized servers.

Server Impersonation, Password Capture, and Password Playback

If the hacker has observed an encrypted logon session to one of your computers, they may not know the username and password being used to log on, but might be able to fool your system anyway. The hacker might simply record the encrypted log-on credentials and send those same credentials to your computer later. It won't matter that the hacker can't discern what the password is because the receiving computer expects its encrypted form anyway.

Older networking protocols are vulnerable to this sort of attack. This attack can be defeated by using challenge and response authentication for passwords.

With challenge and response authentication, the password is never transmitted. Rather, the client indicates that she would like to log on. The server transmits a unique number to the client. Both computers encrypt that number using the client's password as a key. The client transmits the encrypted number back to the server. If the encrypted results match, then the same key was used to perform the encryption and the server knows that the client knows the correct password. By encrypting a random number, the results will be different each time, making it impossible to derive the password used to encrypt it through mechanisms like snooping.

Windows NT and most modern versions of UNIX use this sort of password encryption and authentication by default for NetBIOS connections from network client computers. Unfortunately, Windows NT also supports an older LAN Manager authentication protocol. Networking clients may elect to use an older protocol if they inform Windows NT that they do not support the Windows NT Challenge/Response protocol. Hackers can exploit NT's support for this weaker protocol against newer computers by forging a response packet that appears to come from the server (using source routing, rerouting, or a man-in-the-middle position) and that instructs the modern client to use the weaker LAN Manager protocol. This way, the hacker can make the client use an easily cracked password encryption method or even instruct the client not to use password encryption at all.

The hacker can then eavesdrop on the resulting log-on traffic and capture the password used by the client to log on to the server. The best solution to this security problem is to configure your Windows NT computers not to accept LAN Manager authentication.

Many older UNIX protocols, like Telnet, also don't make use of challenge and response authentication. Hackers can simply sniff these passwords off the network.

One limitation of the NT Challenge/Response protocol as it exists now is that a hacker can set up a server for capturing passwords and either entice users to connect to the server (the hacker can set up a Web site, for example, that accepts Windows NT Challenge/Response authentication), or the hacker can use denial-of-service attacks to redirect network connections to a computer that is masquerading as a valid server for your network. When the hacker configures the deceptive server, the hacker does not have the passwords for the user accounts that will attempt to connect to it. The hacker can specify one number that the server will always send to the client computers as a challenge, however, and can pre-compute passwords encrypted with that seed from dictionary files. If an unsuspecting client computer sends an encrypted password that matches a computed dictionary value the hacker has calculated, then the hacker has found a new username and password to use to get into your network. Currently, the best solution to this kind of network attack is for network users to never select passwords that might show up in a dictionary, that might be easily guessed, or that are under eight characters in length.

Man-in-the-Middle

A special case of the impersonation attack is the man-in-the-middle attack, where the hacker operates between two computers on your network, or between a client computer on the Internet or other WAN network and your server computer in your secure LAN. When the client computer opens a connection to the server computer, the hacker's computer intercepts it (perhaps via a DNS or DHCP impersonation attack or by rerouting the IP traffic from the client to a compromised computer). The hacker computer opens a connection on behalf of the client computer to the server computer. Ideally (from the hacker's point of view), the client will think he is communicating with the server, the server will think it is communicating with the client, and the hacker computer in the middle will be able to observe and alter all of the communications between them.

Depending on the nature of the communications, the hacker computer may be able to use a man-in-the-middle attack to gain greater access to your network. For example, if the connection is an administrator-level Telnet session into a server computer from a client computer, the hacker computer in the middle could (after passing through the log-on credentials to gain entry to the server) download the password file from the server to the hacker computer instead of uploading HTML pages that the administrator may wish to place on the server computer.

On an insecure network such as the Internet it is difficult to defend against a man-in-the-middle attack. Fortunately, a successful man-in-the-middle attack is also difficult to construct. The measures you take to protect your network against data gathering, denial-of-service, and impersonation will help protect you from a man-in-the-middle attack. Nevertheless, you should never connect to your network using an administrative account over an insecure network.

You can use encryption to create secure communication links over a TCP/IP network, and you can use third-party authentication packages (such as S/KEY provided by Bellcore and SecureID provided by Security Dynamics) to ensure that your client computers are communicating directly with a trusted host computer (and vice versa).

Hijacking

One last hacker trick is the hijacking of an already established and authenticated networking connection. This can occur at two layers of the networking protocol—at the TCP connection layer and at the SMB or NFS session layer. In order for a hacker on the Internet to hijack a network share connection, the hacker will have to do both because SMB uses TCP ports to make the connection.

In order to hijack an existing TCP connection, a hacker must be able to predict TCP sequence numbers, which the two communicating computers use to keep IP packets in order and to ensure that they all arrive at the destination. The hacker must also be able to redirect the TCP/IP connection to the hacker computer, and also launch a denial-of-service attack against the client computer so that the client computer does not indicate to the server that something is wrong. In order to hijack an SMB session (such as a drive mapping to a NetBIOS share), the hacker must also be able to predict the correct NetBIOS Frame ID, Tree ID, and the correct user ID at the server level of an existing NetBIOS communications link.

While an exploit of this nature is theoretically possible, tools for hijacking SMB connections are not readily available to the garden-variety hacker (as opposed to TCP hijacking tools, which can be downloaded from the Internet). A properly secured Internet site will not expose NetBIOS to the Internet, however.

The Metamorphosis

24seven **CASE STUDY**

The authors of this book were hackers in high school. We started on simple eight-bit computers like Ataris and Commodores, trading tricks, tips, and software amongst ourselves for such nefarious purposes as copying write-protected floppy disks and unlocking secret codes for games. Back then, the protections afforded to software were so simple that a fifteen-year-old stood a reasonable chance of cracking them. I remember that we once disassembled and printed out a piece of software in its entirety, and then poured through the code by hand to find the routines that checked for the presence of a hardware key.

Back then, nobody knew about the Internet outside of a few government agencies and universities, so modems were our gateway to the wide world of computers. Hackers would hang out on dial-up servers called Bulletin Board Systems (BBS), the archaic equivalent of chat servers, to trade software, secrets, and chat amongst themselves. The coolest of these boards were never in your local city, however, so you had to pay long distance fees to dial into them.

Hacking consisted of "war-dialing" random numbers looking for the carrier tone of a modem. If a human picked up the phone, the computer would drop the line and proceed to the next number in the list. The first pass consisted of simply browsing for carrier tones and printing the phone numbers that were answered by computers. Once a list of computers was generated, we'd browse that list looking for interesting targets.

Because we had to use direct-dialed telephone lines to connect our computers to BBS hosts, we needed a way to pay long distance charges without them showing up on our parents' phone bill. This, too, was an easy problem to solve—we simply dialed a long distance provider and supplied a random number as the access code. When the number worked, we'd print it out. When it didn't work, we just tried again. By leaving a computer running over night while we slept, the method could generate about ten valid access codes a day. We'd use each access code just once so that by the time anyone knew the call had been illegal, it would be too late to trace.

When the FBI raided the home of a twelve-year-old friend of ours because he repeatedly used an illegal phone card number that we generated, we realized the seriousness of what had been just fun for us. His parents were held liable for over twenty thousand dollars in phone charges and fines, and he lost his computer until he reached the age of eighteen. That (along with a few other hacks that went south) ended our hacking careers before we left high school.

Hacking did prepare us for the rigors of network integration, however. We learned a lot of important information early, so when we ran into similar problems as adults, we already knew how to solve them. When Local Area Networks first came on the scene in the 80s, we already understood network technology—so it was easy for us to move into the field.

TCP/IP from a Security Viewpoint

If you are reading this book, you presumably have a good understanding of how computers work and you have a working knowledge of how to use Internet tools such as Web browsers, Telnet, and e-mail. You might not, however, know just how your computer connects to other computers and downloads Web pages, exchanges e-mail, or establishes a Telnet session. This chapter will give you a better idea of what is going on behind the scenes.

You Need to Be a TCP/IP Guru

But why do you care how TCP/IP works if you aren't a computer programmer or network engineer? You should care because the hackers attempting to get past your network security are often computer programmers or network engineers (self-taught or otherwise), and in order to stop them you need to understand and correct the weaknesses in TCP/IP or higher-level protocols that they will attempt to exploit. In other words, know what your enemy knows.

You don't have to be intimidated by the network technology because you just need to know enough to keep the hackers out; not so much that you can recreate a network from scratch. If you were planning the defence of a castle, you wouldn't need to know how to build the stone walls or forge swords, but you would need to know where the openings are, how the invading barbarians typically attack a castle, and what defenses you have at your disposal.

Similarly, you don't need to drop everything and learn how to write device drivers in C, nor do you need to pore over the Internet RFCs that describe the protocols you use. You should know what protocols your network supports, however, and you should have a basic understanding of how the protocols interact with your firewall, the client computers on your network, and with other computers outside your firewall on the Internet. You should understand the risks (and benefits) of opening ports on your firewall for the various services your network clients would like to use. You should be aware of the limitations a firewall places on network traffic, and you should understand which protocols are easily subverted by hackers and which ones are not.

TCP/IP Rules

What is the big deal about TCP/IP anyway? Why, with its acknowledged weaknesses (we'll get to them in a moment), is the world using TCP/IP to "get wired" instead of another protocol, such as IPX/SPX or SNA? TCP/IP has won out over other protocols that might have competed for world domination for the following reasons:

TCP/IP is packet based.   Many communicating computers can send data over the same network connections. The alternative is to use switched networks, which require a dedicated circuit for every two communicating devices. Packet-based networks are less costly and easier to implement. They typically don't guarantee how much bandwidth the communicating devices will get or what the latency will be. The market has shown, through the Internet, that low cost is more important than guaranteed performance.

TCP/IP provides for decentralized control.   Every network that communicates via TCP/IP gets a range of numbers to use for the computers on that network. Those numbers, once assigned to the organization that requested them, are under the control of that organization for assignment, reassignment, and even sub-allocation to other organizations. Internet Service Providers, for example, get a block of numbers and then dynamically allocate them to callers as they attach to the ISP. Similarly, the Internet domain names, once assigned to an individual or organization by a top-level Internet authority, can be further sub-allocated locally without top-level intervention or authorization. If you own sybex.com, for example, you can assign www .sybex.com to one computer, ftp.sybex.com to another, and mail.sybex.com to a third. Similarly, utah.edu is subdivided by the University of Utah into cs.utah.edu, math.utah.edu, med.utah.edu, and law.utah.edu (which is further subdivided into `www.law.utah.edu` and `ftp.law.utah.edu` and a host of other specific Internet names for computers on the Law School network).

Communicating devices are peers. Unlike other contemporary networks that divide computers into clients and servers (such as NetWare) or mainframes and terminals (such as SNA), TCP/IP treats every computer on the network as a peer—able to initiate or accept network connections independently of other computers (presuming, of course, that there is a network path between the two computers). Client and server software can be implemented on top of TCP/IP using sockets, but that is all irrelevant to the TCP and IP protocols. This means that TCP/IP is flexible and less likely to be vulnerable to failures of other computers not in the network path between the communicating computers.

TCP/IP is routable. A routed network protocol makes it easy to pass data between two or more LANs or network links because routers simply retransmit the data in the payload portion of the network packet from one LAN onto another. Network protocols that can't be routed must rely on protocol gateways, which reinterpret the data on one network to allow it to conform to the addressing and data requirements of the other.

TCP/IP is independent of any particular transmitting medium. TCP/IP will work over Ethernet, Token Ring, ARCnet, FDDI, USB, serial links, parallel port cables, shortwave radio (AX.25,) or any other mechanism that allows two or more computers to exchange signals. TCP/IP has even been defined to work using carrier pigeons as a packet delivery service!

TCP/IP is an open standard. All of the documents describing the TCP/IP standard are available on the Internet for anyone to download and implement for free. There are no trade secrets or hidden implementation details limiting who may implement it.

TCP/IP is free. TCP/IP was developed by universities with defense department funding, and anyone may implement it without paying royalties or licensing fees to any controlling body. Nobody "owns" TCP/IP. Or rather, everybody does.

TCP/IP is robust. TCP/IP was designed when telecommunications lines between computers were not completely reliable, so the TCP/IP protocols will detect and correct transmission errors and gracefully recover from temporarily interrupted communications. TCP/IP will even route around damaged portions of the Internet.

TCP/IP is flexible. TCP/IP is a protocol suite, with IP and a few other simple protocols at the bottom, and other protocols providing increasingly more sophisticated services layered on top. A simple network device, such as a router or print server, need only include those components required for it to do its job. Other more complex devices, such as personal computers or domain name servers, implement a wider range of protocols to support their expanded functionality.

TCP/IP is pragmatic. TCP/IP grew from a simple set of protocols. Additional protocols were added as the implementers found more uses for TCP/IP. This contrasts protocol suites designed ex-nihlo (such as the OSI stack) which, since nobody can think of everything, often leads to over-architected and brittle standards that don't quickly adapt to changing network requirements.

TCP is not perfect, however. Two significant limitations are addressing and security. When it was first designed to link university and military computers, the implementers had no idea it would eventually grow to span the whole world. At the time, 32 bits of address space (allowing for approximately four billion computers) seemed plenty. Now, not only computers and routers, but also printers, terminal servers, scanners, cameras, fax machines, and even coffee pots connect to the Internet. Those 32 bits are being used up quickly, especially since address numbers are allocated in blocks and not all of the numbers in a block are actually used. Also (despite the military application of TCP/IP), the designers did not spend a great deal of effort securing TCP/IP against data snooping, connection hijacking, authentication attacks, or other network security threats. The era of electronic commerce lay too far in the future to worry about when they were designing a small communications system for a few elite researchers engaged in the open exchange of information.

So TCP/IP is cool, but how does it work? The next section will show you the nitty-gritty details of how your computer talks to those other computers on the Internet.

The Bit Bucket Brigade

Computer networks are complicated, and there is a lot you need to understand about TCP/IP in order to keep your network safe. Fortunately, you don't have to understand the whole structure of TCP/IP at once; you can start at the bottom of the stack (the TCP/IP suite is often called a protocol stack) where things are relatively simple and work your way up. You can do this because TCP/IP is built in layers, each of which relies on the services provided by the layer below and provides more powerful services to the layer above. Figure 3.1 shows a graphical view of the layers in the TCP/IP protocol suite.

The International Organization for Standardization (which in English goes by the acronym ISO) has developed a useful model for comparing network protocols called OSI (Open Systems Interconnect). The OSI stack is comprised of seven layers; the first five describe well the first five layers of the TCP/IP protocol suite. The bottom three layers describe how data transfers from one computer to another, and are discussed in this section, starting at the bottom.

Figure 3.1 The TCP/IP protocol suite is composed of layers of services roughly corresponding to the layers of services defined in the OSI network model.

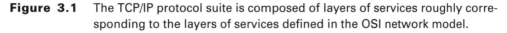

| Application Layer |
| Presentation Layer |
| Session Layer |
| Transport Layer |
| Network Layer |
| Logical Link Layer |
| Physical Layer |

Application
Ping / Telnet / FTP / SMTP / X / Traceroute / DNS / SNMP
TCP / UDP
ICMP / IP / IGMP
Logical Link Control / Media Access Control — Device Driver
Network Adapter

Layer 1: Physical

Computer networking requires that each computer has a physical device (such as an Ethernet card or modem) to use to connect to the network. This device, and the signaling characteristics of it, comprise the Physical Layer in the TCP/IP suite and the OSI stack. TCP/IP doesn't care what kind of device it is (TCP/IP is not dependent on any specific transmission medium, remember?), only that there is one, and that data can be exchanged using it. TCP/IP relies on the operating system to configure and control the physical device.

Although TCP/IP doesn't care how the data physically gets from one place to another, you should. People trying to break into your network may chip away at any level of the network stack, including the Physical Layer. You need to understand the security implications of each physical-network link choice in order to keep your network secure.

For convenience's sake, physical-layer links can be divided into three categories based on connection behavior:

Dial-up Temporary point-to-point connections over a shared infrastructure such as the telephone system

WAN and MAN (Wide Area Network and Metropolitan Area Network) Constantly connected point-to-point connections

LAN Two or more network devices communicating over a shared broadcast media

For each of the physical link options in each category we'll examine the security vulnerabilities and remedies for that option.

Dial-up

Dial-up connections are temporary; they are established when they are needed and reset at the end of the communications session. The biggest problem with dial-up communications (and digital leased lines as well) is that you cannot provide physical security at all points along the communications stream. The cables are run through the public infrastructure (under streets and over power lines) and other private establishments (the basement of your office complex, for example, where only janitors and telecom people dare to go).

Modem   This communications medium uses regular, twisted-pair copper telephone lines for sending and receiving data and attaches to the phone lines just like a regular telephone. The modem modulates the outgoing serial digital signal into analog electrical signals in the same range as a telephone produces for human speech. It demodulates the incoming "tones" (actually just electrical signals corresponding to tones) back into serial digital bits for the computer to receive. Modem bit rates are typically low (up to 56 Kbps).

> **Vulnerabilities**   A physical tap on a phone line (either in the same building or at the phone company) can be fed into another pair of modems (one to receive each channel of the bi-directional communications) which can then demodulate the network traffic and feed it to an eavesdropping computer.

> **Remedies**   Encrypt the data being sent over the modems.

ISDN   This communications medium uses regular, twisted-pair copper telephone lines for sending and receiving data, but rather than connecting like a telephone, the data is sent digitally. Because ISDN does not connect to the phone wires like a regular telephone, the phone wires must be connected to a special, digital service. ISDN bit rates range from fast modem speed (56 Kbps) to almost T1 speed (1.5 Mbps).

> **Vulnerabilities**   As with a regular modem, a physical tap on a phone line (either in the same building or at the phone company) can be connected to a specially programmed ISDN modem which can snoop on the network traffic and feed the intercepted communications to an eavesdropping computer.

> **Remedies**   Encrypt the data being sent over ISDN.

WAN and MAN

WAN and MAN communications channels are typically links that are permanently maintained between locations made either using the telephone infrastructure or wireless technologies such as radio, microwave, or lasers.

Dedicated Digital Leased Lines   The most frequently used, permanent Internet connection for businesses today is a dedicated telephone line leased from the local phone company that is connected by a digital device called a CSU/DSU. These connections are like ISDN connections in that they are digital; however, they are not established and then shut down for each communications session as ISDN connections are. Also, the bit rate of a leased line ranges from modem speed (56Kbps for a fractional T1) to many times faster than typical LANs (an OC12 allows 1.5 Gbps!). Leased lines may also be shared by more than one communicating device (as in the case of Frame Relay), but are typically transparent to the customer. This is true except when the leased line is also being used by another customer; in such cases there will be less available bandwidth. See Figure 3.2 for a comparison of leased line data rates.

Figure 3.2   Leased line data rates range from 56Kbps all the way up to 2.5 Gbps.

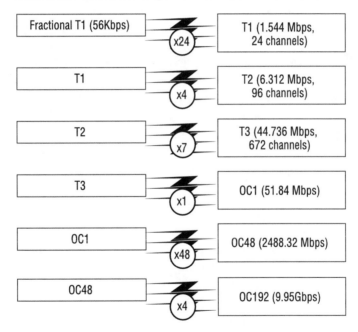

Vulnerabilities   As with a regular modem, a physical tap on a phone line (either in the same building or at the phone company) can be connected to a specially programmed DSU which can snoop on the network traffic and feed it to an eavesdropping computer.

Remedies   Encrypt the data being sent over leased lines.

Radio, Microwave, and Laser   Sometimes it is not feasible to run a physical cable between two locations. Islands, buildings separated by ravines, ships, and isolated communities, for example, need a way to exchange data without wires. NASA uses TCP/IP to communicate with some of its satellites, and for that application copper cables are certainly not an option!

TCP/IP will operate just as effectively over a wireless medium as a wired one. The computer (or other network device) must, of course, have a transceiver for the medium—and there are transceivers for radio, microwave, and even laser communications. Most radio and microwave transmissions have stringent licensing requirements (there is only so much room in the RF spectrum, and government or military applications generally take priority), so there is a lot of paperwork as well as expensive equipment involved in setting up a radio or microwave link.

> **Vulnerabilities**   Broadcast media, such as radio and microwave, are even easier to eavesdrop on than cabled media. A single radio anywhere in the broadcast range of both the sender and the receiver of a radio link can eavesdrop on radio communications, while two receivers, each stationed behind and in the line-of-sight of the target transponders, can record the data being sent between them. Alternatively, two receivers directly between the transponders can eavesdrop on the communications, and since the power requirement is squared at twice that distance, the eavesdropping dishes can be much smaller. (Laser communications cannot be easily eavesdropped on in this manner, but lasers are much more sensitive to environmental effects such as rain and snow.)
>
> **Remedies**   Encrypt the data being sent over radio or microwave links. Consider using lasers for point-to-point communications in areas that are not adversely affected by weather and have adequate line-of-sight between communicating endpoints.

DSL   This communications medium uses twisted-pair copper telephone lines for sending and receiving data, but they must be of sufficient quality and length to handle the greater voltages of the downstream xDSL (Digital Subscriber Line) signal. Also, like ISDN, the data is sent digitally. Because xDSL does not connect to the phone wires like a regular telephone, the phone wires must be connected to a special, digital service. DSL bit rates are much higher than regular modems (up to several Mbps depending on cable quality and filters).

> **Vulnerabilities**   As with a regular modem, a physical tap on a phone line (either in the same building or at the phone company) can be connected to a specially programmed xDSL modem which can snoop on the network traffic and feed it to an eavesdropping computer.
>
> **Remedies**   Encrypt the data being sent over xDSL.

Cable Modems   This communications medium uses the cable TV infrastructure for sending and receiving data. A portion of the cable broadband capacity is reserved for digital communications, and all of the customers in a neighborhood share that bandwidth like an Ethernet (the computer even connects to the cable modem using an Ethernet adapter). Cable modem bitrates are the highest of any low-cost Internet connection service (768Kbps upstream, up to 10 Mbps downstream).

> **Vulnerabilities**   As with Ethernet, an adapter strategically placed (at the cable company head-end) can snoop on the network traffic and feed it to an eavesdropping computer.

> **Remedies**   Encrypt the data being sent over cable modems.

LAN

While dial-up and WAN communications provide network links over large distances and generally connect just two computers together, LAN links are typically tied to a single physical location such as an office building and provide many computers with a shared communications medium.

Adequate site security can alleviate the problem of physical tapping of LAN communications, but when you develop the site security plan, keep LAN security requirements in mind.

Ethernet, Token Ring, FDDI, ARCnet, etc.   Ethernet has become the glue that binds an organization together. Most organizations can still get some work done if the coffee pot breaks, the printer runs out of toner, or the Internet connection drops, but you can forget it if the network stops working! Ethernet's speed, versatility, and ease of configuration has made it the LAN substrate of choice. From a hacker's point of view, however, they all work similarly—cables are run to various locations, and computers are plugged into them. Any one computer on the LAN can transmit using electrical or optical signals to any other computer on the LAN. If a hacker can get control of one of the computers on the LAN, they can listen to all of the communicating computers.

> **Vulnerabilities**   Any computer attached to a LAN can eavesdrop on all of the communication traversing it.

> **Remedies**   Maintain strong physical security. If a portion of the LAN goes through a publicly accessible area (such as between buildings in a campus environment), consider using fiber optic cable for that section. Fiber optics are not easily tapped and any break in the cable will terminate the link.

Serial Connections   Sometimes you just need to link two devices, but you don't need a very fast connection—RS232 serial cables will do that just fine, and most computers come with serial ports built in. Serial cables make a good poor man's LAN, and serial cables have the same vulnerabilities that other LANs do.

Vulnerabilities   A serial cable can be spliced and the data sent over it fed to a third observing computer.

Remedies   Maintain strong physical security.

Layer 2: Data Link

At the very bottom of networking technology, signals are sent from one computer to another using an adapter (as the above section shows, there are many kinds of signals and many kinds of adapters). But how does the computer talk to the device, and how are those signals organized into bits that the computer can make sense of? That's what the Data Link Layer (Layer 2 in the OSI stack) is all about, and that's where the software meets the hardware.

Each networking adapter requires a piece of software, called a device driver, so that the operating system can control the hardware. The device driver must be tailored to the specific hardware device (such as an Ethernet card or FDDI adapter) that it drives. The operating system also requires a consistent way of simultaneously communicating with all of the network devices available to it. For this reason, the Data Link Layer has been split (in the IEEE elaboration on the OSI network model) in to two sublayers:

The Logical Link Control (LLC) Sublayer   Provides the operating system link to the device driver.

The Media Access Control (MAC) Sublayer   Translates generic network requests (send and receive frames, device status, etc.) into device-specific terms.

Media Access Control

The MAC sublayer rests at the very bottom of the software stack, and does its work just before the hardware turns your data into electrical or optical signals to be sent out on the cable. This is the device driver, and it is responsible for controlling the hardware device, as follows:

- Reporting and setting the device status
- Packaging outgoing data received from the LLC sublayer in the format that the network adapter requires (in the case of Ethernet and PPP, a correctly constructed frame)
- Sending outgoing data at the appropriate time
- Receiving incoming data when it arrives
- Unpacking incoming data from the transmission format (i.e. the Ethernet or PPP frame), verifying the integrity of the data, and relaying the data up to the LLC sublayer

A network adapter actually receives all of the network frames transmitted over the link (if it is a shared media link, such as Ethernet) regardless of the intended destination because the network adapter has to read the recipient portion of the frame in order to determine if it is the intended recipient or not. The MAC sublayer discards all frames intended for some other recipient and only forwards data in frames intended for the MAC sublayer to the LLC sublayer above it.

The format of frames varies among link types, depending on the features supported by that networking technology. Ethernet, for example, has 48 bits of address space for identifying network devices, while ARCnet has only eight, and for PPP the addressing is irrelevant (the only device you can be talking to is the one at the other end of the line). Similarly, each supports a different data portion size, the ordering of status and control bytes differ, and some network types support features that others do not (such as compression, encryption, quality of service, authentication, and so on). Figure 3.3 compares Ethernet and PPP frames.

Figure 3.3   The structure of Ethernet and PPP frames are tailored to their uses (Ethernet for fast shared LANs, PPP for slow dial-up links).

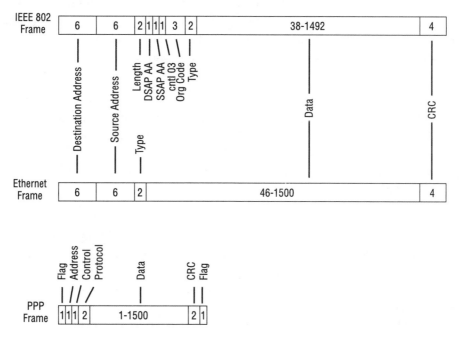

Ethernet   There are actually two frame types for Ethernet. The original Ethernet frame (defined in RFC 894) specified that the last two bytes indicate the type of the frame. The

IEEE's reinterpretation of Ethernet (changed in order to fit it into their network taxonomy and defined in the IEEE 802.2 and 802.3 standards as well as RFC 1042) uses the bytes at that offset as a length indicator. Fortunately, none of the RFC 894 types have the same two-byte value as valid IEEE 802 lengths, so network software can tell the two frame formats apart.

The fields the two frame types have in common are the six-byte address and data fields (giving 48 bits of hardware addressing) and the four bytes of cyclic redundancy check (CRC) at the end. For standard Ethernet frames (as opposed to IEEE 802.3 frames), a type of 0800 indicates that the data portion of the frame is an IP packet. 0806 is an ARP packet, and 8035 is a RARP request/reply packet. The IP packet can be from 46 to 1500 bytes in length, while the ARP and RARP packets are 28 bytes in length plus 18 bytes of padding because the minimum data length for a standard Ethernet frame is 46 bytes.

For both kinds of Ethernet, those six-byte addresses identify the sender and the recipient in an Ethernet LAN. An Ethernet LAN is a network where the computers' communications are mediated only by hubs, switches, media converters, and bridges, not routers or firewalls. Ethernet cards are purchased with addresses pre-assigned to the cards (or to the device if the device, such as a network printer, which comes with Ethernet built in). Because each hardware manufacturer is assigned a different range of Ethernet addresses to build into their devices, every Ethernet card or device should have a unique address. However many Ethernet adapters now allow their addresses to be over-ridden in software, so uniqueness is not guaranteed.

WARNING Don't rely solely on unique Ethernet addresses to identify network frames from authorized computers. A network intruder could perform a denial-of-service attack on the authorized computer and bring up in its place on the network another compromised computer with the same Ethernet address configured in software.

Although the addresses in Ethernet frames are (or should be) globally unique, they can only be used to identify computers on the same Ethernet LAN. This is because the Ethernet frame contains no provisions for forwarding or routing between networks. Ethernet is a shared media network, in that every computer on it should be able to communicate directly with another device on the LAN without the Ethernet frame being reinterpreted and converted by an intervening router or firewall. While the frame may be selectively forwarded to other Ethernet segments and/or converted to new media by bridges and media converters, the actual contents of the frame must remain the same. Other LAN protocols, such as Token Ring, ARCnet, and FDDI have local addresses in their frames, not internetwork addresses that can be used to route data between LANs.

TCP/IP uses IP, ARP, and RARP to move data across the whole Internet, not just the local LAN. For now you can just think of them as the data that has to be exchanged; from the Ethernet point of view, it doesn't matter what is contained in the data portion of the frame. Ethernet will convey other network protocols, such as IPX (used by NetWare,) EtherTalk (AppleTalk on Ethernet,) and NetBEUI (Microsoft's networking protocol) just as easily as it will convey TCP/IP.

NOTE   We'll discuss IP, ARP, and RARP in more detail later on in this chapter.

For IEEE 802 frames, after the length field, there are three bytes containing 802.2 LLC information, and five bytes of SNAP information, the last two of which specify the type of data contained in the payload section. As with Standard Ethernet, a type value of 0800 specifies an IP datagram, 0806 specifies ARP, and 8035 specifies RARP. Because of the 8-byte LLC and SNAP overhead of IEEE 802 frames, the data portion of the frame may be from 38 to 1492 bytes in length, giving a maximum Ethernet packet a length of 1492 and ARP and RARP packets an absolute length of 28 bytes of data and 10 bytes of padding.

PPP   The Point-to-Point Protocol was designed to support multiple network types over the same serial link, just as Ethernet supports multiple network types over the same LAN. It replaces an earlier protocol called SLIP (Serial Line Internet Protocol, which is still in wide use) that only supports IP over a serial link.

PPP frames have a five-byte header. The first three bytes are constant (7E FF 03 for the flag, address, and control bytes respectively), and the last two specify the protocol being transmitted in the data portion of that frame. The frame can hold up to 1500 bytes of data, and is trailed by a two-byte CRC and a one-byte flag (value 7E).

The three protocol types used by IP over PPP are the IP datagram with a protocol value of 0021, the link control data packet (C021), and network control data (8021).

Link Establishment Subversion   There are several tricks that old-school telephone hackers (or phreakers, as they call themselves) can use to subvert or abuse dial-in networks. Call forwarding, for example, can re-route connection attempts to a hacker computer that can then eavesdrop on all your communications at the modem level rather than the IP level. If the computer making the connection supports several network protocols (newer versions of Windows can use IPX and NetBEUI as well as IP over PPP), the hacker can attempt to break in to the dial-in computer with one of these other protocols. Also, dial-up connections made over cellular phones (especially analog cellular phones; digital ones are a little more secure) can be eavesdropped on and even interrupted or captured by hackers with modified radios and cellular telephones.

Media Access Subversion Since it is up to the MAC to discard frames destined for other computers, hackers exploit this behavior by placing the device driver in *promiscuous mode* (replacing the device driver with one that supports promiscuous mode, if the installed device driver lacks it). Promiscuous mode simply relays all packets, regardless of their intended destination, to another program that monitors the data on your LAN.

TIP As a part of your greater security policy (beyond setting up and running a firewall), you'll want to monitor the computers on your network for changes to the device drivers, as well as to other important system files (such as the password lists and network service program files).

Logical Link Control

The LLC portion of the network stack is where the operating system sets up and controls the device driver as a general network device. If you have multiple Ethernet adapters, for example, you may have only one device driver but you will need several instances of it running, one for each Ethernet card. You may also have a Token Ring adapter and several serial port links in your computer, and the operating system will want to treat them all the same—as generic network devices that it can initialize, query the state of, deliver data to, and receive data from. Every operating system has a different specification for this layer, but all the device drivers for the operating system must meet the specification in order to operate as network devices. Windows NT has the Network Driver Interface Specification, (or NDIS) for example, and Unix has its character mode device specification (which, of course, varies among Unix implementations).

Layer 3: Network

TCP/IP doesn't specify how the Physical and Data Link Layers work, it just expects them to provide enough functionality to link two or more computers together into a Local Area Network. That is, because TCP/IP is an Internetwork Protocol suite, it specifies how data can make its way from a computer on one LAN to another computer on a totally different LAN that could be as far away as half-way around the world or out of this world entirely.

TCP/IP does not replace other network technologies such as Ethernet or Token Ring. Instead, it incorporates their functionality and layers its own on top (this is in contrast to the supposed network of the future—ATM—which attempts to provide one specification that works at all layers of the OSI stack). The next layer up in TCP/IP is the Internet Protocol, or IP.

Each layer in the stack exists to perform a specific function. The Data Link Layer moves data across a LAN. The purpose of the Network Layer is to move data across as many

LANs and network links as is necessary to get the data to its destination. IP performs this function well, and it performs only this function—other functions, such as ensuring that the data arrives in order and without duplication, or even that it arrives at all, are performed by other higher-level layers.

How Layering Works

Each layer in the OSI model (and in the TCP/IP suite) operates by using the data portion of the layer below it. IP over Ethernet, for example, places its data structures (called packets) in the data portion of the Ethernet frame. TCP (a layer above IP) places the communications streams it manages in the data portions of IP packets. Application level services such as FTP, which use TCP to establish and maintain the communications channels for exchanging files, write data to TCP sockets, which are placed in IP packets, which are placed in Ethernet (or PPP or Token Ring) frames to be sent out over the network link.

Another way of looking at the protocol stack is to start from the highest level and work your way down. As the data goes down through the TCP/IP networking layers, information specific to that layer is added to the data until it reaches the bottom, at which point it is sent out over the communications link (see Figure 3.4.). When it is received on the other side, the process is reversed, with each layer removing the data specific to that layer, until it is presented to the ultimate recipient of the data.

Frames and Packets   The basic unit of Logical Link Layer data transmission is the frame. The Internet Protocol has a similar basic unit of data transmission—the packet. An IP Packet is quite similar in structure to an Ethernet frame, with source and destination addresses, packet description and option fields, checksums, and a data portion. Because of the way IP is layered on top of the Logical Link Layer, all of the packet structure is nested inside the data portion of the logical link frame (Ethernet, for example).

There are many different types of packets exchanged in a TCP/IP network, starting with the ARP and RARP packets (described in the "Machine vs. IP Addresses" section), and including IP packets (described in the next section of this chapter). For now, just understand that the Internet is based on packets nested in frames. The generic structure of an IP packet is illustrated in Figure 3.5.

Figure 3.4 Each layer of the OSI stack adds layer specific data to what it receives and passes the expanded information to the layer below it. When the layer receives information from the layer below it, the layer removes layer-specific data and passes the information on to the layer above it.

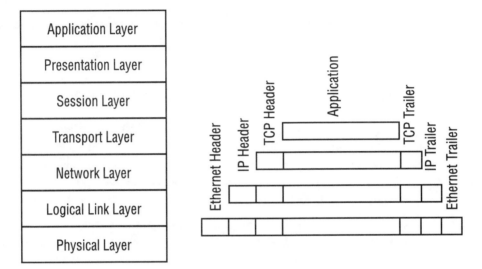

The IP Header As shown in Figure 3.5, the IP header is typically 20 bytes long, but can be up to 60 bytes long if the packet includes IP options. The (non-optional) fields are as follows:

Version These four bits identify which version of IP generated the packet. The current IP version is 4. (IPV6 would, of course, place a 6 here.)

Header length This four-bit value is the number of 32-bit words (not bytes!) in the header, and by default is 20.

Precedence (TOS) These eight bits are an early attempt at implementing quality of service for IP. They are comprised of three bits for packet precedence (ignored by modern implementations of IP), four Type of Service bits, and a bit to be left at zero. Only one of the four Type of Service bits can be turned on. The four bits are: minimize delay, maximize throughput, maximize reliability, and minimize cost. All zeros means the network should use normal priority in processing the packet. RFCs 1340 and 1349 specify TOS use. Most implementations of IP don't allow the application to set the TOS value for the communicated data, which limits the usefulness of this field.

Datagram Length This is the total length of the IP datagram in bytes. Since this is a 16-bit field, the maximum IP packet size is 165535 bytes in length, even if the Data Link Layer frame could accommodate a larger packet.

Figure 3.5   An IP packet has a header that includes the source and destination IP addresses, version, type, and service information, options, and a data section.

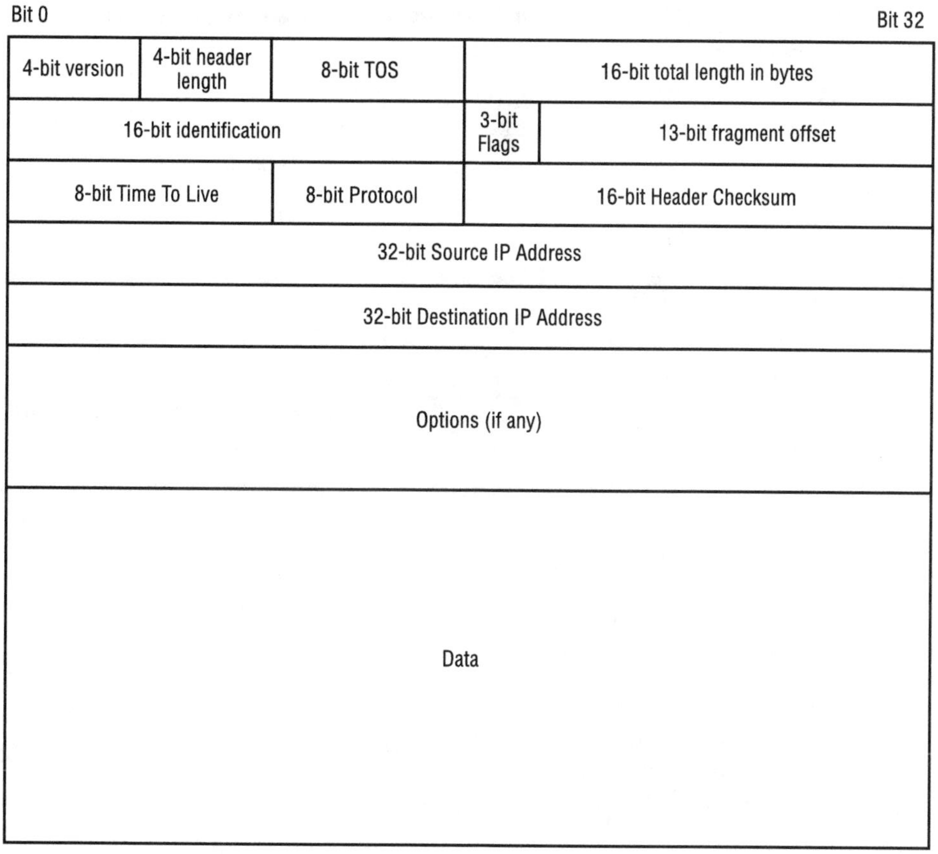

Bit 0   Bit 32

4-bit version	4-bit header length	8-bit TOS	16-bit total length in bytes
16-bit identification		3-bit Flags	13-bit fragment offset
8-bit Time To Live		8-bit Protocol	16-bit Header Checksum
32-bit Source IP Address			
32-bit Destination IP Address			
Options (if any)			
Data			

Identification   To guarantee that packets are unique and to assist in the reassembly of data streams that have been broken down into packets, the sending computer numbers the packets, incrementing the value when each packet is sent. This value doesn't have to start at zero, and isn't necessarily incremented by one on all implementations of IP.

Flags   Flags define whether or not this packet is a fragment of a larger packet.

Fragment Offset   This defines where in the chain of fragments this fragment belongs when reassembling a fragmented packet.

Time To Live   This declares the number of routers through which the packet may pass before it is dropped. This prevents packets from getting caught in routing loops.

This field is typically set to 32 or 64. When a packet is dropped due to TTL expiring, an ICMP message is sent to the sender.

Protocol This field shows which IP protocol (TCP, UDP, ICMP, etc.) generated the packet and should be the recipient of it at the destination.

Header Checksum All of the 16-bit values in the packet header are summed together using one's complement addition and placed in this field.

Source This is the computer or device sending the IP packet.

Destination This is the intended ultimate recipient of the IP packet.

Network Byte Order (Big Endian)

Internet Protocol packets are sent in Network Byte Order, where the most significant bit of a word is sent first. For example, the 32-bit word 0xFFE0A102 would have the byte 0xFF sent first, and the byte 0x02 sent last. For this reason, Network byte order is also called Big-Endian. The other way of doing things is called Little-Endian, where the least significant bits are sent first.

Network Byte Order can be a little confusing to think about. If you number the bits in a word being sent, starting with zero, the most significant bit is the 0th bit and the least significant bit is the 31st bit. This is the opposite of how computer professionals are used to numbering bits.

Of course, regular people (and computer professionals, too) like to count forwards rather than backwards when sending and receiving things, and there are other good reasons to send data in Big Endian order. Plus, the Internet requires a standard byte order. Therefore, Most Significant Bit first, starting the count at zero, is the way to go.

Networks of Networks

The Internet is more than just a really big LAN—it is a network of networks, in much the same way a LAN is a network of individual computers. And just as every computer on an Ethernet has an Ethernet address, every network in the Internet has a network address. In addition, every computer on the Internet also has a station address identifying it on that network. Together, the network address and the station address form the IP address, uniquely identifying that computer on the Internet.

Networks vary in size, from small home or office networks to multinational corporations and large ISPs that may have thousands of computers connected to their network. There are many more smaller networks than there are large ones. The designers of the Internet Protocol took advantage of this fact by making the sizes of the network and station addresses variable, with the network portion getting larger as the station portion gets smaller. That way, the address size as a whole can remain constant. With the eternal optimism of computer programmers everywhere, they decided that 32 bits would be plenty— after all, what is the likelihood that anyone would want to connect more than four billion devices to their little academic network?.

Class and Classless Addressing

It used to be that you could tell the size of a network by the first byte of the network address. If the first bit was zero (i.e. if the byte was from 0 to 127), the address was a class A network. If the first bit was one and the second was zero (if the byte was from 128 to 191), it was a class B network. If the first two bits were one and the third was zero (if it was from 192 to 223), it was a class C network. So, a simple look at the IP address told you how big your LAN was and whether or not another computer was on the same network (it was on the same network if it had identical network address bits as specified by the class, and a different set of station bits in the IP address).

But things have changed. With the advent of classless adressing, you can no longer expect your IP address to reflect the size of the network the computer is on. Instead, you have to examine the subnet mask, which explicitly defines the size of the network address portion and the station address portion of the IP address. Classless addressing started as an easy way for organizations with large networks to efficiently break up their large IP ranges into subnets (that's why it's called a subnet mask), and as the IP address range has filled up, classless addressing has proved itself a useful tool for scavenging smaller class C network numbers out of the large class B and class A spaces.

If you were paying attention you'd have noticed that classes A, B, and C did not fill up the all 32 bits of IP address space. There were two additional classes specified, as follows:

- Class D (with the first three bits set to one and the fourth set to zero), which was reserved for IP multicast (sending packets to multiple networks)

- Class E (with the first four bits set to one and the fifth set to zero), which was reserved for future use

Until address space started to run out, an organization could request a range of addresses in one of three classes that conveniently mapped to byte boundaries, as follows:

Class A   There were only 125 (0,10, and 127 reserved) of these because only seven bits were used for the network address (the first bit was zero and (several network addresses are reserved), but a class A network could have more than sixteen million stations.

Class B   There were about 16,000 of these, each of which could have more than 65,000 stations, because the network portion of the address was 14 bits and station portions of the address were 16 bits in size.

Class C   Almost the opposite of a class A network, there were about two million possible class C networks, each of which could have up to 254 station addresses.

The number of networks and stations are always a little less than the number of bits allocated to the network size because several network and station addresses are reserved for special functions. The lowest and highest address (0 and 255 for class C, 0 and 65536 for class B, etc.) are used for broadcasting to all of the computers in the local network, for example.

So, when an organization wanted to connect to the Internet they got a range of IP addresses sufficient for the number of computers they wanted to hook up. Internally, the computers all shared the same network number, but each had different station addresses.

Machine vs. IP Addresses

If Ethernet addresses are globally unique, why not use them as the Internet address? Ethernet addresses could not be used as a global addressing scheme because a) not every computer has an Ethernet adapter, and b) the sending computer needs to know not only the recipient's address, but also how to send the data to that address (there's no telling where in the world any particular Ethernet adapter might end up).

For this reason, IP uses its own addressing scheme in addition to whatever addressing scheme is used by the network adapter in the machine. IP addresses are four bytes long, and (unlike Ethernet addresses) they are hierarchical in nature. While Ethernet cards from different vendors (and therefore with completely different Ethernet addresses) can be mixed with impunity in a LAN, all of the TCP/IP-capable computers that communicate directly with each other (i.e. that are in the same subdomain) have anywhere from 3 to 30 bits of the address in common, depending on the size of the subdomain the computers participate in.

The Ethernet, Token Ring, ARCnet, FDDI, or AX.25 address (depending on the Data Link Layer media connecting the computer to the Internet) is still used to get the IP data across the LAN. To avoid confusion, the Data Link Layer address is called the Machine

Address, while internetwork addressing is done using an IP address, which is more than just a number.

Network Addresses, Subnet Masks, and Station Addresses   As described in the previous section, every IP address has two parts: those bits it has in common with the other computers in its subdomain (called the network address) and those bits that are unique for computers in the subdomain (the station address). The bits for the network address always come before the bits for the station address. A third IP configuration value, the subnet mask, tells the computer which part of the IP address is the network address and which part is the station address, as shown in Figure 3.6.

Figure 3.6   The subnet mask identifies which part of the IP address is the network address and which part is the station address.

Decimal		Binary		
IP Address	MSB			LSB
128.110.121.213	10000000	01101110	01111001	11010101
Subnet Mask				
255.255.255.192	11111111	11111111	11111111	11000000
Network Address				
128.110.121.192	10000000	01101110	01111001	11000000
Station Address				
21				010101

All of the computers that have the same network address are expected to be able to directly communicate with each other using the Data Link Layer. All of the computers on one Ethernet LAN could be put in one subnet, for example, and all of the computers in a Token Ring LAN could be put in another. Mixed Token Ring and Ethernet computers can't all be put in the same IP subdomain (i.e. they could not be given the same network address) because an Ethernet enabled computer could not send an Ethernet frame directly to a Token Ring enabled computer.

Every subnet that will be connected to a larger network, such as a campus network or the Internet, must have at least one machine that has multiple network adapters so that it can move data between the LAN and the exterior network. This machine is called the gateway in Internet terminology (see Figure 3.7), and can be a special purpose adapter (such as a fast hardware router) or a general purpose computer that routes network data as well as performing other functions (such as firewalling and hosting FTP and Web services). This machine will have two (or more) IP addresses, one for the network adapter residing on the local network and one (or more) for the network adapter(s) residing on the external one(s).

Figure 3.7 A gateway machine has two network adapters and allows network traffic to move between LANs.

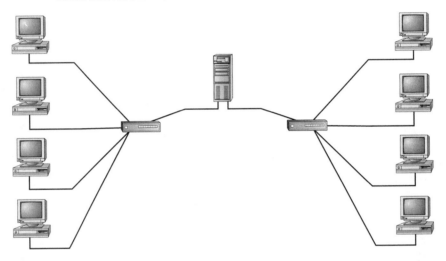

A multi-homed host may reside on networks of different sizes. Therefore, each network adapter (Ethernet, CSU/DSU, modem, etc.) has a different subnet mask associated with its IP address, identifying for that IP address only which part of it is the network address and which part is the station address for that network adapter.

Communicating with a Local Host Sending IP data is a little more complicated than sending Ethernet data, partially because IP uses data link protocols such as Ethernet to do part of its job. With Ethernet, a computer that has data to send just broadcasts it. Every computer on the LAN then receives it and (unless a hacker has put an adapter in promiscuous mode) only the recipient keeps it. IP, on the other hand, needs first to determine whether or not the destination computer is on the local network, and if so, what its corresponding machine address is before it can send the packet embedded in a Data Link frame.

IP operates simply to determine if the destination computer can be communicated with directly. For each of the network devices attached to the computer, the computer compares the network portion of the adapter IP address (as identified by the subnet mask for that adapter) with the same bits (but only those bits, as identified by that same subnet mask) of the destination IP address. If the bits match, the destination computer resides on the subnet that adapter is connected to, and the computer can send the data directly to that computer using that adapter.

But the Data Link Layer, which IP uses to actually send the data, doesn't know anything about IP addresses, so IP needs to get the Machine Address of the destination computer on that LAN before it can put the IP data into a Data Link Layer frame and send it out. The Internet Protocol uses another protocol, called the Address Resolution Protocol (ARP), which every computer on an IP subnet hears and can respond to, to translate IP addresses into Machine Addresses.

ARP works by filling a Data Link Layer frame with a special packet that every computer on the LAN will receive. As you saw in the Data Link Layer section, the frame type for Ethernet for an ARP packet is 0806. Figure 3.8 shows the structure of an ARP packet (which is contained in the data portion of the Data Link Layer frame).

Figure 3.8   An ARP/RARP packet is a broadcast request for data.

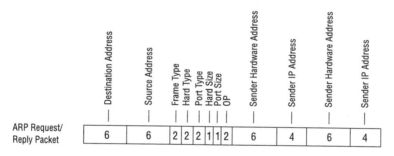

The fields for an ARP/RARP packet are defined as follows (this example is based on Ethernet; other Data Link Layer packets may have different sized values):

- Hardware Type (two bytes)—The type of hardware address (1 for Ethernet)

- Protocol Type (two bytes)—The protocol type (0x0800 for Internet Protocol)

- Hardware Size (one byte)—The size of the hardware addresses in bytes

- Protocol Size (one byte)—The size of the protocol addresses in bytes

- OP (two bytes)—The type of operation: either ARP Request, ARP Reply, RARP Request, or RARP Reply

- Sender Hardware Address (six bytes for Ethernet)—The Ethernet address of the ARP packet sender

- Sender Protocol Address (four bytes for IP)—The IP address of the ARP packet sender

- Target Hardware Address (six bytes for Ethernet)—The Ethernet address of the ARP packet sender

- Target Protocol Address (four bytes for IP)—The IP address of the ARP packet sender

To get the hardware address of a computer in a local subnet, a computer sends out (in a broadcast Data Link Layer frame) an ARP packet with an OP value of 1 and everything but the Target Hardware Address filled in (because only the sender needs to know that). Since the frame is broadcast to all stations on the LAN, all of the computers will receive it, but only the one with the matching Target Protocol Address responds by changing the OP value of the packet to 2, filling in the Target Hardware Address, and broadcasting the packet back.

The computer does not perform an ARP for every IP packet it sends out. The computer maintains a table of IP addresses and corresponding hardware addresses, and only when the computer does not have an entry for an IP address in its subnet does it send out an ARP packet and wait for a reply. The rest of the time it just uses the value it has in its ARP table.

When the computer has the hardware address corresponding to an IP address for a packet, the computer sends the IP packet to the destination in a Data Link Layer frame addressed to just that computer. That computer receives the frame, notes that the destination IP address is its own, and processes the packet according to the protocol information in the header.

NOTE   Why does IP bother with ARP and machine addressing when Ethernet is a broadcast medium anyway? After all, every Ethernet adapter in the LAN can listen to all the packets, not just ones with its own Machine Address as the intended recipient. Why not just send all of the IP packets as broadcast frames, and let the IP protocol on each computer sort them out?

The reason is two-fold: Ethernet hardware can be much more efficient than the IP protocols at determining which frames should be ignored and which ones should be processed, and Ethernet networks are often partitioned into many small collision domains by bridges and switches in order to decrease contention and increase available bandwidth. Broadcasting defeats this optimization by spilling traffic over into collision domains that contain neither the sender nor the recipient.

Communicating with a Distant Host   But what if the destination IP address does not lie on any LAN the computer is connected to? The computer could send out an ARP message, but nobody would reply.

If none of the network addresses of any of the computer's adapters exactly match the destination IP address (as defined by the subnet mask for that adapter), then the computer needs to know where to send the packet so that it will eventually get to its destination. Since it can't send the packet directly to the destination, it needs to know where else it can send the packet that will eventually get it there.

For most networks, that intermediate location is the gateway host or router. As described in the section above on network addresses, subnet masks, and station addresses, the gateway is a machine that has adapters residing on at least two networks. Most LANs connected to the Internet will have one gateway, but some may have more than one. Just one of them should be configured to be the default gateway, where computers in the LAN send an IP packet when they don't otherwise know what to do with it.

All your standard computer needs then is a default gateway entry to send non-local packets to. The gateway can then figure out where to send the packet from there. This means, of course, that the gateway requires a bit more configuration than computers with just one network adapter. The configuration information goes in a routing table that tells the router what to do with packets it receives that have an ultimate destination of somewhere else.

A routing table is simply a list of station and network addresses and a corresponding gateway IP address further along to which it should send packets that match that station or network address. Figure 3.9 shows a sample routing table.

Figure 3.9   The routing table instructs the gateway how to forward IP packets.

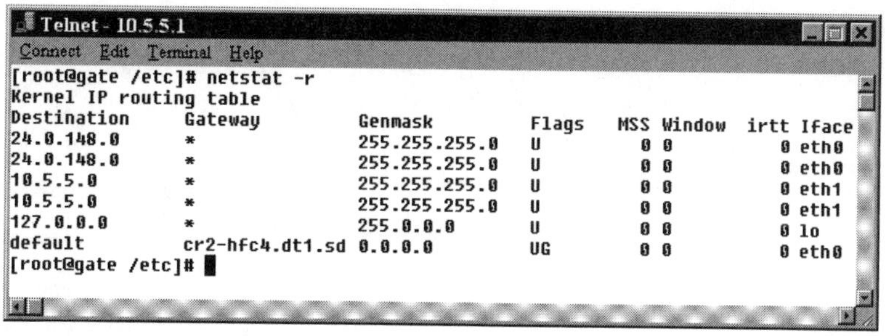

```
Telnet - 10.5.5.1
Connect  Edit  Terminal  Help
[root@gate /etc]# netstat -r
Kernel IP routing table
Destination     Gateway          Genmask          Flags  MSS Window  irtt Iface
24.0.148.0      *                255.255.255.0    U      0 0         0 eth0
24.0.148.0      *                255.255.255.0    U      0 0         0 eth0
10.5.5.0        *                255.255.255.0    U      0 0         0 eth1
10.5.5.0        *                255.255.255.0    U      0 0         0 eth1
127.0.0.0       *                255.0.0.0        U      0 0         0 lo
default         cr2-hfc4.dt1.sd  0.0.0.0          UG     0 0         0 eth0
[root@gate /etc]#
```

The simplest gateway configuration requires just three entries—one for itself (127.0.0.1 is IP shorthand for the computer itself), one for IP addresses in the interior LAN, and one for all other IP addresses (its own default gateway when it doesn't know what to do with an IP address).

Things get a little more complicated when you have a more complex network structure behind your gateway, but the principle remains the same—the routing table explicitly lists all of the networks behind the gateway and where the next closest (internal) gateway is for those internal networks, and the routing table lists a default gateway entry to send packets to that the gateway otherwise doesn't know what to do with. See figure 3.10 for a more complex routing example.

Figure 3.10   A gateway should know how to explicitly route to any internal network and also have a default external gateway to send packets it doesn't know what to do with otherwise.

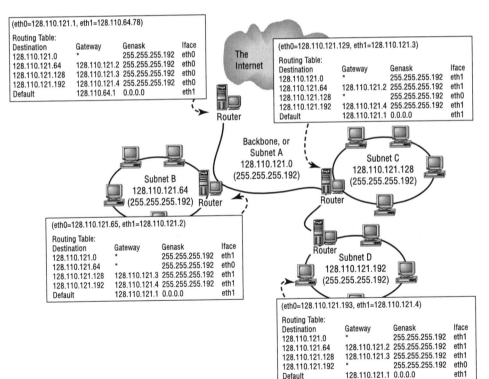

A gateway or router processes a packet as follows (see Figure 3.11 for a graphical view):

1. Accept Data Link Layer frame.
2. Verify CRC strip frame header and trailer; discard if invalid.
3. Verify IP header checksum; discard if invalid.
4. Check IP parameters; discard if invalid or does not match policy.
5. Decrease the Time to Live field in the packet. If the field now reads 0, discard the packet and send an ICMP message back to the sender of the packet.
6. Check the destination IP address against the router's own IP addresses; if there is a match, process the IP packet locally.
7. Find the network or host entry in the routing table that matches the destination IP address of the packet. If there is no match, use the default entry in the routing table.
8. Create a new Data Link Layer frame for the packet with the hardware address of the next closest gateway to the destination (or the hardware address of the destination itself if it is on the same LAN).
9. Send the Data Link Layer frame.

The nice thing about IP routing is that no one computer needs to know how to get the IP packet all the way to the destination—all each computer needs to know is how to get the packet to the next computer on the way. So long as there are no problems along the way, the packet will eventually get to its destination.

ICMP Messages

But what if there is a problem? Let's say, for example, that the default network link for your connection to the Internet has gone down, and (while the network technicians frantically try to get it up) an alternate host has been provided to route data to and from the Internet.

The gateway that would otherwise forward your IP packet to its destination needs a way of telling your computer about the network problem. ICMP packets are the Internet Protocol's way of sending network status information back to the sender. With ICMP, network devices can identify routing problems, congestion problems, quality of service problems, and more. Table 3.1 shows the types of ICMP messages your computer can send or receive.

Table 3.1   ICMP Message with general message type, specific message code, and whether the message is a query or a response to a network event.

Type	Code	Description	Q/E
0	0	Echo reply	Q
3		Destination Unreachable:	
	0	Network Unreachable	E
	1	Host Unreachable	E
	2	Protocol Unreachable	E
	3	Port Unreachable	E
	4	Too Big/Can't Defrag	E
	5	Source Route Failed	E
	6	Destination Network Unknown	E
	7	Destination Host Unknown	E
	8	Source Host Isolated (obsolete)	E
	9	Destination Network Prohibited	E
	10	Destination Host Prohibited	E
	11	Network Unreachable for TOS	E
	12	Host Unreachable for TOS	E
	13	Prohibited by Filtering	E
	14	Host Precedence Violation	E
	15	Precedence Cutoff in Effect	E
4	0	Source Quench	E
5		Redirect	
	0	Redirect for Network	E

Table 3.1 ICMP Message with general message type, specific message code, and
whether the message is a query or a response to a network event. *(continued)*

Type	Code	Description	Q/E
	1	Redirect for Host	E
	2	Redirect for TOS and Network	E
	3	Redirect for TOS and Host	E
8	0	Echo Request	Q
9	0	Router Advertisement	Q
10	0	Router Solicitation	Q
11		Time Exceeded	
	0	TTL Exceeds 0 During Transit	E
	1	TTL Exceeds 0 During Reassembly	E
12		Parameter Problem	
	0	IP Header Bad	E
	1	Required Option Missing	E
13	0	Timestamp Request	Q
14	0	Timestamp Reply	Q
15	0	Information Request (obsolete)	Q
16	0	Information Request Reply (obsolete)	Q
17	0	Address Mask Request	Q
18	0	Address Mask Reply	Q

Backgrounder

PART 1

IP identifies by the Protocol field what kind of packet is being transmitted (see Figure 3.5). ICMP is one of those kinds of packets. The structure of an ICMP packet is shown in Figure 3.11.

Figure 3.11 ICMP messages share a common header format with Type, Code, and Checksum fields.

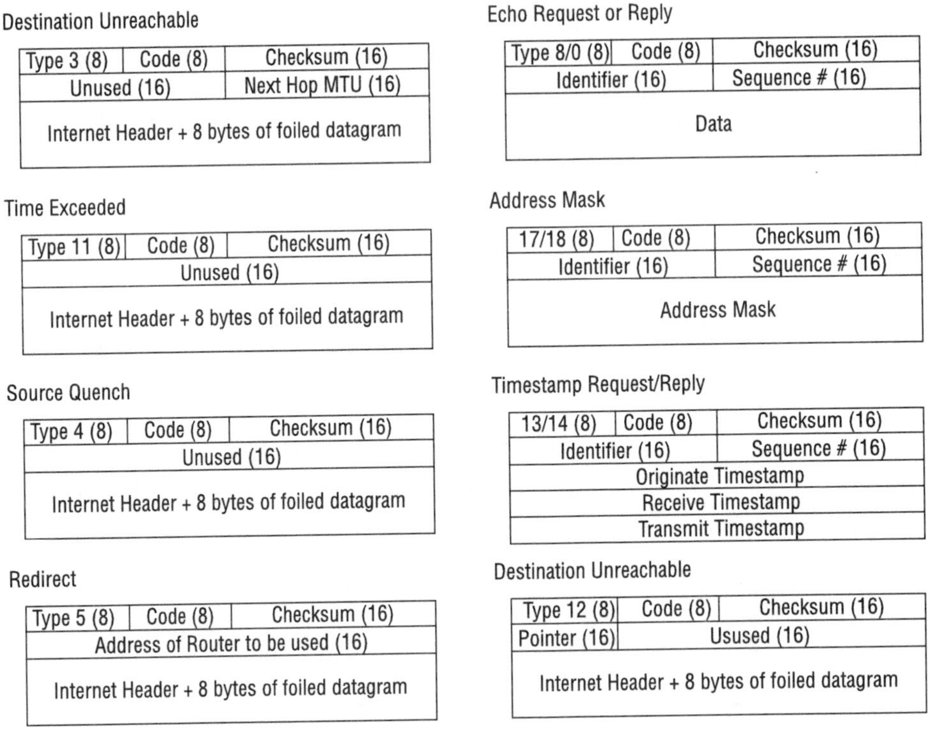

Destination Unreachable

Type 3 (8)	Code (8)	Checksum (16)
Unused (16)		Next Hop MTU (16)
Internet Header + 8 bytes of foiled datagram		

Echo Request or Reply

Type 8/0 (8)	Code (8)	Checksum (16)
Identifier (16)		Sequence # (16)
Data		

Time Exceeded

Type 11 (8)	Code (8)	Checksum (16)
Unused (16)		
Internet Header + 8 bytes of foiled datagram		

Address Mask

17/18 (8)	Code (8)	Checksum (16)
Identifier (16)		Sequence # (16)
Address Mask		

Source Quench

Type 4 (8)	Code (8)	Checksum (16)
Unused (16)		
Internet Header + 8 bytes of foiled datagram		

Timestamp Request/Reply

13/14 (8)	Code (8)	Checksum (16)
Identifier (16)		Sequence # (16)
Originate Timestamp		
Receive Timestamp		
Transmit Timestamp		

Redirect

Type 5 (8)	Code (8)	Checksum (16)
Address of Router to be used (16)		
Internet Header + 8 bytes of foiled datagram		

Destination Unreachable

Type 12 (8)	Code (8)	Checksum (16)
Pointer (16)		Usused (16)
Internet Header + 8 bytes of foiled datagram		

So what happens when your computer tries to send a packet through the obstructed gateway? The steps that the gateway and your computer go through are as follows:

1. Your computer sends a packet with the frame address of the gateway machine, but with the IP address of an exterior computer.

2. The gateway machine reads the packet from the frame and decodes it.

3. The gateway machine discards the packet (because the packet cannot be forwarded) and creates an ICMP message.

4. If the gateway has not been configured to redirect traffic to an alternate gateway, it will send a host-unreachable or network-unreachable ICMP packet back to the sending computer.

5. If the gateway has been configured to redirect traffic, it will send an ICMP redirect packet to the sending computer.

6. The sending computer receives the ICMP packet and decodes it.

7. If the packet is a host- or network-unreachable packet, it generates an error message for the program that attempted to send the data.

8. If the packet is an ICMP redirect packet, it resends the data using a different gateway.

This sort of network reporting and redirection can happen at any point in the string of packet "hops" from the sending computer to the receiving computer. The operations performed are the same.

ICMP Vulnerabilities

ICMP packets do not include any authentication method for the recipient of the message. A clever hacker can forge ICMP packets and cause havoc in an unprepared network. The two greatest threats from malicious ICMP packets are denial-of-service attacks and impersonation or man-in-the-middle attacks.

A forged destination-unreachable packet can isolate a computer from necessary services. Echo Request has been used by hackers to crash computers with a naïve implementation of the ICMP protocols.

Once a computer that performs an important service (such as a DNS server, file server, or web server) is out of the way, an ICMP redirect packet can point unwitting victims to the hacker's computer, where the hacker can accept authentication information (usernames, passwords, etc.).

Routers and Route Discovery

Routers (sometimes called gateways) link IP subnets together. It is up to the router to send IP packets toward their destinations when the end computer resides outside of the subnet. How does the router know where to send the packet?

For small networks with just one or two routers the answer is easy—the network administrator enters routes by hand into the router. This is called static routing because the route information does not change automatically according to network conditions—it is up to the administrator to change the router's settings when a new subnet is added or a network link goes down.

The router must have IP forwarding rules that account for any possible IP address because there's no telling which computer, locally or on the Internet, a client computer may want to talk to. On a simple network the rules are correspondingly simple. On a one-router network, for example, the rule may be as follows: If the destination address is on the local subnet, then send the packet directly to its destination, otherwise send it to an upstream router.

Dynamic Routing In larger networks, the static routing tables get to be a real hassle to maintain. In a university with every college maintaining its own LAN, or a corporation with each department having a different subnet, the configuration of the network is always changing and the router tables must be updated to reflect those changes. In addition, the routers must have a consistent view of the network.

The IP routing protocols reduce the work required to keep those routing tables updated and consistent. The protocols enable the routers to automatically update each other of network changes such as new routes between subnets or network links that are down and must be routed around. The administrator makes a change in just one router's table, and the change will propagate automatically to all of the other routers in the network.

Interior Gateways vs. Exterior Gateways Before you take a closer look at the routing protocols, you need to understand that there are two categories of routers—interior routers (or gateways) that reside entirely within your organization, and exterior gateways that convey IP traffic between your network and the Internet (or any other organization's network). The difference between these two types of gateways is primarily a matter of trust; you want routing changes within your network to move from one router to another with minimum hassle, while you may not want routing information from outside your network to be implemented on your border routers unless it comes from an authorized source and until you've had a chance to review it first.

RIP v1 and v2, IGRP The earliest routing protocol in wide-spread use is called (imaginitively enough) Routing Internet Protocol, or RIP. Routers using version 1 of the protocol simply broadcast their entire routing table every 30 seconds on each of the subnets to which that router has network adapters connected. When a router receives a RIP packet, it compares the contents with its own table and updates its table with new information from the packet (modified, of course, to include the extra hop that it takes to get to the router that sent the RIP packet). It removes routes that haven't been updated for a while, so bad routes eventually disappear from the table.

RIP is a distance-vector protocol because it keeps track of the distance (number of network hops) that it takes to get to a destination listed in the routing table. When multiple routes to the same destination show up in the table, the route with the least number of hops is used to send the packet on its way, regardless of the speed of the network links used in the route. RIP packets are broadcast using UDP.

RIP v1 had a significant security problem—there was no authentication included in transmitted RIP packets, and received RIP packets weren't checked to make sure they came from authorized routers. Anybody could forge a RIP packet and reconfigure your router for you. RIP also has the problem that in complex networks with large routing tables and lots of routers, the RIP broadcasts can soak up a lot of network bandwidth. Also, it can take a long time for network changes to propagate through all of the routers in a complex network using RIP.

RIP v2 fixes the authentication problem by including passwords in the RIP packets. The router discards any RIP packets without a correct password. The bandwidth and convergence delay problems of RIP remain, however.

Cisco developed for their high-performance routing hardware a new protocol called IGRP, which was endorsed by the IETF. IGRP maintains more link information, such as bit rate and cost, allowing the routers to make better decisions about possible routes. IGRP has a 90-second update interval, however, and it can take even longer than with RIP for IGRP routers to converge on a consistent set of routing tables.

OSPF   In 1988 the Internet Engineering Task Force (IETF) came out with a protocol designed to replace RIP for routing within a single organziation's network (i.e. an IGP). That protocol was called Open Shortest Path First, or OSPF. It is a more complicated protocol than RIP, but has reduced network bandwidth use and speedier convergence. This makes RIP a much better protocol for routing in medium-to-large networks.

OSPF is a link-state protocol, unlike RIP (which is a distance-vector protocol). OSPF records in its routing table the state of the link between it and any other routers it can directly connect to, along with those IP domains that its network adapters reside on. In addition to status, it records link characteristics such as bandwidth, cost, and type-of-service restrictions. OSPF uses IP multicast as well as broadcast for transmitting routing table updates. It also performs load-balancing, which sends successive IP packets along different routes to the same destination to reduce congestion on the network.

Route updates in an OSPF routed network propagate much more quickly than they do in a RIP routed network. After the initial update, only the difference between one update and the next is transmitted. This is unlike RIP, which transmits the entire table each update. Also, OSPF imposes a hierarchy on the routers in the network, with Designated Routers for each subnet, a Backbone Router for the network backbone, and Autonomous System Boundary Routers for links between separately administered systems. The hierarchy makes administration a little more difficult, but the centralized collection and redistribution of route data allows the routers to converge on a consistent view of the network in a matter of seconds rather than minutes or hours for a large network.

OSPF, like RIP v2, authenticates the routing packets exchanged between the routers, making it much more difficult for network intruders to subvert them. In addition, the

OSPF packets contain sequence numbers, making forgery difficult even if the authentication mechanism is compromised.

NOTE You should block all RIP, IGRP, and OSPF traffic at the firewall. Because your firewall will be the only connection to the Internet (otherwise, why have a firewall?), you have no need to maintain route information from the Internet on your internal routers. The only Internet configuration your routers need is that IP packets with destinations exterior to your entire protected network should go to the firewall.

BGP and IDRP Unless you run the network for an Internet Service Provider or Network Access Point, you don't need to worry about Exterior (or Border) Gateway Protocols. We'll touch on them here, however, for the sake of completeness.

The original Border Gateway Protocol was designed for the routers at the edges of private networks. These routers must maintain huge routing tables because the Internet is a large place, and there's no telling where on the Internet an IP subnet is going to be until the router containing the subnet announces the fact and the route is propagated across the public network.

BGP is a distance-vector protocol because it maintains hops like RIP. However unlike RIP, BGP uses TCP rather than UDP to exchange routing information.

With the expansive growth of the Internet, BGP began to show its age and its naïve security assumptions. The IETF developed an Inter Domain Routing Protocol (IDRP) to replace BGP for routing between private networks. Like OSPF, IDRP is a link-state routing protocol, which allows multiple routes to destination, and records link attributes such as throughput, delay, and security characteristics. It also supports authentication of the exchanged route data and supports a hierarchical management of domains called Domain Confederations.

Where Is the Data Coming From?

Until you actually take a look at a protocol analyzer, you may not be aware of the importance of knowing exactly how TCP/IP gets data from one place to another. But when you do see all those bytes flowing in and out of your computer, even when (from the user's point of view) the computer isn't actually doing anything, you'll feel much more comfortable knowing which bits are natural and which ones are suspect.

One customer, who manages a medium-size LAN connected to the Internet as well as a number of remote LAN clients that connect over the Internet, called one day after seeing the lights on his modem though he wasn't actually using the computer. He observed that even when he wasn't transferring files or browsing the Web, every second or so the modem lights would flash. Instantly his imagination conjured visions of hackers and Trojan horses burrowing into his hard-drive and sending sensitive corporate data out over the network. An examination of the TCP/IP statistics of his computer (he is relatively knowledgeable in networking) showed that no IP packets were going out.

What the manager did not know was that PPP is a true Data Link Layer protocol, and some PPP implementations (including his) periodically exchange link data even when no protocol data is being transferred over the link. His mind was set at ease after he closely examined what exactly was being sent and why.

24seven CASE STUDY

4

Sockets and Services from a Security Point of View

In Chapter 3 you saw the first four layers of the OSI stack—those layers which transfer data, irrespective of what that data is, from one computer to another over the Internet. This chapter focuses on the security implications of the types of data exchanged between computers using those lower-level protocols. We'll talk about common protocols, such as HTTP and FTP, hidden or problematic ones such as RPC and Finger, as well as obscure ones like BootP and SNMP.

A network intruder will look for security weaknesses at every point in your network architecture. If you have adequately locked down the Physical, Data Link, Network, and Transport Layers of your network, the wily hacker will simply move up to those protocols and services your network does expose to the Internet. These application-specific protocols are actually much easier to exploit, so many hackers start there and drop down to the network or transport level when they need to circumvent a protocol's security mechanisms.

In this chapter we'll go over each of the most commonly used Internet services, briefly examining each for their weaknesses and abuse potential. First, however, we'll discuss sockets and services in general, identifying typical service vulnerabilities so you can identify potential problems when you need to install services on your own network.

Exploiting Socket-Based Services

Which services are safe to allow through your firewall, which are not safe, and which ones do you do need to keep an eye on? When a new service becomes popular, or when you want to give your network clients a new Internet-based tool, what do you look for when you evaluate the service?

Later in this chapter we will examine the most common protocols that use IP as a transport and are passed through firewalls. For those protocols, and for any others you may want to support in your network, you should ask the following questions:

- How complex is the service?
- How might the service be abused?
- What information does the service dispense?
- How much of a dialog does the service allow?
- How programmable or configurable is the service?
- What other services does the service rely on?
- What sort of authentication does the service use?

How Complex Is the Service?

Complex services are easier to exploit than simple services. The Echo service, for example, simply transmits back to the client whatever the client sends to it. The Echo service is useful for debugging and for network connectivity testing, but it is difficult to see how the Echo service could be exploited to gain control of the computer running the service. Since the Echo service accepts data from the client, however, it must be programmed to correctly handle being fed too much data at once.

The mail service, on the other hand, is a large, complex piece of software that accepts data (mail) from and returns data to the client, as well as reads and stores data and configuration information on the computer's hard drive. Many mail services (POP and IMAP, for example) require authentication before the client can use the service. SMTP, on the other hand, allows any connecting user to send mail as though it came from any user—even a non-existent one. If the authentication mechanism can be subverted, the passwords hacked, or the service tricked into sending out private data (such as your password file), the hacker can use the service to get enough information to break into your computer through other means, such as FTP or Telnet.

Buffer Overruns and Denial-of-Service Floods

Buffer overruns are a potential weakness of all services that receive data from the client. Optimistic programmers expect network clients to play by the rules and only send as much data as would be appropriate for the protocol. For example, the destination address portion of an SMTP message should be somewhere between four and two hundred characters. But what if the client sends several megabytes instead?

A correctly written implementation of the protocol will simply discard the excess data and return an error. An incorrectly written implementation, which does not check how much data is being received, may overwrite its own program code and either crash or (if the sender of the data sent it maliciously) begin executing the excess data as a program.

Early versions of Sendmail had exactly this kind of security hole, and the infamous Internet Worm used this weakness to gain control of target computers and to bring the whole Internet to its knees.

A related attack for computers that store data (such as mail), is to keep sending data until the storage space on the server runs out. This is a denial-of-service attack that, although it does not give the hacker control of the computer, renders the computer unusable to its intended clients.

How Might the Service Be Abused?

Some services might be simple and innocuous in themselves, but can be turned to unexpected and detrimental uses. Chargen, for example, is a simple UNIX service that sends out ASCII characters over and over. Chargen is a useful network programming and testing tool because there are certain classes of networking problems that become evident when you can look at a stream of data spanning a whole range of binary representations. A communications channel that clears (or sets) the top two bits of every data word, for example, becomes obvious because the pattern of characters from Chargen will change as well.

An unscrupulous hacker, however, might exploit this protocol by forging a SYN packet (connection request) that redirects the output of Chargen to another computer and port. This way the hacker can flood the target computer with data that doesn't even originate from his own computer!

What Information Does the Service Dispense?

Some services may be simple, terse, and still dangerous to your network security. Finger, for example, was designed to help Unix users contact each other. A Finger request will tell you whether or not there is an account for an individual on a computer, what that account name is, when the user last logged on, additional contact information for the user, and whatever else that user would like to tell the world.

That information is certainly useful if you need to know a co-worker's email address or phone extension. It is also incredibly useful for a hacker who wants to verify the existence of an account, find a dormant one, and get clues to the identity and personality of an account holder. You won't find many computers on the modern Internet that support the Finger protocol. The Whois service is another one that you might not want to run on your network due to the amount of information it can give to a network intruder.

Services such as Whois and Finger are excellent time-saving tools for use within an organization, but you should never allow access to these services from beyond your internal network or your Intranet.

How Much of a Dialog Does the Service Allow?

A simple service with a regular interface is easier to secure than a complex service that uses an extensive dialogue with the client to provide its functionality. HTTP, for example (disregarding CGI, server applets, and Active Server Pages for the moment), is easy to secure because all the client can do is ask for a resource, and the server does not maintain data about the state of the connection between client requests (i.e. the protocol is stateless).

A stateful protocol is more difficult to secure, especially if the protocol requires client authentication at the beginning of the session and allows for many requests, replies and state changes after authentication. A stateful protocol must be tested for security holes for every state the client may place the server in. It is possible, for example, to hijack a Telnet session after an authorized client has established the connection and provided correct credentials.

Also, the more dialog a service allows, the more dangerous the service is when compromised. If a hacker arranges the Finger service to run at the wrong permissions level (such as root or Administrator), the hacker would still just get account and contact information from it. An FTP session at the supervisor level, however, could send the hacker any file in the computer. A root Telnet session would allow the intruder to do anything at all, including running programs, shutting down or starting services, replacing operating system code, as well as creating and deleting accounts.

Service Separation

FTP sites, Web sites, and Telnet hosts perform vital functions in today's Internet-connected networks. They create an Internet presence and facilitate communication within the organization as well as with outside customers and the rest of the world. You can't just decide not to run these services, but you can be careful about how you do it.

Because computers running these services are more vulnerable to being compromised, these services should not be run on computers that also host other internal services (i.e. the file server or a database server). Ideally, each Internet service would be run on its own server, but some services work well together (FTP is often used to update Web server content, for example).

How Programmable or Configurable is the Service?

The more configurable a service, the easier it is to get the configuration wrong. The more programmable the service, the more likely bugs are to pop up, creating loopholes for network intruders to jump through. So, Exchange Server (which has more configuration options than you can shake a stick at) and Internet Information Server (or any other Web server that allows you to run arbitrary scripts to generate Web pages) are more likely to contain a security weakness than simpler services such as the POP service that comes with the NT 4 resource kit.

What Sort of Authentication Does the Service Use?

Any service that requires authentication from the client is a potential security risk for two reasons: the authentication protocol may be weak, and users tend to use the same account names and passwords across multiple services.

POP is one example of weak authentication. The username and password is sent from the client to the server unencrypted, and the password is sent complete and unsalted. In POP, the server asks for the username and password, and the client just sends them. Compare this to MAPI (used by Microsoft Exchange), which uses a challenge-and-response protocol. With MAPI, the server requests the username and password, but also sends a value for the client to salt (pre-pend to) the password before the client hashes (scrambles) the password. The username and hashed password are then sent to the server. The server can compare the hash to a known hashed password to determine if the client should have access to the service. No eavesdropping computer can determine what the password is from the hash, and the same hash cannot be used more than once because the server changes the hash every time.

Anther common problem with authentication is insufficiently long passwords. LAN Manager style passwords, which are used in Windows for Workgroups and Windows 95, are weak because case sensitivity is ignored in the hash, and because the hash is comprised of two sections using the same seed that may be cracked in parallel. In addition, older Microsoft networking clients send the same password hashed with both the LAN Manager protocol and the Windows NT challenge and response protocol, seriously compromising the Windows NT hash.

The purpose of a strong password hash is to keep the hacker from intercepting the passwords as they travel from the client to the server. If the hacker can't intercept the password, he may just try to guess it. This is another area in which many protocols fail. A properly implemented protocol will detect an unusual number (three or greater) of failed password attempts and not allow any more logon attempts to that username or from that client. A weak protocol will allow as many attempts as the hacker can perform, and a clever hacker can write a program to perform hundreds of attempts per second, determining the true password by brute force. Windows NT by default will lock out any account but the Administrator account when there are too many failed password attempts.

It is easier to remember one password than a half-dozen, so many computer users use exactly the same password for all of their computer accounts. This means that if a network intruder penetrates one computer and captures the password list for that computer, one or more passwords and usernames from that computer are very likely to also work in another computer that is otherwise secure. Your password-protected service gives the hacker a double resource—if the hacker can find a password that works on that service, she'll try it elsewhere, and if she can find a password elsewhere, she'll try it on that service as well.

One Key Fits All

For convenience's sake, some services use the operating system username and password instead of recording a separate username and password pair for the service. While this feature makes life easier for the user, it also makes life easier for the hacker. When the hacker has obtained access to the service, it means that he has also obtained access to the underlying operating system. Internet Information Server for Windows NT (for password-protected Web pages) works this way, as do the POP and SMTP services that come on the NT 4 resource kit. Surprisingly, Microsoft's Exchange Server maintains a separate set of usernames and passwords for access to its services.

Internet Names

One of the most important higher-level services in the Internet Protocol Suite is the Domain Name Service. The lower-level Internet protocols all use IP addresses to identify source and destination computers, but people have a hard time remembering numbers. So, the architects of the Internet developed a service that will translate human-friendly Internet addresses like www.microsoft.com and www.linux.org into their corresponding computer-friendly IP addresses.

Dot Com and All That

In the beginning, people just kept a list of the human-friendly Internet addresses and their corresponding IP addresses (the host file is a remnant of this), but as the Internet grew these files got unwieldy, and a more flexible method was needed. The Internet architects came up with a new scheme that allowed an organization (or a person) to request an Internet address from a central authority and then expand on that name using their own authority. Thus was born the Internet Domain Name Registration system.

Human-readable Internet addresses, like IP addresses, contain dots. But Internet addresses can have as few as one dot or many more than four (although it is a rare address that will have more than a half-dozen). The dots function as separators, and the last portion of the address is called the top-level domain. Common top-level domains include .com, .org, .net, .mil, .gov, .edu, and two-character country codes such as .uk, .us, .cz, .au, and .oz.

When you request a domain name such as memetech.com, tribalgame.net, or robinson-crusoefamily.org, you are staking out space on the Internet in a similar manner to when you obtain a range of IP addresses. It is up to you to further subdivide the name space. When you request the name, you provide the top-level service with the IP address of two servers that will handle name requests from your name space. When a computer wants to contact www.tribalgame.net, for example, it is up to the domain name servers that you specify to perform the translation from www.tribalgame.net to the actual IP address. Your servers can put any computer name you want below tribalgame.net, including this.is.a.very.long.domain.name.tribalgame.net.

A large organization or a service may further subdivide the name space. BigCorp, for example, might have separate domain name servers for each of its divisions in Asia, Europe, the US, and Africa. In this scenario, one domain name server would handle requests such as www.asia.bigcorp.com and a different one would handle requests such as www.us.bigcorp.com, allowing each division to configure their networks independently but maintain overall BigCorp control of the bigcorp.com domain.

DNS Queries

When you type www.microsoft.com into your Web browser, your computer needs to know what IP address corresponds to that Internet address. Microsoft's DNS (Domain

Name System) server is the computer that contains that information. How does that information get from the Microsoft DNS server into your computer?

Your computer has the IP addresses of one or two DNS servers that it can ask about domain names (and unless you work in Redmond, neither one is likely to be the Microsoft DNS server that has the resolution you need). Your DNS servers most likely contain only Internet address to IP address mappings for your local network, and for a few frequently accessed external locations. When your local DNS server cannot satisfy a DNS mapping request, it will either redirect your computer to another DNS server query that DNS server itself and pass the results back to your computer.

If the mapping query is for an address in a domain foreign to the DNS server, the DNS server redirects the query up the chain of servers toward (or to) a root server (such as the server for the .com, .edu, or .gov domains). A server that has recorded and delegated name service for a domain will redirect the query down to the DNS server that has responsibility for the domain. See Figure 4.1 for an example.

Figure 4.1   The DNS system distributes control of Internet domain names.

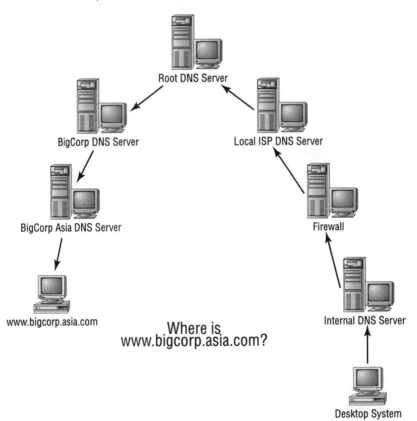

DNS Messages

Your computer makes a DNS request by sending a UDP packet in the DNS message format to port 53 of the DNS server. DNS uses UDP rather than TCP because it has one short message that will fit in a UDP packet to send to the server, and the connection establishment overhead of TCP is not necessary for DNS. The message has a fixed 12-byte header and four variable-length fields as shown in Figure 4.2.

Figure 4.2   A single DNS message may contain multiple address resolution queries or responses in the Question RR and Answer RR fields of the DNS UDP packet.

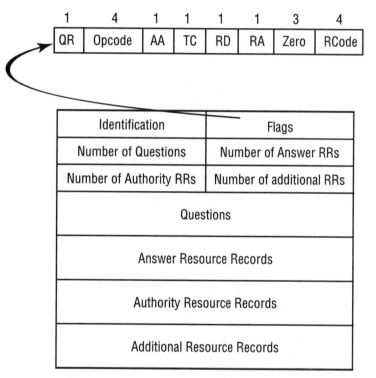

The DNS message fields are as follows:

- Identification—This is set by the client so that it can identify the DNS server response.
- Flags—This field classifies the message as follows (See Figure 4.2):
  - QR—0 for query or 1 for response.
  - Opcode—0 for standard query, 1for Inverse query, or 2 for Server Status Request.
  - AA—Authoritative Answer (True/False).

- TC—Truncated (True/False).
- RD—Recursion Desired (True/False).
- RA—Recursion Available (True/False).
- Zero—These three bits are zero.
- Rcode—0 for No Error, or 3 for Name Error.
- Number of Questions—1 or more for query, 0 for reply
- Number of Answer RRs—0 for query, 1 or more for reply
- Number of Authority RRs—0 for query, 1 or more for reply
- Number of Additional RRs—0 for query, 1 or more for reply
- Questions—Each question is composed of a string containing the Internet address being queried, a query type, and a query class (which is 1 for Internet addresses). Common types are as follows:

1	A	The IP Address
2	NS	The Name Server for the domain
5	CNAME	The Canonical Name (if a computer responds to more than one name, this is the main one)
12	PTR	The Pointer Record (looks up the name corresponding to an IP address)
13	HINFO	Host Information (computer details)
15	MX	The Mail Exchange Record (which host handles mail for this Internet Address)
252	AXFR	The Request for Zone Transfer
255	ANY	The Request for all records

- Answers, Authority, and Additional Information—all share the same Resource Record format, as follows:
  - Domain Name—This is the Internet address that information was requested for.
  - Type—This is the same as the Type field in the query.
  - Class—This is usually set for 1 for Internet addresses.
  - Time-To-Live—The number of seconds that the data may be cached by the client (typically two days).
  - Resource Data Length—The amount of space taken by the resource data.
  - Resource Data—The four-byte IP address for a type 1 (a record) response.

So when you type www.microsoft.com into your Web browser, your computer fires off a UDP packet to your DNS server asking where Microsoft is. The DNS server either sends back a UDP packet containing that information, or it redirects your computer to another DNS server that might have it instead. Eventually, your computer gets back an Answer record containing the IP address, and the Web browser can then use it to open a TCP socket to Microsoft's Web server.

in-addr.arpa

Sometimes you already have the IP address to a computer, and you want to know what the Internet address for that computer is. Web server administrators, for example, often need to know which domains most of their traffic is coming from. More importantly, if you suspect that a hacker is breaking into your system, you need to be able to translate the IP address into a domain so that you can contact the administrator of the network that the hacker is coming from. How do you look up an IP address?

> **NOTE** The different kinds of Internet addresses can be confusing to people who are just learning how the Internet protocols work. Just remember—IP addresses are for computers and are made up of four numbers separated by dots. Internet addresses (also called Internet names) on the other hand are meant to make sense to humans, and have the familiar endings such as .com, .edu, .mil, .net, or .org.

When you are allocated a block of IP addresses and you request a domain name to go with it, you are also given control of a portion of the DNS name space corresponding to the IP addresses you have control over. The top level domain name for this portion of DNS is not .com or .org, but rather .in-addr.arpa, which (like the rest of the DNS system, and unlike IP addresses) gets more specific as values are added to the left of it.

If you want to look up the address 128.110.121.144, you would request the CNAME record for 144.121.110.128.in-addr.arpa, and you would receive back the actual Internet address for that computer if there is one registered for it. This is why your own DNS server must be configured for that weird numerical in-addr.arpa domain in it as well as the domain you requested.

Reverse Lookup

Many services will not allow a network client to connect to it if the client does not have an Internet name as well as an IP address configured for it. While a computer without an Internet name is not proof positive of hacking, it is indicative of a domain with lax administration. If the protocols you support allow it, and your network can handle the overhead of looking up every IP connection attempt, lock out these name-less computers.

Coordinating Name Servers (and Subverting Them)

When you obtain a domain name (or more than one), you are required to provide the IP addresses of at least two DNS servers that will handle DNS requests for your domain(s). Why two? So that if one fails, the other can take over its responsibilities. One is designated the primary DNS server and has several secondary servers to backup its data.

Primary and secondary DNS servers are typically configured to stay in sync through the exchange of zone transfer messages. The primary can preemptively send the zone transfer message, or the secondary can request that the primary send one. Zone transfers can be incremental or complete.

DNS servers make juicy targets for hackers because the hacker can use a compromised name server to redirect unwitting clients to her own computer. As a result, impersonation and man-in-the-middle attacks are easy to perform. If your DNS servers aren't particular about where zone transfer packets come from, the hacker can feed false information to the secondary server and then perform a denial-of-service attack on the primary (perhaps through a ping-of-death or smurf attack). The hacker is then in charge of your network name space, not you.

> **NOTE**   With a very small network you can disable zone transfers and simply update the tables of your internal DNS servers by hand. For larger networks this becomes impractical, and you must have either firewall software that discriminates between regular DNS queries and zone transfers, or you must have DNS proxy software that will allow only safe domain name requests.

The Protocols

DNS is one service you must allow through your firewall in one manner or another because without it your network clients won't be able to find anything. There are many more services you may want to support on your network, or that you may elect to block depending on the needs of your network users. Each has its strengths and vulnerabilities, which we'll examine using the criteria established at the start of this chapter. The protocols we'll discuss are:

- BootP/DHCP (67 and 68 UDP)
- Chargen (19 UDP and TCP)
- Daytime (13 UDP)
- Discard (9 UDP and TCP)
- DNS (53 UDP)

- Echo (7 UDP)
- Finger (79 TCP)
- FTP (20 and 21 TCP)
- Gopher (70 TCP)
- HTTP (80 TCP)
- IMAP (143 TCP)
- LDAP (389 TCP and UDP)
- NetBIOS (137, 138, and 139 TCP)
- NFS (2049 TCP and UDP)
- NTP (123 UDP)
- POP3 (110 TCP)
- Quote (17 UDP)
- RPC(sun) (111 UDP)
- RSH (514 TCP)
- SMTP (25 TCP)
- SNMP (161 UDP)
- Telnet (23 TCP)
- TFTP (69 UDP)

BootP/DHCP (67 and 68 UDP)

BootP was developed as a simple mechanism for allowing simple network terminals to load their operating system from a server over the LAN. Over time it has expanded to provide for centralized control of many aspects of a computer's identity and behavior on the network, including allocating IP addresses, configuring gateway, DNS, and router settings, dispensing NetBIOS names, as well as downloading operating system files. The following bulleted items summarize this protocol's security profile (we'll provide a similar bulleted list for each protocol we discuss).

- Complexity—BootP is simple, DHCP is a little more complex.
- Abuse Potential—Medium. The greatest danger from BootP and DHCP is from a network intruder impersonating a DHCP server on your network and thereby misconfiguring the DHCP clients. If you do not allow DHCP to pass your firewall you should be able to use DHCP internally without problems.
- Information Sensitivity—Medium. The DHCP server responds with machine information about your network, but not user account information, when queried.

- Dialog—Minimal.
- Programmability and Configurability—Medium.

Chargen (19 UDP and TCP)

Chargen continuously sends out the printable ASCII characters. It is useful for testing network applications. Any service that could be stopped or swamped by a stream of ASCII characters is broken anyway and shouldn't be let past your firewall. It is extremely unlikely that a network intruder could use Chargen to break into your system.

- Complexity—Simple.
- Abuse Potential—Chargen can be redirected to flood other unsuspecting computers.
- Information Sensitivity—none.
- Dialog—none.
- Programmability and Configurability—none.

Daytime (13 UDP)

This service sends the date and time at the server to the client. It would take a very clever hacker to find a security weakness in this protocol.

- Complexity—Simple.
- Abuse Potential—Minimal.
- Information Sensitivity—None.
- Dialog—Minimal.
- Programmability and Configurability—None.

Discard (9 UDP and TCP)

This protocol throws away any data sent to it. It is useful for developing network tools.

- Complexity—Simple.
- Abuse Potential—Minimal.
- Information Sensitivity—None.
- Dialog—Minimal.
- Programmability and Configurability—None.

DNS (53 UDP)

While this protocol is a prime target for network intruders, you can't disable it without disabling all your network clients as well. You should protect your DNS servers (as described in the previous section, "Dot COM and All That") by blocking zone transfer packets or by using a DNS proxy service.

- Complexity—Complex.
- Abuse Potential—High.
- Information Sensitivity—Minimal.
- Dialog—Minimal.
- Programmability and Configurability—High.

Echo (7 UDP)

Echo repeats to the connected client whatever the connected client sends to it. It is useful for testing network applications. It is extremely unlikely that a network intruder could use Echo to break into your systemas long as Echo properly manages its input buffers.

- Complexity—Simple.
- Abuse Potential—Minimal.
- Information Sensitivity—None.
- Dialog—Minimal.
- Programmability and Configurability—None.

Finger (79 TCP)

The Finger service was designed to help network users communicate by providing system information, such as the last time a user checked their e-mail, and real-world data, such as the user's office hours, telephone number, or current projects. Unfortunately, this data is as good as gold to hackers looking for potential account names and passwords. Also, some hackers will even go so far as to call an office pretending to be the help desk staff and trick users into giving up their account names and passwords over the phone.

- Complexity—Simple.
- Abuse Potential—Average.
- Information Sensitivity—High.
- Dialog—Minimal.
- Programmability and Configurability—Average.

FTP (20 and 21 TCP)

FTP is a useful command-line protocol for transferring files over the Internet. FTP is often used to remotely update Web content on HTTP servers. For this reason it may be necessary to allow FTP traffic through your firewall.

The FTP protocol's development predates the development of firewalls and is therefore a little more difficult to pass through a firewall than newer protocols such as HTTP. When a client opens a connection with the service (using port 20, the command channel) the server opens a second connection to the client (using port 21, the data channel). If the firewall is using IP translation to hide the client computers behind a single public IP address, the data channel connection attempt will fail unless special measures are taken in the firewall to identify and pass through the incoming data channel.

You should be exceedingly careful in configuring FTP security because FTP establishes a dialog with the client in which the client can browse files on the FTP server and download them, and because FTP authentication is made using operating system usernames and passwords. Even if someone accesses the FTP server as the "anonymous user," the user can gain access to critical operating system files if you have set up file and directory security incorrectly (especially if you have established symbolic links that allow the anonymous user out of the typical safety sandbox).

When you set up an FTP server for access that is external to your network, do not use the same account names and passwords on the FTP server as are used for LAN log on.

- Complexity—Complex.
- Abuse Potential—High.
- Information Sensitivity—Medium.
- Dialog—Complex.
- Programmability and Configurability—High.

Gopher (70 TCP)

The Web was not the first widespread hypertext system on the Internet—Gopher actually predates the Web by a year or two. Gopher, like the Web, displays pages of information and has links you can select that lead to other pages. Gopher is text-based, however, while HTTP supports graphics, sound, etc.

Gopher's simplicity makes it a safer service to support than HTTP, but you still need to make sure that the directories served by Gopher don't contain sensitive data.

- Complexity—Simple.
- Abuse Potential—Minimal.
- Information Sensitivity—Low.
- Dialog—Minimal.
- Programmability and Configurability—Low.

HTTP (80 TCP)

The Web uses the HTTP protocol to transfer text, video, sound, and even programs over the Internet. Initially, Web servers were very simple (merely sending out to a client whatever page the client requested), but the exploding World Wide Web demands more and more features from Web servers. Now a Web server is a complex piece of software, with many configuration options, a complicated dialog, and infinite programmability.

The hacker exploitation of HTTP can go both ways—a hacker may try to exploit your Web site using HTTP, and a hacker Web site may contain dangerous Web page components such as malicious ActiveX controls or Java applets.

ActiveX controls are an Internet Explorer feature. An ActiveX control, once downloaded and run on a client computer on your network, can do absolutely anything any other program on that computer can do. You should require that on your network only those ActiveX controls that have been digitally signed by organizations you trust will be downloaded. You can use the Internet Explorer Administration Kit to lock down this Internet Explorer setting. If you can get away with it, disable ActiveX controls entirely.

Java is a little safer. Make sure that all of the computers in your network are configured not to allow Java applets access to hardware resources unless they are digitally signed by organizations you trust.

On the server side, be extremely careful with remote Web administration software. Most of the Web site hacking done by Internet vandals has been accomplished by exploiting security holes in remote Web site management tools.

Scrutinize server-side applets and CGI scripts. Do not make script directories browsable. Do not allow arbitrary scripts to be uploaded. Do not allow scripts to be executed from directories that contain other Web data.

If you can, maintain Web page usernames and passwords separately from operating system usernames and passwords. Log Web access, and look for unusual patterns (excessive 404 errors, etc.).

- Complexity—Complex.
- Abuse Potential—High.
- Information Sensitivity—Medium.
- Dialog—High.
- Programmability and Configurability—High.

IMAP (143 TCP)

This is the protocol used by network clients to retrieve mail from servers configured to retain e-mail on the server rather than transferring it to the client. The protocol itself, while more complex than POP or SMTP, is more secure (passwords aren't sent in the clear, at least).

- Complexity—Simple.
- Abuse Potential—Minimal.
- Information Sensitivity—Medium.
- Dialog—Low.
- Programmability and Configurability—Low.

LDAP (389 TCP and UDP)

The Lightweight Directory Access Protocol is a flexible and distributed way of maintaining contact information (including usernames and passwords) over the Internet. Several Internet services use LDAP to maintain user information rather than relying on the operating system user accounts. This is more secure because it separates operating system functionality from service functionality, and a hacker who gets a service password will not necessarily be able to log on to the server with it. If you want to maintain contact information on your network to facilitate communication with people in your organization you should consider using LDAP instead of Finger and Whois.

- Complexity—Complex.
- Abuse Potential—Minimal.
- Information Sensitivity—Medium.
- Dialog—Medium.
- Programmability and Configurability—Medium.

NetBIOS (137, 138, and 139 TCP)

NetBIOS is the protocol used by Microsoft Windows networking to connect LAN clients to file and print servers. NetBIOS will run over IPX, NetBEUI, and TCP.

You should definitely not allow NetBIOS traffic to pass your firewall in either direction. NetBIOS is easily hacked and many exploits exist on hacker Web sites. If you want to link your LANs over the Internet, you should use an encrypted IP tunnel to convey the NetBIOS IP packets through the Internet.

- Complexity—Complex.
- Abuse Potential—High.

- Information Sensitivity—High.
- Dialog—High.
- Programmability and Configurability—Low.

NFS (2049 TCP and UDP)

NFS is the UNIX equivalent of NetBIOS—it gives LAN clients access to file server storage. If you need to allow remote clients access to NFS resources, establish an encrypted tunnel to do it, don't just open up the NFS ports.

- Complexity—Complex.
- Abuse Potential—High.
- Information Sensitivity—High.
- Dialog—High.
- Programmability and Configurability—Medium.

POP3 (110 TCP)

The Post Office Protocol allows clients to check their e-mail over the LAN or over the Internet. POP is easy to configure and use, but the protocol is a little too simple—it doesn't encrypt usernames or passwords. Avoid allowing access to internal mail accounts from outside the firewall using POP—and if you do, do not allow POP account names and passwords to be the same as LAN usernames and passwords.

- Complexity—Simple.
- Abuse Potential—Medium.
- Information Sensitivity—Medium.
- Dialog—Minimal.
- Programmability and Configurability—Low.

Quote (17 UDP)

This protocol merely sends to any connecting client a random selection from a file full of quotes. Quote provides little leverage for abuse.

- Complexity—Simple.
- Abuse Potential—Minimal.
- Information Sensitivity—None.
- Dialog—Minimal.
- Programmability and Configurability—None.

RPC (111 UDP)

Remote Procedure Call is a protocol that allows two computers to coordinate in executing software. A program on one computer can use RPC to transfer the execution of a subroutine to another computer, and have the result returned via RPC to the first.

RPC is a fragile service, and most operating systems cannot handle arbitrary data being sent to an RPC port. RPC is best used in trusted LAN environments, and you should not let RPC traffic through your firewall.

- Complexity—Medium.
- Abuse Potential—High.
- Information Sensitivity—High.
- Dialog—High.
- Programmability and Configurability—High.

RSH (514 TCP)

The Remote Shell protocol makes up for deficiencies in Telnet. There are always dangers when you allow remote command line access to computers through your firewall, but if you are going to do so, use RSH rather than Telnet. RSH at least protects the passwords as they are exchanged between the client and the server.

- Complexity—Medium.
- Abuse Potential—High.
- Information Sensitivity—High.
- Dialog—High.
- Programmability and Configurability—Low.

SMTP (25 TCP)

Most of the mail exchanged over the Internet is done using the Simple Mail Transport Protocol. All the protocol does is accept mail in a simple dialog (without checking the authority or even the identity of the sender).

Although the protocol is simple, the software that processes the mail (once it's received) is often not so simple. Many SMTP packages have complex configuration options and forwarding rules, and, if incorrectly configured, can adversely affect network performance or crash the mail server when large amounts of mail are being processed. Also, the lack of sender authorization leaves SMTP open to spam attacks and e-mail flooding.

Unfortunately, if you want to receive Internet mail you need to support SMTP. You should choose mail server software that is as bullet proof as possible and use care when configuring it, paying attention to details like available hard disk space, network bandwidth, and so on. Install a server-based virus scanner to sanitize e-mail attachments as well.

- Complexity—Complex.
- Abuse Potential—Medium.
- Information Sensitivity—Medium.
- Dialog—Minimal.
- Programmability and Configurability—High.

SNMP (161 UDP)

The Simple Network Management Protocol is a useful tool for remotely managing network devices such as routers, servers, hubs, clients, and terminal servers. You can use it to enable and disable ports, measure bandwidth, reboot devices, and gather statistics. However, it should be used to manage your network only, not to allow hackers to watch every aspect of the data flow on your network. Block SNMP traffic at your firewall.

- Complexity—Medium.
- Abuse Potential—High.
- Information Sensitivity—High.
- Dialog—Minimal.
- Programmability and Configurability—Medium.

Telnet (23 TCP)

Telnet is extremely simple—it's just a connection opened to a command line interpreter. Whatever you type is sent to the interpreter on the server, and the interpreter's response is returned to you. The data traffic is not encrypted, and when you log on, the username and password are readable by any computer on any intermediate LAN.

Do not allow Telnet access to computers inside your firewall. If you require command-line access use a more secure protocol such as RSH.

- Complexity—Simple.
- Abuse Potential—High.
- Information Sensitivity—High.
- Dialog—Minimal.
- Programmability and Configurability—None.

TFTP (69 UDP)

TFTP is used with BootP and DHCP to allow diskless workstations to load their operating system and other configuration over the LAN. TFTP does not have the two-channel problem that FTP has (and therefore interoperates well with a firewall), but there is little reason to allow TFTP through a firewall when you already have FTP and HTTP for file distribution. Also, hackers have developed tools for using unprotected TFTP servers as pirated software dumping grounds, so only allow TFTP through your firewall if you have a good reason to.

- Complexity—Simple.
- Abuse Potential—High.
- Information Sensitivity—Medium.
- Dialog—Minimal.
- Programmability and Configurability—Low.

Leaving the Barn Door Open

One of the benefits of being a consultant who actually fixes things and makes life easier for the client company is that when an employee leaves for greener pastures he or she often will take you with them to fix problems in those new, greener pastures. One day, a former employee of a customer of mine called up and asked if I could evaluate the security of his new employer's network. I said that of course I could—and that for this excellent customer I would perform an initial, over-the-Internet evaluation for free. I agreed that I would present the over-the-Internet results to the customer and, at that point, discuss the cost of a full security evaluation of their network, including hardware, software, internal, and external practices.

I then gathered a few widely available Internet tools and began my remote evaluation. The first thing I discovered was that their Web server computer (accessible through their firewall) had ports 137 through 139 open. Not only did this identify the computer as a Windows NT machine, it showed that the NetBIOS service was accessible over the Internet, protected only by Microsoft LAN authentication. A quick check showed that the administrative account was still Administrator, and I crafted a small program to repeatedly try passwords (distilled from common password lists I generated or grabbed from Internet Web sites). I then got to work looking for other ways into the system.

I didn't get very far, though, because an hour and a half later the password testing program came up with the Administrator password and allowed me in. The password was short and simple and all lowercase. I immediately phoned our contact, let him know that he did indeed have at least two problems, and set up a time to come in and do an exhaustive evaluation.

Encryption

For hundreds of years people have used codes and ciphers to protect important information from the view of others. Computers store, manipulate, and transmit information swiftly and accurately. Codes and ciphers that were difficult and time-consuming to perform by hand now take only milliseconds on a computer, so encryption has found a new home in computer operating systems and networks.

Firewalls use codes and ciphers for two vitally important purposes:

- To prove the identity of a user (authentication)
- To hide the contents of a data stream (encryption)

This chapter will first examine what encryption is and how it has developed from a tool for spies and diplomats to become an integral part of modern communications. Next, you'll see how computer networks use encryption to secure your files, keep out unauthorized users, provide a secure channel for communications, and identify trusted computers or users. Finally, you'll be introduced to the several kinds of encryption and the strengths of and uses for each. In addition, you'll be given a glimpse of how a network intruder might attempt to circumvent encryption measures on your network.

This chapter covers encryption in general. Encryption as it is used in firewalls specifically for virtual private networking is covered in Chapter 9.

How to Keep a Secret

The primary purpose of encryption is to keep secrets. Encryption was first used to protect messages so that only the person knowing the "trick" to decoding the message (or the *key* in the jargon of cryptographers) could read the message. History is full of clever codes and ciphers used by kings and princes, spies, generals, business people, and inventors. As you read through this chapter you'll see examples of historical codes and ciphers, and learn how the concepts illustrated by those examples are used in computers today.

A *cipher* protects a message by rearranging it or performing modifications to the encoding, rather than the meaning, of the message. A *code* is an agreed-upon way of keeping a secret between two or more individuals. A *key* is a bit of information that is required to decrypt a message, usually in the form of a value that is used with a cipher to encrypt a message. The key must be kept secret in order for the message to remain private.

Ciphers

A cipher used by children around the world is pig Latin (no offense is intended towards pigs or aficionados of Latin). The secret is simple—the first consonant is moved to the end of the word and the "ay" sound is appended to it. If the word begins with a vowel, simply append "ay." Thus: "Isthay isay anay iphercay orfay implesay essagesmay."

Many dialects of the pig Latin cipher exist; you could use the keys "oi" or "ah" instead. What makes this cipher different from the backwards day code (wherein words take on their opposite meanings on the agreed upon "backwards day") is that you can encode any message in pig Latin. This ability to encode any message (or plaintext, as unencrypted messages are called) regardless of subject is a common feature of all ciphers. This is not a feature of codebooks. Codebooks operate by obscuring the meaning of words in messages, and are limited to the words in the book, whereas ciphers obscure the words being used regardless of what the words actually are. Backwards day is a code; pig Latin is a cipher.

A cipher almost as simple as pig Latin that is being used on the Internet and on computer bulletin boards around the world today is the Rot(13) cipher. If you've seen an e-mail or newsgroup message that looks like a jumble of random letters and has `<rot13>` at the top, then you have seen a message using this cipher. The trick to decoding it (the trick is called the *algorithm* in the jargon of cryptographers) is to rotate each letter through the alphabet 13 places. For example, A would be replaced with N, B would be replaced with O, W would be replaced with J, and M would be replaced with Z. Vg'f abg n irel pbzcyvpngrq pvpure. This is a simple *substitution cipher*, so called because each letter of the alphabet is replaced with a substitute letter. The key is to know which letters are replaced with which other letters—in this case, the letter 13 letters away from it (it doesn't matter if you rotate backward or forward, because there are 26 letters in the English alphabet). Figure 5.1 shows how the Rot(13) substitution cipher works.

Figure 5.1   In the Rot(13) substitution cipher the plaintext is rotated 13 characters for encryption into ciphertext, and then rotated 13 characters back into plaintext for decryption.

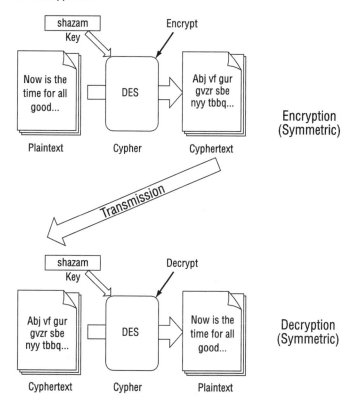

Rot(13), like pig Latin and backwards day, is not very hard to figure out. Any message encoded with a simple substitution cipher (if the message is long enough—25 characters is enough for most messages) can be decoded simply by counting the frequency of each letter. The letter E, for example, is the most common English letter and will probably be the one at the top of the frequency list. Common two- and three-letter combinations of letters are also clues to the hidden identity of substituted letters.

Another kind of cipher is the *transposition cipher*. Instead of replacing the letters in a message, this kind of cipher rearranges them. Imagine writing the letters of a message in the squares of a piece of graph paper. You would then copy the message to another sheet of paper, but instead of copying the letters from left to right you would do so from top to bottom. To decipher the message, you would put the letters back on graph paper from top to bottom and then read them from right to left, as usual.

A weakness of ciphers is that if someone knows the cipher you are using and the key you have chosen (say you are using the cipher PigLatin97 with the secret key "chu"), then everything you send or have sent with that cipher and key can be read by that person. This makes it very important to choose a cipher that is difficult to crack and a key that is difficult to guess.

Keeping Secrets Automatically

Encryption and decryption take a long time to perform by hand, and when your computing tools are limited to a pencil and paper (and, of course, the substitution alphabets or codebook) you can only use the simplest of ciphers. However, for hundreds of years the manual process was the only way, until the advent of the Industrial Revolution and the invention of calculating machines.

The various national governments of the 1920s developed rotor machines to automate the encryption and decryption process of cryptographic substitution. The ability to send secure and lengthy messages from the headquarters of the various armed forces to remote locations over a medium that anyone could eavesdrop on (the newly invented radio) proved to be a crucial aspect of modern warfare. Secure communications often meant victory, and broken codes often meant defeat. The most popular encryption machines had rotors and were primarily mechanical.

Each machine contained a number of rotors, and each rotor was wired to replace one letter with another letter. The rotors would rotate at different rates, so a machine with rotors that had 26 positions (one for each letter of the English alphabet) would have a period of 26 times the number of rotors. This means that a rotor machine with three rotors would encode the same letter with the same encrypted value every 78 letters of the message. The Enigma machine used by the Germans in the late '30s was the most famous rotor machine of the time and was fiendishly difficult for British cryptanalysts to crack.

Keeping Secrets Electronically

The development of electronics and computers gave code makers and code breakers a whole new arsenal to work with. They were able at last to develop ciphers that were much too complex to perform by hand. They could also program computers to automatically try many different combinations of keys and ciphers much more quickly than a human being was able to. Many ciphers were developed in secret, and only governments or large corporations had the computing power necessary to use or break the codes.

One algorithm that was developed in secret but then released for use by the public as well as the government (but only for "Unclassified but Sensitive" information) is the *Data Encryption Standard*, or *DES*. It is a symmetric algorithm, which means the same key is used for encryption and decryption, and uses a 56-bit key. DES is widely used in commercial software and in communication devices that support encryption. There is lingering suspicion, however, that the DES algorithm might contain a weakness that could allow the National Security Agency (NSA), which has a vested interest in maintaining its ability to decrypt communications and which cooperated in the development of DES, to more easily break messages encrypted with DES.

RSA (which was named after its inventors) is an algorithm that was not developed by a government agency. Its creators—Rivest, Shamir, and Adleman—exploited the computationally difficult problem of factoring prime numbers to develop a nonsymmetric, or public key algorithm, which can be used for both encryption and digital signatures. RSA has since become a very popular alternative to DES. RSA is used by a number of software companies that produce products that must negotiate secure connections over the insecure Internet (such as Web browsers) including Microsoft, Compaq, Sun, Netscape, and IBM.

The NSA and the Executive branch of the U.S. Government have developed a new encryption technology and are attempting to convince the rest of the government as well as the private industry to use it. First called "Clipper" and then "Capstone," the encryption scheme uses hardware that embodies a classified algorithm (called the "Skipjack" algorithm). The algorithm uses a secret key in combination with an escrow key or keys. The escrow keys are meant to be given to a pair of government or other key escrow agencies. Authorized law enforcement officials can then obtain the keys to the hardware device and decrypt any messages encoded by that device. The ostensible purpose is to make further digitally encrypted communications devices wiretappable.

> **NOTE** The Clipper and Capstone efforts have gained very little support from the private sector because they are viewed as a threat to privacy.

The ciphers described here are not the only ones available for use in computers and networks today—other governments (such as the former USSR) were just as active as the United States in developing codes and ciphers, and many private individuals (especially in the last decade) have made contributions to the field of cryptography. GOST was developed in the former USSR, FEAL was developed by NTT Japan, LOKI was developed in Australia, and IDEA was developed in Europe. Most of these ciphers use patented algorithms that must be licensed for commercial use, but there are some (such as Blowfish, which is described later in this chapter in the section on symmetric functions) that are not. Each cipher has strengths and weaknesses, some of which will be explored later in this chapter.

Backgrounder

PART 1

NOTE   All of the ciphers described in this section have the same weakness: If you know the cipher being used to encode a message but not the key, there are a number of attacks you can use to attempt to decode the message, including the "brute force" method of trying all of the possible keys.

The purpose of ciphers, after all, is to hide information. Hiding information would not be a useful activity (especially for wartime governments that have other pressing areas to spend time and money on) if no one were interested in the information being hidden. The converse of hiding information is attempting to discover what is hidden, and advances in breaking codes (or deciphering codes without the key) have progressed hand-in-hand with developments in creating codes. The practice of attempting to break codes is called *cryptanalysis,* and the people who break codes are called *cryptanalysts.*

Cryptographers have developed other key discovery methods than brute-force cryptanalysis. *Differential* and *linear cryptanalysis* are two examples of the esoteric art of breaking codes; they are complex mathematical analyses that would take a book each to explain. Some ciphers are more vulnerable to these two methods of cryptanalysis than other ciphers. Some ciphers use a longer key than others (a longer key contains more bits) and therefore require more time or compute power to go through all of the possible keys. Some ciphers can accept a variable number of bits in the key (you can choose how strong you want the encryption to be). Once the key is discovered, however, all of the messages encrypted using that cipher with that key are compromised.

The Almost Perfect Cipher

There is one encryption cipher—the *one-time pad*—which cannot be compromised if you do not have the key, even with all the time left in the universe and all the compute power that is theoretically possible. It is not simply improbable that the key would be discovered or the message retrieved by using brute force; it is impossible. Unfortunately, the requirements of the cipher make it impractical for use in anything but certain kinds of low-bandwidth communications.

A one-time pad uses a key that is exactly the same length as the message being encoded. The key must be completely random (anything less than random leaves your message open to certain kinds of cryptographic analysis), and no portion of it can be re-used without compromising the security of your message. Each letter (or byte) of your message is combined mathematically with an equal-sized portion of the key (often by the XOR mathematical function or addition with modulus mathematical function), which results in the ciphertext and uses up the key.

The reason that the one-time pad is so secure is that, from the ciphertext being decoded, any resulting plaintext (of the same length) and associated key is equally likely. For example, "henryjtillman" encoded with the one-time pad key "lfwpxzgwpoieq" results in the ciphertext "tkkhsjafbavfe." While the ciphertext decoded with the correct key produces the original message, the ciphertext can also be decoded using the possible key "swgpn-mquypciq" resulting in the message "andrewjackson," or using the key "gbywrvwcm-lkwz" resulting in the message "milkandcookie." The attacker has no way of knowing which key and resulting plaintext is correct.

The problem with the one-time pad is that it requires a key as big as the message being sent, and both the sender and the receiver must have the same key. If you must encrypt a 10Mbps Ethernet link you could use up a CD-ROM worth of key data in just 10 minutes!

NOTE   Clearly, the one-time pad is best used in cases where communication is infrequent or uses very little bandwidth, such as e-mail messages that must have the most secure encryption possible.

Encryption in Your Network

The previous section took a look at how cryptography developed and how it works in a cursory manner. The next section, "A Conspiracy of Cryptographers," will examine the world of cryptography in greater detail, explore the advantages and disadvantages of specific algorithms, as well as give you a glimpse of how they can be broken. This section focuses on how you can use encryption in your network.

After all, what good is a secret decoder wheel if you have no secrets to keep? You can use encryption to protect the following types of network data:

- Private communications
- Secure file storage
- User or computer authentication
- Secure password exchange

You should encrypt any communications containing sensitive or proprietary information that go over an insecure medium such as radio, a telephone network, or the Internet. Use file system encryption to protect sensitive data when operating system features are not effective (when the hard drive has been removed or the operating system has been replaced).

Private Communications

The most common use for encryption with computers is to protect communications between computer users and between communications devices. This use of encryption is an extension of the role codes and ciphers have played throughout history. The only difference is that instead of a human being laboriously converting messages to and from an encoded form, the computer does all the hard work.

E-Mail

Many e-mail packages include the facility to encrypt an e-mail message before sending it—even those programs that do not can include encrypted text that comes from a separate encryption program such as Pretty Good Privacy (PGP). When you receive an encrypted e-mail message you can have the e-mail package decrypt it for you (if your e-mail supports encryption—basic LAN e-mail products such as Microsoft Exchange and cc:Mail often don't, but advanced packages such as Microsoft Exchange Server do) or you can use an external program to decrypt the message.

In order to encrypt or decrypt a message you must have the key to the message. You'll usually use the same key for messages to the same person, so if you regularly exchange encrypted mail with a lot of people, you'll have a lot of keys to keep track of. Your e-mail package or your encryption package can make keeping track of keys easier by storing your keys in key rings (files on your disk drive that keep track of your keys for you). The key rings are, of course, encrypted and protected by a key as well. The benefit of this is that you only have to remember one key.

Communications Links

Encryption can protect the communication between network devices as well as between computer users. Any time two network devices are communicating over an *insecure* medium (that is a medium that an intruder can listen in on), you should consider encrypting the communication. For example, you might encrypt the data transferred over a microwave link between buildings if sensitive data flows over the link.

Encryption can be expensive, however, either in terms of the processing power required to encrypt or decrypt data, or in terms of the cost of specialized hardware to do the same thing. The more data there is to encrypt (the greater the bandwidth of the encrypted link), the more processing power is required. So, while any modern personal computer can encrypt a 56Kbps modem link without slowing down the user's applications all that much, encrypting a 100Mbps fast Ethernet link will tax even the most powerful RISC and Pentium processors.

Dedicated encryption hardware also costs much more than regular unencrypted communications devices like Ethernet adapters and modems. For these reasons you probably would only encrypt those portions of your network that are exposed in a way that they are accessible to an eavesdropper.

Secure File Storage

Encryption isn't just for communication. It can also be used to protect data in storage, such as data on a hard drive. All UNIX implementations and Windows NT have many sophisticated security features. You may have configured your OS to allow only authorized users to access files while the operating system is running, but when you turn your computer off all those security features go away and your data is left defenseless. An intruder could load another operating system on the computer, or even remove the hard drive and place it in another computer that does not respect the security settings of the original computer.

Encryption Utilities

You can use encryption software to encrypt specific files that you want to protect, and then decrypt them when you need to access them. The encryption and decryption process can be cumbersome, however, and you may end up having to remember a lot of encryption keys. Using encryption in this manner can also allow you to easily leave behind temporary files or files that are erased but still present on the hard drive containing sensitive information after you delete the original encrypted document. This is obviously not what you want.

Encrypted File Systems

A better approach to security is to have the operating system encrypt and decrypt the files for you. You can get encrypted file systems for Windows NT and most versions of UNIX that will encrypt all the files on your hard drive, even temporary ones created by the applications you use.

You must supply the cryptographic key when you start your computer, but otherwise you can treat the files on your hard drive as regular, unencrypted files. This doesn't protect your files from being accessed while the operating system is running—that is what the operating system security features are for—but it does keep the data safe even if someone steals the hard drive.

User or Computer Authentication

In addition to keeping secrets (either stored or transmitted), encryption can be used for almost the opposite purpose—to verify identities. It's used to authenticate users logging on to computers, it's used to ensure that software you download from the Internet comes from a reputable source, and it's used to ensure that the person who sends a message is really who they say they are.

Logon Authentication

You may not know it, but your operating system already uses encryption. When you log on to a Microsoft operating system such as Windows 95 or Windows NT, the operating system does not compare your password to a stored password. Instead, it encrypts your password using a one-way cryptographic function, and then compares the result to a stored result. Other operating systems such as UNIX and OS/2 work the same way.

This seems a roundabout way of verifying your identity when you log on, but there is a very good reason the operating system does it this way. By only storing the encrypted version of your password, the operating system makes it more difficult for a hacker to get all of the passwords in your system when they gain access to the system. One of the first things a hacker goes for in a compromised system (that is, one where the hacker has gotten at least one password) is that computer's password list, so that the hacker can get account names and passwords that may be valid on other computers in your network.

With a one-way cryptographic function, it's easy to generate an encrypted value from the password, but it's difficult or impossible to generate the password from the encrypted value. Since only the encrypted values are stored, even a hacker who has complete access to the computer can't just read the passwords. The best the hacker can do is to supply passwords one by one and see if they match any of the hashes in the password list. The hacker can run a program to do this instead of typing them all in by hand, but it can take a while if the users of the computer have chosen good passwords.

Digital Signatures and Certificates

One problem with Internet e-mail is that it was not designed with security in mind. Messages are not protected from snooping by intermediate Internet hosts, and you have no guarantee that a message actually came from the person identified in the e-mail's From: field. Internet newsgroup messages have the same problem: you cannot really tell whom the message actually came from. You can encrypt the body of the message to take care of the first problem, and digital signatures take care of the second.

Digital signatures are useful because while anyone can check the signature, only the individual with the private key can create the signature. The difference between a digital signature and a certificate is that you can check the authenticity of a certificate with a certificate authority.

In Chapter 2 you read about the danger in downloading files from the Internet. Hackers can (and do) upload programs and utilities that contain Trojan horses, which can leave your network wide open to intrusion. One way to make sure that those programs and utilities are safe to download is to only download files that have certificates signed by a reputable certificate authority.

> **NOTE** The exploreZip.worm virus outbreak that occurred during the writing of this book is an example of a Trojan horse passed as an executable attachment to e-mail that claimed it was sent from associates of the recipient. A digital signature standard would have prevented its spread because users would have been warned that the file was not signed by the sender.

A software company can transmit a certificate along with a file you download that certifies the file as free of viruses and Trojan horses. You can check the certificate with a certificate authority you trust (VeriSign is the certificate authority that Microsoft uses; Thawte provides cryptographic certificates free for personal use like e-mail encryption) and hackers cannot forge the certificates. Certificates and digital signatures are explained in more detail later in this chapter.

Secure Password Exchange

When you log on to your network file server, or when you connect to your Internet Service Provider, you supply a username and password. These two pieces of information control your access to the network and represent your identity on the network. They must be protected from eavesdropping.

Most network operating systems (Windows NT and all modern versions of UNIX included) protect your username and password when you log on by encrypting the username and password before sending them over the network to be authenticated. The file server (or ISP host) checks the encrypted username and password against the list of legitimate users and passwords. The host can check the password either by decrypting it and checking the database of passwords stored in the clear, or it can encrypt the stored password and check the result against what has been sent from the client over the network.

To keep the same encrypted data from being sent every time, the client can also include some additional information such as the time the logon request was sent. This way your network credentials are never sent unprotected over your local LAN or over the telephone system. Windows NT does accept unencrypted passwords from older LAN Manager network clients, however, so you should be careful about allowing older clients on your network.

> **NOTE** Not every authentication protocol encrypts the username and password. SLIP, for example, does not. Telnet and FTP do not. PPP may, if both the dial-up client and server are configured that way. Windows NT by default requires encrypted authentication.

A Conspiracy of Cryptographers

Cryptography is the study of codes and ciphers. Like any other group of specialists, cryptographers have a language of their own to describe what they do. You don't have to be a theoretical mathematician to evaluate and use cryptography in your network, but it helps to have a general idea about them when you are evaluating cryptography options for your network. Before we continue, there are a few terms you should know the precise meanings of as they are used in this book:

Algorithm Detailed steps for performing a function.

Asymmetric Algorithm An algorithm in which different keys are used for encryption and decryption. Public key algorithms are asymmetric.

Block Cipher A cipher designed to operate on fixed-size blocks of data.

Breakable A cipher that, given a reasonable amount of time and resources, can be compromised by a competent cryptanalysist.

Computationally Secure A cipher that, given all the computational power that will be available to the most powerful governments over the next hundred thousand years, is unlikely to be compromised.

Keyspace The range of all possible keys for a cipher. A cipher with a large keyspace is harder to crack than one with a smaller keyspace because there are more keys (numbers or combinations of letters) to try.

Restricted Algorithm An algorithm that is kept secret to make it more difficult to break.

Secure A cipher that, even given a reasonable amount of time and resources, most likely cannot be compromised by a competent cryptanalysist.

Stream Cipher A cipher designed to operate on a continuous stream of data.

Strong A cipher that, given the computational power that may reasonably be brought to bear on it any time in the near future, is unlikely to be compromised.

Symmetric Algorithm An algorithm in which the same key is used for encryption and decryption. Private key algorithms are symmetric.

Unconditionally Secure A cipher that, given an unlimited amount of time and an infinitely powerful processor, cannot be compromised.

Algorithms

When you encode a message (transform a plaintext into a ciphertext), you must perform a series of steps. For example, to encode a message using the PigLatin93 cipher, you do the following:

1. Take the first word of the plaintext.

2. Replace each vowel in the word with "ra" followed by that vowel.

3. Write the modified text down (this is the ciphertext).

4. If you have words left, take the next word of the plaintext and then go to step 2. Otherwise, you're done.

A set of instructions, like the steps outlined above, is an *algorithm*. Ciphers are algorithms that describe how to encode or decode messages; therefore, ciphers are *cryptographic algorithms*. Not every algorithm is a cipher, of course—algorithms are used for many other things, especially in computers. In fact everything that computers do is detailed in an algorithm of one sort or another.

Algorithms can be performed by people (recipes are algorithms), but the all-time-champion algorithm followers are computers. This, combined with the fact that most ciphers are meant to be performed by a computer, means that most ciphers are detailed in computer languages such as C rather than in English steps like the example above. The following is an example of a cipher in C:

```c
/*
ROT(n)
Usage: rot [e|d] number inputfile outputfile
The number should be between 0 and 26, exclusive
Assumes a contiguous linear character encoding (i.e. ASCII)
*/

#include <stdio.h>
#include <string.h>

int do_rotate( char isencrypt, int key, int thechar ){
  if(isencrypt=='d')
    key *= -1;
  if( thechar >= 'A' && thechar <= 'Z'){
    thechar+=key;
    if(thechar>'Z')
      thechar-=26;
  }
```

```
    if( thechar >= 'a' && thechar <= 'z'){
       thechar+=key;
       if(thechar>'z')
          thechar-=26;
    }
    return(thechar);
}


void main(int argc, char *argv[]){
   FILE *infile,*outfile;
   int thischar, keyval, isencrypt;

   isencrypt=(char)argv[1];
   keyval = atoi(argv[2]);
   if(keyval>0&&keyval<26&&(isencrypt=='e'||isencrypt=='d'){
      if((infile = fopen(argv[3], "rb")) != NULL){
         if((infile = fopen(argv[4], "wb")) != NULL){
            while((thischar = getc(infile)) != EOF){
               putc(do_rotate(isencrypt,keyval, thischar), outfile);
            }
         }
      }
   }
}
```

If you examine the above cipher, you will notice that there are two basic parts to it: the main part that takes care of opening, reading, stepping through, and writing files, and the do_rotate part that performs a specific function (in this case, adding or subtracting the key value) to a portion of the file (in this case, one character). This is the function that is performed by the cipher. (It is also defined as a function written in the C programming language, but that's beside the point. If it were written in BASIC it might be called a subroutine, but it still performs a cryptographic function.)

You can implement other ciphers by replacing the do_rotate function with a different function, such as one that performs an XOR on the character with a specific key. You would then be implementing an XOR cipher instead of a ROT cipher. There are many different ciphers that you can implement in this manner, each performing a specific mathematical function on input text (plaintext) with a key to produce the output text (the ciphertext).

Symmetric Functions

If the same key can be used to encrypt or decrypt the message (as in the ROT example in the *Algorithms* section), then the cipher uses a symmetric function. Both the sender and receiver must have that same key. Good symmetric ciphers are fast, secure, and easy to implement using modern microprocessors.

Some ciphers are more secure than others. The XOR cipher, for example, is not very secure. A competent cryptanalyst can decode an XOR-encoded message in short order. There are two general features of a symmetric algorithm that make it secure:

- The algorithm produces ciphertext that is difficult to analyze.
- The algorithm has a sufficiently large keyspace.

Cryptanalysts test ciphertext for correspondences in the text, an uneven distribution of instances of numbers, and essentially anything that differentiates the ciphertext from a series of truly random numbers. A good algorithm will produce a ciphertext that is as random-seeming as possible. This is where the XOR cipher fails miserably—an XOR-ed message has a lot in common with a regular ASCII text message. Cryptographers will exploit these commonalities to recover the key and decode the whole message.

A cryptanalyst who cannot exploit the nonrandom in ciphertext has little choice but to simply try all the possible key combinations to decode the message. This is a lot like the hacker trying to guess the password to your system—if they don't know that the password is a birthday or the name of your dog, then they must try all the possible passwords.

NOTE Just as a longer password is safer than a shorter one, a longer key is more secure than a shorter key.

There are a number of symmetric ciphers used in both software and hardware. You can get a feel for what is available by comparing the following three ciphers.

Data Encryption Standard (DES)

IBM and the U.S. National Security Agency cooperated to develop this cipher (see the "How to Keep a Secret" section earlier in this chapter). It has been designed to be resistant to differential cryptanalysis, but has been shown to be susceptible to linear cryptanalysis (linear and differential cryptanalysis are described later in this chapter in the section on "Attacks on Ciphers and Cryptosystems."). Its key length is only 56-bits, which makes it increasingly easy to perform a brute-force examination of all of the possible keys for an encrypted ciphertext. DES is an ANSI standard and commonly found in encryption hardware and software.

International Data Encryption Algorithm (IDEA)

This cipher has a key length of 128 bits—considerably more than DES uses. While a sufficiently motivated and financed organization can break a DES-encoded message, the large key space makes a brute force attack on IDEA impractical. IDEA was designed to be immune to linear and differential cryptanalysis, and you can reasonably be assured that not even the NSA can decode an IDEA-encrypted message without the key. IDEA is patented both in Europe and United States.

Blowfish

This cipher can use a key with anywhere from 32 to 448 bits, allowing you to select how secure you want to make your message. It was designed to be immune to linear and differential cryptanalysis. Its developer, Bruce Shneider, has not sought a patent on the algorithm so that a good, freely implementable algorithm would be available to both private individuals and the public sector.

One-Way Functions

When you type your password to log on to Windows 95 or Windows NT, it is encrypted and compared against the stored encrypted value of your password (see the section "Logon Authentication" earlier in this chapter). The reason the password is stored using a one-way function (also called a hash, trap-door, digest, or fingerprint) is to make it difficult for a hacker or other network intruder to determine your password even if the hacker has gained access to the operating system's stored settings.

Hash functions can also be used for other purposes. For example, you can use a hash to "fingerprint" files (create a digital fingerprint or hash that is unique to that file). A hash function can produce a result that is much smaller than the input text; a hash of a multi-megabyte word-processor document, for example, may result in a 128-bit number. A hash (or fingerprint) is also unique to the file that produced it—it is practically impossible to create another file that will produce the same hash value. You might use this kind of hash to make sure that your Internet-distributed software product is delivered free of viruses and other malicious modifications. You can allow your customers to download the software, and then tell them what the hash value for the software files is. Only your unmodified software files will hash to the same value.

> **NOTE** One feature of a hash function (especially one that produces short hashes) is that any hash value is equally likely. Therefore, it is practically impossible to create another file that will hash to the same value.

Some hash functions require a key, others do not. Anyone can calculate a hash that does not use a key; this kind of hash is good for distributing software or making sure that files have not been changed without you noticing. A hash function with a key can only be calculated by someone (or something) that has the key.

Public Key Encryption

While symmetric ciphers use the same key to encrypt and decrypt messages (that's why they're called symmetric), public key encryption (or a public key cipher) uses a different key to decrypt than was used to encrypt. This is a relatively new development in cryptography, one that solves many longstanding problems with cryptographic systems, such as how to exchange those secret keys in the first place.

The problem with symmetric ciphers is this: Both the sender and the recipient must have the same key in order to exchange encrypted messages over an insecure medium. If two parties decide to exchange private messages, or if two computers' network devices or programs must establish a secure channel, the two parties must decide on a common key. Either party may simply decide on a key, but that party will have no way to send it to the other without the risk of it being intercepted on its way. It's a chicken-and-egg problem: Without a secure channel, there is no way to establish a secure channel.

In 1976, Witfield Diffie and Martin Hellman figured a way out of the secure channel dilemma. They found that by using a different key, the one-way function could be undone. Their solution (called public key cryptography) takes advantage of a characteristic of prime and almost prime numbers—specifically, how hard it is to find the two factors of a large number that has only two factors, both of which are prime. Since Diffie and Hellman developed their system, some other public key ciphers have been introduced. For example, the difficulty of determining quadratic residues (a subtle mathematical construct that few people other than mathematicians and cryptologists really understand) has been exploited to make a public key cipher.

With a public key cipher, one key (the public key) is used to encrypt a message, while the other one (the private key) is the only key that can decrypt the message. This means that you can tell everyone your public key, even complete strangers and NSA agents. Anyone who has your key can encrypt a message that only you can decrypt. Even the NSA agent who has your public key cannot decrypt the message.

One problem that plagues secure public key ciphers is that they are slow—much slower than symmetric ciphers. You can expect a good public key cipher to take 1,000 times as long to encrypt the same amount of data as a good symmetric cipher. This can be quite a drag on your computer's performance if you have a lot of data to transmit or receive.

Although it is much slower than symmetric systems, the public key/private key system neatly solves the problem that bedevils symmetric cryptosystems. When two people (or devices) need to establish a secure channel for communication, one of them can just pick a secret key and then encrypt that secret key using the other's public key. The encrypted key is then sent to the other party, and even if the key is intercepted, only the other party can decrypt the secret key using the private key. Communication may then continue between the two parties using a symmetric cipher and that secret key. A system that uses both symmetric and public key encryption is called a *hybrid cryptosystem*.

Protocols

There is a lot of mathematics in cryptography, and to be a good cryptographer you almost have to be a theoretical mathematician, but there is more to cryptography than mathematics. There is even more to cryptography than ciphers that use math. The ciphers all by themselves are merely a computational curiosity—they only become useful when secure communications systems are built using them.

Communications systems are built out of protocols. Protocols, in turn, describe how the entities in a communications system (such as the computers in a network) cooperate. Protocols also perform the same function in human terms. Robert's Rules of Order, for example, contains the protocols for people communicating in a meeting or assembly, including who may speak at any particular time and how to excuse yourself from the meeting.

For a computer, the protocols describe who will transmit when, what will be transmitted, how it will be formatted, and what (and who) will transmit next. A protocol is very much like an algorithm, but while an algorithm describes the steps for one computer to take, a protocol describes the steps that two or more communicating computers must take.

> **NOTE**   The parts of a protocol that one computer performs comprise an algorithm. You can think of a protocol as a set of algorithms that communicating computers use.

Every time you log on to your network or connect to the Internet, you use protocols. The Internet uses TCP/IP, which is a set of protocols that all communicating Internet computers use. Windows NT uses the NetBIOS protocol along with either the TCP/IP, NWLink, or NetBEUI protocols to provide access to shared files and printers. These are general-purpose protocols that allow networked computers to communicate, and they are designed more for efficiency and scalability than for security.

Cryptographers have a very narrow view of protocols. A cryptographer will consider such aspects as the computation time required for a protocol, or whether or not it is feasible for a hundred thousand computers to use it, but the cryptographer is more concerned with whether the protocol is susceptible to such network malfeasance as the man-in-the-middle attack (see the "Attacks on Ciphers and Cryptosystems" section).

The following is a simple protocol for two people (let's call them Alice and Bob, in the tradition that real cryptographers follow) to establish a symmetrically encrypted communications channel using public key encryption. Here are the steps:

1. Alice sends Bob her public key (or Bob gets Alice's public key from a public key directory).

2. Bob selects a secret key for use with a symmetric cipher, encrypts it using Alice's public key, and then sends it to Alice.

3. Alice decrypts the secret key using her private key.

4. Alice and Bob use the secret key and the symmetric cipher to send private messages to each other.

However, this protocol has a problem. We'll explore this problem in the next section.

Attacks on Ciphers and Cryptosystems

Throughout history, cryptography has been a race between those trying to keep secrets and those trying to find out what those secrets are. (These code makers and the code breakers are often the same people.) It's no different today. If you are really serious about keeping information private using cryptography, you should be aware of what others may do to ferret out that private information. Cryptographers call these attempts *attacks*, and they come in two forms: cryptanalysis and protocol subversion.

Cryptanalysis

Cryptanalysis is the process of examining encrypted information to try to determine what the encrypted message is, or what the key that encrypted the message is (which, of course, gives you what the message itself is). There are a number of different techniques a cryptanalyst can use, including:

Keyspace Search   This is the hard way to crack an encrypted message. A keyspace search involves checking all of the possible keys that might have been used to encrypt the message. This is like trying all of the possible combinations on a bank vault in order to open it. A keyspace search is only feasible when there are not very many possible keys. A cryptanalyst might use this technique if the key length is 32 or 48 bits, and perhaps if it were 56 bits and the message were really worth the million-dollar hardware that would be required. Keyspace searches of larger keyspaces are impractical at the present level of computing technology.

Known Plaintext   A cryptanalyst can reduce the number of possible keys to be searched for many ciphers if the cryptanalyst already has the plaintext of the encrypted message. (Why would the cryptanalyst want the key if the message is already out? Perhaps there is another message encrypted with the same key.) If even a portion of the message is always the same, especially at the beginning of the message (for example, the headers in an e-mail message are always the same), your ciphertext may be vulnerable.

Linear and Differential Cryptanalysis   A cryptanalyst may also look for mathematical patterns in collections of ciphertexts that have all been encrypted with the same key. Some ciphers (not all) are vulnerable to either or both of these kinds of analysis, and a cryptanalyst may then have a much smaller range of keys to search.

Protocol Subversion

Just choosing a good cipher doesn't make your network safe. Recall the protocol example in the previous section with Alice and Bob. They both used a pretty good public key encryption system to exchange a secret key that they then used with a very secure symmetric cipher. That wasn't enough to ensure their privacy, though, because their protocol was weak. Consider the following scenario with a determined and powerful adversary, Mallet:

1. Alice sends Bob her public key.
2. Mallet intercepts Alice's public key and sends Bob his own public key (alternatively, Mallet intercepts Bob's request for Alice's public key from the directory and substitutes his own).
3. Bob selects a secret key for use with a symmetric cipher, encrypts it using Mallet's public key (which he thinks belongs to Alice), and then sends it to Alice.
4. Mallet intercepts Bob's response. He then encrypts the secret key he received from Bob with Alice's own public key and sends it to her.
5. Alice decrypts Mallet's secret key using her private key.
6. Mallet maintains the illusion that Alice and Bob are talking to each other rather than to him by intercepting the messages and retransmitting them.

Obviously, this man-in-the-middle attack scenario requires that Mallet be able to intercept messages and substitute his own. This is possible in some media (such as the Internet) and not others (such as radio). A protocol can be modified to be resistant to man-in-the-middle attacks. Consider the following modification (called the Interlock Protocol and invented by Ron Rivest and Adi Shamir) and how it affects Alice and Bob's negotiation of a secure key:

1. Alice sends Bob her public key.
2. Bob sends Alice his public key.
3. Alice selects a secret key and sends Bob a message encrypted with that secret key. Neither Bob nor Mallet can read the message, since neither of them have the secret key.
4. Bob selects a secret key and sends Alice a message encrypted with that secret key. Neither Alice nor Mallet can read the message, since neither of them have the secret key.

5. Alice encrypts her secret key with Bob's public key and then sends it to Bob. Bob can then read Alice's message.

6. Bob encrypts his secret key with Alice's public key and then sends it to Alice. Alice can then read Bob's message.

7. Bob and Alice continue to communicate, using the secret keys they have established.

The above protocol is not perfect, but it does make it much more difficult for Mallet to impersonate Alice and Bob. Mallet cannot read Alice's message until step 5, and cannot read Bob's message until step 6. In both cases, it is too late for Mallet to change the message already sent to the other party. In order for Mallet to subvert this protocol, he must correctly guess what is being sent in steps 3 and 4 in order to create a convincing counterfeit.

Digital Signatures

In the above examples using public key encryption, the message is encrypted with the public key and decrypted with the private key. You can also do it the other way—encrypt with the private key and decrypt with the public key.

Why would you want to encrypt a message that anyone can decrypt? That seems a bit silly but there is a good reason to do so—only the holder of the private key can encrypt a message that can be decrypted with the public key. This encryption is in effect a digital signature, proving that the holder of the private key produced the message.

Since the purpose of a digital signature is not to conceal information but rather to certify it, the private key is often used to encrypt a hash of the original document, and the encrypted hash is appended to the document or sent along with it. This process takes much less processing time to generate or verify than does encrypting the entire document, and it still guarantees that the holder of the private key signed the document.

Steganography

Cryptography can be very effective at keeping a secret. With a sufficiently powerful cipher and a sufficiently long key, even major world governments cannot read your diary. What if you don't want people to know that you're keeping secrets? After all, an encrypted file or an encrypted hard drive is pretty strong evidence that you're hiding something. *Steganography* is the process of hiding those encrypted files where it is unlikely that anyone will find them.

Encrypted files look like random numbers, so anything that also looks like random numbers can be used to hide an encrypted message. In graphics images that use many colors, the low-order bit for each pixel in the image doesn't make much difference to the quality of the image. You can hide an encrypted message in the graphic file by replacing the low-order bits with the bits from your message. The low-order bits of high-fidelity sound files are another good place for encrypted data. You can even exchange encrypted messages with someone surreptitiously by sending graphics and sound files with those messages hidden in them.

Random Sequence Generation

Most cryptographic systems manage the selection of keys and the negotiation of protocols for you. Systems that do this must be able to select keys that are not easily guessed, because one way to attack a cryptographic system is to predict the keys that might be used in the system. These keys are selected by generating random numbers.

It is difficult for a computer to generate good random numbers. Computers, by their very nature, are extremely predictable, and hundreds of thousands of engineers have labored (collectively) millions of years to make them more so. If you run a computer program twice and give it the same input the second time as you did the first, you will get the same output the second time as you did the first. Since the whole point of a truly random number is not to be able to guess the output based on the input, computers (unassisted) make lousy dice-throwers.

The best that computers can do by themselves is good *pseudorandom numbers*. Pseudorandom numbers are created by a deterministic means (that is, given identical starting conditions, identical numbers will be produced). Good pseudorandom numbers have a long periodicity and satisfy the other conditions of random numbers, such as incompressibility and having an even distribution. Random numbers, on the other hand, are unpredictable (a series of random numbers cannot be reproduced, even from identical starting conditions).

In order to get a good random number (to use as a seed value, for example) the computer must look outside itself because computers are inherently deterministic. There are many sources of randomness in the real (non-computer) world—the weather, ocean waves, lava-lamp wax gyrations, the times between one keystroke and the next—and a computer can measure these events and use them to generate random numbers. Keystroke timing is commonly used to generate secret keys. Another way is to ask the user to type in a paragraph or two of text; there are no published algorithms that will predict arbitrary user input (yet).

If a random number is going to be used as a seed for pseudorandom numbers, it should have enough bits to make it difficult to guess. For example, you don't want to protect a 128-bit cryptosystem that uses IDEA with a password of 8 characters or less for a seed—this is effectively only about 48 bits of security if you just use printable ASCII characters in the password.

Encryption Measures

While working for a network services company as a network integrator, I received a request for help from a government contractor who had been hired to decrypt the contents of a hard disk that had been seized by a federal law enforcement agency.

There are two kinds of encryption in common use on computers today: encryption that will keep coworkers out of your files, and encryption that will keep everyone out of your files.

An examination of the contents of the hard drive revealed that this drive (which contained an encrypted NTFS volume protected by a pass phrase that we did not have) used the latter kind of encryption. I had to inform the contractor that our organization did not have the resources that were required to break the encryption, and it was likely that no organization would.

In a related incident, the same contractor asked us to take a look at another server with an encrypted disk. (This contractor had won a bid to provide cryptographic services to the government for a slew of related cases.) The disk encryption was remarkably similar in quality, and just as difficult to crack—but this server came with a backup tape left in the DAT drive that contained the entire contents of the server in unencrypted form.

Part 2

Firewall Technology

Topics Covered:

- How packet filtering works
- Problems with packet filtering
- How Network Address Translation works
- Problems with Network Address Translation
- How proxies work
- Problems with proxies
- How Internet tunnels and Virtual Private Networks work
- Problems with tunnels and VPNs
- How to determine the level of security your network requires
- How to implement your required level of security

Packet Filtering

Packet filters were the original firewalls. The first attempts to make TCP/IP secure were based on the idea that it's pretty easy for a router to inspect the header of TCP/IP packets and simply drop packets that don't conform to the specifications you want to accept.

Packet filters have problems that make them insufficient to provide total security for an internal network. They are now combined with proxy servers and Network Address Translators to solve those problems.

Proxy servers were originally designed to make the World Wide Web faster. Network Address Translators were originally designed to increase the address space available to private organizations and to solve IP address numbering problems associated with attaching existing private TCP/IP networks to the Internet. The serendipitous security benefits of both of these functions were integrated with packet filtering to create the modern effective firewalls in use today.

Neither proxy servers nor Network Address Translators can be properly secured without a packet filter, and a packet filter cannot provide total security without the services of a proxy server or a Network Address Translator. Because these services must be combined into a single coherent security function to be effective, you should use firewalls that make effective use of all three methods to truly secure your network.

There are two primary types of packet filtering:

- Standard, or "stateless" packet filtering
- Stateful inspection packet filters

This chapter discusses "pure" packet filtering: packet filtering when not combined with proxy or Network Address Translation functions. Pure packet filters are still in use all over the place, so this discussion remains very current.

How Stateless Packet Filters Work

Packet filters are border routers that increase security by determining whether or not to forward a packet based on information contained in the header of every individual packet. Filters can theoretically be configured to determine this based on any part of the protocol header, but most filters can be configured only to filter on the most useful data fields:

- Protocol type
- IP address
- TCP/UDP port
- Fragment number
- Source routing information

The following sections detail each of these fields.

Protocol Filtering

Protocol filtering filters packets based on the content of the IP protocol field. The protocol field can be used to discriminate against entire suites of services, such as:

- UDP
- TCP
- ICMP
- IGMP

For example, if you have a single-purpose server serving a TCP-based service like HTTP, you could filter out all UDP services. Unfortunately, the protocol field is so general (only four common protocols are available to filter on) that most servers and routers will have to leave all of them open.

IP Address Filtering

IP address filtering allows you to limit connections to (or from) specific hosts and networks based on their IP address. Most filters allow you to either deny access to all hosts except an accepted list or allow access to all hosts except a denied list.

Specific denial of certain hosts is almost worthless, since you'd have to keep track of every hacker that had ever attacked your network and assume that they have no way to gain information from a different IP address, which they always will. Relying on specific denial is not a strong security policy.

Specific acceptance of certain host addresses provides particularly strong security, however; it is the strongest form of security that a stateless packet filter can provide. By denying access to all hosts except a list of known IP addresses, you can ensure that your routers can only be reached by the IP addresses of machines or networks you know about. This list could be other networks in your organization, the networks of your customers, or the networks of work-at-home users. By denying access to all other IP addresses, you make it nearly impossible for a hacker to exploit your network. To hack into your network, a hacker would have to have access to your list of allowed IP addresses.

It is possible for hackers to use source-routing, (explained in detail in the next section), to "spoof" IP addresses. Source routing would allow a hacker to put an allowed address into a packet and then capture the return by specifying that responses are routed back to his computer. For this reason, packet filters should always be configured to drop source routed packets.

Good packet filters will allow you to specify hosts on a per-protocol basis, so (for example) you could allow all hosts to access TCP port 80 for HTTP service but only hosts from your company network to access TCP port 23 (Telnet). Most simple filters don't have allowed lists per protocol, so you can only assign a single list of hosts allowed for all protocols.

It's important to remember that a filter can only limit addresses based on the IP address field's contents, which could be different than the actual source host. It's easy for hackers to forge the IP address field of a packet, so it's certainly possible for them to get a packet past a packet filter if they know an address that the filter will pass. This would be useful in instances where a round-trip is not necessary, such as in a denial-of-service attack or where the return address for the protocol is contained in the payload of the packet as well as the header (as in FTP).

TCP/UDP Ports

TCP or UDP port information is the most commonly used information to filter on because this data field indicates most specifically what the packet is for. Port filtering is also commonly referred to as protocol filtering because the TCP or UDP port number identifies higher-level protocols. Figure 6.1 shows how a stateless packet filter discriminates based on TCP or UDP port number.

Figure 6.1   A packet filter rejects undesired traffic

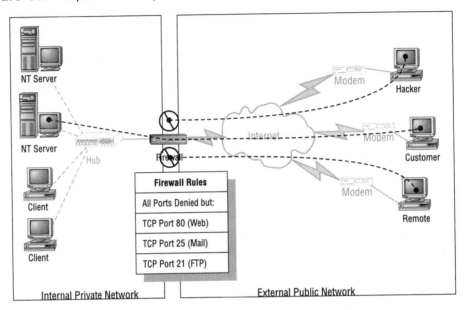

Common protocols that can be filtered based on the TCP or UDP port field are:

Daytime	DNS	NetBIOS Session
Echo	HTTP	IMAP
Quote	Gopher	NFS
FTP	POP	Whois
Telnet	SNMP	RSH
SMTP	NNTP	

As with IP addresses, most packet filters allow you to either pass all protocols except a denied list or pass no protocols except an allowed list, and as with IP addresses, passing no protocols except an allowed list is more secure. Unlike IP address filtering, blocking only certain ports is still useful because most hacking exploits target only a few specific protocols. The most important protocols to block are:

- Telnet—Leaving this port open on a host will allow hackers to open a command prompt with a large amount of access to your machine.

- NetBIOS session—Leaving this port open to the Internet on Windows or SMB serving hosts will allow hackers to attach to your file servers as if they were local clients.

- POP—You should implement a VPN connection for remote clients who need to check their mail because POP uses plain-text passwords to allow access, which will allow hackers to sniff user's passwords off the network.

- NFS—Unix clients should not leave open access to NFS ports for the same reason Windows clients should not leave open access to the NetBIOS ports.

- X Windows—Running X client software (the terms "client" and "server" in X environments are opposite their usual meanings) will leave your server vulnerable to attack.

These ports are especially sensitive to attack because of the high level of functional control they give the attacker. Other ports, like DNS, could be used to damage some specific information, but they can't be used to control the machine directly and are therefore of less value to attackers.

Other ports you should block include any sort of remote access or remote control software such as pcAnywhere or VNC.

Filtering on Other Information

In addition to the standard fields, headers contain other information that can be used to determine whether or not a packet should be passed.

Source routing and fragmentation are two techniques supported by the IP protocol that are largely obsolete and frequently exploited by hackers. Most packet filters will allow you to simply drop any packets that are source routed or fragmented.

Source Routing

Source routing is the process of defining the exact route a packet must take between hosts in an IP connection. Source routing was originally used for debugging and testing purposes, but it is now frequently used by hackers because a hacker can put any address in the source field and still ensure the packet will return by specifying her own machine in the source route.

Two types of source routing exist:

- Loose source routing, which indicates one or more hosts the packet must flow through, but not a complete list.

- Strict source routing, which indicates the exact route a packet must follow back to it's source.

Of the two types, loose source routing is most often used because the hacker can simply plug in the IP address of his machine to make sure the packet comes back to her by any means.

Unless you use source routing in your network, configure your filters to drop any source-routed packets. No protocol or ISP requires source routing.

Fragmentation

Fragmentation was developed to support the passage of large IP packets through routers that could not forward them due to the frame size constraints encountered in some early networks. Fragmentation gave any router in the path between two hosts the ability to chop up an inbound IP packet into multiple smaller packets and then forward them on size-constrained networks. The receiving system simply waited for all fragments of the packet to reassemble it to its original form.

The problem with fragmentation comes from the fact that the most useful filter data, the TCP or UDP port number, is only provided in the beginning of an IP packet, so it will only be contained in fragment 0. Fragments 1 and higher cannot be filtered based on port information because they don't contain any port information. So most early filters simply forward all subsequent fragments with the assumption that if the 0 packet had been dropped, the subsequent packets would be worthless.

But that's not always the case. Many flawed versions of TCP/IP running on internal hosts might reassemble the packet anyway, and if the 1 through n packets contained a valid TCP packet, they'd go ahead and use it. This meant that a hacker could modify his IP stack to start all fragment numbers at 1 and effectively bypass the filter altogether.

Problems with Stateless Packet Filters

Packet filters suffer from two problems that prevent them from being completely effective:

- They cannot check the payload of packets.
- They do not retain the state of connections.

These problems make packet filters alone insufficient to secure your network.

No Service-Specific Security

Packet filters make pass/drop decisions based solely on header information—they do not inspect content for the presence of dangerous or malformed data to determine whether or not that data should be passed. For this reason, packet filters alone do not constitute effective security.

For example, HTTP content flowing back into your network could contain Trojan horses embedded in Active-X controls. Your packet filter cannot determine this, so it simply passes the content through. Or you may allow SMTP port 25 through to your mail server to receive e-mail, but the filter can't determine that a malformed e-mail passing through it will crash your e-mail server.

Service-specific security can only be implemented by the service-specific filters used by proxy servers and true firewalls.

No Connection State Security

Most packet filters are stateless—that is, they do not retain information about connections in use—they simply make pass/drop determinations packet by packet and based only on the information contained within that packet. Stateless packet filters cannot determine whether or not to drop fragments because they retain no information about the fragment's service port. Stateless packet filters also cannot determine when a return socket connection applies to a connection established from inside the network, so they must be configured to simply pass all TCP ports in the range of a normal return socket. For this reason, many early packet filters simply pass all TCP ports above 1024.

Modern port filters and all modern firewalls use state information to keep track of connection status and thereby more positively control the routing of packets through your network.

If you can't use proxy servers to eliminate routing at your border, use state-based packet filtering and Network Address Translation.

OS Packet Filtering

Most modern operating systems, UNIX and Windows NT included, include packet filtering as part of the TCP/IP stack. This means that you can configure unique packet filtering rules for each server based on its individual function. This is called end-system packet filtering because the final computer in the route, the host to which the packet is actually addressed, performs the filtration.

Intermediate systems like packet filtering routers and firewalls can be configured to drop or pass packets based on the ultimate address, so end-system packet filtering may seem unnecessary. But no border system can protect your server from an internal attack or from an attack that somehow sidesteps your border security by exploiting an improperly secured VPN or dial-up connection.

By including backup packet filtering directly on servers, you can provide an extra level of security that will still be in place if your border security fails or if the attack comes from inside your network.

You should use the packet filtering functionality of your server's operating systems to guarantee that you are only serving those protocols you intend to serve publicly. Host-based packet filtering allows you to ensure that each server exposes only those services you intend.

How Stateful Inspection Packet Filters Work

Standard packet filters have a number of flaws, all of which stem from the fact that a single packet in a communication does not contain enough information to determine whether or not it should be dropped because it is part of a larger communication. Stateful inspection packet filters solve this problem by retaining the state of all the communication flowing through the firewall in memory, and using that remembered state to determine whether or not individual packets should be dropped. Stateful inspectors filter entire communication streams, not just packets.

Stateful packet filters remember the state of connections at the network and session layers by recording the session establishment information that passes through the filter gateway. The filters then use that information to discriminate valid return packets from invalid connection attempts or hacking.

Most stateless packet filters simply allow all ports above 1024 to pass through the firewall because those ports are used for the return sockets of connections initiated inside the firewall. This is extremely poor security—nothing prevents Trojan horses from waiting inside your network on a service port above 1024, so stateless packet filters cannot prevent this sort of intrusion.

Stateful packet filters, on the other hand, do not allow any services through the firewall except services they're programmed to allow and connections that they already maintain in their state tables.

When a trusted internal host connects to a TCP socket on an external untrusted host, it transmits with the connection synchronization packet the socket (IP address and port) on which it expects to receive a response. When that SYN packet is routed through the stateful inspection filter, the filter makes an entry in it's state table containing the destination socket and the response socket, and then forwards the packet onto the untrusted network. When the response comes back, the filter can simply look up the packet's source and destination sockets in its state table, see that they match an expected response, and pass the packet. If no table entry exists, the packet is dropped because it was not requested from inside the network. Figure 6.2 shows the establishment phase of a stateless filter.

The filter removes state table entries when the TCP close session negotiation packets are routed through, or after some period of delay, usually a few minutes. This ensures that dropped connections don't leave state table "holes" open. Figure 6.3 shows a filter removing the table entry that allows return data from a connection.

Stateful filters are then programmed with rules (usually called policies) that modify that basic behavior. Policies usually include rules for packets that are always dropped, packets that are never dropped, services that are allowed to pass from the outside to specific hosts inside, and so forth. On multi-function firewalls, the policies also control network address translation and proxying, and generally abstract IP addresses, networks, and ports into objects, areas, and services.

Figure 6.2   A stateful inspection packet filter allows return data.

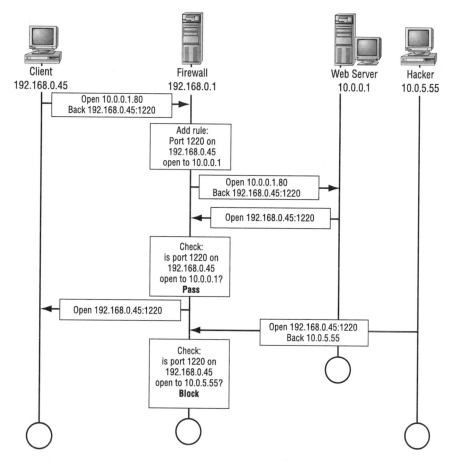

Because stateful filters can filter on all the same information that stateless filters can, plus fragment membership, which side of the firewall a connection is initiated from, and other more complex information, stateful filters are considerably more secure.

Stateless packet filters still don't solve the problem of internal protocol analysis for higher-level protocols like HTTP and FTP, but firewalls like Firewall-1 do provide a "proxy-like" higher-layer filtration service for common protocols like HTTP, FTP, and SMTP. While far more secure than not having higher level inspection, the packets are still

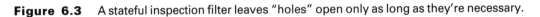

not regenerated the way they are on a proxy server, so there's still a chance that mal-formed original data could pass through the filter to a target inside your network.

Figure 6.3 A stateful inspection filter leaves "holes" open only as long as they're necessary.

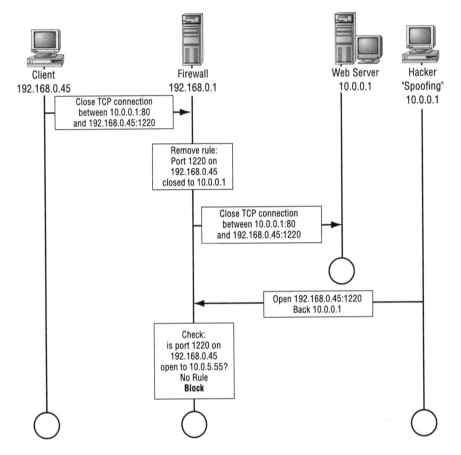

Hacking Through Packet Filters

Hackers use a number of well-known methods to bypass packet filters and get inside your network. They exploit the following security problems with packet filters:

- TCP can only be filtered in the 0th fragments.
- Many packet filters pass all ports above 1024.
- Trojan horses can defeat packet filters using NAT.

These hacks are detailed in the following sections.

TCP Can Only Be Filtered in 0th Fragments

Stateless packet filters inspect each packet on its own merits without retaining information about previous packets. For this reason, when a fragmented packet comes through, the TCP header will only be available in the 0th fragment, which means that although the packet filter will drop the 0th fragment, it won't drop fragments past 0.

Because many operating system TCP/IP stacks don't actually pay attention to fragment ordering, these operating systems will reassemble a fragmented packet until they get a packet with the final fragment flag set. If the data in their IP buffer constitutes a valid packet, they'll pass it along to the operating system.

Hackers exploit this to pass data right through a packet filter to a specific host inside your network. By transmitting all packets with the fragment number set to 1, but containing the entire TCP packet, the filter will ignore the TCP payload allowing it to pass to the internal network. The addressed end system sees that the final fragment message is set and passes the TCP packet along to the operating system. In this way, hackers can connect directly to hosts inside your network as if the packet filter didn't even exist.

The two solutions to this problem are to use only hardened TCP/IP stacks on your internal hosts and to use state-based packet filters like true firewalls. Windows NT 4 Service Pack 3 hardens the TCP/IP stack against this vulnerability, but earlier editions of NT are vulnerable. Many UNIX implementations are hardened against this attack, but many are not. Search the Web for your specific version and variation to determine if this exploit will work against your operating system.

Low Pass Blocking Filters Don't Catch High Port Connections

Stateless packet filters and the packet filtering services provided by ISPs usually open ports above 1024 so that the return socket of a connection can be established back to a host. This means that any protocol running with a TCP port higher than 1024 cannot be protected by these packet filters.

Make sure your packet filter is state-based and blocks all inbound connection attempts except those you want to allow and those connections that were initiated from inside your network.

Internal NATs Can Defeat Filtering

If a user inside your network sets up a Network Address Translator on a machine (a Linux computer, for example), then that machine can be used to perform port and address translation to change a protocol inbound on a high, unfiltered port (say 8080) back down to a protocol on a filtered port (80) and then pass it to an internal server. Internal proxy servers could also be used to cause this vulnerability. This would allow uncontrolled access to your internal services.

Trojan horses perform exactly this sort of protocol translation for the purpose of allowing hackers to access your internal network directly. Unsuspecting users might get e-mail from your e-mail address with instructions to click the setup file of the attached program, which would then install the Trojan horse. Hackers could then exploit the network address translator in the Trojan horse to bypass your filter.

Packet Filtering Best Practices

Pure packet filters are subject to a few glaring security problems. Use these recommendations to keep your packet filtering secure:

- Use at least a stateless filter if you can't use a proxy.
- Disable all ports by default.
- Secure the base operating system.

These practices are detailed in the following sections.

Use a Real Firewall

First and foremost, use a strong firewall. Examine the firewall comparisons that constitute the second half of this book for firewalls that perform correct state-based packet filtering in combination with service-specific, proxy-based filtering and Network Address Translation.

Do not rely upon simple packet filters or the packet filtering functionality of your operating system to keep your network secure. Pure packet filters cannot adequately secure a network.

Disable All Ports By Default

Do not pass all protocols by default and then block those you consider dangerous. Although this is convenient, it opens you up for attack by Trojan horses and unintended user mode services like pcAnywhere.

Block all ports by default, and pass only the ports you intend to serve and the return channels from connections initiated from inside your network.

Secure the Base OS

Make sure the base operating system is secure. As with all security software, the security of a packet filter is based on the security of the device upon which it's run. Most packet filter appliances (routers) can be configured via Telnet. This means that a hacker could telnet into your packet filter and reconfigure it to allow more useful ports to be opened.

Leaky Filters

When a customer of mine attached their network to the Internet in 1994, we put a "firewall" in place on the routed connection. In those days, a firewall was a router with a packet filter. We used Telnet to block all inbound ports except ports 80 (they ran a Web server on a SPARC machine), 21 (FTP), and 25 (SMTP). We felt perfectly secure.

Then a scientist downloaded a Trojan horse embedded in a freeware utility without knowing about it. Since it wasn't a virus, the virus scanning software didn't pick it up.

One day a few months later, the scientist was working at his desk when an MS-DOS commands prompt popped up on the screen. At the C:\> prompt, the letters "format c:" slowly appeared one at a time, as if they were being typed by someone directly—except he wasn't typing them.

The hacker apparently paused before hitting the return key for some reason, and during that pause, the scientist wisely unplugged his network connection. He immediately got on the phone to me and I came in to take a look.

I had never seen such a brazen intrusion before. Until then, Trojan horses to me were a theoretical possibility that were too esoteric to bother thinking about. I knew how difficult it would be to write a useful one, so I didn't worry about them.

This specific Trojan horse set itself up as a server on port 12345 and waited for connections. Upon receiving a connection, it would open a command prompt and vector the I/O to that command prompt over the TCP connection. This effectively gave hackers a remote command prompt on infected machines. Hackers could simply scan wide ranges of IP addresses browsing for open connections on port 12345 to find running instances of the Trojan horse.

Of course, I was called to the mat to explain how the firewall had failed. It hadn't, I explained, it just wasn't designed to prevent that sort of intrusion. The budget for security went up considerably, and we used it to install a Firewall-1 based stateful inspection gateway. We also bought port scanning tools to search for other instances of unknown services running inside the network.

24*seven* **CASE STUDY**

7

Network Address Translation

Network Address Translation (NAT) converts private IP addresses in your private network to globally unique public IP addresses for use on the Internet. Although NAT was originally implemented as a hack to make more IP addresses available to private networks, it has a serendipitous security aspect that has proven at least as important: Internal host hiding.

Network Address Translation effectively hides all TCP/IP-level information about your internal hosts from hackers on the Internet by making all your traffic appear to come from a single IP address. NAT also allows you to use any IP address range you want on your internal network even if those addresses are already in use elsewhere on the Internet. This means you don't have to register a large, expensive block from InterNIC or reassign network numbers from those you simply plugged in before you connected your network to the Internet.

NAT hides internal IP addresses by converting all internal host addresses to the address of the firewall (or an address responded to by the firewall) as packets are routed through the firewall. The firewall then retransmits the data payload of the internal host from its own address using a translation table to keep track of which sockets on the exterior interface equate to which sockets on the interior interface. To the Internet, all the traffic on your network appears to be coming from one extremely busy computer.

> **NOTE** RFC 1631 describes Network Address Translation.

NAT is actually a fundamental proxy: A single host makes requests on behalf of all internal hosts, thus hiding their identity from the public network. Windows NT does not provide this function—you must use a third party firewall if you want to use Network Address Translation. Many versions of UNIX provide or can use publicly available IP masquerade software.

NAT is implemented only at the transport layer. This means that information hidden in the data payload of TCP/IP traffic could be transmitted to a higher-level service and used to exploit weaknesses in higher-level traffic or to communicate with a Trojan horse. You'll still have to use a higher-level service like a proxy to prevent higher-level service security breaches.

> **TIP** NAT is so effective at IP address re-use that the implementation of IP version 6 has been practically stalled due to lack of interest, and the threat of IP address scarcity has been eliminated for the foreseeable future. NAT allows entire class B sized networks to hide behind a single IP address.

NAT Explained

To perform Network Address Translation, firewalls maintain a table of interior sockets matched to exterior sockets. When an interior client establishes a connection to an exterior host, the firewall changes the source socket to one of the firewall's exterior sockets and makes a new entry in the translation table indicating the actual interior source socket, the destination socket, and the mated firewall socket.

When an exterior host sends data back to the interior hosts socket, the firewall performs the reverse translation. If no entry exists in the translation table for the socket addressed or if the IP address of the source is different than the address the firewall expects to see, then the packet is dropped.

This is easiest to explain with an example. Let's say that interior host 10.1.1.7 wants to establish a Web session with exterior host 192.168.13.15. Using the next available port, 10.1.1.7:1234 transmits a TCP packet to 192.168.13.15:80.

Router/Firewall (10.1.1.1 interior address, 128.110.121.1 exterior address) receives the packet, and makes the following record in its translation table:

Source   10.1.1.7:1234

Public Host	192.168.13.15:80
Translation	128.110.121.1:15465

It then transmits the packet on the Internet using the translated IP address and port number, so 192.168.13.15:80 (the public host) receives a connection attempt coming from 128.110.121.1:15465 (the firewall's exterior address). When the public host transmits back, it responds to the source that it thinks originated the request: 128.110.121.1:15465 (the firewall's exterior address).

Upon receiving the packet, the firewall searches its translation table for a matching socket and finds it. It then verifies that the source of the packet is the same as the public host recorded in the translation table when the entry was made. The presence of a table entry confirms that the packet was requested by an internal host—had the packet not been requested, no translation entry would be present matching both the translated socket and the recorded public host socket. If no matching entry is found, the packet is dropped and logged.

The firewall then modifies the packet with the internal source client's socket number and passes it to the interior network for transmission to the ultimate client. Figure 7.1 illustrates this process.

Figure 7.1   Network Address Translation

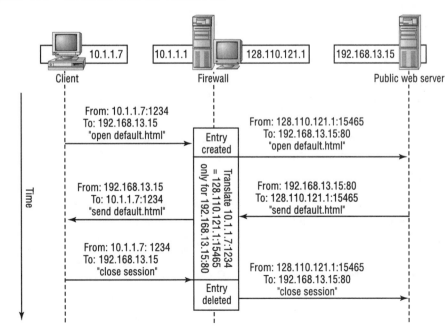

Because NAT changes the IP address in the packet, it is almost always necessary to make entries in your routing tables to make sure translated packets reach their proper destination inside your network.

Since NAT performs only simple substitutions at the packet layer, it does not need to perform complex analyses on the contained data, as application proxies must. This means that most implementations of NAT are nearly as fast as straight routing. NAT requires far less processor overhead than higher-level application proxying.

> **WARNING**   Firewalls performing Network Address Translation must have at least one valid public IP address, and that address cannot be concealed.

Translation Modes

Many firewalls support various types of Network Address Translation. The four primary functions of a NAT firewall are defined below in order of their popularity and availability:

Static Translation (also called Port Forwarding)   Wherein a specific internal network resource (usually a server) has a fixed translation that never changes. Static NAT is required to make internal hosts available for connections from external hosts.

Dynamic Translation (also called Automatic, Hide Mode, or IP Masquerade) Wherein a large group of internal clients share a single or small group of internal IP addresses for the purpose of hiding their identities or expanding the internal network address space.

Load BalancingTranslation   Wherein a single IP address and port is translated to a pool of identically configured servers so that a single public address can be served by a number of servers.

Network Redundancy Translation   Wherein multiple Internet connections are attached to a single NAT firewall that it chooses and uses based on load and availability.

> **WARNING**   Not every firewall supports each type of NAT. Read the firewall's documentation carefully before you purchase it to make sure its form of NAT is the type you need.

Dynamic Translation

Dynamic translation, also referred to as IP Masquerade or just "masking," protects internal hosts by replacing their IP address with an address that routes to the firewall.

Individual hosts inside the firewall are identified based on the port number in each connection flowing through the firewall.

> **NOTE**   RFC 1631 does not describe the use of port addresses to extend the applicability of a single IP address, but every existing NAT implementation I know of uses this method. Purists call this method NAPT, for Network Address and Port Translation.

Because a translation entry does not exist until an interior client establishes a connection out through the firewall, external computers have no method to address an internal host that is protected using a dynamically translated IP address. And since most firewalls create translations that are valid only for the addressed host and port, there's no way for any computer except the computer addressed to attack the host because no other route exists back to it.

It's important to note that NAT does nothing to protect the client other than to keep external hosts from connecting to it. If the client is seduced into connecting to a malicious external host, or if a Trojan horse is somehow installed on the computer that connects to a specific external host, the client can be compromised just as easily as with no firewall. For this reason, NAT alone is not sufficient to protect your network.

Seducing a client into connecting to a malicious site is surprisingly easy. For example, if your boss sent you e-mail saying, "Check this site out. It's remarkably close to what we want to do," you'd probably click on the hyperlink included in the e-mail without a second thought. That's all it takes, and forging e-mail is child's play for a hacker.

> **WARNING**   The paragraph above was written just days before the Explore.Zip worm wreaked havoc upon corporate networks using exactly that strategy. You should strongly consider filtering executable files from HTTP downloads and e-mail attachments.

Some protocols do not function correctly when the port is changed. These protocols will not work through a dynamically translated connection. Any protocol that relies upon the ability to establish a separate reverse connection to the source client will only work correctly if the firewall is designed to make exceptions for that specific protocol.

When you use dynamic translation, you must establish an IP address to translate the internal addresses to. This is the address that will be visible to the outside world for outbound connections. Most firewalls allow you to use the firewall's own address or another address that routes to the firewall and for which the firewall will answer using ARP.

Each IP address can only support a theoretical maximum of 65,536 (2^{16}) connections because the port address pool used for multiplexing the client connections is only 16 bits wide. Most firewalls are further limited to about 50,000 connections because many ports are reserved for other uses. Linux's default IP Masquerade settings make only 4096 ports available for translation, but that number can be easily modified.

In any case, the number of ports is large and shouldn't cause a problem unless your users maintain hundreds of simultaneous Internet connections while they work. If you do find yourself running out of ports, you'll have to have more than one IP address behind which to hide hosts.

Static Translation

Static translation (also called port forwarding) is used when you have a resource inside your firewall that you want to be publicly available, or (in rare cases) when you use a protocol that must have certain port or IP addresses to operate.

For example, if you want to put your e-mail server inside your firewall, you can establish a static route through the firewall for that service.

Let's say your e-mail server's IP address is 10.1.1.21, and your firewall's external IP address is 128.110.121.1. You can statically map socket 128.110.121.1:25 to address 10.1.1.21:25. This static connection will cause the firewall to translate any connections to its SMTP port to the e-mail server inside your firewall.

Static translation can be used to establish a number of different complex services on a single IP address. For example, you could have an e-mail server statically translated on the SMTP and POP ports, a Web server statically translated on the HTTP port, and a news server on the NNTP port. Since the translations can specify any IP address, these services can be split among many machines inside your firewall.

Load Balancing

Some firewalls support IP load balancing using the static NAT facility. This allows you to spread the load of one very popular Web site across a number of different servers by using the firewall to choose which internal server each external client should connect to on either a round-robin or balanced load basis. This is somewhat similar to dynamic translation in reverse—the firewall chooses which server from among a pool of clones each connection attempt should go to.

To choose based on load, the servers in the pool must have some facility to transmit their load levels to the firewall. Since there is no standard way to do this, your firewall must implement a proprietary method. For that reason, many simpler firewalls assume that each connection creates about the same amount of load and assign connections to the next server in the list.

IP load balancing only works with protocols that are stateless or which maintain their state on the client. For Web sites, IP load balancing is perfect because the server does not maintain any information about the client between page transmittals, so it doesn't actually matter if a specific client gets the same server each time they load a page. Consider the problem with mail, though. If a firewall provides load-balancing for a number of e-mail servers, each of a user's e-mail messages would arrive on any on the of the servers depending on which server the firewall selected for the SMTP connection. When the user connects to a server, the firewall will again select one server for the POP connection so the only messages that user would serve see are the messages that happen to have been received by that server—the user would not see all of her received messages.

IP load balancing is particularly important for e-commerce sites that have a heavy processing load because they make heavy use of Active Server Pages, CGI or Perl scripts, or Java Servlets. These technologies all put a heavy compute burden on a Web server, which reduces the maximum number of clients that server can support. Figure 7.2 shows a complex e-commerce Web site being load balanced by a firewall.

Figure 7.2   Using firewalls to perform load balancing.

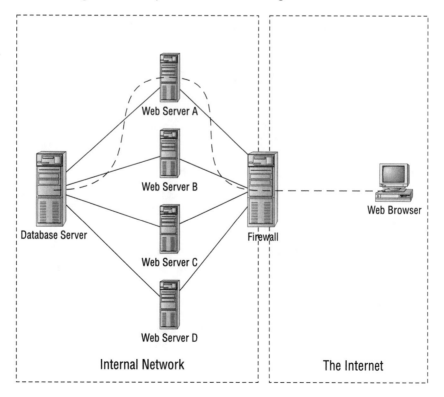

Network Redundancy

It is possible to use a NAT-based firewall to perform Internet network redundancy either to balance the load of clients across multiple low cost Internet connections or to compensate automatically for the failure of any given link.

Network redundancy works with dynamic translation in much the same way that IP load balancing works with static translation. In network redundancy, the firewall is connected to multiple ISPs through multiple interfaces, and has a public masquerade address for each ISP. Each time an internal host makes a connection through the firewall, the firewall decides on a least-loaded basis which network to establish the translated connection on. In this way, the firewall is able to spread the internal client load across multiple networks.

The failure of any network is then treated as if that network is completely loaded; the firewall simply will not route new clients through it. Although session-based protocols will have to be reestablished from the client hosts, stateless protocols like HTTP could then survive a link failure without the client even knowing anything had occurred. Figure 7.3 shows network redundancy. Notice that because the IP address is translated, it does not matter which ISP the firewall uses to connect to the public Web site.

Figure 7.3 Network redundancy

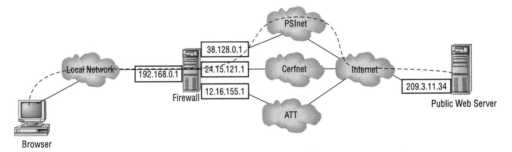

Router Configuration for NAT

When you use Network Address Translation with IP addresses other than the IP address of the firewall, you'll have to configure the routing in your network to make sure that packets reach the firewall, and you may have to configure routing on the firewall to make sure that packets are relayed to the correct interfaces.

Whether or not you have to configure routing separately from the firewall's configuration depends upon whether the firewall routes packets itself or whether it relies upon the host system for routing. If the firewall relies on the host operating system to perform the routing function, you then need to know whether the firewall translates addresses before or after the routing function has occurred.

You can tell whether or not the firewall relies upon the host system for routing in Unix by checking whether the firewall requires the use of the routed daemon. If the firewall requires the routed daemon, then it relies upon the routed daemon to perform the routing function.

In Windows NT, you can tell if the firewall relies upon the operating system to route if the firewall enables the Enable IP Forwarding setting in the network control panel, or if it instructs you to enable it manually.

If the firewall relies on the operating system for routing, you must ensure that the internal routing tables are correct for the various translation modes you establish. Some firewalls configure the routing tables for you—others do not. If the firewall performs the routing function, you can assume that the firewall will correctly route packets without intervention. In either case, you should thoroughly read the firewall documentation on routing and test the routing through your firewall once it's completely configured.

The first router between your firewall and your ISP is usually the biggest routing problem, because it may assume that it can use ARP (Address Resolution Protocol) to determine where a packet should be routed, especially if there's no static route between the router and your firewall. This means that your firewall will have to respond to ARP requests for all the IP addresses that you want to pass through the firewall.

Most true routers will allow you to manually set a route to the correct interface on the firewall, so this isn't an issue. But many new high-speed data link devices like cable-modems and DSL interfaces aren't actually routers—they're just bridges, and they assume that every device they talk to will be connected to the same collision domain as their Ethernet adapter.

In UNIX, this is no problem. Just use the ARP command to set the IP addresses for which the external interface will ARP (or respond as the correct interface for said IP address), and add routing entries to make sure the packets will be routed to their correct location as shown in the example below.

In Windows NT, this is a serious problem. Windows NT includes an ARP command, but it does not properly implement the ARP protocol for proxy ARP (when an interface responds to ARP requests for multiple IP addresses). Manual ARP entries remain cached for only about an hour, after which time your routing will fail.

The only way to handle this problem is for the firewall software to implement some method to properly implement proxy ARP for the IP addresses that the firewall uses for translation.

Adding IP addresses to the external adapter will not solve the problem because these addresses are automatically used to create the routing tables for NT, which will then be incorrect for further routing to the interior of the network.

An example will explain why this is the case. If the firewall has two interfaces, 10.0.0.1 and 128.110.121.1, then there will be default entries in the routing table that look like Table 5.1.

Table 7.1   Firewall routing table entries

Network	Mask	Gateway
10.0.0.0	10.0.0.255	10.0.0.1
128.110.121.0	128.110.121.255	128.110.121.1

Say host 10.0.0.12 has its address translated to 128.110.121.44 as it goes through firewall 128.110.121.1. A return packet will be addressed to 128.110.121.44. When that packet reaches the firewall router, the packet will be routed to interface 128.110.121.1 by default because the address translation will have occured after the routing function had already happened. The firewall will then translate the address to 10.0.0.12, but it will have been too late—the packet will have already been routed to the incorrect interface so it will be transmitted on the 128.110.121.0 network.

If you try to solve the problem by adding IP address 128.110.121.44 to the 128.110 .121.1 interface or the 10.0.0.1 interface, Windows NT will automatically generate routing rules for that interface that unfortunately stipulate incorrect routing—and these automatically generated rules cannot be removed.

To solve the problem, use the firewall's ARP facility and make a routing entry on the firewall that specifies a route for each IP address that the firewall proxy ARPs:

Route add 128.110.121.44 10.0.0.1 1

This will ensure that packets coming in on the proxy ARP address will be routed to interface 10.0.0.1. Then they will be transmitted on the correct interface once the address is translated.

IANA Private Use Network Numbers

The Internet Assigned Numbers Authority (IANA) has designated three blocks of addresses for private use without coordination:

- 10.0.0.0 to 10.255.255.255
- 172.16.0.0 to 172.31.255.255
- 192.168.0.0 to 192.168.255.255

> **NOTE**   IANA is in the process of converting its operations to a non-profit corporation called The Internet Corporation for Assigned Names and Numbers (ICANN). ICANN will eventually assume ultimate naming authority from Network Solutions, Inc. for domain names. I use the more familiar IANA acronym since at the time of this printing, ICANN is not yet functional.

Internet routers are configured not to route these addresses on the Internet backbone. You can use these addresses in your own network with a certain amount of impunity, unless your ISP also uses them. Most ISPs use portions of the 10.0.0.0 domain for their own internal routing, with Network Address Translation into and out of the range.

For that reason, I generally recommend that clients use the 192.168.0.0 network range for their own private networking. This prevents conflicts with ISPs that use the 10 domain for internal routing, and you don't have to remember which block of addresses is valid inside the 192.168.0.0 domain. You can use all 16 bits of address space with impunity.

Problems with NAT

There are a few protocols that cannot be used with NAT because they either require the ability to open a back channel to the client, embed TCP/IP address information inside the higher level protocol, encrypt TCP header information, or use the original IP address for some security purpose.

- Back channels will not work because no separate route back to the internal hosts exists. This occurs with H.323 video teleconferencing.
- Software that embeds TCP/IP address information inside TCP/IP packets and then relies upon that information will not work because the interior TCP/IP address information will be incorrect. This occurs with FTP and some other protocols.
- Software that encrypts the TCP header information will not work correctly with NAT because the TCP information must be accessible to the firewall. Solve these problems by making the firewall the encryption end point. This occurs with PPTP.

- Software that relies upon TCP/IP address information for security checking will fail because the IP address information has changed. This occurs with sqlnet2.

More advanced firewall software can inspect outgoing connections for these protocols and establish a translation entry to wait for the destination public host to respond with the back-channel open request. Most firewalls do not support service specific NAT; rather, they use service specific proxy software in combination with the NAT mechanism to perform these functions.

NAT cannot be used with the following services without some form of higher-level proxying or a patch to the basic NAT code:

H.323, CUSeeMe, and VDO Live These video teleconferencing software programs cannot be used because they rely upon the ability to establish a back channel to the host. Some firewalls may make special entries in their translation tables to allow a specific host to create the back channel.

Xing This software fails for the same reason.

Rshell This software fails for the same reason.

IRC This software fails for the same reason.

PPTP This software fails because it relies on encrypted IP information inside its stream, but other non-TCP/IP protocols can be tunneled inside PPTP with an end point on the firewall to get around this problem.

Sqlnet2 This software requires the numerical difference between the host and client IP addresses to be the same as if both IP addresses were not translated. This means that the protocol will nearly always fail unless you design your network around this strange restriction.

FTP This software must be RFC 1631 compliant to work with NAT. FTP embeds IP address information in ASCII text inside the TCP packets, the length of which is likely to change through an address translation.

ICMP This software sometimes embeds the first part of the original packet in ICMP messages. This first portion will contain the untranslated address. The secure solution is simply not to pass ICMP traffic through your firewall.

Hacking Through NAT

If Network Address Translation makes clients invisible, it's impossible to hack them, right? Wrong. Here's where NAT can fail:

- Static translation does not protect the internal host.
- If the client establishes the connection, a return connection exists.

- If the connection can be intercepted or subjected to a man-in-the-middle attack, the man-in-the-middle is the end point.

- If the firewall's NAT implementation is flawed, it could be subject to exploitation.

These hacks are further explained in the following sections.

Static Translation = No Security

Static translation merely replaces port information on a one-to-one basis. This affords no protection to statically translated hosts—hacking attacks will be just as efficiently translated as any valid connection attempt.

The solution to security for statically translated hosts that must provide public services is to reduce the number of attack vectors to one, and then to use (if necessary) application proxy software or other application-based security measures to further protect the internal host.

For example, to protect e-mail servers inside a firewall, Checkpoint's Firewall-1 software has a simple SMTP store-and-forward mechanism that eliminates the nasty problem of e-mail buffer overflows. Firewall-1's e-mail proxy receives all e-mail inbound on its port 25 (SMTP) and writes each message to the hard disk. A separate service running in a different process reads the e-mail messages and transmits them to the internal e-mail server. This mechanism eliminates the possibility that a buffer overflow from a malformed e-mail message will affect anything but the firewall, and in that case, it will only shut down the e-mail receiver. The firewall's internal consistency checker can then simply restart the e-mail receiver afresh.

Internal Host Seduction

Even if hackers can't get inside your network, you can't prevent your users from going to the hackers. Forged e-mail with a Web site link, a Trojan horse, or a seductive content Web site can entice your users to attach to a machine whose purpose is to glean information about your network. HTTP is a reasonably robust protocol, and extensions to it by the major browser vendors have made it a potent source for exploitation. Since nearly any type of content can be downloaded through an HTTP connection, your users can be easily compromised once they connect to a hacker's machine.

Higher-level, application-specific proxies are once again the solution. By inspecting the contents of those protocols for what will most likely be exploited (like HTTP), your firewall can sniff for suspicious content like Java applets, Active-X controls, downloadable executables, malformed URLs, and other tools hackers use to perform their mischief. By filtering out or at least logging and alerting on the presence of this content, you can keep your users from being exploited through seductive means.

The State Table Timeout Problem

Network Address Translation has one hackable aspect to its function. When a client connects to the outside world, the firewall must remember which internal host has connected to which external host so that it can route the return portion of the TCP connection back to the source host. Without this functionality, only unidirectional (and therefore worthless) transmissions can be made.

But how does the firewall know when the client is finished with the connection? If the firewall relies only upon TCP information, it can sniff for close session information. But many protocols don't have an obvious ending negotiation, and there's always the possibility that a connection may be dropped without proper closing negotiation. In those cases, to remain as protocol generic as possible, most firewalls implement a timeout value. The length of this timeout varies greatly, and firewall publishers never tell you how long it is.

Before the timeout occurs, a connection through the firewall to the originating internal host exists. This connection could potentially be exploited by a hacker, although the hacker would have to know exactly which IP address and port to use, and would probably have to know the IP address of the original destination in order to get through the firewall. This information would only be known if the hacker had been snooping on the connection.

The theoretical possibility of this exploitation exists, but would require a lot of information to execute. Even if the client had closed the connection, the client wouldn't be listening on the high number port the client had opened to initiate the connection. This attack could be most effectively used to send malformed packets to a host in a denial-of-service attack.

24seven Case Study: Trial by Firewall

A customer of mine wanted to implement Network Address Translation in their network for security reasons and because they used a DSL adapter that only provided sixteen public IP addresses. Since they were an all-Microsoft shop and a small business, we decided to use Checkpoint Firewall-1, which has good automatic support for Network Address Translation.

After setting up the firewall for standard use and creating the appropriate policies, I set up Network Address Translation for the internal client computers to use the firewall's IP address. I then created a static translation for the mail server, which was internal.

The client access worked fine, but I realized that I'd have to set a route in the DSL adapter to route the static IP address for the mail server. Since the DSL adapter was owned by the ISP, I called their technical support number and asked to have a route programmed into the adapter.

Much to my surprise, the support technician had no idea what I was talking about. He'd never heard of adding a route to anything. I asked to speak with his supervisor, who then informed me that the DSL adapter was not a router at all—it was merely a data link layer bridge. Any devices it talked to would have to be present on the same Ethernet collision domain.

This was problematic because we needed to protect the e-mail server (and because I didn't want to buy a hub to put between the firewall and the DSL adapter). So I decided to use proxy ARP, which I was familiar with

from the UNIX world, but which I'd never used in Windows NT.

I sat down to the NT server and typed ARP. The command existed and it worked as expected. I typed in the ARP command to bind the static translation address to the MAC address of the external adapter. It accepted the command, and viola! Traffic began to flow. I verified that I could connect from the outside world to the e-mail server and that mail could flow from the ISP. Everything seemed fine.

After chatting with my contact at the client site, I packed up my laptop and tools and began to leave. At that point, one of the employees said that the e-mail service seemed to have gone down. I checked for connectivity again, and found that indeed the static mapping no longer worked.

I was stumped. I checked the firewall—no difference. I re-issued the ARP command with the parameter to indicate a static mapping. That worked as it had the first time, and traffic flowed again.

This time I was wary. I left my laptop in place running a constant ping from the Internet (through a dial-up account) to the mail server's static address mapping. Sure enough, about an hour later the ping began to fail.

For some reason, Windows NT would not retain the ARP mapping. I fired up Internet Explorer and searched Microsoft's tech support site to no avail. Almost no information existed on the default ARP command.

So I went to Alta Vista and did a net-wide search. Surprisingly few pages matched, but I did find one that specifically mentioned that NT's ARP command could not retain address resolutions—exactly the problem I was having.

I figured Firewall-1 must have some sort of solution to the problem. I pulled up the documentation on the CD-ROM (which is normally very complete) and dug around. All I found was a description of the proxy ARP problem with the solution that you should manually enter a proxy ARP command to solve it, which I'd already done.

Next, I added the statically mapped IP address to the protocol stack of the NT machine as a second IP address on the external adapter. Unfortunately, Firewall-1 performs late translation, which means that the IP addresses are translated after the operating system has routed the packet. This means that the packets bound for the statically translated address were being "bounced" back out the external adapter by the default routing NT adds for each adapter, which I could not defeat. Only true proxy ARP, which NT didn't support, would solve my problem.

I couldn't imagine that I was the first person to have had this problem, so I called Checkpoint's tech support. They told me they could open up a support incident for $500, which frosted me, but which I would gladly pay if they could guarantee me a solution. They would not, so I decided not to pay them.

I sat and stewed about the problem when my phone suddenly rang. It was the Checkpoint support technician, who said he'd send me e-mail with a URL to click on. I checked my mail, read the message, and clicked into a private area in Checkpoint's support Web site that described the exact problem and how to solve it.

It seems that Firewall-1's firewalling engine for NT is designed to support proxy ARP because NT doesn't, but that there's no user interface for doing it or documentation on how to do it. Firewall-1 will ARP by adding entries to a file in Firewall-1's configuration directory called config.arp. The file is a simple list of Ethernet MAC addresses for the adapter and the IP address to respond to.

I added the entry for the static mapping and restarted the firewall. Everything worked fine after that.

This problem highlights my basic problem with the fee-for-support arrangements that nearly all firewall vendors set up. Vendors are naturally inclined to "hold out" on users until they pay for support, and to provide minimal documentation so as to increase the number of paid support calls. Vendors claim that they have to pay their support costs, but making user interfaces and completely documenting software can nearly eliminate support calls. Be sure to do a thorough search on the Internet and at Deja news (www.deja.com) on your issue before paying for technical support.

8

Application-Level Proxies

Proxy servers were originally developed to cache Web pages that were frequently accessed. In the early days of the Internet, wide area links were slow, the Web was relatively small, and Web pages were static. The entire Web consisted of only a few thousand Web sites shared by scientists and academicians. Whenever an important news element hit a Web site, many scientists in the same organization would visit that page (how many times have you forwarded a link inside your company?). By caching that page on a local server, proxies could eliminate redundant Internet access to retrieve the same page over and over. So, proxies were originally very effective at Web caching.

When the Web went supernova, proxies became markedly less effective at caching—the Web is now vast, Web pages are frequently dynamic, expiring as soon as they're transmitted, and the users of a single organization might range across a million Web pages before the same one is hit three times. These factors present a difficult caching problem indeed. But the new Web also has its seedier element, and proxy servers have shown their remarkable serendipitous side effect: They can hide all the real users of a network behind a single machine, they can filter URLs, and they can drop suspicious or illegal content. The primary purpose of the majority of proxy servers is now firewalling rather than Web caching.

Proxy servers regenerate high-level service requests on an external network for their clients on a private network. This effectively hides the identity and number of clients on the internal network from examination from the external network. Because of their position between a number of internal clients and public servers, proxies can also cache frequently accessed content from the public network to reduce accesses to the public network through high-cost wide-area links.

This chapter discusses only "pure" proxies—those that operate on the principle of service protocol forwarding. Most actual implementations of security proxies include the services of packet filtering and Network Address Translation to form a complete firewall. Those technologies can be combined with proxies to eliminate some of the attacks to which pure proxies are vulnerable.

Many proxy service alternatives exist, ranging from the application layer filter functionality of true firewalls like Checkpoint's Firewall-1, to general-purpose pure "proxy only" applications like WinGate, to simple single-service proxies like Jigsaw for HTTP. Pure proxies are subject to a number of problems, most based on the fact that the base operating system is not protected by the proxy software against denial-of-service attacks and the exploitation of other services that may be running on the server.

Proxy servers are most often associated with the HTTP World Wide Web service because proxies were first developed for this service. Since that time, proxy functionality has been applied to most other common Internet services. Examples in this chapter will use the HTTP service, but the functionality remains largely the same for other services.

How Proxies Work

Proxies work by listening for service requests from internal clients and then sending those requests on the external network as if the proxy server itself was the originating client. When the proxy server receives a response from the public server, it returns that response to the original internal client as if it were the originating public server. Figure 8.1 shows this process in detail.

The next sections discuss the advantages and disadvantages of proxy servers in detail.

Security Advantages of Proxies

The process of request regeneration and the fact of a proxy's location between the external and internal networks provide a number of security advantages:

- Proxies hide private clients from external exposure.
- Proxies can block dangerous URLs.
- Proxies can filter dangerous content such as viruses and Trojan horses before passing it to the client.

- Proxies can check the consistency of returned content.
- Proxies can eliminate the need for transport layer routing between networks.
- Proxies provide a single point of access, control, and logging.

Figure 8.1   A service proxy

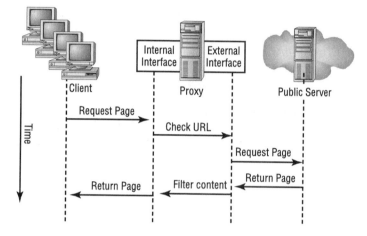

Each of these security advantages is detailed in the following sections.

Client Hiding

The major security feature of proxy servers is client hiding. Like Network Address Translation, proxy servers can make an entire internal network appear to be a single machine from the Internet because only a single machine passes requests onto the Internet.

Like Network Address Translators, proxy servers prevent external hosts from connecting to services on internal machines. In the case of proxy servers, no route to the clients exists because the address domains of the internal and external networks may be incompatible and because transport layer routing does not exist between the two networks.

Proxies perform this feature by completely regenerating service-level requests rather than simply changing and recalculating address headers. For example, when a Web client makes a request through a proxy server, the proxy server receives the request as if it were the destination Web server on the internal network. It then regenerates the request on the external network as if it were a typical Web browser. When the proxy receives the response from the ultimate Web server, it serves that response to its internal client. Only HTTP passes through the proxy, not TCP or IP. TCP/IP (and other low-level protocols) are regenerated by the proxy—they do not route through it unless the proxy is misconfigured.

Another aspect of client hiding is that of connection multiplexing; a proxy server can be used to share a single Internet connection and IP address among an entire network. For this reason, light proxy servers like WinGate are extremely popular in home and small office environments where only a single dial-up or dedicated connection is available.

URL Blocking

URL blocking allows administrators to disallow the provision of certain Web sites based on their URLs. In theory this will keep your employees from viewing Web sites you don't want them to have access to. This function in easy to implement. The proxy simply checks every request for a Web page (or other service URL) against a list of denied pages before it regenerates the request. If the URL is blocked, the proxy will not request or return the page.

URL blocking is easy to circumvent, however, because a Web site can be just as easily addressed by its IP address or even by the whole number address. For example, a user could type in any of the following in their Web browser to access exactly the same home page:

http://www.gamehound.com/default.html

http://192.168.13.12/default.html

http://3232238860/default.html

But your URL blocker will (probably) only be checking for the full text URL.

URLs can contain DNS names or IP addresses. Most people are familiar with the first two examples of site references, but have never heard of the third: an IP address specified as a whole number rather than as a "dotted quad notation." The concept is simple: An IP address is just a 32-bit number, and though we refer to them in dotted quad (10.0.0.0) notation for convenience sake, there's no reason why they can't be referred to as a whole number. To convert a dotted quad number to a whole number, use the following formula ("a" is the most significant quad, "d" the least): $a \times 2^{24} + b \times 2^{16} + c \times 2^{8} + d$. Converting everything to easily calculable numbers, the formula becomes: $a \times 16777216 + b * 65536 + c * 256 + d$. So, for example, turning www.starlingtech.com's IP address of 209.68.11.152 into a whole number makes it $209 \times 16777216 + 68 \times 65536 + 11 \times 256 + 152 = 3510897560$. Put 3510897560 into your Web browser's address bar and you'll see the starlingtech home page come up. Note that Web sites behind proxy servers (like microsoft.com) don't come up because the whole number IP address must be programmed into the proxy for the proxy to recognize it.

The other major problem with URL blocking for security administrators is simply keeping up with sites to block. Problem sites like hacking depositories, pornographic sites, and game sites have the ephemeral life of a mayfly—they pop up and disappear just as quickly. Most people who engage in the activities ascribed by these sites just use search engines or Usenet news lists to keep up with where their favorite sites have moved. You will not be able to stay ahead of that activity with your URL blocked database.

Sage Advice: Don't Make Me URL

When you're dealing with adults, it's much easier to use policy to enforce appropriate Web use. Just make sure everyone knows that every Web site accessed is cached on your proxy server, and that the proxy uses content filtering to search for suspicious content like games, pornography, and the city of San Francisco in Web site content. Once they know that you could check up on their browsing after the fact, they won't risk it, and you won't have to deal with trying to stay ahead of a blocked URL database.

(Disclaimer: The San Francisco joke is a reference to the fact that Sybex, the publisher of this book, is located in the San Francisco Bay Area. It should not be construed as an endorsement or denigration of vegetarianism or any other lifestyle choice.)

Content Filtering

Because proxies retransmit all protocol payloads and are protocol specific, the proxy service can be used to search the payload for suspicious content. This means that you can configure your HTTP proxy service to strip out Active-X controls, Java applets, or even large images if you felt they could present a security problem. You could use an SMTP proxy to strip out executable file attachments and archived zip files if you felt they were a security problem.

Content filters can also be used to check Web pages for the presence of certain words or phrases, such as the trademarks of your competition or some current news item.

You should filter Active-X controls in Web sites, Java applets, and executable files in e-mail because they can be used to install Trojan horses inside your network. If someone needs to transfer an executable file, have him or her transmit it as a zip file or use BinHex or some other encoder to transfer it in a text format. This will require effort to decode, thus preventing the accidental transfer of a virus or Trojan horse into your network.

Consistency Checking

The same buffer overrun problem was discovered in MS-IIS4 during the writing of this book. Consistency checking refers to checking the content of a protocol to be sure it makes sense for that protocol. Consistency checking ensures that specifically malformed types of content can't be used to exploit a security weakness in your internal network.

For example, earlier versions of the UNIX sendmail SMTP daemon is notoriously susceptible to various buffer overflow problems. These occur when an e-mail message is sent and is longer than it says it is. Sendmail will allocate a memory buffer that is the size the message claims to be, but will then scan the message until it hits an end-of-file marker. If the area between the claimed end and the actual end contains executable code, a hacker could gain root access to your e-mail server.

Sage Advice: Beware the Open Filter

I have customers who use content filtering to keep employees from reading news sites, posting their resumes on job sites, and basically doing anything even remotely fun on the Web. The problem they've run into is that the employees now feel that any site that isn't blocked is fair game—if they can get to it, they can waste as much time as they want on it. The whole thing has turned into a sort of escalating cold war between the IT department and the rest of the company. Once an unblocked site is found, it's passed around discreetly (and not through e-mail) amongst the employees until everyone knows about it.

Again, my earlier advice of simply treating people like adults and making sure they know that you could check up on their activities if you wanted to is a far more effective method than blocking or filtering specific types of content.

Another example of a buffer overflow occurs in URLs that are longer than 256 characters. Early Web browsers were flawed because the end of the URL beyond 256 characters could contain executable code that would be executed by the browser software.

Consistency checking with your proxy software can ensure that these sorts of problems are eliminated at the proxy so they won't affect internal machines. Unfortunately, the problems to check for usually are not known until some hacker exploits them, so most consistency checks are only available after an exploit has been found.

Route Blocking

Transport layer packets need not be routed because the request is completely regenerated. This eliminates transport layer exploits like source routing, fragmentation, and various denial-of-service attacks. By eliminating routing, you can also ensure that no protocol for which you have not established a proxy service can be passed to the public network.

Route blocking is perhaps the most important advantage of proxy servers. Because no TCP/IP packets actually pass between the internal and external networks, a vast number of denial-of-service and exploitation attacks are prevented.

Unfortunately, route blocking is not used often enough. Because many protocols exist for which there are no good proxy services, administrators often must enable routing on the proxy server, which completely eliminates the security gain achieved by route disconnection. If you can, avoid allowing low-level network packets to pass through your proxy server. Most proxy server software will allow you to create generic TCP proxy services for any port using a generic SOCKS proxy. These generic proxies, although they cannot perform content filtering, still allow you to keep TCP/IP packets from flowing between your networks.

Logging and Alerting

The final security advantage of proxies is the logging and alerting facilities they provide. Proxies ensure that all content flows through a single point, which gives you a checkpoint for network data. Most proxy software will log the usage characteristics of the proxy by user, and can be configured to retain a log of sites they visit. This will allow you to reconstruct the user's Web browsing sessions if you suspect some illegal or unethical activity has occurred.

The alerting facility provided by some proxies can alert you to attacks in progress, even though the proxy facility of a server is not generally subject to attack. But the facility can alert you to attempted proxy connections from the external interface, which hackers frequently try to exploit to launder their connections.

Performance Aspects of Proxies

In addition to their security aspects, proxy servers can also perform important performance enhancements:

- Proxies can cache frequently requested data to improve performance by eliminating redundant access to the slower external network.
- Proxies can balance the service load across a number of internal servers.

Caching

Proxies were originally developed as a performance improvement, not as a security device. In the early Web days, there were only tens of thousands of sites. They were mostly scientific in nature and didn't change often. Because wide area links to the Internet were slow, a proxy could be used to cache large portions of the Web locally, so internal users could simply browse from the local proxy. Content didn't change very fast, so that made sense.

Caching now only makes sense in those instances where a large number of users frequently access the same Web pages over and over. This usage is currently somewhat rare, so the caching aspects of proxy servers are all but obsolete.

As e-commerce becomes more prevalent, caching will again become an important function because many people will perform their jobs by interfacing to a few frequently accessed sites. Consider for example a travel agency that uses `Expedia.com` and `Travelocity.com` to perform their work. Many agents would access the same two sites over and over, so caching the main site elements, graphics, and applets makes sense.

Reverse Proxy Load Balancing

Newer proxy servers can be used to "reverse proxy," or provide the proxy service to external clients for internal servers. This functionality is used to balance the load of clients across a number of Web servers. Many high functionality Web sites make use of complex applications in the form of ISAPI applications, Active Server Pages, Java servlets, or CGI applications. These applications execute on the server, so they considerably reduce the number of clients a single server can handle. For example, an NT server running IIS that could reasonably handle 100,000 browsers of standard HTML pages may only be able to handle 5,000 browsers of an ASP page that is executed on the server.

This means that most e-commerce functions cannot actually be handled on a single server, so the site must be run in parallel across a number of machines. For example, www .microsoft.com is currently run on 30 identical Web servers. DNS provides a rudimentary load-sharing scheme by which subsequent access to a DNS name will provide one of a number of IP addresses, but this does not actually balance the load. Only after a statistically large number of equivalent accesses occurs does this scheme serve to actually balance the client load.

A proxy server can be used to respond to a single IP address and then funnel client connections to one of a number of site servers behind it. The proxy server can use some measurement provided by each Web server to maintain awareness of which server has the most remaining capacity. Each connecting client can then be funneled to whichever server has the most capacity to handle it. Because the proxy actually does very little work compared to the effort of serving e-commerce Web pages, it can handle many orders of magnitude and more client connections than the e-commerce servers behind it. Figure 8.2 shows a proxy server load balancing a number of e-commerce servers.

Security Liabilities of Proxies

Proxies suffer from some of the following security liabilities:

- Proxies create a single point of failure.
- Client software must be capable of working with proxies. They cannot be configured to work transparently on the network.
- Proxies must exist for each service.
- Proxies do not protect the base operating system.
- Default configurations are often optimized for performance rather than security.

Figure 8.2 Load balancing with a proxy server

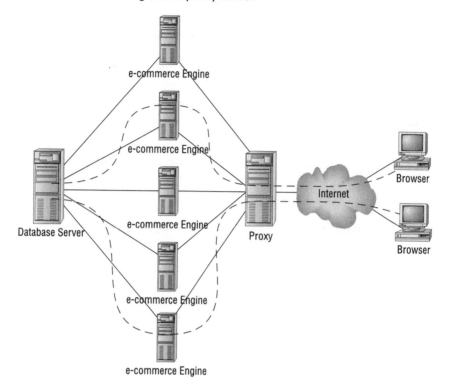

Single Point of Failure

Inherent with any single point of control is a single point of failure. If a hacker can disable your proxy, your entire organization could be cut off from the Internet.

Proxies, routers, and firewalls all suffer from this problem to some degree. With routers the problem is easily fixed by simply having more than one route to the Internet. Firewalls are far more secure than pure proxies because they include low-level packet filtering to eliminate the problems caused by denial-of-service activities. Pure proxy servers do not include the functionality to protect themselves from attack however, so they are very vulnerable both to intrusion and denial of service.

For this reason, your proxy server should either include the services of a strong packet filter or use the operating system's packet filtering mechanism for protection. Your packet filter should be capable of filtering out ICMP as well as IP, TCP, and UDP protocols.

Clients Must Be Made to Work with Proxies

A proxy-enabled client must exist for each service you wish to proxy. For example, your Web browser must support connection to a proxy server by including in the configuration options which proxy service all requests should transmit to. If the client software cannot be configured to use a proxy, a proxy service cannot be used except in conjunction with a true Network Address Translator. This can be a major problem for services like FTP where the client software that ships with most operating systems does not support connection to a proxy server. You can purchase proxy clients for these services, however.

Proxy services included with address translating firewalls can get around this restriction because they can modify inbound and outbound network addresses. This means that clients need not know or be configured to work with proxies that exist as part of a true address translating firewall.

Proxies Must Exist for Each Service

A different proxy service is required for each supported service protocol. Network Address Translation is universal and works with any protocol except those that rely upon payload-embedded IP address information or require the ability to open a back channel to the client. Protocols for which no proxy service is available cannot be connected through a proxy except by a generic TCP proxy service (like the generic SOCKS proxy) that would work much like a Network Address Translator. Any such service would not have the advantage of content filtering, however.

Many services cannot be easily proxied because they require the establishment of a back channel. Only proxy servers that maintain a table of expected return sockets can proxy services like H.323 (the protocol used by NetMeeting for voice and video conferencing).

Many services exist for which there are no effective content filters. Stream-based services like RealAudio or RealVideo are very difficult to filter for content because the content must stream through in real time, and an interruption in the compressed stream will make the remainder of the stream undecipherable. Since content like this cannot be reliably filtered, it should be blocked if considered a security threat.

Lax Default Configurations

Many proxy server software packages suffer from lax default configurations that can cause serious security problems. For example, WinGate, the most popular proxy server for home and small office environments, is used to share a single Internet connection rather than for security. For this reason, the software producer made it easy to set up for people who didn't understand proxies, and set it up to work by default for most common protocols.

For versions before 3.0, the default installation opened up a Winsock proxy to the external interface, which allowed hackers to connect to the external interface as if they were an internal client. The hackers could then use the proxy to connect to other Web or Internet services as if they were working from the unsuspecting home user's computer directly. This effectively laundered their connection and made it appear as if the owner of the computer running WinGate was performing the illegal activities the hackers actually performed. Version 3.0's default configuration disabled connections coming from the external interface.

Many proxy servers suffer from the problem of lax default configuration because they are often designed for less experienced computer users and put performance and functionality ahead of security. Most can be configured correctly, but users frequently ignore the software once they've got it completely installed.

Performance Liabilities of Proxies

Proxy servers only have one performance liability, but for the sake of uniformity, I'll present it as a bulleted list:

- Proxy servers create a service bottleneck.

Proxies Create a Network Bottleneck

Like firewalls or routers, a single proxy server connection to the Internet can create a bottleneck if it's not properly upgraded as the number of network users increases. Although proxies initially improve performance through their caching mechanism, you'll make everyone wait behind a slow machine if you've got more clients than the server can support effectively. But beware of blaming your proxy for a bottleneck that's actually caused by a slow Internet pipe. If you have only one Internet connection, and it is a T1 (1.5MB) or slower connection, any computer that actually meets the minimum requirements for the operating system and the proxy server is fast enough to handle the load. Proxy bottlenecks only occur on network connections faster than 1.5MBs or when something is actually wrong with the proxy server.

This problem is easy to solve—add more proxy servers. Unlike Web sites or public servers, a proxy server doesn't need to have the exact same configuration across a number of machines. You can directly attach any number of proxy servers to your external network connection and assign each client inside your network to one of the servers on a random or fair share basis. For example, if you've got four proxy servers running, just assign every fourth client to the same proxy server. You'll lose some of the caching effect because a client on a different proxy who accesses a site won't make that site available to the other proxies.

You can also use sophisticated, high availability software and TCP/IP load balancing to handle the connection to multiple proxies, but that involves considerable expense and is not much more efficient. It does provide proxy redundancy though, because otherwise a segment of users would lose service if their assigned proxy went down.

Proxy Best Practices

Proxies are useful for a number of different purposes, and for that reason security often takes a back seat to performance or connection multiplexing. Proxies can be extremely dangerous if they're used incorrectly (okay, people can't actually get hurt—just dangerous in the legal risk sense) because hackers can exploit them to make it appear as if their activities are coming from within your network. This can make your company liable for their activities.

This section details proxy servers' best practices that you should implement whenever you use proxy services to connect to the Internet.

Use a Real Firewall

The most important thing you can do to protect yourself is to either use the proxy functionality of a real firewall or put a firewall in front of your proxy server to protect it. There's no reason why a proxy server has to be directly connected to the external network unless the proxy is used for reverse proxy load balancing of a Web site. Figure 8.3 shows the strong firewall use of proxy servers both for client proxy and reverse proxy functions.

The firewall's purpose is to protect the proxy server from exploitation or attack from the network since pure proxies do not include protective features like packet filtering or network address translation.

Disable Routing

If you use proxies as your primary protection against hackers on the Internet, be sure you disable routing through the proxy. If you allow routing through the proxy, the proxy is not performing a significant security function for your network because your clients will all be directly addressable from the Internet. Proxies' client hiding feature relies upon disabled routing to prevent a number of low-level protocol attacks.

Proxies are usually set up initially with routing disabled, but after some time a service or protocol is needed for which you do not have a specific proxy service or which cannot be proxied. Don't be tempted to simply enable routing in this case. If you find you need services that cannot be proxied, use Network Address Translation. If the service can neither be translated nor proxied, don't use it at all.

Figure 8.3 Place proxies behind firewalls

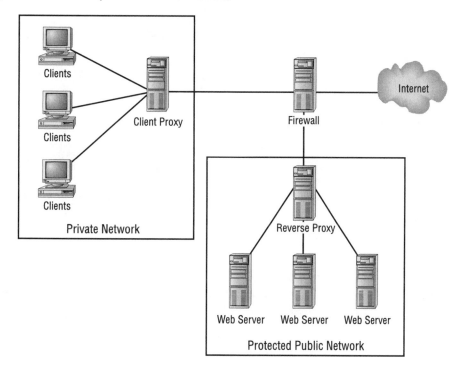

Secure the Base Operating System

Securing the base operating system is crucial to the effective use of proxies as security devices. If hackers can exploit the server upon which your proxy runs, they can reconfigure the proxy security settings to bypass it completely.

This is especially important in UNIX and Windows environments. Both operating systems are notoriously susceptible to well known hacking exploits, so proxies that run upon them are just as susceptible.

Use strong user-based security permissions as well as port and protocol filtering at the operating system level to make sure your proxy server is serving only those protocols you intend for it to serve. Stay up to date on the latest hacking exploits for your operating system and be certain that you apply patches and hot-fixes to your external security servers as they are released. It's more important for a publicly exposed server to be secure than it is to be stable. A crash due to an untested patch or hot-fix only causes a temporary loss of service—it doesn't allow a security breach.

Disable External Access

Never allow external network clients to proxy through your server, even if it seems like it would make sense for remote users to do so. By allowing external proxy access to your server, you make it possible for hackers to exploit your proxy server to launder their IP connections and make it appear as if your proxy server is the origin of their attacks. This could make you legally liable for the damages they cause.

Disable Excess Services

Don't pile all your public services on the same machine as your proxy server. This general rule is especially important when applied to security mechanisms like proxy servers. If a service like FTP or SMTP allows a hacker access to your proxy server, the hacker can disable the proxy server's security settings to gain further access to your network. If these services are divided amongst several machines, however, an FTP specific attack will only yield access to the FTP server—not the rest of the network.

On Windows NT, it's especially important to unbind the NetBIOS session ports from the external TCP/IP interface through the network control panel. Leaving these ports open will make it possible for hackers to use automated password guessing tools to attempt to log directly into your proxy server. Once that's accomplished, they have free reign to modify your security settings.

24seven Case Study: Guilt by Association

A small-business client of mine used a copy of WinGate to share their cable-modem among a group of five computers at one of their offices. Cable-modems are constantly connected Internet interfaces that operate asynchronously at a fairly high speed—up to 10Mb down from, and 768Kb up to, the ISP. They provide more than enough bandwidth to share in a small office.

WinGate is simple enough that they set the software up themselves. Running on a Windows NT Workstation, they established Web and e-mail (POP and SMTP) proxies.

After about a year, they noticed that their Internet connection had become comparatively slow, and that the computer seemed to be doing quite a bit of hard disk access. They called me to determine why. I enabled the WinGate logging mechanism and immediately determined that the proxy was working overtime with a number of WinSock connections—a function that they did not use. Within a few seconds, I determined that their proxy server was being exploited by hackers to launder their IP address through an unsecured WinSock proxy service that WinGate established and allowed access to on the external interface by default.

Hackers love WinGate. By running through someone else's proxy server, a hacker can launder their IP address and keep from being found. If they're caught hacking, the IP address shows up in logs as the address of the proxy server, not their own. By scanning for the default WinGate administration port (808) that the default installation leaves open to the outside interface, they can

quickly find hosts for their parasitic activities. They scan the address ranges of ISPs that they know provide constantly connected services with static IP addresses (like cable-modem providers) so they can exploit the proxy whenever they want.

We recorded all the incoming address information we could, and then I set about the task of properly configuring the WinGate proxy for security by disabling connections from the external interface and shutting down the WinSock proxy. I warned my client that they may be subjected to numerous denial-of-service attacks because the hackers who'd been routinely exploiting their server would probably be angry that the server had been secured—and that they'd been caught.

Once I had the hacker's IP addresses, I set about contacting their ISPs to get their service shut off. Using tracert and the InterNIC Web site, I located the actual bottom tier ISPs (those that provide the dial-up service directly to the customer) and contacted them by phone. We'd determined that two of the three hackers were in Canada and one was from Israel. I called the support number for the Israeli company and explained the situation to their support technician. He escalated the call to their network administrator, who told me flat out that they would not pursue the issue even enough to find out which of their customers was to blame, and that I had no legal recourse. Upsetting as that was, he was right. There's no effective way to sue a foreign network service provider to force them to identify their customer in countries where that's not required by law.

Canada is a different story, however. I called their ISP and was greeted by much the same initial response of being elevated to a network administrator. This time the problem wasn't one of indifference as much as incompetence. The administrator admitted that they had no time accounting system or logging in place—they simply billed all their customers a flat rate because they couldn't figure out how to bill for time used or even to keep track of when which users were using what. He admitted that they had no way to determine which customer had been online or using a specific IP address at any specific time. When I warned him that the law made his company responsible for how their network is used, he assured me that they were working on an accounting system that would take care of the problem.

So although I was able to secure the proxy and prevent its future exploitation, I was not able to hold the hackers who'd exploited it liable for their actions.

9

Virtual Private Networks

Virtual Private Networks (VPNs) are a cost-effective way to extend your LAN over the Internet to remote networks and remote client computers. VPNs use the Internet to route LAN traffic from one private network to another by encapsulating the LAN traffic in IP packets. The encrypted packets are unreadable by intermediary Internet computers and can contain any kind of LAN communications, including file and print access, LAN e-mail, Remote Procedure Calls, and client/server database access.

Virtual Private Networks between LANs can be established using server computers, firewalls, or routers. Client access to the VPNs can be made using VPN software on the client computers or by dialing in to ISPs that support the VPN protocol. Using this second method, however, makes the ISP a partner in your network security in the same way that relying on an ISP for your firewall does.

Pure VPN systems do not provide adequate network protection. You also need a firewall and other Internet security services to keep your network safe. You should be particularly aware of the security problems of PPTP and take steps to correct them in your own network.

Using the Internet to link LANs and give remote computers LAN access causes security, performance, reliability, and management problems. Your LAN is a protected environment that is only available to members of your organization. The LAN clients and servers should be protected from the Internet by a firewall and proxy servers so that (ideally) network intruders can't even identify their existence, much less target them for individual attack. In order to make it more difficult for hackers to capture private company information, most firewalls are configured not to pass typical LAN service protocols such as NetBIOS, the NetWare Core Protocol, or NFS.

You could link your Windows-based LANs together over the Internet and, by simply configuring your firewall to pass NetBIOS traffic, allow your employees to have remote access to file and print services. You could open your firewall to NFS to allow UNIX hosts to communicate directly over the Internet, or open your firewall to AppleTalk traffic for Macintosh clients. But this would allow hackers to access your data simply by providing a valid account name and password or by attacking the protocol to exploit a bug that would allow access.

Exposing your LAN file-sharing protocols (like NetBIOS, NFS, or AppleTalk) in this manner effectively makes the whole Internet your LAN. It is virtual, but not private. Not only could your sales force print to your engineering department's printers or log on to your accounting department's file server, anyone on the Internet could print to the printer or log on to the file server. An intruder would have to guess a password, of course, but hackers have a lot of experience in guessing passwords.

Virtual Private Networking Explained

Virtual Private Networks solve the problem of direct Internet access to servers through a combination of the following fundamental security components:

- IP encapsulation
- Cryptographic authentication
- Data payload encryption

All three components must exist in a true VPN. Although cryptographic authentication and data payload encryption may seem like the same thing at first, they are actually entirely different functions and may exist independently of each other. For example, Secure Socket Layer performs data payload encryption without cryptographic authentication of the remote user, and the standard Windows logon performs cryptographic authentication without performing data payload encryption.

IP Encapsulation

When you plan to connect your separated LANs over the Internet, you need to find a way to protect the data traffic that travels between those LANs. Ideally, the computers in each

LAN should be unaware that there is anything special about communicating with the computers in the other LANs. Computers outside your virtual network should not be able to snoop on the traffic exchanged between the LANs or be able to insert their own data into the communications stream. Essentially, you need a private and protected tunnel through the public Internet.

An IP packet can contain any kind of information: program files, spreadsheet data, audio streams, or even other IP packets. When an IP packet contains another IP packet, it is called IP encapsulation, IP on IP, or IP/IP. There are many ways you can encapsulate one IP packet in another—the way Microsoft does it is specified in the Point-to-Point Tunneling Protocol (PPTP). Other hardware and software vendors, such as Cisco and Alta Vista Software, do it differently, but the principle is the same.

Why encapsulate IP within IP? Because doing so makes it possible to refer to a host within another network when a routed connection may not exist. IP encapsulation can make it appear to network computers that two distant networks are actually adjacent—separated from each other by a single router. But they are actually separated by many Internet routers and gateways that may not even use the same address space because both internal networks are using address translation.

The tunnel end point—be it a router, VPN appliance, or a server running a tunneling protocol—will remove the internal packet, decrypt it, and then apply its routing rules to send the embedded packet on its way in the internal network.

As an example, consider two IP networks linked by a router. Both are class C IP subnets, one with the network address of 10.1.1 and the other with the network address of 10.1.2. In this example, the fourth number in each network is reserved for the station address, in the range 1 to 254. The router must have a network interface adapter on each network so that it can move IP traffic between the two LANs. The .1 and .127 station addresses are typical addresses reserved for routers and gateways, so in this network the router has one adapter with the IP address of 10.1.1.1 and another with the IP address of 10.1.2.1. All of the computers in both networks have a netmask of 255.255.255.0, since both networks are class C subnets.

When a computer in the 10.1.1 network (for example, 10.1.1.23) needs to send an IP packet to a computer in the 10.1.2 network (such as 10.1.2.99), the communication proceeds as follows:

1. The originating computer first notices that the network portion of the destination address (10.1.2.99) does not match its own network address.

2. Instead of attempting to send the packet directly to the destination, the originating computer sends the packet to the default gateway address for its subnet (10.1.1.1).

3. The router at that address reads the packet.

4. The router determines that the packet should be placed on the 10.1.2 network subnet.

5. The router sends the packet from its adapter (10.1.2.1) to the destination address (10.1.2.99) on that network subnet.

6. The destination computer reads the packet.

In comparison with the preceding example, consider two IP networks linked by RAS servers using PPTP. One LAN has the network address 10.1.1, and the other has the network address 10.1.2. In this example, the RAS computers on each network provide the network connection to the Internet. One RAS server has a LAN IP address of 10.1.1.1 and an Internet address of 250.121.13.12 assigned by its ISP, while the other has a LAN IP address of 10.1.2.1 and an Internet address of 110.121.112.34 assigned by its ISP.

Communication in the PPTP-connected LANs starts and ends the same way it does in router-connected LANs. The IP packets have further to go, though, so more work is done in the middle. Compare the following example to the earlier one:

1. The originating computer (10.1.1.23) first notices that the destination address (10.1.2.99) is not in the same subnet as itself.

2. Instead of attempting to send the packet directly to the destination, the originating computer sends the packet to the default gateway address for its subnet (10.1.1.1).

3. The RAS server on the 10.1.1 network reads the packet.

4. The RAS server on the 10.1.1 network determines that the packet should be placed on the 10.1.2 network subnet, for which it has a PPTP connection established over the Internet.

5. The RAS server encrypts the packet and encapsulates it in another IP packet.

6. The router sends the encapsulated packet from its network interface, which is connected to the Internet (24.121.13.12), to the Internet address (110.121.112.34) of the RAS server of the 10.1.2 network subnet.

7. The RAS server of the 10.1.2 network subnet reads the encapsulated and encrypted packet from its Internet interface.

8. The RAS server of the 10.1.2 network decrypts the embedded IP packet, verifying that it is a valid packet that has not been tampered with and that it comes from a trusted source (another RAS server).

9. The RAS server of the 10.1.2 network sends the packet from its adapter (10.1.2.1) to the destination address (10.1.2.99) on that network subnet.

10. The destination computer reads the packet.

Note that from the point of view of the two network client computers, it doesn't matter how the packet got from one IP subnet to the other. As far as the network client computers are concerned, a router is the same thing as two RAS servers and a PPTP connection.

Cryptographic Authentication

Cryptographic authentication is used to securely validate the identity of the remote user so the system can determine what level of security is appropriate for that user. VPNs use cryptographic authentication to determine whether or not the user can participate in the encrypted tunnel, and may also use the authentication to exchange the secret or public key used for payload encryption.

Many different forms of cryptographic authentication exist:

Private Key Encryption   Also called Shared Secret encryption, relies upon a secret value known to both parties. Simply knowing the value proves to the provider that the requester is to be trusted. Challenge and response can be used to make sure that only hashes of the secret, not the secret itself, are transmitted on the network, and one-time password variations can be used to ensure that the secret changes each time it's used.

Public Key Encryption   Relies on the exchange of unidirectional keys—keys that can only be used to encrypt data. This means that the decryption key is held on the receiver and never transmitted over a public network, which makes the encrypted data secure during its transmission because it can't be decrypted by anyone else even if they have the encryption key. Tunnel-end systems may exchange pairs of public keys to form a bidirectional channel, or the public key receiver may encrypt a shared secret key and transmit it to the public key transmitter to use for future communications (because secret key encryption is faster than public key encryption).

If a hacker intercepted the public or encrypting key, the only thing they could do with it is encrypt data and transmit it to the receiver—they could not decrypt the contents of data they intercept.

Data Payload Encryption

Data payload encryption is used to obfuscate the contents of the encapsulated data. By encrypting the encapsulated IP packets, both the data and the internal nature of the private networks is kept secret. Data payload encryption can be accomplished using any one of a number of secure cryptographic methods, which differ based on the VPN solution you chose.

Characteristics of VPNs

When you consider establishing a VPN for your company, you should understand the advantages and disadvantages of VPNs when compared with traditional LANs and WANs.

VPNs Are Cheaper Than WANs

The primary consideration, in many cases, is that a VPN is often much cheaper than a WAN of similar size, especially when you want Internet connectivity for your LANs. A single dedicated leased line through a metropolitan area (from one part of a city to another) can cost from hundreds to thousands of dollars a month, depending on the amount of bandwidth you need. A company's dedicated connection to an ISP is usually made with a leased line of this sort, but for each LAN to be linked with a VPN, only one leased line to an ISP is required and can be used for both Internet and VPN traffic. ISPs can be selected for proximity to your operation to reduce cost.

You can also establish a business Internet connection to some ISPs using regular analog modems, ISDN, xDSL, or cable modems, depending on the services available in your area. These methods of connecting to the Internet can be much less expensive than dedicated leased telephone lines, but you must evaluate whether the bandwidth provided by these connection methods is sufficient for use with your VPN.

VPNs really shine compared to traditional WANs in the way they deal with LANs being connected over widely separated geographical areas (in different cities, different states, or even different countries). The costs of dedicated long distance phone lines are much greater than the costs for local-loop circuits (connections between locations that share the same local telephone switch). You can use the Internet instead of expensive long-distance lines.

When considering a VPN, you have to take into account your total monthly bandwidth requirements as well as your peak, short-period bandwidth requirements. Many ISPs apply a surcharge when the total amount of data transferred in a month exceeds a certain amount. It is unlikely that even intensive long-term use of the Internet connection will exceed the costs of leasing a long-distance line of similar capacity, but you should still check the policies of the ISPs in your area and make plans accordingly.

The VPN advantage in terms of remote user dial-in is that you don't have to provide and support your own specialized dial-in equipment, such as modems and terminal servers, or maintain dial-up phone lines. You can rely on an ISP to provide that service for you. The management and equipment depreciation costs alone should justify paying for your users' ISP accounts (and many users have arranged for their own ISP accounts for their home computers, anyway).

VPNs Are Easier to Establish

The two most difficult issues in WAN creation and management have to do with establishing communications links over the dedicated leased phone lines (using specialized communications devices) and routing WAN traffic over those links using routers and gateways.

When you establish a VPN over the Internet, your Internet Service Provider will help you make the initial IP connection to their service. Once you configure your firewall for tunneling, you can let the Internet do your routing for you. You don't have to learn how to program and manage specialized routers and gateways (unless you use them in your local network, as when several LANs in a campus are linked together). You do have to establish and manage the VPN connections, however, and you must maintain a connection to the Internet (you will most likely be maintaining an Internet connection anyway).

VPNs Are Slower Than LANs

You will not get the same performance out of your VPN that you would with computers that share the same LAN. Typical LANs transfer data at 10 or 100 Mbps while the Internet limits VPNs to the slowest of the links that connect the source computer to the destination computer. If, for example, the dial-in PC is connected to the Internet by a 56Kbps modem, then data transfer will go no faster than 56Kbps. If your LANs are connected to the Internet to the ISP with T1 leased lines, then the maximum you can expect for inter-LAN traffic is 1.5 Mbps (each way). Of course, WANs are no different; if you linked the same LANs directly via T1 leased lines, you would still have a 1.5 Mbps (each way) bandwidth limit.

Even if you have a very fast connection to your ISP, you may not get to use the full bandwidth of that connection because there may be a lower-speed link between your ISP and the ISP that serves the remote LAN. You may connect to the ISP via FDDI (a 100Mbps medium), for example, but the ISP may only have a T3 connection to the Service Access Point that links ISPs, limiting your total throughput to about 45Mbps. Also, you must share the Internet bandwidth with other Internet users, which means you actually get considerably less than the maximum theoretical bandwidth.

Furthermore, you may find that Internet congestion between your VPN end points will put a serious drag on your network. If your VPN travels over more than ten intermediate systems between end-points as shown by the tracert command, it will probably be uselessly slow, especially if those ten systems are owned by different major ISPs. The best way to take care of this problem is to use the same national or global ISP to connect your systems. This way, all your data will travel over their private network, thus avoiding the congested commercial Internet exchange network access points.

VPNs Are Less Reliable Than WANs

With a WAN, you retain far greater control over your network than you do with a VPN. When you use a WAN, you configure the routers and gateways, you negotiate the leased line service for the entire distance between your LANs, and you configure and maintain the specialized devices that maintain the WAN. You do not share the WAN bandwidth with any other organizations or individuals. With a VPN, on the other hand, you delegate all of those decisions to individuals outside your company. You and the ISP cooperate to establish the first stage of the VPN (from your LAN to the ISP), but someone else manages every other stage. This means that you have less control in the event of network outages. Also, unexpected surges in Internet activity can reduce the bandwidth available to users of your VPN. On the other hand, these service providers often have considerable experience in solving communications problems and can fix them much more quickly than the typical LAN administrator. Also on the plus side, Internet capacity has been growing consistently.

The reliability problem is most effectively dealt with in the same manner as the speed problem: Use the same national ISP throughout your network. If you have remote home users, make sure your ISP also provides commercial dial-up service so those users won't have to route through the CIX NAPs to get to your network. By using a single national ISP, you only have one company to hold accountable when things go wrong—you won't have competing companies pointing the finger at each other in an attempt to avoid responsibility.

VPNs Are Less Secure Than Isolated LANs or WANs

One drawback of VPNs (and the point that is most relevant to this book) is that they are less secure than LANs and WANs that are not connected to the Internet. Before a hacker can attack your network, there must be a way for the hacker to reach it. But how many LANs or WANs today are not connected to the Internet? A VPN is marginally more vulnerable to network intrusion than a LAN or WAN that is connected to the Internet because the VPN protocol is one more interface for the hacker to try to subvert.

VPN solutions like Microsoft's implementation of PPTP provide attack vectors for hackers to exploit. Any method that provides access to your network is a potential vector for attack, and VPNs force you to expose a vector into your network on the public Internet. Strong encryption and authentication can reduce the risk of intrusion, but they can't eliminate it. And any flaws in the implementation of a VPN protocol will considerably weaken your security posture.

Remote access clients present special security problems. Although they connect securely to your computers, they also participate directly on the Internet. This makes the remote client vulnerable to attack from the Internet since client operating systems are far less robust than server operating systems in most cases. Because very few strong security packages exist to secure individual clients, you will have difficulty ensuring that a remotely connected client doesn't present a hole in your security posture. Firewall vendors have just identified this potential vulnerability, and a few of them offer strong firewall services for some types of client computers. Your best bet to prevent this problem is to allow only Windows NT Workstation or UNIX remote hosts that have been secured as strongly as their native security will allow to attach to your network. Macintosh and Windows clients are not capable of providing the level of security required for facilities that need a strong security posture.

Types of VPNs

The example described earlier in this chapter is simplistic because it doesn't include such common Internet security components as firewalls and proxy servers. It does represent one type of VPN, however: the server-based VPN. Many firewalls also include IP tunneling functionality on which a VPN can be based. Many medium to large networks use routers to manage traffic routed within, as well as into and out of, the LAN. And many routers include VPN features that perform the same function as PPTP. A number of VPN-only routers also exist; these devices are called VPN appliances because they perform only one function. Regardless of how the VPN is set up, any properly secured network with an Internet connection will include firewall and possibly proxy server services. A VPN must be configured to work with these services.

There are three types of VPNs:

- Server-based VPNs
- Firewall-based VPNs
- Router-based VPNs including VPN appliances.

Server-Based VPNs

In a Windows NT-based network, perhaps the easiest and least disruptive way to establish a VPN between LANs is to dedicate a Windows NT Server computer to routing the PPTP traffic. Existing firewall, router, and proxy server services can be left in place, and the only modification to the Internet security setup required is for the firewall to pass the PPTP ports through to the Windows NT RAS server.

While Windows NT is a full-featured operating system that can run firewall software, maintain PPTP links using RAS, and provide file and print services to network clients all at the same time, it is not a good idea to do all that with just one computer. A security failure in any one of these services would compromise the entire network instead of just the affected computer. The RAS server, for example, doesn't have to be a privileged computer in the network; all it has to do is encapsulate and un-encapsulate network traffic. A hacker who has compromised a properly isolated RAS server will still have regular LAN security to defeat (such as usernames and passwords) and will have to get through the firewall to get to the RAS server. If the file server also hosted the RAS services, the hacker would have access to all of the network files.

You should be aware that VPN traffic destined for a remote network in the VPN travels over each LAN twice—once in the form of regular LAN traffic to the RAS server, and once again encapsulated in PPTP from the RAS server to the firewall. While the duplication of LAN traffic is inefficient, the amount of traffic is usually insignificant compared to regular LAN traffic because the bandwidth of the Internet connection limits the amount of information that can be sent over PPTP.

Windows NT Server 4 comes with everything you need to establish a Virtual Private Network over the Internet using PPTP, but their implementation of PPTP is flawed and should only be considered somewhat secure. You may want to rely on additional software to protect your network from IP intrusion, even if the RAS service that comes with the operating system is sufficient to establish an encrypted link between secure LANs.

Linux's IP masquerade/IP Chains features can be used with additional open-source software to create fairly robust VPNs as well. However, integrating numerous packages from different vendors isn't easy to do correctly, and can lead to a "Swiss-cheese" security effect, where all the pieces are in place but holes exist because they aren't well integrated.

Microsoft's PPTP software isn't the only server-based IP tunneling solution. Alta Vista's Tunnel is a popular and secure alternative for providing secure LAN connections over the Internet, and most firewalls have VPN modules you can use. Additionally, a number of tunnel solutions exist for UNIX.

Firewall-Based VPNs

Every LAN that is connected to the Internet needs a firewall to isolate LAN traffic (NetBIOS traffic in the case of NT networks; NFS, telnet, or X-Windows in the case of UNIX networks; AppleTalk in the case of Macintosh networks; and IPX in legacy NetWare networks) from Internet traffic. A firewall should at least block certain ports—especially the NetBIOS, NFS, Telnet, or X-Windows ports—from being accessed from outside your network, and should specify which computers inside your network are allowed to access the Internet.

That is not all that modern firewalls can do, however. Popular firewalls can perform address translation; take care of protocol and port filtering; redirect common services such as mail, news, and FTP; and even proxy such protocols as HTTP, SMTP, NNTP, Telnet, and FTP. (The remainder of this book contains overviews of various firewalls.) Since firewalls already do every other sort of analysis and transformation of network packets, it is a simple matter to include IP tunneling capability in the firewall.

The tunneling protocols included with most firewalls are proprietary and will only establish a VPN link with the same brand of firewall on the remote LAN or with client software written specifically for that firewall. This situation is beginning to change with the widespread adoption of the IPSec+IKE (IP Security with Internet Key Exchange) encryption and negotiation protocols. Although many vendors now support IPSec+IKE encryption, their specific versions are not always compatible. If you intend to use IPSec+IKE in a multi-vendor firewall network, contact each vendor to make sure they've tested their software to work with your other firewalls and to identify any configuration issues you'll have. A completely standardized implementation of IPSec+IKE should eliminate the compatibility problems caused by proprietary encryption systems.

Many of the firewalls include VPN software for individual remote client computers to connect to the firewall and establish a tunnel. If you need to connect remote computers to your LAN, you should check to make sure the client software is available for all your supported platforms.

Router-Based VPNs

Large networks (such as those in a business, school, government, or campus environment) are often comprised of several LAN segments linked together by routers. The routers isolate internal LAN segment traffic while conveying inter-LAN traffic quickly and efficiently. The routers are custom hardware devices with specialized circuitry and programming for handling network packets.

Simple routers merely transport the network packets from one segment to another, but the more complex and expensive routers can also act as firewalls, examining the network traffic and manipulating it (blocking ports, redirecting packets, and so on) according to rules established by the network administrator. Some routers even include the ability to encapsulate network traffic and establish VPN links between routers. IBM's 2210 router family, Cisco's routers running IOS, and Ascend's MAX switches are three popular router solutions that support VPN capabilities.

Secure Remote Access

Virtual Private Networks are great for connecting LANs, but what about people with isolated computers such as telecommuters, roving troubleshooters, salespeople, executives on the move, or anyone else lucky (or unlucky) enough not to work in an office or cubicle?

The traditional (read: expensive) way to provide these users with LAN access is to install modem banks and purchase phone lines so that they can dial up to your LAN using modems. Dial-up services provided in this manner require a modem and a phone line for each simultaneous dial-in connection supported. If you want two people to be able to connect at the same time, you'll need two modems and two phone lines for your dial-up server. If you want to support two hundred people at the same time, you'll need two hundred modems and two hundred phone lines (and some esoteric serial connection hardware as well). Also, either your company or the dial-up users will have to pay any long-distance toll charges if the users aren't a local phone call away from the dial-up server.

Just about anywhere you can go in the industrialized world today, an Internet Service Provider is a local phone call away. Internet service from these providers is relatively cheap because the ISPs can spread the cost of supporting dial-up connections across a wide base of customers. It makes sense to use these dial-up services just for your own network connections rather than to duplicate them. The problem is this: How do you protect the network communications between the remote computer and the computers on your LAN?

There are two ways to extend a Virtual Private Network to include individual remote computers connecting over the Internet. One way is to have your users dial up to ISPs that include a VPN port in their dial-up service, essentially making the ISP a partner in your LAN security management. The other way is to move the VPN port into the remote computer.

VPN in the ISP

Internet Service Providers use special devices called remote access switches, remote access servers, terminal servers, or serial concentrators to connect a large number of phone lines and modems to their dial-up network. The serial concentrators allow a server computer (often a UNIX workstation but sometimes a Windows NT Server computer) to accept a large number of dial-in connections. The remote access switches, servers, and terminal servers are special-purpose computers designed just to connect dial-in users to the network. In either case, the dial-up server (a general purpose computer or specialized device) performs the functions of authenticating the user and connecting the user's computer to the ISP's LAN.

Many newer dial-in switches (Windows NT Server computers as well, of course) support the PPTP protocol. When the user establishes an account with the ISP, the user (in cooperation with the network administrator of the LAN the user wants to connect to) can specify which VPNs the user's computer should be allowed to connect to. When the user connects to the remote access switch (typically using the PPP protocol), the ISP's remote access switch first gets the user's ISP account name and password, and then makes an encrypted connection over the Internet to the RAS server specified by the user's network administrator. The remote user can (after providing a valid account name and password for the LAN, of course) then participate in the LAN like any other network client.

Having the ISP establish the encrypted tunnel connection as well as authenticate and encapsulate the remote users' network traffic provides equivalent security as having your LAN's ISP manage your firewall for you. Many companies rely on the ISP to provide firewall services, and this can be a cost-effective solution when you have confidence in the security and responsibility of the Internet service provider. However, as mentioned elsewhere in this book, depending on people outside your network to keep it secure is not a good idea if you're serious about security.

VPN in the Dial-Up Client

In most cases, the remote user will not be able to rely on the Internet service provider to establish a VPN session with your remote users. The vast majority of firewall and encrypted tunnel vendors provide small client-side versions of their tunnel software that can be run directly on the remote access client. This allows the client to connect directly to the firewall over the Internet and appear as if it is a workstation on the local network.

In order for the client computer to establish a VPN session, it must first connect to the Internet. This connection can be made through any ISP or can even be made from a computer on a foreign LAN (one that's not a part of your VPN) that is connected to the Internet. Once the client computer is on the Internet, the client VPN software can establish the encrypted connection to your firewall or server using TCP/IP.

In the case of Microsoft's PPTP protocol, the encapsulation process is quite clear. The user must first connect (using their dialer) to the Internet, and then connect using their dialer to the firewall with PPTP. From the user's point of view, they have to use the dial-up software twice—once to connect to the ISP and then once to connect to the RAS server over that IP connection.

VPN Best Practices

Virtual Private Networks are convenient, but they can also create gaping security holes in your network. The following practices will help you avoid trouble.

- Use a real firewall.
- Secure the base operating system.
- Use a single ISP.
- Use packet filtering to reject unknown hosts.
- Use public-key encryption and secure authentication.
- Compress before you encrypt.
- Secure remote hosts.

Use a Real Firewall

As with every other security component, the best way to ensure you have comprehensive security is to combine security functions on a single machine. Firewalls make ideal VPN end points because they can route translated packets between private systems. If your VPN solution wasn't combined with your NAT solution, you'd have to open some route through your firewall for the VPN software or the NAT software, both of which can create a vector for attack.

Real firewalls are also most likely to use provably secure encryption and authentication methods, and their vendors are more likely to have implemented the protocol correctly. Ideally, you'd be able to find an open-source firewall whose source code you (and everyone else) could inspect for discernable problems. The remainder of this book discusses various firewall solutions to help you decide what will work best in your environment.

Secure the Base Operating System

No VPN solution provides effective security if the operating system of the machine is not secure. Presumably, the firewall will protect the base operating system from attack, which is another reason why you should combine your VPN solution with your firewall.

Implementing PPTP on a Windows NT Server without also implementing PPTP filtering is asking for trouble—without a secure base operating system, the VPN can be easily hacked to gain access to your network from anywhere.

Use a Single ISP

Using a single ISP to connect all the hosts acting as tunnel end points will increase both the speed and security of your tunnel because ISPs will keep as much traffic as they possibly can on their own networks. This means that your traffic is less exposed to the Internet as a whole and that the routes your ISP uses will avoid congestion points in the Internet. When you use multiple ISPs, they will most likely connect through the commercial Internet exchange network access points—the most congested spots on the Internet. This practically guarantees that your VPN tunnel will be slow—often uselessly slow for some protocols.

Chose an ISP that can also provide dial-up service to your remote users who need it. Alternatively, you may choose a local ISP that is down-stream from your national ISP because they are also on the national ISP's network and many national ISPs don't provide dial-up service.

Use Packet Filtering to Reject Unknown Hosts

You should always use packet filtering to reject connection attempts from every computer except those you've specifically set up to connect to your network remotely. If you are creating a simple network-to-network VPN, this is easy—simply cross filter on the foreign server's IP address and you'll be highly secure. If you're providing VPN access to remote users whose IP address changes dynamically, you'll have to filter on the network address of the ISP's dial-up TCP/IP domain. Although this method is less secure, it's still considerably more secure than allowing the entire Internet to attempt to authenticate with your firewall.

Use Public-Key Encryption and Secure Authentication

Public key authentication is considerably more secure than the simple, shared secret authentication used in some VPN implementations—especially those that use your network account name and password to create your secret key the way PPTP does. Select VPN solutions that use strong public key encryption to perform authentication and to exchange the secret keys used for bulk stream encryption.

Microsoft's implementation of PPTP is an example of a very insecure authentication method. PPTP relies upon the Windows NT account name and password to generate the authentication hash. This means that anyone with access to a valid name or password (like a malicious Web site one of your users has visited that may have initiated a surreptitious password exchange with Internet Explorer) can authenticate with your PPTP server.

Compress Before You Encrypt

You can get more data through your connection by stream compressing the data before you put it through your VPN. Compression works by removing redundancy. Since encryption salts your data with non-redundant random data, properly encrypted data cannot be compressed. This means that if you want to use compression, you must compress before you encrypt. Any VPN solution that includes compression will automatically take care of that function for you.

Secure Remote Hosts

Make sure the remote access users who connect to your VPN using VPN client software are properly secured. Hacking Windows 98 home computers from the Internet is depressingly easy, and can become a vector directly into your network if that home computer is running a VPN tunnel to it. Consider the case of a home user with more than one computer using a proxy product like WinGate to share his Internet connection, who also has a VPN tunnel established over the Internet to your network. Any hacker on the planet could then proxy through the WinGate server directly into your private network. This configuration is far more common than it should be.

Alert users to the risks of running proxy software on their home machines. Purchase client firewalling software to protect each of your home users; remember that a weakness in their home computer security is a weakness in your network security when they're attached to your network.

Prefer Compatible IPSec+IKE VPNs

To achieve the maximum flexibility in firewalls and remote access software, choose IPSec+ IKE VPN solutions that have been tested to work correctly with each other. IPSec+IKE is the closest thing to a standard encryption protocol there is, and although compatibility problems abound among various implementations, it is better than being locked into a proprietary encryption protocol that in turn locks you into a specific firewall vendor.

VPNyone?

A client called me in to evaluate why his users were having such a hard time exchanging mail with their main office. Their San Diego facility consisted of a small, leased office space for ten users with a single server and a firewall connected to a 56K ISDN connection. They used PPTP to connect over the Internet to their main office in Cleveland. They ran MS-Exchange Server at both sites and had them configured to exchange e-mail through the PPTP tunnel. The server in San Diego was configured as a Backup Domain Controller to the PDC in Cleveland. Other traffic transmitted through the tunnel included Windows NT domain control synchronization, the occasional remotely opened file, and license control software information for the application packages that they used. Central license managers in Cleveland were relied upon to allow access to locally installed applications.

They complained of excessive e-mail transmission times and in some cases, altogether missing e-mail messages.

Checking the event logs showed numerous RPC communication failures from the Exchange service, occurring about every 30 minutes. This corresponded to the timeout delay for the exchange servers to connect to one another to synchronize mail. So, the exchange servers were failing to authenticate with one another and therefore were not exchanging mail. Early in the morning and late in the day, the servers would correctly authenticate and begin transmitting mail.

I surveyed their usage patterns to get a feel for how much bandwidth they might be using. As it turned out, the entire company was well used to e-mail. The average employee expected to receive upwards of 100 mail messages per day, which they would usually respond to, creating a mail overhead of 200 messages per employee per day. Each message took up an average of 2K bytes including header information, for a daily transmission of about 400Kbps per user per day. Multiplied by 10 users, that figure came to 4MB of mail traffic per 8-hour work period. The only other significant traffic transmitted between the two networks was license information each time certain applications were started, but that data was negligible and it generally worked.

I first began throughput testing through the ISP connection to a fast server in the local area to make sure that the Network Layer to the ISP was working fine. It performed flawlessly.

Ping testing the server in Cleveland was disappointing: only about 33% of ICMP packets made the round-trip. Applying that efficiency to the pipe meant that at most, they were getting 33% of the speed of their 56K link, or about 18Kbps.

After talking to the Cleveland office and verifying that their own Internet links could connect at 100% to local hosts in their area, we had determined that it was, in fact, the low connection efficiency of the VPN that was causing the exchange servers to frequently fail when communicating with one another. And, considering the fact that the Exchange servers would transfer no mail until they correctly authenticated, and that there were 30 minute delays between authentication attempts, most of the day would go by without any mail transfers occurring at all.

I then issued a tracert command to check the route between the Cleveland and San Diego servers. The connection between servers traveled through more than 20 intermediate systems from 15 different ISPs and through three of the four major CIX NAPs. I'd never seen a more circuitous route. It became quite clear that through that many crowded exchanges, a VPN would never get enough data through to be effective.

I then recommended that they switch to a single ISP, so they decided to switch the San Diego office to the same ISP as they used in Cleveland. They had to change from 56K ISDN to 56K frame relay, but the circuit cost was only slightly more and the data rate was unchanged. Once the cutover was performed, everything began humming along smoothly. A quick ping check showed 100% of ping packets returning, and a tracert showed only six routers between their servers—and none going through the CIX NAPs.

10

The Ideal Firewall

The following chapters will review a number of commonly used (and a few less commonly used) firewall packages and toolkits. They detail the strengths and weaknesses of each, but as firewall implementation changes with time (they get better, usually) only those firewalls that are currently available will be covered. What should you look for when you are examining firewalls? How would you set up the ideal firewall for your network? These are the questions that will be answered here.

First, you'll determine the security needs for your organization and network. Second, you'll see how the ideal firewall should be configured for varying degrees of paranoia. Third, you'll learn about the various ongoing tasks you'll need to perform with even the most automated and secure firewall. Finally, you'll find out what you should do when your network is actually under attack.

This chapter is broken down into two major parts. The first part, Defining Your Security Requirements, will help you figure out what general type of security your business requires. The second part will then explain exactly how to configure your border gateways to achieve that level of security. You may find that you'll read back and forth between the two sections to gain a full understanding of the problem.

Defining Your Security Requirements

No two networks have exactly the same security requirements. A bank, for example, is going to be a bit more concerned than a retail clothing store about network intrusions.

The type of security concern varies as well as the degree—in a university computing lab the administrator is just as concerned about hosting the source of hacking attacks as well as being the target.

To decide just how much effort to expend in securing your network, you need to know the value of the data in your network, the publicity or visibility of your organization, and the harm that could be caused by loss of service. You should also consider how much disruption or imposition in the name of security you can live with on your network.

Similar organizations have similar requirements, so you can compare the needs of your network to those organizational types listed below.

Home Office

A home office is the simplest Internet connected network. Usually, a home office has two to three computers connected in a peer-to-peer fashion on a small LAN. These networks either have a modem attached to each computer so users can dial the Internet or they have one computer that dials the Internet whenever any of the users need an Internet connection. Sometimes the computer that dials the Internet is an inexpensive network hub and router device.

The typical home office budget can't afford to dedicate a computer to be a network firewall. Instead, the Internet Service Provider is relied upon to keep the hackers out. But this is not a particularly effective technique because ISPs vary in competence and workload, and they never customize security to fit your needs—they provide only a "one-size-fits-all" solution that is necessarily lax because they don't know how their customers will use the Internet.

Just because most firewalls are prohibitively expensive for home use doesn't mean you are helpless. Small firewall-less networks can still (and should) install current operating system patches to protect the computers from TCP/IP attacks such as Ping of Death and the Out of Band attack. File sharing should be turned off for computers that are connected to the Internet (or, for more advanced operating systems such as Windows NT and Unix, those services should be disconnected from the network adapter or modem that is connected to the Internet). Any unnecessary services should also be turned off so network intruders can't exploit them.

The reason home office networks aren't exploited more often is because their network connections are intermittent. Most hackers exploit random targets of opportunity, so a computer that spends most of its time detached from the Internet isn't going to make a very juicy target. The biggest threat to the home office network is from someone who knows about the network and has a specific reason to attack it. Disgruntled employees or former employees, business competition, or an individual with a personal axe to grind are the most likely culprits.

Small Service Business

Small service business networks, with a typical computer count of around a dozen or so, often have a dedicated computer for file and print services, and in many cases a dedicated connection to the Internet. Although few small service businesses have firewalls, they all should. The potential loss of data and business productivity due to a network intrusion more than justifies the cost of one extra computer and some software.

You don't want to go overboard with security in a small service business, however, and very few small service businesses will go to great lengths to bulletproof their networks because a cost/benefit analysis will usually show that less stringent security is sufficient. Consider, for example, a heating and air-conditioning company that has a small network with an Internet connection. The company's computers have little that would interest either a random hacker or rival companies that might engage in industrial espionage. The network users want as few restrictions as possible on how they access the Internet, so it is difficult to justify draconian network policies.

> **TIP** The small service business network administrator should be concerned about security, but the appropriate policy for the firewall is to permit by default, and to specifically deny packets, protocols, and services on the firewall that the administrator judges to be dangerous.

Professional Firms

Like the small service business, a small confidential practice such as a law firm, accounting firm, psychiatry practice, or medical specialist may have a half dozen to a dozen or more computers connected in a LAN with an intermittent or permanent Internet connection. The small confidential practice should have a more stringent security requirement than the typical small business, however, because the practice's computers contain confidential information that invite specific and targeted attack from network intruders over the Internet.

> **TIP** Because of the sensitivity of the information and the attraction this type of network presents to hackers, the network administrator of a small confidential practice should be cautious about security (denying packets, protocols, and ports by default unless the rules established specifically allow them) or strict about it (not routing IP packets at all and allowing only proxied network traffic through the firewall).

Manufacturers

A large network with fifty to a hundred computers is a much more tempting target to the average hacker, especially if the network has expensive network equipment and VPN links to other large computer networks. This is the type of network used by medium-to-large corporations, and the very size and complexity of corporate networks make them easier for hackers to attack.

Large corporate networks also may be subject to specific targeted attacks for the purposes of industrial espionage or anticompetitive denialofservice. Since corporations have more employees (and former employees) than smaller businesses do, the corporations are also much more likely to come under attack from insiders or former insiders.

A corporation with a lot of public visibility (such as Sony, Microsoft, Pepsi, or Disney) also has the problem of hackers trying to penetrate their networks for the greater bragging rights than would be achieved by hacking other less well-known companies (such as McMaster-Carr or Solar Turbines).

> **TIP**   Network administrators of large corporate networks need to take extra care that their networks are not compromised because the potential cost of lost productivity is proportionately greater in the larger networks than it is in small ones, and because the large corporate network makes a much more tempting target for hackers. A cautious (deny routing by default) or strict (no routing at all) policy is most appropriate for these kinds of networks.

Government Bureaus

The networks used by governmental bureaus have all of the characteristics of corporate networks (they are often large, have interesting hardware, and provide links to other networks), but governmental networks are also tempting targets because of their political nature. The Bureau of Reclamation has little to worry about, but the FBI, on the other hand, is under almost constant siege from the very hackers they chase. As a general rule, the more visible the organization, the more likely it is to attract the ire of a hacker with an agenda.

> **TIP**   Network administrators of governmental bureaus should be either strict (allowing no routing) or paranoid (minimizing any sort of Internet risk, regardless of the constraints that places on their own network use), depending on the visibility and sensitivity of the organization. Special care should be taken to secure Web sites in order to deny hackers an easy way to embarrass the bureau and to advertise their own causes.

University or College

University network administrators have the vexing problem of having to defend their systems from internal attacks as well as external ones. The periodic influx of new students ensures a fresh crop of hackers who will always be pushing at the security boundaries of the network. The students must have computers and access to the Internet, but the administrative staff of the school also needs a secure work environment.

Most schools cope with this problem by having two (or more) separate networks, each with a different security policy and with carefully controlled access between the networks. The public access student network typically has a severely restrictive policy and is frequently checked for viruses, Trojan horses, modified system settings, and so on.

> **TIP**   The university or college network administrator usually takes a cautious (deny by default) or a strict (proxy only, no routing) approach to managing the school's administrative networks. The network administrator also takes a fairly open approach to managing the student's network, while taking special care to keep the networks separate and while keeping a close eye on the state of the student network.

Internet Service Provider

The ISP network administrator has a problem similar to that of the university network administrator. The ISP network administrator must keep hackers from the Internet at bay and internal hackers contained, for the customers of the ISP expect to be protected from each other as well as from the outside. In addition, customers expect to have full Internet access—they want to decide for themselves which protocols and services to use.

> **TIP**   Most ISPs use a firewall to protect their network service computers (DNS server, mail server, and so on) in a cautious or strict configuration and use a packet filter in a more liberal configuration (permission by default) to stop the most obvious Internet attacks (Ping of Death, source-routed packets, malformed IP and ICMP packets, etc.) from reaching their clients. At the client's request, many ISPs will apply more strict security policies to the client connection on a per-client basis.

Online Commerce Company

For most companies, the Internet connection is a convenience. For online commerce companies, the reliable operation of the connection and the services that flow over it are the lifeblood of the company. A used bookstore that accepts inquiries for titles over the Internet can afford for its Web site to be down every once in a while, but an online bookstore that transacts all of its business over the Internet cannot.

In addition to preventing denial-of-service attacks, the administrator of an online commerce network must be aware of a more dire threat—the theft of customer information, including financial transaction data (especially credit card numbers). Consumers expect that the data they provide to your online company will remain confidential, and there may be severe public relations problems if the data gets out, as well as legal repercussions if the company is found negligent in its security precautions.

TIP   Because of the severe repercussions of both denial-of-service and data-theft attacks, the smart network administrator for an online commerce company will implement a strict (proxy only, no routing) firewall policy for the company's Internet servers. The administrator may establish a more permissive (cautious or concerned) policy for a separate administrative network if the staff needs freer Internet access for business activities that are not business critical.

Financial Institution

As a general rule, if there is money or there are things worth money flowing over the network, the administrator is going to be particularly careful about who can access the network and how they go about it. The more money there is, the more strict the rules for access will be. Therefore, banks and credit unions never allow any direct Internet access to their financial networks (the ones that directly convey money from one account to another) or even to the administrative networks that bank officials use to perform more mundane tasks.

A growing trend in financial institutions is to allow customers to perform online banking through their Web browsers over the Internet. This, of course, means that a Web server of some sort must be linked both to the Internet and to the protected financial computers. If you work for a financial institution, you should be sure that every possible measure is taken to secure that Web server and protect the customers' account information.

TIP   Those banking systems that allow any sort of Internet access implement strict (proxy access only) or paranoid (custom crafted with special purpose network software) policies to protect their computers.

Hospital

In a hospital network, unlike all the previous types of networks, people can die if the computers stop working. For this reason, the patient care hospital networks that have medical equipment attached to them are seldom connected to the Internet in any form. Administrative networks may be connected, but those links are carefully secured because of the risk of divulging or destroying confidential patient data. The networks in research labs, however, are typically closely and permissively attached to the network because scientists work best in an open environment where information exchange is made easy.

> **TIP** Like those of banks and universities, the hospital network administrator breaks his networks into several mutually untrusting sections. Life-critical equipment simply is not connected to the Internet. A strict policy is adopted for administrative computers (they still need e-mail, after all) while research LANs have a cautious or concerned policy.

Military

Military networks, like hospital networks, can have terminal repercussions when security is penetrated. Like governmental bureaus, hackers or espionage agents often have a specific target or axe to grind with the military. But not all military networks are the same—the civilian contractors managing a contract to purchase, warehouse, and distribute machine tools will have a different set of security requirements than the navy war college's academic network, and neither of those will be designed with anywhere near the level of paranoia that goes into constructing the real-time battle information systems that soldiers use to wage war.

> **TIP** The administrator of a military network must match the firewall policy of the LAN to the type of work performed on it. Most networks will have at least a cautious (default deny) or strict (proxy only, no routing) policy, while critical information systems will be divorced from the Internet entirely.

Intelligence Agencies

Some organizations have the dual goals of safeguarding their own networks while simultaneously finding ways to circumvent the walls keeping them out of other people's networks. You can be sure that the professional agents in these organizations have a dossier on and an action plan to exploit every operating system bug or protocol weakness there is. But knowing about a hole and plugging it are two different issues, and sometimes the hackers can steal a march on the spooks.

TIP   It is a good bet that the administrators of these kinds of networks go one step beyond implementation of a strict firewall security—I would be very surprised if these secrecy professionals used any commercial software to firewall their networks. The true paranoid will only trust software that they personally examine for back doors and weaknesses compiled with similarly inspected software tools.

Configuring the Rules

Once you've determined the degree of paranoia that is justified for your network (or networks if you manage more than one), you can set up the firewalling rules that keep the hackers out. Every firewall allows you to establish a set of rules that will specify what trans-firewall traffic will be allowed and what will not, as well as to establish and manipulate these rules. The following chapters will discuss the specifics of how each firewall is configured.

In the remainder of this chapter, however, you'll learn about these rules generically and how you should establish them so that your firewall won't have any obvious and easily avoided weaknesses. You'll also learn about the care and feeding of a running firewall and what you can do when you discover it has come under attack.

Rules about Rules:

Every firewall worth its weight in foam packing peanuts will have a number of features or characteristics of rules in common. You need to understand these rules and features because they form the building blocks of the logic that will either keep the hackers out or let them in. They are:

Apply in Order

When deciding whether or not to allow a packet to pass the firewall, well constructed firewall software will start with the first rule in its rule set and proceed toward the last until the packet is either explicitly allowed, explicitly disallowed, or until it reaches the end of the rules (whereupon the packet is allowed or dropped by default). The rules must always be evaluated in the same order to avoid ambiguity about which rule takes precedence.

Some strong firewalls take a "best rule fitting the problem" approach rather than an ordered rule set approach. While this may in fact provide stronger security, it can be very difficult for an administrator to determine which rule will be applied in a specific circumstance.

Per Interface

Firewall software should be able to discriminate between packets by the interface they arrive on and interface they will leave the firewall from. This is essential because the firewall can't really trust the source and destination addresses in the packets themselves; those values are easily forged, while a packet arriving on an external interface that says it is from inside your network is an obvious flag that something fishy is going on.

Per Type of Packet (TCP, UDP, ICMP)

Your firewall must be able to filter based on packet type because some are essential to network operation, while other types are just recipies for trouble. For example, you will want to allow ICMP echo reply packets to pass into your network from the outside (so your client computers can verify connectivity to outside hosts), but you may not want to pass ICMP echo request packets in to those same clients. After all, there's no sense letting hackers build a list of potential targets on your LAN. Some protocols use UDP on a particular port while others use TCP, and you don't want to let UDP traffic through on a port that has been opened for TCP or vice versa.

Per Source and Destination Addresses

Your firewall must classify traffic according to where it comes from and where it is going. You may want to allow external computers to establish connections to publicly accessible internal or DMZ Web and FTP servers, but not to establish connections to internal client computers. You probably want to allow internal clients to establish connections going the other way, however. Your firewall should be able to permanently block troublesome hosts and networks from performing any access at all, and should be able to deny all access to sensitive computers inside your network that don't need Internet connectivity.

Per Source and Destination Ports

Similarly, you will want to control TCP and UDP packets according to which ports they're coming from and going to. You should allow external users to connect from any port on their own computers to just those internal ports that are used by externally visible services (such as HTTP and FTP). Don't allow external users to connect to just any port on internal computers because Trojan horses such as Back Orifice work by opening up a port above 1023 (most operating systems restrict user programs from opening ports below this value) for hackers to connect to. However, users inside your network need to be able to initiate connections using source ports greater than 1023 with the destination port of any common TCP protocol ports (such as HTTP, FTP, Telnet, and POP). You might want to limit your users to just a few destination ports, or you may allow connections to arbitrary external ports.

Per Options

Originating hosts and routers can set a variety of options in the header of IP packets. Some options are notorious for being used to circumvent security, with source routing as the most abused of all the options. Most firewalls simply drop source-routed packets. Because none of the IP options are required for normal Internet traffic, strong firewalls simply drop any packets that have options set.

Per ICMP Message Type

As mentioned above, some ICMP packets are required for the Internet to cope with network problems. But, many ICMP packets (sometimes the same essential packets) can also be used in unconventional ways to crash computers on your network. The firewall must be able to determine from the message type and from how it is used whether or not that ICMP packet is safe to pass.

Per ACK Bit for TCP

The firewall must be able to tell the difference between a packet that is requesting a connection and one that is merely sending or replying over an already established connection. The difference between these two types of packets is just one bit—the ACK bit. Packets requesting a connection have it cleared, all others have it set. You will use this rule characteristic most often with the source and destination characteristics to allow connections to only those ports you specify and in only the direction you allow.

Protocol Specific Proxying Rules

For strong security, packet filtering rules aren't secure enough. The above packet rules only concern themselves with the header of IP or ICMP packets; the data payload is not inspected. Packet rules won't keep viruses out of e-mail nor will they hide the existence of internal computers. Proxies provide greater security but also limit any ICMP, IP, TCP, or UDP level attacks to the gateway machine. Proxies also ensure that the data flowing through the firewall actually conforms to the format specified by the protocols that the firewall is proxying for those ports.

Logging

A good firewall will not only block hazardous network traffic but will also tell you when it is doing so both with alerts and with messages written to a log file. You should be able to log (at your discretion) every packet dropped or passed through the firewall.

These logs should be able to grow large enough to track activity over days or weeks, but the logs should never be allowed to grow so large that they fill all of the firewall's hard drive space and crash the computer.

The alert mechanism should not only pop up windows on the firewall's console but also send e-mail to an arbitrary address (such as your pager e-mail gateway if you are really serious about responding quickly to network attacks and you don't mind those occasional midnight false alarms).

Graphical User Interface

While not necessary for firewall security or performance, a graphical user interface for manipulating rule sets makes it much easier to set up and configure firewalls.

Rules for Security Levels

We've divided the spectrum of security into five levels that will be a good fit for most organizations. Using the first half of this chapter, you should be able to identify which of these levels applies most closely to your organization. Once you've matched your organization to one of the following security levels, you can use the rules we lay out as a starting point for your firewall policy. The general levels are:

- Aware
- Concerned
- Cautious
- Strict
- Paranoid

For each security level we'll explore the rules, restrictions, and procedures that a network administrator will enact to provide that level of security in the network.

Aware

There are some things every security network administrator should do regardless of the degree of security warranted by the network contents or the type of organization the network serves. These actions and prescriptions plug obvious security holes and have no adverse affect on Internet accessibility. The security aware administrator should:

- Install the latest operating system patches on both the client and server computers in the network.
- Keep network user accounts off of Internet service computers such as Web servers, FTP servers, and firewalls, and have separate administrative accounts with different passwords for these machines.

- Regularly scan the system logs for failed logon attempts to network services and failed connection attempts to Web servers, ftp servers, etc.

- Regularly scan system user accounts for the unauthorized addition or modification of user accounts for network services.

- Disable all unnecessary services on network and Internet servers.

- Use virus scanners on your server (at least).

- Perform regular backups.

Concerned

A network administrator that is concerned about security will at least install a packet filter and take the above security aware steps. The packet filter will not stop a concentrated network attack from exploiting service protocol weaknesses, but it will stop the simplest denial-of-service attacks—those based on malformed or maliciously configured ICMP or IP packets.

A packet filter in its most lax configuration allows packets to pass by default unless a rule specifically tells the filter to drop them. Proxy servers may be used to enhance network services (by caching HTML pages, for example) but provide no extra security because network clients can easily bypass them. The packet filter can also lock out troublesome external IP addresses and subnets, as well as deny external access from the outside to specific internal computers such as file and database servers.

Packet Rules (Filtering)

The packet rules control the flow of several different kinds of packets through the filter or firewall. They are as follows:

- ICMP Rules
- IP Rules
- UDP Rules
- TCP Rules

ICMP   ICMP controls the flow of IP packets through the Internet. IP is therefore essential to the correct operation of the Internet, but ICMP packets can be forged to trick your computers into redirecting their communications, stopping all communication, or even crashing. The following rules (see Table 10.1) protect your LAN from many ICMP attacks.

Firewall
Technology

PART 2

Table 10.1

Rule	In Interface	Out Interface	Src IP	Src Port	Dest IP	Dest Port	Opt	Ack	Type	ICMP Type	Act
1	*	*	*	*	*	*	*	*	ICMP	Source Quench	Pass
2	*	Ext	*	*	*	*	*	*	ICMP	Echo Request	Pass
3	Ext	*	*	*	*	*	*	*	ICMP	Echo Reply	Pass
4	*	Ext	*	*	*	*	*	*	ICMP	Destination Unreachable	Pass
5	Ext	*	*	*	*	*	*	*	ICMP	Service Unavailabe	Pass
6	Ext	*	*	*	*	*	*	*	ICMP	TTL Exceeded	Pass
7	Ext	*	*	*	*	*	*	*	ICMP	Parameter Problem	Pass
8	*	Ext	*	*	*	*	*	*	ICMP	Echo Request	Drop
9	*	Ext	*	*	*	*	*	*	ICMP	Redirect	Drop
10	Ext	*	*	*	*	*	*	*	ICMP	Echo Reply	Drop
11	Ext	*	*	*	*	*	*	*	ICMP	Destination Unreachable	Drop
12	Ext	*	*	*	*	*	*	*	ICMP	Service Unavailable	Drop
13	Ext	*	*	*	*	*	*	*	ICMP	TTL Exceeded	Drop
14	*	*	*	*	*	*	*	*	ICMP	*	Drop

Note that while we assume that the concerned (but not cautious) administrator allows packets to pass the firewall by default, the above rules work both for permit-by-default and deny-by-default configurations. Rules are (or should be) evaluated in order from first to last, and if an ICMP packet is not specifically allowed or denied in rules 1-13, rule 14 will cause it to be dropped. A short description of each rule follows:

1. Allow source quench: You want external hosts to be able to tell your client computers when the network is saturated.

2. Allow echo request outbound: You want your clients to be able to ping external computers to verify connectivity.

3. Allow echo reply inbound: You want your clients to be able to hear the reply of pinged hosts.

4. Allow destination unreachable inbound: These packets inform your clients that an exterior resource is not available.

5. Allow service unavailable inbound: These packets inform your clients that an exterior resource is not available.

6. Allow TTL exceeded inbound: These packets inform your clients that an exterior resource is too far away.

7. Allow parameter problem: These packets inform your clients that they are not sending correctly formatted packets.

8. Drop redirect inbound (log it instead): You don't want external agents to be able to mess with your internal computers' routing tables without your supervision.

9. Drop echo request inbound: Echo request ("ping") packets can be used to survey your internal network for computers to attack. Malformed ping packets are also often sent in an attempt to crash computers.

10. Drop echo reply outbound: Why make it easy for hackers to find computers to attack?

11. Drop destination unreachable outbound: You should protect the identity of interior networks just as you would the identity of individual interior hosts.

12. Drop service unavailable outbound: It is not a good idea to advertise to network attackers what services are available inside your network.

13. Drop TTL exceeded outbound: Hackers can determine the number of hops or LAN boundaries exist inside your network by trying different TTL values.

14. Drop all other ICMP packets: Just to be safe. The ICMP packets you have specifically allowed should be sufficient.

IP There are some rules that you will want to configure for all IP packets regardless of whether they contain TCP or UDP traffic inside them. See Table 10.2 for an overview of the rules, then read further for an explanation of each.

Table 10.2

Rule	In Interface	Out Interface	Src IP	Src Port	Dest IP	Dest Port	Opt	Ack	Type	ICMP Type	Act
15	*	*	*	*	*	*	Source Route	*	*	*	Drop
16	Ext	*	Internal	*	*	*	*	*	*	*	Drop
17	Int	*	*	*	Internal	*	*	*	*	*	Drop
18	Ext	*	*	*	Protected Servers	*	*	*	*	*	Drop
19	Ext	*	*	*	*	RIP, OSPF	*	*	*	*	Drop
20.	*	*	192.168 .0.1	*	*	*	*	*	*	*	Drop

These rules govern the general flow of IP traffic in and out of your network. If you want to forbid certain computers or networks from accessing your computers, you would place a rule there, as in rule 20.

15. Drop all source-routed packets: Nobody redirects packets around damaged connections anymore, they just fix the broken equipment. A source-routed packet is a red flag indicating a network intrusion attempt.

16. Drop all packets arriving on the external interface that have a source field indicating that the packet came from inside your network: If the packet claims it originated from inside your network, it should only come from the internal interface.

17. Drop all packets arriving on the internal interface that have a source field indicating that the packet came from outside your network: Like in rule 16, this behavior is an indicator that there's something fishy going on, and you're safest if you just drop the packet and log the event.

18. Drop incoming packets to interior computers that have no externally accessible services (file server, etc.): People outside your network have no business connecting to your LAN file server unless they do it through secure encrypted tunnels that you specifically set up for them.

19. Drop RIP, OSPF, and other router information exchange protocols: You don't need external agents reconfiguring your routers for you.

20. Drop packets from a specific host: This is where you put rules banning hosts and networks that have been bugging you.

UDP   Once you have set rules for generic IP traffic, you will want to further specify some UDP rules to block egregious security holes, such as X-windows, as shown in Table 10.3.

NOTE   By default, the concerned-but-not-cautious administrator allows packets to pass through the firewall unless a rule specifically denies that kind of packet.

Table 10.3

Rule	In Interface	Out Interface	Src IP	Src Port	Dest IP	Dest Port	Opt	Ack	Type	ICMP Type	Act
21	*	*	*	*	*	0-20	*	*	UDP	*	Drop
22	*	*	*	*	*	6000-6003	*	*	UDP	*	Drop
23	*	*	*	*	*	161-162	*	*	UDP	*	Drop

Each rule specifically denies a port or a range of ports (some firewalls require you to repeat the rule for each port specifically disallowed).

21. Drop packets using ports below 21: There are no services below port 21 that your average Internet user will find helpful.

22. Drop X-windows (packets using ports 6000-6003): You don't want a hacker gaining control of your mouse and keyboard, do you?

23. Drop SNMP (packets using ports 161 and 162): You don't want network intruders to reconfigure your hubs and routers using this protocol either.

TCP   The TCP rules you create are like the UDP rules with one difference—you can use the ACK bit of a packet to stop connections from being initiated from one direction or the other. Blocking inbound packets with the ACK bit cleared (C) for a particular port allows only outbound connections to be initiated, but allows subsequent data traffic for that connection—all of which will have the ACK bit set (S). See Table 10.4 for a typical set of TCP rules.

Table 10.4

Rules	In Interface	Out Interface	Src IP	Src Port	Dest IP	Dest Port	Opt	Ack	Type	ICMP Type	Act
24	*	*	*	*	*	0-20	*	*	TCP	*	Drop
25	*	*	*	*	*	6000-6003	*	*	TCP	*	Drop
26	*	*	*	*	*	161-162	*	*	TCP	*	Drop
27	Ext	*	*	*	*	23	*	*	TCP	*	Drop
28	Ext	*	*	*	*	8080	*	*	TCP	*	Pass
29	Ext	*	*	*	*	>1023	*	C	TCP	*	Drop
30	Ext	*	*	*	*	20-21	*	C	TCP	*	Drop
31	Ext	*	*	*	*	Not SMTP Server	25	*	*	TCP	*	Drop
32	Ext	*	*	*	*	Not Web Server	80	*	*	TCP	*	Drop

You'll note that some of the TCP ports here are the same as the UDP ports listed in the previous section—some protocols operate over UDP as well as TCP.

24. Drop packets using ports below 21: There are no services below port 21 that your average Internet user will find helpful.

25. Drop X-windows (packets using ports 6000-6003): You don't want a hacker gaining control of your mouse and keyboard, do you?

26. Drop SNMP (packets using ports 161 and 162): You don't want network intruders to reconfigure your hubs and routers using this protocol either.

27. Disallow incoming telnet connections (incoming packets with destination port 23 and source port > 1023): Telnet is an insecure protocol because the account name and password exchange are not encrypted and neither is the data channel once a telnet session is established.

28. Specifically allow any internal services that use ports greater than 1023: This way you can use the next rule to stop back door software such as Back Orifice, which open ports internally for remote unauthorized control of your computers. In the rule base above, we've shown an example of allowing external traffic to a Web server running on port 8080. Your custom rules will vary depending upon your needs.

29. Drop SYN packets from outside to internal ports > 1023): Most legitimate services are configured on ports <1024 so this rule stops connection requests to ports higher than 1023. Rule 28 and others like it (which must be placed before this rule) specifically allow any exceptions.

30. Disallow incoming FTP data connections thus allowing passive FTP only.

31. Disallow SMTP connections (port 25) from the outside to other than your mail server.

32. Establish service destination rules for other services such as HTTP.

Cautious

Most network administrators feel that the above rules are not enough; a dedicated hacker with time and resources can find a way around the above rules. A cautious network administrator will take a more conservative track and block all traffic by default, only allowing the traffic that seems safe after careful consideration. This approach takes much more time and effort to set up correctly, but the result is a much more secure firewall.

Network Address Translation One feature that cautious administrators really like is Network Address Translation, or NAT. This nifty feature allows you to expose just a handful (or even one) of IP addresses to the outside world, while it hides a whole LAN of tens, hundreds, or even thousands of computers behind it. To the computers on your

LAN there is little difference between existing on a NAT hidden LAN and being directly connected to the Internet. The firewall keeps track of connections and rewrites packet source and destination and port values on the fly.

Fragmentation   A cautious network administrator won't allow fragmented packets into the network. Until recently, fragmented packets were considered safe because it was understood that only the first fragment of a fragmented packet needed to be examined and dropped if necessary. Any subsequent packet fragments would be dropped by the destination computers because they lack an initial packet with the header information.

Because of a bug discovered in common TCPIP protocol implementations (including that of Windows NT), that is no longer the case. The bug (since fixed) ignored improper fragment offset values which allowed the second (or later) fragment to occupy the memory location of the first fragment and to provide the header information the network stack was looking for (header information that had not been checked by the firewall). Although the bug has been fixed, most cautious network administrators choose to reassemble fragmented packets at the firewall or just drop them since the fragmentation feature is largely obsolete.

ICMP, TCP and UDP   Some of the packet rules listed in the previous sections become redundant when the cautious administrator denies all packets by default. You may want to leave them in your rule set so you can switch from deny-by-default to allow-by-default and back again when you are diagnosing network connectivity problems.

One rule that is not listed here (because it is denied by default) is that you shouldn't allow telnet connections (connections to port 23) to travel through your firewall at all. Use the Secure Shell (SSH) instead because it provides much greater security for a remote terminal. In addition, we don't explicitly list the rule you should block access out to ports above 1023 because the commonly accessed services live below 1023. See Table 10.5 for a few additional rules that the cautious administrator will want to configure in the firewall.

Table 10.5

Rules	In Interface	Out Interface	Src IP	Src Port	Dest IP	Dest Port	Opt	Ack	Type	ICMP Type	Act
33	*	*	SMTP Server	*	*	25	*	*	TCP	*	Pass
34	*	*	NNTP Server	*	Ext NNTP Server	119	*	*	TCP	*	Pass
35	*	*	Ext. NNTP Server	119	NNTP Server	*	*	*	TCP	*	Pass
36	Int	*	*	>1023	*	80	*	*	TCP	*	Pass
37	Ext	*	*	80	*	>1023	*	S	TCP	*	Pass

33. Allow outgoing SMTP connections (port 25) from your mail server.

34. Allow NNTP from your news server to external news server (source Port of 119, destination port >1023).

35. Allow NNTP from external news server to internal news server (source Port of 119, destination port >1023).

36. Allow clients to establish HTTP connections (source port >1024, destination port 80).

37. Allow data traffic from an already established HTTP connection to travel back from port 80 on the Internet to the client port (>1023) on your LAN.

You can repeat rules 36 and 37 for any additional Internet services that you want internal clients to be able to connect to.

Service Rules (Proxying)

General rule: Disallow proxy requests from the Internet by filtering out packets with the ACK bit clear that connect to your proxy from the external interface. This prevents hackers from connecting to your proxy server and using it to launder their connections.

Proxy DNS using a DNS server or a proxy server that supports DNS proxy transparently, but disallow zone transfers. You don't want anyone outside your network reconfiguring your network names.

Use SOCKS to proxy stream-oriented (circuit level) TCP and UDP going out of your network for protocols you intend to allow that do not have specific security proxy software.

Proxy SMTP by having your mail servers write e-mail messages to disk and having another mail process read and forward those messages inside the network. This prevents any single process from being compromised, which would allow a connection all the way through the machine. It also guarantees that any malformed e-mail will either crash the inbound process and be dropped or will be completely regenerated by the forwarding process without the deformity. This prevents buffer overrun conditions on mail servers inside your network.

Proxy NNTP by establishing an NNTP server in your demilitarized zone. Inbound NNTP should be forwarded only to that machine, and internal newsreaders should only be able to read news at that machine. This prevents Trojan horses or other non-NNTP traffic from exploiting the open NNTP port on the packet filter.

Proxy FTP using a dedicated FTP proxy application in the firewall. FTP service filters on stateful firewalls may also be used as long as they are specific to the FTP protocol.

Proxy HTTP through a secure HTTP proxy. Your HTTP proxy should be capable of virus checking and stripping executable content.

Disable SOCKS proxies because of the wide protocol access SOCKS allow.

Do not provide POP access at your exterior border gateway. Your SMTP servers should be inside your DMZ. For remote users, force the establishment of an encrypted tunnel for mail access. This prevents e-mail from being exposed in an unencrypted form on the Internet. Internal users who wish to access their private POP accounts should use one of the many free gateway services available on the Internet so they can use their Web browser to check their private e-mail.

Do not provide a Telnet proxy. Telnet is far too insecure to allow public access through your gateway.

Strict

The basic strategy for strict control is to completely disallow network layer routing between the public and private networks. Strict policies use only application layer proxies (and not many of them) to provide only the most useful Internet services. Stateful packet filters should be used to protect the application proxies on the bastion host, which should perform no packet routing.

The bastion host may perform Network Address Translation to make itself "invisible" to internal hosts so that client applications don't have to be explicitly set to use a proxy. In this mode, the proxy host looks like a router to internal hosts; it receives all traffic as if it were going to forward it directly onto the public network. That traffic is routed to proxy applications on the bastion host instead of being routed, so the connections are in fact regenerated to eliminate any undetected deformities. This mode also makes it easy to proxy difficult protocols like FTP and H.323.

Packet Rules (Filtering)

No routing should exist between the external public and internal private interfaces of the bastion host. The same ICMP and IP rules described for the previous section should be applied to protect the bastion host from denial-of-service attacks.

Service Rules (Proxying)

The basic strategy behind strict security is to proxy only the most useful protocols: HTTP and SMTP. These two protocols, which are easy to control and keep track of, allow most of the functionality of the Internet to be utilized. Your attack risk increases linearly with the number of special cases you define on your bastion host. So, the policy here is to limit to the utmost practical degree.

Proxy DNS using a DNS server, but disallow zone transfers. You don't want anyone outside your network reconfiguring your network names. Make sure your DNS proxy does not publish internal names.

Proxy HTTP through a secure HTTP proxy, like NAI Gauntlet. Strip all executable content including EXE, ActiveX, and Java applets.

Proxy SMTP by having your mail servers write e-mail messages to disk and another mail process read and forward those messages inside the network. Configure your mail server to strip all executable attachments and perform virus checking on ZIP compressed and office documents. The only allowable method to transfer executable content through the firewall should be in a non-executable form like BIN-HEX or compressed format. This prevents users from clicking on Trojan horse attachments and executing them. The extra level of indirection ensures that they will at least manually inspect the files before running them.

Paranoid

The strategy for paranoid installations is to either not connect to the Internet or connect a separate "Internet only" network to the Internet. The U.S. government does both to protect its classified networks from the Internet: they are completely disconnected, and a separate pool of "disposable" machines are available for users to work on the Internet. You should simply use a pool of dedicated Internet machines behind a standard stateful inspection filter.

Packet Rules (Filtering)

Allow no direct routing between the public and private networks.

Service Rules (Proxying)

Allow no proxying between the public and private networks.

All The King's Firewalls

As I wrote this chapter, I agonized over the case study: What could I talk about that would justify the "paranoid" strategy? Reality intruded on my behalf. While this chapter was being written, the Explore.zip e-mail attachment worm appeared and passed unscathed through even the most rigorous firewalls in the world, wreaking havoc and causing uncountable millions of dollars in damages.

Worms are malicious programs that exhibit characteristics of both Trojan horses and viruses. In fact, Explore.zip was both a worm and a Trojan horse that propagated using the methods of a virus that required user activation.

The worm typically worked like this:

An e-mail message appeared in the victim's inbox containing the message text

"I received your e-mail and shall send you a reply ASAP. Till then, take a look at the attached zip docs." The sender's address would be the valid address of a close friend or co-worker. The attached executable file was called zipped_files.exe.

Upon clicking the attachment, the Trojan horse functionality was activated. The worm would create e-mail messages to everyone in the user's personal address book,

thus propagating itself to all of them and appearing to come from the activating user. The worm would also rifle through the shared directory structure on the computer and propagate itself to other machines on the local network.

The worm then went on a rampage, destroying programming code, office documents, and other useful work-related materials, as well as modifying system files on the computers.

Because the virus was attached to e-mail and transmitted by the users who had privileged access through the firewall, it passed through even the strongest firewalls unmolested. Only those organizations whose administrators had insisted on stripping executable attachments from e-mail were safe.

I predicted this sort of psychology-based attack in the NT4 Network Security book, but until now, the attack had remained only a theoretical possibility discussed by arcane security experts.

The only way to truly protect an organization from Internet-based attacks is not to connect to the Internet. Using the paranoid model discussed above is protection against even the most devious schemes.

Part 3

Operating Systems and Firewalling

Topics Covered:

- Firewalling features provided by Windows NT

- Firewall features not provided by Windows NT

- How to configure Windows NT to protect itself

- The limitations of Windows NT's built-in firewalling features

- Problems that NT's firewalling cannot solve

- Situations where NT's firewalling support is appropriate

- Firewalling features of open-source operating systems like Linux and NetBSD

- Firewall software not included in standard distributions of open-source operating systems

- How to configure an open-source operating system to perform firewalling

- Problems with open-source firewall systems

11

NT as a Firewall

The Windows NT operating system is not a firewall—yet. Windows NT supports simple packet and PPTP filtering, but not Network Address Translation or application proxy services without additional software. In addition, its TCP/IP stack is not hardened completely against malformed packets. Windows NT was not designed to operate as a firewall; rather, it was designed for higher network performance. The consistency checks that firewalls must perform on each received TCP/IP packet requires a considerable compute load, which would be too much for a heavily loaded server to deal with. This is one reason why firewalls should be isolated on dedicated machines.

Windows NT's TCP/IP stack is not hardened and is vulnerable to a number of well-known exploits. For example, prior to the release of Service Pack 3, Windows NT did not check for the presence of a proper 0th packet in a fragment; rather, when a packet arrived with its end-of-fragment bit set, NT would simply conjoin the data it had already received, regardless of fragment numbering, and pass the data up. This meant that any hacker with a copy of Linux could build his TCP/IP stack to make every IP packet claim to be the 1st packet instead of the 0th packet. The packet could then pass right through most packet filters, which only check for TCP port information in the 0th packet of a fragment, and go straight to an NT machine. This exploit made simple packet filtering firewalls pointless. It's one of the reasons that packet filtering alone does not constitute real firewalling.

Other exploits that can cause a denial of service are various ping-of-death attacks. These attacks either send ping packets that contain more data than NT's packet buffers can deal with, or they deform the packet in a way that NT isn't prepared to deal with. For example, the attack could set the reply address to the address of the NT machine, which causes it to ping itself repeatedly at high speed.

Microsoft releases hotfixes on a regular basis to solve or deal with these hacking exploits, but you can count on at least a three-month turnaround between the development of an exploit and the release of a hotfix. Furthermore, many hotfixes are not fully tested, so even Microsoft does not recommend installing them unless you are subject to the problem they fix. Waiting for service packs that solve these problems can take up to a year. And so far, service packs have been hit-or-miss—service packs 2 and 4 actually caused numerous problems and were quickly supplanted.

That said, Windows NT does support some important firewalling functions natively without the addition of extra software. Although we do not recommend using Windows NT as a firewall to protect your network, these packet-filtering capabilities can be used to protect NT machines that must be exposed outside your firewall (Internet servers and PPTP end points). This means that you can put your Internet servers outside your firewall without having to put a firewall between them and the Internet. They won't be absolutely secure against attack, but they'll be in much better shape than they would be without these features.

Windows 2000 will support Network Address Translation, which could make it a strong contender for the title of a true firewall. The IP stack would have to be considerably more consistent than the IP stack provided with Windows NT 4 to withstand a concerted attack, however.

Capabilities

Windows NT supports three primary firewalling features:

- Packet filtering
- Encrypted tunneling
- Encrypted authentication

Unlike most modern firewalls, Windows NT cannot easily share firewall policy with other servers, but sophisticated NT administrators can create registry scripts that can be applied across a range of machines by clicking the script on each machine. Nonetheless, this minimal functionality makes it difficult to configure security consistently across a range of machines.

Windows NT's firewalling features are most appropriate in the role for which they were created: additional security on multipurpose servers. You can (and should) configure all your Windows NT servers to allow only those TCP protocols for services you intend to provide.

Packet Filtering

Windows NT provides a stateless packet filter. Stateless packet filters make their decisions based only on information contained within each packet; they do not retain information about connections or other higher-level constructions.

The packet filter is capable of blocking TCP, UDP, or IP protocols individually for each interface. The filter can only be configured to pass all protocols or to pass specific protocols. It cannot be configured to block specific protocols. The packet filter blocks only inbound packets. All outbound packets are transmitted.

Packet filters are configured by opening the network control panel to the TCP/IP protocol and clicking the advanced button in the IP address panel. PPTP filtering, which blocks all packets except PPTP packets, can be enabled by checking the Enable PPTP filtering option.

Enabling all other forms of packet filtering is performed by checking the Enable Security option and then clicking the configure button. You can then select the Allow Only radio button and enter the protocols you want to allow for each transport. Figure 11.1 shows the Windows NT packet filtering dialogs.

Figure 11.1   Windows NT Packet Filter Configuration

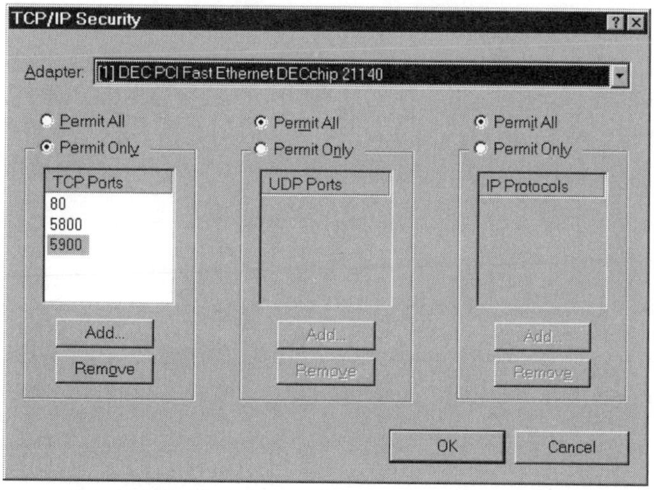

Tunneling

Microsoft has included the Point-to-Point Tunneling Protocol (PPTP) with Windows NT to allow secure remote access. Microsoft provides two levels of security with PPTP corresponding to the U.S. government's limitations on export grade security and the security grade Microsoft considers to be ideal for encrypted communications. The 40-bit export grade security level is not particularly strong. The 128-bit domestic grade security package is strong enough for most uses. Unfortunately, it's not always clear which version you have installed, and the version will automatically change if you install certain service updates or use the wrong version of a service pack. You'll also have to make sure that both the server and all the clients support 128-bit encryption, and that your servers are configured to reject connections to 40-bit clients. Careful administration is the only way to be sure you're using the 128-bit domestic grade version.

In order to use the Windows NT Remote Access Service to create a VPN, you will, of course, need a Windows NT Server computer to host the RAS software. The computer must have sufficient RAM, hard drive space, and processing power to run Windows NT Server 4 adequately (this means 64MB of RAM, a 4GB drive, and a Pentium or higher microprocessor running at least 150MHz should be sufficient for a VPN with Internet connections of T1 speed or slower). Of course, you will need the Windows NT Server 4 operating system itself. The same computer can be used to establish dial-in RAS sessions via modem as well as VPN RAS connections over the Internet, but (as mentioned in previous sections) the computer should not also function as the file and print server for your network or the firewall for your network.

You will also need a connection to the Internet for your LAN. The RAS server does not have to be the computer that establishes the connection; in fact, it is better if a different computer, which runs firewall software, performs that role. In summary, to use RAS to establish a VPN over the Internet you will need:

- A dedicated Pentium-class computer
- Windows NT Server 4 (preferably running service pack 3 or higher)
- RAS
- PPTP
- A constant connection to an Internet service provider
- A LAN connection to your network

Client Requirements

There are two sets of requirements for connecting remote computers via PPTP to your LAN. If you set up a class of service with the ISP that the client computer will be using and that service includes establishing a PPTP tunnel, the client computer needs only to dial up the ISP using the PPP protocol. The client computer will then be able to do anything that it would be able to do if it had dialed directly into the RAS server on your LAN. Before the client can connect in this manner, however, you will have to negotiate with the ISP to set up the service.

On the other hand, if the ISP does not offer the PPTP service (or if you don't want to use the ISP's service), the client computer must support the PPTP protocol itself. Microsoft has provided client software for Windows 95, Windows 98, Windows NT Workstation, and the MacOS that allows these operating systems to connect to an RAS server via PPTP.

The client computer must also have a connection to an Internet service provider. This connection can be a temporary connection made via a regular modem, ISDN, or xDSL, or it can be a permanent connection made by a cable modem or a leased line. In summary, the requirements for a remote client are as follows:

- NT 4 Workstation, Windows 95, Windows 98, or MacOS

- PPTP-capable dial-in software

- A temporary or permanent Internet connection

Establishing and Securing the VPN

To establish a VPN, you need the RAS software and the PPTP protocol on at least one server computer in each LAN. The RAS and PPTP software can be found in the i386 (or Alpha) directory of the Windows NT 4 Server installation CD-ROM. You should add RAS from the Services tab and PPTP from the Protocols tab of the Network Control Panel program.

When you add PPTP to the services supported by NT, you must specify how many Virtual Private Networks RAS will support. You can enter a number from 1 to 256. This number should equal the number of other LANs this RAS server will maintain connections to, in addition to the maximum number of simultaneous remote computer users.

In Remote Access Setup, you will need to add the VPN ports that will appear in the RAS-capable devices list. The number of VPN ports that will appear will match the number of PPTP connections that you selected (to be supported).

By default, all of the VPN ports will be configured to only accept connections. To establish a connection to another RAS server you will have to configure a VPN port for a dial-out connection. In any pair of communicating RAS servers, one must have a port configured for a dial-in connection and the other a port for dial-out connection. When establishing a dial-out connection to another RAS server you will also have to create a phone book entry so that RAS can make the connection.

Operating Systems and Firewalling

PART 3

You should find the security features for VPN ports familiar; they are the same as the security features for any other RAS connection. As with regular dial-in connections, you can configure which protocols may be used for dialing out, which protocols may be used for dialing in, and the encryption settings for VPN communications. You should require Microsoft-encrypted authentication and data encryption.

Since PPTP can support more than one transport protocol (NetBEUI, TCP/IP, and NWLink), the use of PPTP for your VPN doesn't limit you to using TCP/IP for your file and print services. Consider using a different protocol for file and print services in order to make it more difficult for network intruders to penetrate your security.

PPTP Vulnerabilities

The PPTP protocol as implemented by Microsoft has some problems you should be aware of before you implement your VPN using Microsoft RAS servers. (Counterpane Systems has a white paper exploring them in detail at www.counterpane.com.) Some of the weaknesses are easily dealt with by a diligent network administrator; others are less easily solved. The sections that follow cover some of the topics you should be aware of.

LAN Manager Authentication Makes Password Cracking Easy   Windows NT supports LAN Manager authentication and Windows NT password authentication to allow older network clients to connect to Windows NT networks. Windows 95 provides both LAN Manager and Windows NT–style passwords to support connection to older LAN Manager servers and to Windows NT. The problem is that LAN Manager passwords are simplified (reduced to eight characters or less and shifted to one case) before being presented to the server. A network intruder that eavesdrops on the PPTP authentication process or redirects the remote client computer in order to capture the password can easily crack the LAN Manager password and use that simplified password to gain access to PPTP servers supporting LAN Manager authentication. With a bit more processing, the intruder can use the simplified password to determine the full password.

TIP   Disable LAN Manager authentication on both the PPTP client(s) and server(s). (In Windows 98 LAN Manager authentication is disabled by default.)

Microsoft's 40-Bit Encryption Is Weak and Flawed   With Windows 95, 98, and NT you have the option of using 40-bit encryption or 128-bit encryption for authentication and encrypted communication. In addition to being weak (the 40-bit key makes the encrypted communication relatively easy to crack using brute-force cryptanalysis), the 40-bit protocol used by Microsoft does not salt (modify with a random number provided by the server) the key used to establish the session. The key is simply generated from the

LAN Manager hash of the user's password, and since the password will not change from one session to the next, neither will the key.

On the other hand, the 128-bit encryption does salt the key with a number provided by the server, thereby resulting in a different key for each session. Note, however, that the key is still based on a hash of the user's password, and most passwords contain much less than 128 bits of randomness (unguessability). Passwords with non-alphanumeric characters in them are much more difficult to crack than short, alphanumeric passwords.

TIP   Use only 128-bit encryption on PPTP clients and servers. Require passwords with non-alphanumeric characters for PPTP users.

PPTP Clients Are Vulnerable to Internet Attack   The remote PPTP clients to your network have two network connections--one network connection to their ISP and another (through the ISP) to your network. You must make sure that hackers can't penetrate the client computer through the IP connection at the ISP and then come in through the PPTP connection established by that client (or establish a PPTP connection of their own after having captured the passwords and network configuration information stored on the client).

A properly secured client will not export network services that can be compromised by network intruders, such as Web or FTP servers. By no means should the client have file and print sharing enabled; Internet users would be able to see the NetBIOS ports as well as members of your VPN. The Internet client software (Web browsers and mail software) should be kept up to date; bug fixes and security updates should be applied promptly. Disable file and print sharing and disallow Internet service hosting on PPTP client computers. Promptly apply bug fixes and security updates to Internet client software.

If possible, get strong client-based software that puts a stateful inspection firewall on every PPTP client. This type of software is new but increasingly available.

Control Data May Be Intercepted   PPTP has a problem for which there is no easy solution. While the data exchanged by the client and server are encrypted, some control information used to establish the session is not. Information that can be gleaned by an eavesdropper includes:

- Client and server IP addresses
- Number of PPTP virtual tunnels available on the server
- Client RAS version
- Client NetBIOS name
- DNS servers handed to the client by the server
- Client username and the password hash

There is no quick fix to this problem other than to use a different software or hardware package for establishing your VPN. PPTP control channel spoofing can crash the PPTP Server; an additional vulnerability of PPTP is that it is easy to crash an RAS server by sending it spurious and wrong PPTP control information. Your only defense against this sort of attack is to limit who can communicate with your PPTP server by implementing connection restrictions in your firewall.

TIP Use your firewall to restrict the IP addresses or address ranges that are allowed to connect to your PPTP server. Drop source-routed frames to make IP spoofing of valid addresses more difficult.

PPTP Filtering

When you install the PPTP protocol there is a new check box that shows up in the TCP/IP Properties settings. (To access these settings go to the Network control panel, click the Protocols tab, select TCP/IP, click the Properties button, and then click the Advanced button.) The Enable PPTP Filtering option gives you the ability to restrict the client traffic that will pass through the RAS server by the IP address of the client.

The option by itself doesn't give you a great deal of control over what is filtered, but by adding a key and two values to the RAS server's registry, you can explicitly list the allowed IP addresses for PPTP clients.

PPTP filtering does not protect you from denial-of-service attacks that use the PPTP control channel to crash your RAS server. IP restrictions more properly belong in your firewall.

Encrypted Authentication

Authentication in a Windows NT system consists of shared secret authentication by providing an account name and a password. The password authentication mechanism is performed through a hashed challenge and response mechanism so that the password is never transmitted on the network.

Unfortunately, Windows NT passwords are limited to a maximum length of just 14 from a selection of 96 possible characters. Since most people tend to choose words they can remember easily, password protection is not sufficient for Internet-based authentication.

Consider the following scenario: The commonly available NetBIOS Auditing Tool can perform automated password attacks against a Windows NT server at a rate of one password attempt per second. Assume that a hacker actually wanted to compromise the administrative account of your machine and used ten simultaneous NetBIOS Auditing

Tool sessions from a single machine to do it. Table 11.1 lists how long it would take to crack various types of passwords.

Table 11.1   Time required to crack common sets of passwords

Password Set	Members in Set	Time to Crack
Most common passwords	50	5 seconds
Slang word	200	20 seconds
First name	7,500	13 minutes
Last name	40,000	67 minutes
Common English (CE)	25,000	42 minutes
English	750,000	21 hours
Top 10 common languages	250,000	7 hours
Name + Any character	4,560,000	126 hours
CE + Any character	2,400,000	66 hours
CE + Any character + CE	60,000,000,000	190 years
Completely Random 14 char	5.6×10^{27}	17 quintillion years

*Top 10 common languages include the 25,000 most commonly used words of the 10 most common languages. This is why the set is smaller than the complete English language.

Notice that at ten attempts per second, a completely random 14-character password would take a billion times longer than the universe has existed to crack. This is long enough, and statistics like these led Microsoft to believe that a 14-character limitation on password length would be sufficient.

But humans are not computers. The vast majority of passwords (my most commonly used password, in fact) can be broken in less than a single work day because they fall into very small known sets like those shown in Table 11.1. My experience tells me that humans simply will not accept memorizing random garbage longer than a telephone number or a social security number, and that they're simply not capable of reliably repeating that task once a month when the system invalidates their old passwords.

Operating Systems and Firewalling

PART 3

To compensate for these problems, I recommend linking two randomly chosen words and salting the combination with any other random character. The resultant password is easy to remember and sufficiently difficult to crack to satisfy most security requirements.

Passwords in Windows systems are further compromised by a number of extremely poor convenience choices that Microsoft has built into their client operating systems and applications:

- Windows 95 and 98 store all entered passwords in password files that are easily pilfered from nonsecure client computers and trivial to decrypt.
- Internet Explorer will automatically respond to challenges for an encrypted password from a Web server—yielding a decodable hashed value to the server because the server knows the random seed value it provided for the hash. This is a serious flaw in all challenge-and-response systems, but is made especially bad in the case of Internet Explorer because the entire negotiation occurs without the user's awareness.
- Backward compatibility with LAN Manager's far weaker authentication system is built into Windows NT and difficult to disable.

More disturbing than the presence of these features is the fact that Microsoft does not allow the user to eliminate or disable them in favor of security.

NOTE Windows 2000 allows passwords of up to 256 characters, which considerably improves the security of the operating system if consistently used.

Limitations

The firewalling functions of Windows NT 4 are not sufficient to provide border security for a number of reasons:

- NT's packet filtering is simplistic, providing only minimal stateless functionality.
- There is no NAT or proxy service, so internal hosts are not hidden.
- The tunneling protocol relies upon shared secret passwords that are generally easy to discover and use for other services.
- The authentication service, while reasonably strong theoretically, suffers from numerous well-known exploits and is weakened by its default support for weaker authentication.
- There is no specific security-based logging and alerting mechanism, although the operating system's strong support for logging and alerting can be used to compensate for this deficiency.

- There is no managed method to propagate consistent security policy in an enterprise beyond authentication policy, which is automatically handled through the single logon functionality of domain security.

Most of these limitations have already been discussed, but the important ones are reiterated below.

No NAT

Windows NT does not currently include the ability to perform Network Address Translation, although this capability has been announced for Windows 2000. This means that if you cannot complete your connection requirements using a proxy server, you must allow routing from the Internet inside your private network using public numbers.

No Proxy

Windows NT does not include proxy services, although Microsoft Proxy Server, an add-on BackOffice component designed for Windows NT, is a reasonably good proxy server application. However, despite Microsoft's use of the word in their advertisements, it is not a firewall because it does nothing to protect the source operating system from denial of service or intrusion.

Limited Logging and Monitoring

Microsoft's security monitoring is spotty and incomplete because it was designed to support more generalized operating system monitoring and logging. Logging and monitoring is only performed on higher-level operating system objects like files and user accounts. Indicators of hacking activity like malformed packets or source-routed packets are impossible to track in Windows NT.

Performance

Routing performance in Windows NT is lower than that of most UNIX implementations on the same hardware, and lower than most comparably priced dedicated routers. Windows NT's routing performance is perfectly sufficient for routing to the Internet, however, because any Internet link a server is directly attached to is bound to be slower than what the server could comfortably handle.

Enabling packet filtering does not put an appreciable load on an NT server. Because the filtering is stateless, it does not consume any more memory than the routing function itself. The tunneling performance is also lackluster, but sufficient for most Internet connections.

Windows 2000

Windows 2000, the successor to all Microsoft operating systems, is based on the Windows NT kernel with the interface of Windows 98. The operating system supports many convenience features missing in Windows NT but present in Windows 98, such as USB support and support for hot swapping PCMCIA cards.

None of the interface features are especially important for server functions, but the Server and Advanced Server packages also include the following network-related services that, in addition to those provided by Windows NT 4, are very relevant to firewall operations:

- CryptoAPI/Public Key Infrastructure
- Kerberos authentication
- Network Address Translation
- Improved Packet Filtering
- IPX Packet Filtering
- Layer-2 Tunneling Protocol (L2TP)
- IPSec

The only missing feature is network proxying, which is provided by the addition of Microsoft Proxy Server (a BackOffice product). Each of the supported firewall features of Windows 2000 is discussed in the following sections. MS-Proxy Server is discussed in Chapter 13.

Windows 2000 Professional Edition, the direct successor to NT Workstation, includes a lightweight Network Address Translator designed for sharing dial-up and consumer Internet subscriber line technologies like xDSL and Cable modems. The feature allows you to install two network adapters and automatically establish NAT and a DHCP server for interior clients. As of Windows 2000 beta 3, the service has a bug that forces you to use the first bound network adapter on the Internal network, but otherwise works flawlessly and is very easy to set up.

CryptoAPI

CryptoAPI is a set of operating system routines that make any encryption algorithm look the same to the operating system and other programs. This means that you can install any cryptographic module (called a Crypto graphic Security Provider, or CSP), such as DES, RSA, Blowfish, or GOST into Windows NT to be used pervasively. It also means that as existing algorithms are weakened by greater computing power or found to be flawed, they can be replaced easily and completely. CryptoAPl was actually released in Windows NT Server 4 Service Pack 3, but had no important effect on that already functional operating system. It is an integral part of Windows 2000.

For example, the Encrypted File System of Windows 2000 relies upon CryptoAPl to perform key and certificate generation, encryption, and decryption. So, although by default it uses the RSA encryption for key generation and the RC4 stream cipher for bulk data encryption, you could replace the default RSA CSP with a Blowfish CSP to change Windows NT's EFS encryption to use the Blowfish cipher. This not only gives the end users complete control over the encryption methods, it allows them to create their own encryption modules if they feel the need.

CryptoAPl passes generic service requests from applications to the various installed CSPs to perform the following functions:

- Public key generation
- Encryption/decryption
- Digital signing
- Hashing

There's no reason that the CSP has to use the same algorithm for each of these functions; in fact, the default CSP does not. A CSP need not perform all of these functions because multiple CSPs can be installed in the system and used for different purposes.

Public Key Infrastructure (PKI) is Microsoft's term for the pervasive changes that CryptoAPl allows. Nearly all security services in Windows 2000, including EFS, IPSec, and RAS authentication, rely upon CryptoAPl.

The Default CSP Windows 2000 comes with default CSP written to implement RSA for public key generation, RC2 for bulk block encryption, RC4 for bulk stream encryption, and MD4 and MD5 for digital signing and hashing. This CSP can be set up to use the local registry, a group security policy, or a key server for the storage of public keys.

WARNING Storing your cryptographic keys in the registry of the protected machine makes it possible for someone who has seized your equipment to extract the key and decrypt your encrypted content. Always store Cryptographic keys on a foreign server or removable device.

Kerberos Authentication

Kerberos authentication—an Internet standard for user authentication—is the basis for the new security features that will be available with Windows 2000. Like the Windows NT domain model, Kerberos is a trusted authentication system, meaning all the servers in the domain hierarchy use (and trust) the same system.

Kerberos does not rely upon a secure network, the physical security of network clients, or the host's IP address for security. Kerberos was designed from the ground up with the assumption that traffic on the network could be read, written, and changed at will by a hacker who was theoretically perfect and who would understand all of the security-related issues in the network and the Kerberos system. Kerberos does not rely on security through obscurity at all.

Kerberos keeps a database of the private keys of its clients. Those clients may be users or network services. If the client is a user, that private key is an encrypted password. In this respect, the system behaves very much like NT security.

Once a Kerberos client has been authenticated by the Kerberos system, the Kerberos server generates unique session keys that two clients (the user and the service being used) use to authenticate messages between one another. Kerberos supports three levels of encryption security:

Authentication Proves to each client that the other is who it says it is initially, but provides no further identification midstream.

Message Signing Includes an encrypted signature with each packet of data, proving to each client that the message originates from the other client and is not a forgery. Message signing is often referred to as safe messages in Kerberos documentation.

Encryption Makes the contents of each packet indecipherable to parties other than the clients engaged in the conversation. These are called private messages. They are used by the Kerberos system for the transmission of passwords over the network. In most Kerberos systems, any or all of these methods can be used for any session, depending upon the level of security required and the amount of load that the system can tolerate for the encryption process.

Kerberos is based on DES encryption. DES (Data Encryption Standard) was developed by the U.S. government for public use. That being the case, many people have theorized that the government may have some method for decrypting the contents of DES-based systems that is faster than a simple brute-force attack. This has not been proven, and no statistical evidence has implied any abnormal weakness in DES security. Kerberos is not dependent upon DES encryption, and it is not yet clear whether Microsoft will use DES encryption in its implementation or will rely upon CryptoAPl, which would allow the use of any encryption method.

Kerberos session keys have a short valid lifetime. If an intruder gains access to a session key, it's only useful until it expires. If your session key's lifetime is set to a reasonably short value, such as one day, even if compromised, it can only be used for that day. Copying a valid session key and attempting to reuse it is called a replay attack because the session key, although not decrypted, is simply used again by a third party to gain access. Most Kerberos implementations attach to each message a time stamp that must be valid to within a few minutes or the message is assumed to be an attempt at a replay attack.

Kerberos also allows authentication to take place using public keys rather than an account name and password. This means you could generate keys that associated businesses could install in their systems to prove their identities to your network and allow whatever limited access you've defined for that key. Kerberos' controllable public security is an important part of Microsoft's long-term strategy for Windows NT.

Network Address Translation (NAT)

Support for Network Address Translation in Windows 2000 is strong and very easy to configure; in fact, it's the easiest NAT configuration around. Because the NAT is built into the router software, there's no silliness to deal with concerning routing table additions, specific interface problems, or any of the other issues you deal with when using NAT software that sits above or below the router layer. With Windows 2000, you simply define the range of internal addresses you want to translate for, and you're done.

The NAT software allows reverse translation mappings so you can configure each port on the NAT to map to a specific internal host and port. This makes it easy to create a DMZ using Windows 2000 to shunt Internet services to a group of hosts behind your firewall.

The NAT software also allows for static internal mappings so you can assign a public IP address to an internal host. This feature allows you to make services on that host visible to the external network. It is generally more secure to translate services on a service-by-service basis using the IP address of the firewall, however.

Network Load Balancing

Windows 2000 includes a network load-balancing feature that can be enabled on a per-interface basis. Network load balancing allows a group of servers to provide services using the same public IP address and share the load on a fair share basis. You can assign various load weights to servers in the group based on their various service capacities, or you can specify that all hosts should be loaded equally.

Because Windows 2000's load-balancing feature is performed by all hosts simultaneously, there's no requirement that all data stream through a single NAT host. This makes it possible to service extremely busy network services that would overwhelm the routing capabilities of a NAT. All hosts in the IP cluster must be able to receive routed data to the shared IP address and must be able to communicate with one another for the load balancing to operate correctly.

NOTE Windows 2000 Advanced Server will and Windows 2000 Professional Edition will not include the load-balancing feature, but it is not clear as of this writing whether Windows 2000 Server will include it.

Improved Packet Filtering

Packet filtering in Windows 2000 is much improved, but it remains stateless. Windows 2000 is capable of performing both incoming and outgoing packet filtering, as well as specific protocol blocking and specific allowance. Configuring the IP filter is easier in Windows 2000 than in Windows NT 4 once you're familiar with the Microsoft Management Console (MMC) that is used to administer all administrative features of the operating system. Because the packet filter is stateless, it is still not as strong as the filter in a true stateless inspection firewall.

The packet filter also allows filtering of various ICMP message types, so you can protect against certain denial-of-service attacks while retaining the useful services of the ICMP protocol.

IPX Packet Filtering

Windows 2000 supports filtering of IPX packets, even though Microsoft is trying to deprecate support for IPX. This deprecation is a shame, because IPX is an excellent transport inside a network while WinSock compatible proxies are available to perform TCP/IP translation at Internet borders.

IPX packet filtering allows basically the same level of packet filtering control as does the IP filter.

Layer-2 Tunneling Protocol (L2TP)

Layer-2 (datalink layer) Tunneling Protocol is a derivative of PPTP refined by Cisco Systems to create a tunneling protocol that is independent of IP. PPTP can only be carried inside IP packets; any connected frame forwarding mechanism can rout L2TP. One benefit of the decoupling between the tunnel and the transport is that L2TP can support multiple tunnels between the same two end points, whereas PPTP supports only one. One use for this functionality might be to create different tunnels for different quality of service requirements.

Microsoft's implementation of L2TP uses IPSec encryption to encrypt the payload. Microsoft's implementation of L2TP can be accurately thought of as PPP with an IPSec payload.

IPSec

IPSec is a Layer-3 (network layer) encryption technology. It provides encrypted transportation services similar to PPTP and L2TP, except that there is no concept of a connected session or tunnel.

Individual IPSec packets can be transmitted between hosts, and it is simply assumed that some prior authentication has occurred that will enable the hosts to decrypt the packets when they arrive. This is entirely different from the concept of tunnels, which are sessions between two machines that maintain the state of the connection. When the tunnel is closed, the information necessary to decrypt the tunnel's contents is gone. IPSec is merely IP with encrypted payloads; there is no encapsulation within another protocol.

Because there is no overhead for tunnel establishment or maintenance, IPSec is more appropriate for message-oriented communications than either L2TP or PPTP.

Operating Systems and Firewalling

PART 3

NT Naked on the Net

I use a cable-modem to access the Internet from home. My home machine is a Windows NT Server that acts as a proxy (running WinGate, no less) for the other machines in my house (yes, I'm a serious geek). I have no firewall.

I have actually used Windows NT directly attached to the Internet for three years now without incident, using only NT's simple packet filter for protection. I open only my Web port and on rare occasions my NetBIOS session port.

In my situation, this level of security is appropriate because

- I have no significant secrets.
- I have a strong backup policy.

- I have no significant cost associated with downtime.
- I provide no public services.
- My ISP filters many ICMP and denial-of-service attacks.

Because my security requirements are low, Windows NT's direct security is sufficient to handle my problem. Some smaller businesses have very little requirement for security, but I cannot recommend taking as cavalier an attitude about security as I have. Despite my personal use of Windows NT's security mechanisms, I cannot recommend them for use alone on the Internet. If you feel you cannot afford the cost of a firewall, use an open-source firewall like Linux.

12

Firewalls for Free

This chapter could also be titled "How Hackers Protect Themselves." Hackers have computers too and want to keep their own machines free of intrusion from the Internet. Paradoxically, these computers may be the most secure computers on the Internet because the hackers use free software they can examine for security problems, they are the first to discover (or create) security weaknesses, and they fix their own systems as soon as loopholes are discovered. They share the security fixes with anyone who wants them, and you can take advantage of this fast response to new threats in your own network by using the same software they do.

There are several free software packages that you can use to craft a firewall for your network. Most of these packages run on free operating systems such as Linux, BSD, or DOS. We'll examine three popular packages—IPChains for Linux and Trusted Information System's Firewall Toolkit (TIS FWTK) as a proxy server, DrawBridge on FreeBSD, and IPRoute on top of DOS.

Free firewalls all suffer from a few of the same class problems:

- Weak or missing logging and alerting features
- No real-time firewall monitoring capability
- Weak or missing graphical user interface
- Difficult command prompt based configuration

These problems all stem from the fact that the software is developed primarily by a single individual or small team rather than by a corporation. Small teams don't have the time or money to spend on ancillary problems like ease of use or sophisticated alerting and logging mechanisms. These features, when present, are nearly always provided by an add-on package developed by a different developer. Free software is developed for people who deeply understand the problem to be solved and the operating system upon which the software runs. Essentially, this makes free software an option only for those who are completely familiar both with the operating system (usually UNIX) and TCP/IP.

Linux and IPChains

Linux is an Internet phenomenon that baffles many people in the traditional computer software industry. Linux was an educational project of a Finnish college student named Linus Torvalds that has gone much further than originally expected. Using free software tools developed for Richard Stallaman's GNU (Gnu's Not Unix) project, he wrote a simple operating system for his computer because he didn't like DOS and Windows, and nothing else was available for which he could get source code. He posted his code to the Internet and other people got interested, suggested changes, and (most importantly) sent Linus additional code of their own to extend the little operating system. Now the little operating system is nearly as complex and powerful as Windows NT or traditional UNIX, and all of the source code is still available for anyone to browse, change, and fix for security problems.

> **NOTE**   The biggest security advantage to Linux, according to Linux advocates, is that once a security problem in the operating system is understood, it can be diagnosed and fixed in hours or minutes, and a security patch will be posted to the Internet minutes later. Software or detailed instructions for stopping any intrusion threat is typically made available through security newsgroups and Web sites within a day of the threat being found. Contrast this to the time it usually takes commercial operating system companies to acknowledge a security problem, prepare a work-around, and then deliver an operating system update (hint: it usually takes longer than a day).

A recent addition to the Linux core operating system is the ability to perform packet filtering and Network Address Translation in the operating system itself. Originally called IP Masquerade because of its NAT ability, the system is now called IPChains because it allows the administrator to set up chains of rules that a packet must satisfy when it arrives at the Linux computer, is routed within the computer to another adapter, and exits the computer to another network.

IPChains provides NAT and packet filtering. Protocol inspection must be provided by a higher-level service. TIS FWTK (described later in this chapter) is an excellent proxy server package that interoperates well with IPChains on Linux. Another less secure option is to use Jigsaw, which is a Web server that also makes a good HTTP proxy. Other stream-based protocols (such as SMTP, NNTP, POP, and DNS) can just be redirected to other computers using IPChains, which redirects socket connections according to rule sets you define.

Major Feature Set

Linux with IPChains supports the following major features:

- Packet filtering rules are applied to every packet as it arrives, transits the Linux routing stack, and exits.

- Protocol specific content filters must be provided by higher-level services such as TIS FWTK, Apache, or Jigsaw. Generic stream redirection is performed by IPChains.

- Network Address Translation is performed for packets transiting the routing stack to hidden, internal networks.

- VPN firewall-to-firewall and firewall-to-remote client is provided as additional Linux components that can be downloaded from the Internet at no cost.

Minor Feature Set

Linux with IPChains supports the following minor features:

- Performance of Linux with IPChains is fast. Since it is integrated with the Linux IP stack, IPChains avoids the overhead of other firewalls that are implemented as user-level programs. Linux with IPChains can easily handle a busy LAN connection to the Internet even with Network Address Translation enabled.

- Command-line based configuration requires more skill in administration, but allows you to store policies in text files and use scripting tools for dynamic policy management. IPChains provides graphical interfaces that drive the command-line programs, making the software easier to set up and configure.

- Remote management (using a remote shell (RSH) or remote control software such as VNC) allows you to manage your firewall from other computers in your LAN.

- IPChains rules allow you to use NAT and fowarding for sockets to redirect traffic for particular services (such as HTTP, SMTP, and POP) to protected internal servers.

Security

IPChains filters packets before they are delivered to the IP stack for processing, allowing you to protect your computer from malformed packets and other IP-level attacks. IPChains provides the full range of options for packets filtering on: the SYN bit, source and destination IP addresses, source and destination ports, packet type, and most other TCP/IP header data elements. Network Address Translation is built into the packet filter, so you can use the same rules to specify the kinds of packets that will be translated and the kinds that will not.

Since IPChains does not inspect the data portions of the packets it manipulates, you will need a proxy server to ensure that the traffic traversing a particular port conforms to the protocol for that port (that only HTTP requests and replies are going over port 80, for example). See the section on the TIS FWTK package below. Also, many Web servers will also act as HTTP proxies, and you can use servers for store-and-forward protocols (such as SMTP and NNTP) without modification as protocol proxies for their services. Ideally, you will run these services on a different computer than your firewall, and you will use address translation to redirect the appropriate traffic to and from these servers.

IPChains evaluates every packet received by the network adapters in the firewall computer according to a set of rules you established when you installed IPChains. The rules are applied in order, one at a time, until IPChains finds a rule that matches the packet and specifies a terminal action, such as ACCEPT or DROP. Since the rules are applied in order, it is vitally important to craft the rules in the right order.

A useful feature of IPChains (and the feature that gives it its name) is the bundling of sets of rules into chains. IPChains starts out with three—INPUT, FORWARD, and OUTPUT. You can establish additional chains and use a rule in INPUT, FORWARD, or OUTPUT to direct packet analysis to the appropriate chain for that type of traffic. This structured rule management makes it easier to reason about the security of the firewall and thereby makes it easier to secure the firewall.

Interface

IPChains is administered using the `ipchains` command, which takes as its arguments the rules to be established or modified in the IPChains packet filter. Its syntax is illustrated in the IPChains Command Syntax sidebar.

IPChains Command Syntax

The following shows the result of typing "ipchains -h" at the Linux command line:

```
ipchains 1.3.5, 26-June-1998


Usage: ipchains -[ADC] chain rule-specification [options]

       ipchains -[RI] chain rulenum rule-specification [options]

       ipchains -D chain rulenum [options]

       ipchains -[LFZNX] [chain] [options]

       ipchains -P chain target [options]

       ipchains -M [ -L | -S ] [options]

       ipchains -h [icmp] (print this help information, or ICMP
list)
```

Commands:

```
   -A chain      Append to chain

   -D chain      Delete matching rule from chain

   -D chain rulenum

                 Delete rule rulenum (1 = first) from chain

   -I chain [rulenum]

                 Insert in chain as rulenum (default = 1 = first)

   -R chain rulenum

                 Replace rule rulenum (1 = first) in chain

   -L [chain]    List the rules in a chain (or all chains)

   -F [chain]    Flush (delete all rules) chain or all chains

   -Z [chain]    Zero counters in chain (or all chains)
```

Operating Systems
and Firewalling

PART 3

IPChains Command Syntax *(continued)*

-C chain   Test this packet on chain

-N chain   Create a new user-defined chain

-X chain   Delete a user-defined chain

-P chain target

              Change policy on chain to target

-M -L   List current masquerading connections

-M -S tcp tcpfin udp

     Set masquerading timeout values

Options:

-b   insert two rules: one with -s & -d reversed

-p [!] protor   protocol (tcp, udp, icmp, all or a number)

-s [!] address[/mask] [!] [port ...]

   source specification

-d [!] address[/mask] [!] [port ...]

   destination specification

-i [!] name[+]

   network interface name (or wildcard)

-j target [port]

   target for rule if it matches ([port] for REDIRECT)

-m [+-]mark number to mark on matching packet

-n   numeric output of addresses and ports

-l   turn on kernel logging for matching packets

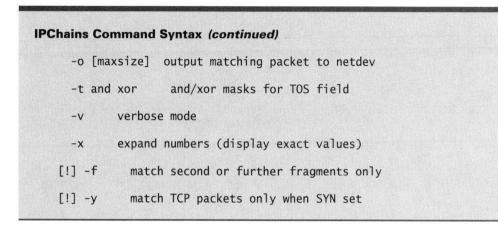

IPChains Command Syntax *(continued)*

```
-o [maxsize]  output matching packet to netdev

-t and xor    and/xor masks for TOS field

-v       verbose mode

-x       expand numbers (display exact values)

[!] -f   match second or further fragments only

[!] -y   match TCP packets only when SYN set
```

Most network administrators that use IPChains create shell scripts to configure the packet filter. The Example IPChains Shell Script sidebar shows you an example of an IPChains packet filter configuration.

Example IPChains Shell Script

The following example creates a simple, permissive filter policy:

```
#!/bin/sh

echo 1 > /proc/sys/net/ipv4/ip_forward

ipchains -F

ipchains -A input -p icmp --icmp-type destination-unreachable -j ACCEPT

ipchains -A input -p icmp --icmp-type source-quench -j ACCEPT

ipchains -A input -p icmp --icmp-type time-exceeded -j ACCEPT

ipchains -A input -p icmp --icmp-type parameter-problem -j ACCEPT

ipchains -P forward REJECT

ipchains -A forward -j MASQ -s 10.5.5.0/24 -d ! 10.5.5.0/24
```

Example IPChains Shell Script *(continued)*

```
ipchains -A input -i lo -j ACCEPT

ipchains -A input -i eth0 -p TCP -d 24.0.148.207 81:519 -j DENY

ipchains -A input -i eth0 -p UDP -d 24.0.148.207 81:519 -j DENY

ipchains -A input -i eth0 -p TCP -d 24.0.148.207 530:1024 -j
DENY

ipchains -A input -i eth0 -p UDP -d 24.0.148.207 530:1024 -j
DENY
```

Documentation

IPChains is documented in the typical UNIX manner—readme and install files come with the software installation package (which may already be installed on your Linux system) and documentation of the ipchains command can be found from the man (manual) command.

> *TIP* You can find step-by-step instructions for installing IPChains on the Internet; go to http://howto.linuxberg.com/LDP/HOWTO/IPCHAINS-HOWTO.html or just search on IPCHAINS from any search engine.

Cost and Support

IPChains is distributed at no cost. Install it on as many servers as you feel like, and protect as many clients as you want. The biggest costs for using IPChains are the cost of the computer used to run it and the cost of the time spent by you or the administrator to configure and manage it.

Minimum platform requirements for Linux with IPChains are easy to meet and should not be expensive:

- Linux or any UNIX platform for which you can compile the IPChains source code.
- 486 processor or better, including any processor architecture for which a version of Linux exists.
- At least two network interfaces.
- 200MB of disk space.
- 32MB RAM.

Source code for IPChains is included with most Linux distributions, so a talented programmer should be able to port the code to any version of UNIX that includes a complete C development environment.

The Trusted Information Systems Firewall Toolkit (TIS FWTK)

The TIS FWTK is the granddaddy of freely available firewalls. You can download versions for Linux, NetBSD, Solaris, as well as just about any other flavor of Unix you can think of. If you need a firewall and you have a spare Unix workstation collecting dust in a corner, this may be the firewall for you.

TIS FWTK was created for the Defense Advanced Research Projects Agency (DARPA) by TIS when DARPA realized that no packet filter would be secure enough to filter protocol content. After fulfilling the terms of their contract with DARPA (which includes making the code public domain), TIS further extended the firewalling concept into a commercial suite known as the Gauntlet Firewall. TIS was acquired by NAI recently, making Gauntlet Firewall a component of the PGP Active Security Suite. TIS FWTK is now maintained by an Internet consortium at www.fwtk.org.

TIS is not a packet filter. Instead it comes with protocol-scrubbing proxies for Telnet, Rlogin, SMTP, FTP, HTTP, and X-Windows. In addition, it comes with a generic TCP pass-through redirector (a SOCKS proxy). TIS also extends its security controls into the Unix LAN environment providing centralized network login and resource control using the netacl and authserv utilities.

Major Feature Set

TIS FWTK supports the following major features:

- Protocol specific content filters are provided by included proxy components.
- Centralized network login and resource access control for Unix computers is maintained using the TIS security mechanisms.

Minor Feature Set

TIS FWTK supports the following minor features:

- Performance of TIS FWTK is relatively fast.
- Command-line based configuration requires more skill in administration, but allows you to store policies in text files and use scripting tools for dynamic policy management.

Operating Systems
and Firewalling

PART 3

- Remote management using a remote shell (RSH) or remote control software such as VNC allows you to manage your firewall from other computers in your LAN.
- Address Translation and forwarding for sockets is performed using the TIS FWTK generic TCP plug-board.

Security

TIS FWTK does not filter packets before they are delivered to the IP stack for processing. You must use some other package to protect your computer from malformed packets and other IP-level attacks (IPChains is a good choice).

TIS FWTK is a proxy server; it examines the data portions of IP packets to ensure that the traffic traversing a particular port conforms to the protocol for that port (that only HTTP requests and replies are going over port 80 for example). This ensures, for example, that a hacker doesn't use port 80 to access a Trojan horse with its own protocol because your packet filter allows packets in the network to port 80 for HTTP services.

TIS FWTK evaluates data received by the network adapters in the firewall computer according to a set of rules established in its net-perm rule table. The rules are defined according to the port to which the data was sent, while permissions are defined according to the source and destination of the data.

Interface

You enable TIS FWTK by replacing the services to be proxied in the `inetd.conf` file with the corresponding TIS filter for that protocol (see Example TIS FWTK Configuration Entries below).

The TIS proxies read their configuration from the net-perm table, which describes for each protocol those hosts (source and destination) that are allowed to use the proxy. The Example TIS FWTK Configuration Entries sidebar shows sample configurations for FTP, Telnet, and HTTP.

IPChains is administered using the `ipchains` command, which takes as its arguments the rules to be established or modified in the IPChains packet filter. Its syntax is described in the previous section.

Example TIS FWTK Configuration Entries

This example creates the files indicated containing the text listed after the file.

    /etc/inetd.conf

Example TIS FWTK Configuration Entries

```
### standard config:

#ftp    stream tcp nowait root /usr/sbin/tcpd    /usr/sbin/
wu.ftpd

#telnet stream tcp nowait root /usr/sbin/tcpd    /usr/sbin/
in.telnetd

### firewall config:

 ftp    stream tcp nowait root /usr/local/etc/netacl wu.ftpd

 telnet stream tcp nowait root /usr/local/etc/tn-gw  tn-gw

 www  stream  tcp  nowait  root  /usr/local/etc/http-gw httpi-
gw

netperm-table

# netacl rules:

# ---------------------

# local FTP users connect to proxy ...

netacl-wu.ftpd: permit-hosts 192.168.* -exec /usr/local/etc/
ftp-gw

# ... while foreigners may use anonymous FTP

netacl-wu.ftpd: permit-hosts *        -exec /usr/sbin/wu.ftpd


# ftp gateway rules:

# --------------------------

# only local users may use FTP proxy

ftp-gw:         timeout 3600

ftp-gw:         denial-msg  /usr/local/etc/ftp-deny.txt

ftp-gw:         welcome-msg /usr/local/etc/ftp-welcome.txt

ftp-gw:         help-msg    /usr/local/etc/ftp-help.txt
```

Example TIS FWTK Configuration Entries

```
ftp-gw:            permit-hosts 192.168.* -log { retr stor }


# telnet gateway rules:

# ----------------------------

# only local users may use Telnet proxy

tn-gw:          timeout 3600

tn-gw:          denial-msg  /usr/local/etc/tn-deny.txt

tn-gw:          welcome-msg /usr/local/etc/tn-welcome.txt

tn-gw:          help-msg    /usr/local/etc/tn-help.txt

tn-gw:          permit-hosts 192.168.*



# http gateway rules:

# ----------------------------

http-gw: deny-hosts unknown

http-gw: permit-hosts 192.168.*

http-gw: permit-hosts * -httpd www.mybiz.com



# smap and smapd rules:

#----------------------------

smap, smapd:    userid 20

smap, smapd:    directory  /usr/local/var/spool/smap
```

Example TIS FWTK Configuration Entries

```
smapd:          executable  /usr/local/etc/smapd

smap:           maxbytes 2097152

smap:           maxrecip 4000

smap:           timeout 3600
```

Documentation

TIS FWTK is documented in the typical UNIX manner—readme and install files come with the software installation package (which may already be installed on your Linux system) and documentation of the TIS FWTK commands can be found from the man (manual) command.

TIP You can find step-by-step instructions for installing TIS FWTK on the Internet—go to http://www.fwtk.org.

Cost and Support

The TIS FWTK is freely downloadable and you can use it without licensing fees. The greatest costs are the time it takes to set it up and the time spent by you or the administrator to configure and manage it.

Minimum platform requirements for TIS FWTK (on Linux) are easy to meet and should not be expensive:

- 486 processor or better
- At least two network interfaces
- 200MB of disk space
- 32MB RAM

FreeBSD and Drawbridge

Linux isn't the only free operating system out there—another free Unix operating system shares its tradition of software freely distributed with source code. It is called FreeBSD, and is also used widely (although less visibly) on the Internet to provide network services including Web serving, routing, and firewalling. When the Texas A&M University found themselves under concerted network attack from a horde of hackers they needed a flexible and stable platform that they could build on to create a firewall that fit their specific needs; they chose FreeBSD and they called the resulting packet filter Drawbridge.

Drawbridge, unlike IPChains, is not a part of the operating system; it's a user-level program that directly controls the network adapters of the host computer. Like other packet filters, Drawbridge uses lists of rules to process packets. Since it was developed at a university where all of the computers are expected to be a part of the Internet as a whole, Drawbridge does not perform Network Address Translation.

Where the TAMU software shines, however, is in its ability to report and act on suspicious activity using the components called tcplogger, udplogger, netwatch, and netstat. Universities have lots of interesting computers that are juicy targets for hackers. Unfortunately, the threat doesn't just come from the outside—university network administrators have to protect themselves from attacks from within their computer labs as well. Since universities are based on the precept of fostering communication, not restricting it, a draconian security policy isn't practical. Instead the administrators keep a watchful eye on network activity and stay ready to swiftly respond to threats.

Major Feature Set

FreeBSD with Drawbridge supports the following major features:

- Packet filtering rules are applied to every packet by Drawbridge before being passed to the FreeBSD network stack.
- Protocol specific content filters are provided by higher-level services such as Apache and Jigsaw.
- VPN firewall-to-firewall and firewall-to-remote client is provided as additional FreeBSD components that can be downloaded from the Internet at no cost.
- Threat detection and response is performed using the tcplogger, udplogger, netwatch, and netstat tools.

Minor Feature Set

FreeBSD with Drawbridge supports the following minor features:

- Performance of FreeBSD with Drawbridge is fast. It can easily handle a busy LAN connection to the Internet.

- Command-line based configuration requires more skill in administration but allows you to store policies in text files and use scripting tools for dynamic policy management.

- Remote management using a remote shell (RSH) or remote control software such as VNC allows you to manage your firewall from other computers in your LAN.

Security

Drawbridge filters packets before they are delivered to the IP stack for processing, allowing you to protect your computer from malformed packets and other IP-level attacks. Drawbridge provides the full range of options for packets filtering on: the SYN bit, source and destination IP addresses, source and destination ports, packet type, and so on.

Since Drawbridge does not inspect the data portions of the packets it manipulates, you will need a proxy server to ensure that the traffic traversing a particular port conforms to the protocol for that port (that only HTTP requests and replies are going over port 80, for example). Many Web servers will also act as HTTP proxies, and you can use servers for store and forward protocols (such as SMTP and NNTP) unmodified as protocol proxies for their services. Ideally, you will run these services on a different computer than your firewall, and you will use address translation to redirect the appropriate traffic to and from these servers.

Drawbridge evaluates every packet received by the network adapters in the firewall computer according to a set of rules stored in its database in RAM (loaded when Drawbridge starts). The rules are applied in order, one at a time, until Drawbridge finds a rule that matches the packet and specifies a terminal action, such as ACCEPT or DROP. Since the rules are applied in order, it is vitally important to craft the rules in the right order.

The tcplogger, udplogger, netwatch, and netstat utilities (which don't necessarily have to run on the same computer as Drawbridge) scan all of the packets crossing or passing by the computer they are run on. Sophisticated analysis algorithms identify suspicious activity such as root logon attempts from off-campus, excessive FTP traffic coming from a computer that shouldn't be hosting an FTP server, and so on.

Interface

Drawbridge packet filtering rules are created in text files and then compiled with the Drawbridge Filter Compiler into the tables used by the Drawbridge packet filter. Instead of entering them one at a time or making a shell script (as you do with IPChains) you type all the rules out at once in a text file, then you compile the file.

Because universities are heterogenous computing environments with many special cases about what kind of traffic can go where, packet filtering rules for them are often large and complex. Drawbridge rules files reduce the complexity by allowing you to specify groups of permissions and groups of affected computers or subnets. This way you can have one set of rules for department Web servers, for example, and another for the various open-access computer labs on campus.

Example Drawbridge Filter Source File

```
#------------------ Group Definitions ----------------------#



#

# Make some useful definitions

#



# Allow all TCP out and no TCP in except:

# src=ftp-data, smtp, auth, gopher, and www

define tcpdefault      <1-65535/tcp out>, <src=ftp-data/tcp in>,

                       <smtp/tcp in>, <auth/tcp in>,

                       <gopher/tcp in>, <www/tcp in>;



# Allow all UDP except ports 7-19, tftp, sunrpc, snmp, xdmcp,
and nfs

# Note: we don't use '!' to exclude ports because it can't be
overridden

define udpdefault      <1-6/udp in>, <20-68/udp in>, <70-110/
udp in>,  <112-160/udp in>, <162-176/udp in>, <178-2048/udp
in>,

                       <2050-65535/udp in>;
```

Example Drawbridge Filter Source File *(continued)*

```
# Allow all known ICMP except redirect

define icmpdefault        <0-4/icmp in>, <6-18/icmp in>;


define telftp             <telnet/tcp in>, <ftp/tcp in>;

define popmail            <109-110/tcp in>;

define blockall           <!1-65535/tcp in-out>, <!1-65535/udp
in>,

                          <!0-255/icmp in>;


#

# The special name 'default' defines access for hosts not
listed in this file

#

define default            icmpdefault, udpdefault, tcpdefault;


#----------------------- Table Definitions ------------------#


#

# Reject all incoming packets with a source address of local-
host or broadcast.

#

reject 127.0.0.0          255.0.0.0;

reject 0.0.0.0            255.255.255.255;

reject 255.255.255.255    255.255.255.255;
```

Example Drawbridge Filter Source File *(continued)*

```
#

# Reject all incoming packets with a source address that is
within our # class C network.  Make an exception for our out-
side router.



#

reject 192.168.0.0      255.255.255.0;

reject ~192.168.0.1     255.255.255.255;



#

# Accept only outbound packets with a source address that is
within our

# class C network.

#

accept 192.168.0.0      255.255.255.0;



#---------------------- Broadcast Addresses --------------------
------#



# Block all packets directed to the broadcast addresses within
our

# network

host 192.168.0.0                    blockall;

host 192.168.0.255                  blockall;
```

Example Drawbridge Filter Source File *(continued)*

```
#---------------------- Host Definitions ------------------#


# The Drawbridge host - UDP ports must be open for DNS queries
# Allow src=ftp-data and ssh; block ICMP echo request
host drawbridge.mybiz.comudpdefault, <1-65535/tcp out>,
                              <src=ftp-data/tcp in>, <ssh/tcp
in>,

                              <0-7/icmp in>, <9-18/icmp in>;


# No access in/out
host accounting.mybiz.com          blockall;
host transactserv.mybiz.com          blockall;


# Allow domain to hosts running dns for zone transfers
host dns.mybiz.com          default, <domain in>;
host dns2.mybiz.com         default, <domain in>;


# NNTP host and phonebook server
host mailnews.mybiz.com          default, telftp,
                              <nntp in>, <time in>,
                              <csnet-ns in>, <domain in>,
                              <finger in>;


# Intranetapp server using port 4211
```

Example Drawbridge Filter Source File *(continued)*

```
host intranetapp.mybiz.com              default, telftp, <4211/
tcp in>;


# Block www and gopher to internal server

host fileserver.mybiz.com      default, <!gopher in>, <!www in>;


# Telnet and FTP servers

host ftp.mybiz.com             default, <ftp in>;

host intranet.mybiz.com              default, telftp;

#------------------------------------------------------------
```

Drawbridge has a command-line manager called dbmgr, which you can use to initialize the filter, start and stop it, load rule sets, monitor packet filter statistics, and set log criteria. This last option (logging) is particularly useful because you can set Drawbridge to report packets with any or all of the following criteria to the log file:

```
unknown event
initialized
incoming class D
outgoing class D
incoming port
outgoing port
incoming type
outgoing type
outgoing via accept table
```

```
incoming via reject table
outgoing via override table
incoming header too short
outgoing header too short
incoming D-O-S attack
outgoing D-O-S attack
incoming IP
outgoing IP
incoming fragment with IP offset == 1
outgoing fragment with IP offset == 1
incoming fragment
outgoing fragment
incoming MAC layer protocol
outgoing MAC layer protocol
```

The tcplogger, udplogger, and netwatch utilities each allow you to specify ports and protocols to watch for and log data in those areas to a text file. The netstat utility keeps network statistics and can be used to generate usage graphs and traffic patterns for your network.

Documentation

The Drawbridge comes with documentation but you can find additional information (as well as instructions on getting the package) at http://www.drawbridge.tamu.edu.

Cost and Support

Drawbridge is distributed at no cost. Install it on as many servers as you feel like, and protect as many clients as you want. The biggest costs for using Drawbridge are the cost of the computer used to run it and the cost of the time spent by you or the administrator to configure and manage it.

Operating Systems and Firewalling

PART 3

Minimum platform requirements for FreeBSD with Drawbridge are easy to meet and should not be expensive:

- 486 processor or better
- At least two network interfaces
- 150MB of disk space
- 8MB RAM

Packet Filtering with DOS and IPROUTE

Some readers who have been using the Internet for a decade or more may be wondering why modern packet filters require a computer as powerful as a supercomputer used to be just to push packets around. After all, a Pentium computer is a fast processor, and even 8 megabytes of RAM is a lot compared to the computers of a decade ago, all of which operated on the Internet just fine. Many organizations have plenty of obsolete 286 and 386 computers laying around.

IPROUTE is a packet filter and Network Address Translator that runs on DOS allowing you to use those older, less powerful computers. IPROUTE is not exactly free (there is a $50 license fee) but then neither is DOS. They are both cheap enough to merit being a part of this chapter because the money you will save by recycling your otherwise useless computers more than makes up the difference in cost.

Just because IPROUTE runs on DOS doesn't mean it is limited in functionality. It is a fully functional packet filter, and NAT, and even provides dial-on-demand IP connections for home networks and workgroups that use modems to connect to the Internet. This functionality makes IPROUTE especially useful for home offices and very small companies that don't have a constant IP connection.

Major Feature Set

IPROUTE supports the following major features:

- Packet filtering rules are applied to every packet as it arrives, transits the IPROUTE routing stack, and exits.
- Network Address Translation is performed for packets transiting the routing stack to hidden, internal networks.
- IPROUTE will automatically establish dial-up connections for intermittent IP links.

- VPN between IPROUTE installations is included in U.S.-only distributions of the software.

- IPROUTE includes the ability to combine dial-up connections to increase available bandwidth.

Minor Feature Set

IPROUTE supports the following minor features:

- Performance of IPROUTE on top of DOS isn't the fastest, especially on an older and slower computer, but then IPROUTE is most often used for slower Internet connections such as dial-up analog modems or ISDN anyway. IPROUTE is entirely sufficient for connection speeds less than 1Mb/sec.

- Command-line based configuration requires more skill in administration but allows you to store policies in text files and use scripting tools for dynamic policy management.

- Address Translation and forwarding for sockets is performed using the IPROUTE rules allowing you to redirect traffic for particular services (such as HTTP, SMTP, and POP) to protected internal servers.

Security

Since DOS doesn't have a built-in IP protocol stack, IPROUTE implements one, as well as the packet filtering and NAT functions. All packets are processed by the packet filter before being routed or translated. IPROUTE provides the full range of packet filtering options, including the SYN bit, source and destination IP addresses, source and destination ports, packet type, and so on.

Because IPROUTE does not inspect the data portions of the packets, and because DOS is a single-tasking operating system, you will need a proxy server running on another computer to ensure that the traffic traversing a particular port conforms to the protocol for that port (that only HTTP requests and replies are going over port 80 for example). Many Web servers will also act as HTTP proxies, and you can use servers for store and forward protocols (such as SMTP and NNTP) unmodified as protocol proxies for their services. Ideally you should use address translation to redirect the appropriate traffic to and from these servers.

IPROUTE evaluates every packet received by the network adapters in the firewall computer according to a set of rules stored in its database in RAM (loaded when IPROUTE starts). The rules are applied in order, one at a time, until IPROUTE finds a rule that matches the packet and specifies a terminal action, such as ACCEPT or DROP. Since the rules are applied in order, it is vitally important to craft the rules in the right order.

Operating Systems and Firewalling

PART 3

Interface

Like the other free firewalls discussed in this chapter, IPROUTE is configured using command-line scripts. One script starts the service and establishes the telnet command interpreter (so you can administer the firewall remotely), and other scripts manage such functions as dialing the ISP and establishing the packet filtering and Network Address Translation rules. The Typical IPROUTE Configuration Scripts sidebar illustrates these rules

---

Typical IPROUTE Configuration Scripts

• IPR script for PPP using a static IP address

```
;  We have an ethernet adapter (and configured packet

;  driver) for the local LAN.

packet en0 0x60 192.168.0.1/24

;  We connect to the Internet using a serial port modem

async sl0 0x3f8 4 57600 do_sl0

;  We make it the default route

route * sl0 perm

;  use RIP on the local LAN.

rip en0

;  Start up the command interpreter

command

exit
```

• Filter and NAT configuration script

```
do_sl0:

set trace on


;
```

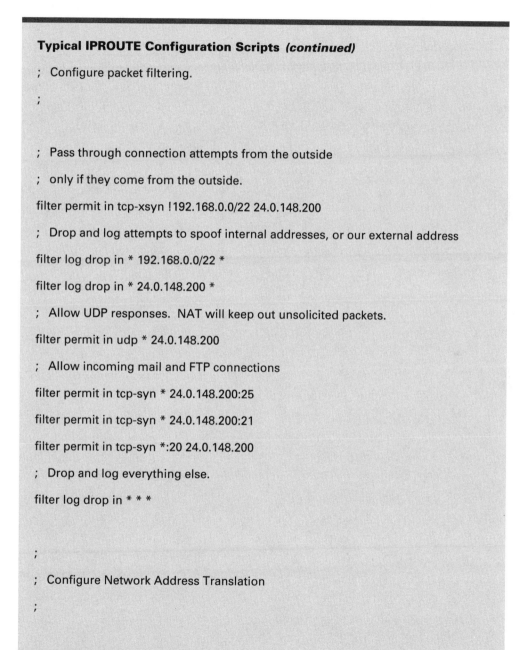

Typical IPROUTE Configuration Scripts *(continued)*

```
;  Configure packet filtering.

;


;  Pass through connection attempts from the outside

;  only if they come from the outside.
filter permit in tcp-xsyn !192.168.0.0/22 24.0.148.200

;  Drop and log attempts to spoof internal addresses, or our external address
filter log drop in * 192.168.0.0/22 *

filter log drop in * 24.0.148.200 *

;  Allow UDP responses.  NAT will keep out unsolicited packets.
filter permit in udp * 24.0.148.200

;  Allow incoming mail and FTP connections
filter permit in tcp-syn * 24.0.148.200:25

filter permit in tcp-syn * 24.0.148.200:21

filter permit in tcp-syn *:20 24.0.148.200

;  Drop and log everything else.
filter log drop in * * *


;


;  Configure Network Address Translation

;


;  Redirect SMTP mail to our mail server.
```

Operating Systems
and Firewalling

PART 3

Typical IPROUTE Configuration Scripts *(continued)*

nat tcp 192.168.0.2:25 24.0.148.200:25

; Redirect FTP to our FTP server.

nat tcp 192.168.0.3:21 24.0.148.200:21

nat tcp 192.168.0.3:20 24.0.148.200:20

; Let outgoing connection requests go out.

nat * * 24.0.148.200

;

; Configure modem control and set up for demand dial.

;

set interface rts flow

hangup:

set interface dtr off

delay .5

set interface dtr on

on packet dialout

wait 0

;

; Dial and establish a PPP connection.

; Hang up after 10 minutes of inactivity.

;

Typical IPROUTE Configuration Scripts *(continued)*

```
dialout:

send "ATDT 555-1212\r"

wait 1

on timeout hangup

wait 45 "CONNECT"

;  Read the rest of the CONNECT message into symbol "speed".

on cd lineup

read 5 "\r" speed

wait 60

lineup:on cdloss hangup

on timeout hangup

log "Connected at $speed"

set ppp login somebody somethingsecret

ppp 600 24.0.148.200/24

goto hangup
```

Documentation

The IPROUTE software comes with documentation but you can find additional information (as well as instructions on getting the package) at the IPROUTE Web site: www.mischler.com/iproute/.

Cost and Support

IPROUTE is commercial software—you have to pay a $50 license to run it. You can download a 30-day, time-limited evaluation copy to try it out, however.

Minimum platform requirements for IPROUTE can be met by almost any IBM compatible computer that you can actually get to boot:

- 286 processor or better
- At least two network interfaces, with DOS packet drivers
- A floppy or hard drive (capacity unimportant)
- 640K RAM

Roll-Your-Own Firewall

Even expensive firewalls are justifiable for most businesses, but there are situations when technical talent is more available than money. Case in point: my home network (yes, I'm a geek, I have a network at home).

Having a cable modem for Internet access at home is terrific—they're blazing fast for downloads, they work all the time, and they don't occupy the phone line. They do have some drawbacks however: They're always on, so your computer is always exposed to the Internet; they only provide a single IP address so you can only attach one computer to the Internet with them; and they don't do anything to protect you from intrusion from hackers. Hackers love people with cable modems, especially because they often use proxy servers like WinGate to share their network connection. This allows hackers to exploit innocent people's computers and launder their IP addresses.

So what's a cost-conscious security professional to do? Use Linux, of course. I've configured a "roll-your-own" firewall out of Linux, IPChains, and TIS FWTK to both protect my home network from intrusion and share my cable modem among my various home computers using the following network architecture:

My oldest PC, a Pentium II 400 with a single 6GB hard disk and 64MB RAM acts as a Web server (don't tell the Cable Company!) and firewall and is directly connected to the cable modem. Although the Cable Company provides DHCP, their DHCP server assumes you run Windows and will only assign an IP address if your computer has a NetBIOS name. So I assign my TCP/IP address, router, and DNS information manually.

The firewall is configured to perform Network Address Translation to the internal adapters, which I've configured to use the 10.0.0.x domain for the 100Mb adapters and 10.0.1.x for the wireless adapter. The firewall provides DHCP to internal clients, so no configuration of client computers is necessary. I use Apache Web server to serve a personal interest Web site with TIS FWTK filters requests going to it to make sure they're properly formed. I don't bother to filter HTTP requests from clients inside the network because I know better than to click on executable attachments from people I don't know.

The firewall's filter is configured to allow inbound connection only to the Web server port, which is proxied by TIS FWTK. Outbound connections are restricted to those protocols I use, and none other.

24*seven* CASE STUDY

Part 4

Topics Covered:

- Feature comparison of firewalls

- Technology details of firewalls

- Recommended firewalls for various platforms

- Commercial firewalls for Windows NT

- Commercial firewalls for UNIX

- Commercial firewalls for Open-Source operating systems

- Commercial firewalls for OS/2

- Commercial firewalls for NetWare

- Dedicated firewalls that include their own operating systems

13

Windows NT Firewalls

There are now so many firewall products available that it's difficult to determine what you should use. This chapter will familiarize you with the firewall market apply the theoretical information in the first part of this book to the practical selection of a real firewall. This chapter is specific to firewalls specific to Windows NT, although most of them also have versions that run under other operating systems as well.

This chapter details the following firewalls:

- Checkpoint Firewall-1
- NetGuard Guardian NCC
- NAI Gauntlet
- Axent Raptor
- Microsoft Proxy Server

These firewalls represent the high-end firewall market for firewalls that run on the Windows NT base operating system. These firewalls use the user, service, and in some cases the network interface functionality of Windows NT, and add only those components related directly to security of the operating system. Basing the firewall on an existing operating system is a double-edged sword. It allows the security systems vendor to concentrate on writing security software rather than operating system software, but it can also make the resulting product vulnerable to flaws in the operating system if the vendor hasn't taken special preventative precautions. With the solitary exception of Microsoft

Proxy Server, the firewalls profiled in this chapter support a remarkably similar set of technologies. With the exception of MS Proxy Server, they all cost about the same amount of money and are ICSA certified. The group is divided into two types based on their primary security posture:

- **Stateful Inspection Filters** Use complex filters based on retained information about connection state and protocols to either block or pass traffic. Firewall-1 and Guardian fall into this group.

- **Proxy Servers** Receive and then completely regenerate allowed services through the gateway, and ignore protocols for which there is no established proxy. Gauntlet, Raptor, and Proxy Server fall into this group.

The primary security posture of a firewall doesn't tell the whole story; most stateful inspectors include proxy or proxy-like services, and most proxy servers include stateful packet filters. The division in this case depends upon which philosophy the architecture of the firewall is based, and which services are added on to shore up deficiencies in the basic architecture.

There are two things you will not find in this chapter:

- Performance ratings
- Hacking tests

We decided not to include performance information in this chapter because we believe that performance should not be a deciding factor in your security posture. This would be something like comparing the top speeds of tractors—performance isn't the point. The essential problem is that more inspection and rigor takes more time, so the better a firewall is, the slower it will perform. If you are in the rare circumstance that you must use a high-performing firewall, use a stateful inspector. Otherwise, proxy servers provide more security, albeit at considerably reduced performance rates.

We performed a number of hacking tests against these products once they were properly secured using publicly available hacking tools. We were not able to find any case in which a firewall was susceptible to intrusion or denial of service except when we knew architectural flaws existed in the software. So we decided not to write about our lack of results. Psychological attacks using forged e-mail or rogue Web sites remain the only ways we know of to penetrate these firewalls, with the exception of MS-Proxy Server, which is subject to numerous security flaws, as discussed in the "MS-Proxy Server" section of this chapter.

Each firewall is detailed in its own section throughout the remainder of this chapter.

Firewall-1

Checkpoint Firewall-1 is a policy-based stateful inspection filter with an integrated Network Address Translator and a small set of nonintegrated protocol-specific security filters for common Internet protocols. Checkpoint Firewall-1 is the best-selling firewall in the world.

Checkpoint developed the concept of stateful inspection to improve the security of packet filters without requiring the overhead of proxy servers. Once a packet passes the suite of tests applied by the inspector module, the original packet is forwarded into the network. This means that any deformations not detected by the inspector module are passed through without modification by the firewall module.

Stateful inspection is a middle ground between simple packet filters and application proxies. Because stateful inspectors maintain state information about each connection, they can make more rigorous pass/fail checks on packets. But they do not usually have the ability to monitor the internal content of the various protocols, so they are more closely related to packet filters than to proxy servers.

Firewall-1 solves this problem to some degree by allowing plug-in protocol filters that are similar to actual proxies. These protocol filters understand the content of popular protocols like HTTP, SMTP, and FTP (the three provided with Firewall-1), so they can inspect and make pass/fail decisions on those protocols. These filters are able to perform high-level filtering functions like Java blocking and attachment stripping. Filters remain less secure than proxies because the packets are routed through the firewall rather than being re-created as they are in proxies. The Firewall-1 SMTP filter is a true proxy, as it writes

Commercial
Firewalls

PART 4

e-mail to its disk and then has a separate service forward the e-mail through the gateway. This method is designed to prevent the buffer overflow problems that plague e-mail systems.

Don't confuse content filters with simple protocol support. Firewall-1's documentation claims to support over 120 protocols out of the box. By support, they mean they've defined an object that encapsulates a protocol's protocol header number, not a content filter. Firewall-1 provides content filters for just three common protocols: HTTP, FTP, and SMTP.

The management console requires a Win32 or UNIX host. Supported UNIX variations are AIX, HP-UX, Solaris, and SunOS. The firewall modules can run on UNIX or NT computers or on numerous commercial routers from Cisco, Bay Networks, and others. Perhaps the coolest design feature of Firewall-1 is that with it you can convert your existing inventory of border routers into strong firewalls.

Firewall-1's documentation assumes you have a working knowledge of TCP/IP and the platform upon which you are installing the software.

Major Feature Set

Firewall-1 supports the following major features:

- Stateful Packet filter.
- Protocol specific content filters (HTTP, SMTP, and FTP).
- Network Address Translation.
- VPN firewall-to-firewall and firewall-to-remote client add-on components are provided at additional cost.
- User authentication is handled transparently through the various protocol content filters.

These features have been described in the previous section.

Minor Feature Set

Firewall-1 supports the following minor features:

Firewall-1 Performance   Makes it extremely difficult to tell the difference between a firewalled router and a non-firewalled router, even on the fastest connections. This makes Firewall-1 a strong contender for high-speed networks where performance is paramount. Firewall-1 is very appropriate, for example, as the first firewall closest to the Internet backbone for ISPs who wish to provide firewall support for their customers, or for major corporations that will then use proxy servers inside their networks for stronger internal security on lower speed links.

Policy-based configuration and management   Makes it easy to view, manage, and understand the configuration of the firewall. Like most GUI-based firewalls, Firewall-1 lets you create protocol definitions called objects that associate a friendly name with a collection of protocol identifiers like the port number and IP protocol type. This way, you can work with objects like FTP instead of TCP Port 21, so you won't get confused during the configuration process. Because the abstraction allowed by identifying protocols, addresses, users, and time ranges as named objects is easy to understand, management is simple. This tends to reduce the number of mistakes made when configuring the firewall.

Content Vectoring Protocol   Allows you to plug in filters to handle very specific protocols like HTTP, mail, and FTP. CVP-compatible filters can strip attachments and executable content, perform virus checking, URL blocking, or any other protocol-specific filtration. NAI and Symantec both make CVP-compatible virus scanners that work with Firewall-1 and are available at additional cost.

Client/Server management   Allows you to control any number of firewall modules from a centralized set of management consoles. The management consoles can be Win32 or X/Motif UNIX hosts.

Automatic Address Translation   Handles objects on an individual basis. Once an object is defined and an address translation mode assigned to it, address translation rules will be automatically generated for every case the object is used in the rule base. Address translation rules can be manually created for those cases where automatic translation doesn't accomplish your goals.

Firewall Module Synchronization   Allows firewalls to trade state with each other. If two firewalls on the same connection are used, one can fail without affecting the connections running through them. This feature can also be used to perform load balancing across a range of firewalls.

Interface

Firewall-1 is a client/server architecture that allows you to centrally control any number of firewall modules from a single management console. The GUI is easy to read and comprehend without being overly busy. It suffers from some poor design problems; for example, many windows can't be properly sized. Guardian (covered in the next section) suffers from very similar interface irregularities. For some reason, Firewall vendors think it's okay to charge many thousands of dollars for software with incomplete user interfaces. Nonetheless, the interface is very useable.

Commercial
Firewalls

PART 4

Firewall-1 encapsulates devices, users, and networks as objects defined by IP or network addresses and referred to by a uniquely assigned name identifier. Pass/drop rules are defined by selecting a source object (including "Any" to encompass the Internet), a destination object, one or more protocols, the action to apply, and the logging or alerting level. The collection of rules is called a rule base; it is synonymous with the strategies used by Guardian. Figure 13.1 shows the Firewall-1 interface with a complete rule base showing.

Figure 13.1 Firewall-1's rule-based interface

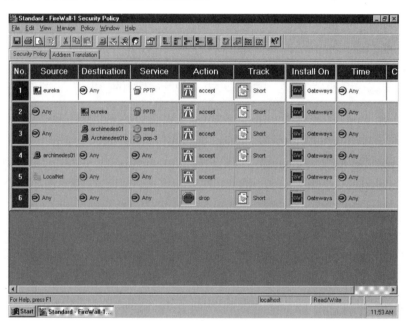

Rules are interpreted from the top to the bottom of the rule base as it is displayed on the screen. The first rule that applies to a packet is used, so a number of rules pertaining to the same protocol can be added in a very intuitive and obvious manner. This allows you to create various levels of security for different groups. The last rule in the rule base is "Any source, any destination, any protocol: drop with no logging." This rule is implicit and is not shown in the rule base, but it guarantees that anything not specifically allowed is specifically denied.

Network address directives are assigned per object, so once the rule base is complete, a NAT strategy is automatically defined. You can add manual address translation rules, but that is usually not necessary.

Once a policy is defined, it must be compiled and applied to the appropriate gateways. This is easy to complete; but unfortunately it is possible for the GUI to allow you to create policies that won't correctly compile. In that case, you must go through something of a compile/debug cycle to create a working policy. A solid user interface would simply prevent you from creating problem policies in the first place.

Security

Checkpoint devised the idea of the stateful inspection packet filter, which improves on the basic packet filter by more closely examining the packets used to set up connections and store connection information (the state). This stored state is used to determine which packets should be passed and which should be dropped based on their participation in a connection. Stateful inspection is very fast because the computation done to examine packets is fairly slim, and once a connection has been established, the filtering of packets through the connection takes very little time. Stateful inspection filters are capable of operating nearly as fast as a standard IP router.

But throughput is not the purpose of a firewall; it is merely a feature. Strong security, which can only be achieved through rigorous examination of all possible protocol information, remains paramount. Because stateful inspectors like Firewall-1 perform only cursory examination of TCP-layer information and do not typically filter the contents of packets, they are not as secure as pure proxy servers like NAI Gauntlet or even a properly protected installation of Microsoft Proxy Server.

To close that security boundary, Firewall-1 includes a small set of security filters for common services like SMTP and HTTP; these filters are not well integrated into the management paradigm, however. Firewall-1 also includes a protocol filter for HTTP that is capable of stripping out dangerous content like executable files and Java applets.

Documentation

Firewall-1's online documentation is among the best in the business. It teaches firewall theory, application, user interface, and is packed with examples. It is professionally written and appropriate for the target audience. Most network administrators will be able to establish a firewall without technical assistance as long as they don't need to use the proxy ARP functionality for Windows NT. This functionality is undocumented because the documentation is oriented more towards the UNIX edition of the firewall, which doesn't require a hack to shore up the operating system's lack of proxy ARP support.

If you intend to purchase and install a firewall by yourself without prior experience, you should consider Firewall-1 based on the strength of its documentation. Any Microsoft

Certified Systems Engineer (MCSE) or equivalent should be able to figure out Firewall-1 from the documentation alone and construct a reasonable, secure firewall policy for it.

Cost Support

Firewall-1 is sold a number of different ways:

- Single gateway products support a specific number of users. The management console and gateway are installed on a single machine. This product is sufficient for small businesses with less than that number of IP addresses on their network (which is how the firewall determines how many hosts it will work with).

- Enterprise products protect an unlimited number of internal hosts and are sold on a per module basis. You purchase the number of firewall modules you require (one per border gateway) and the number of encryption modules you require to support the VPN functionality.

Minimum platform requirements for Firewall-1 are easy to meet and should not be expensive:

- Pentium processor
- At least two network interfaces
- 40MB of disk space
- 32MB RAM
- CD-ROM drive

Checkpoint is stingy with online support and charges an exorbitant $400 per incident for telephone technical support (for which they will not guarantee a solution to your problem). I can understand not wanting to deal with first time network integrators, but it seems that Checkpoint has decided that technical support is a lucrative market. Competition will inevitably change their minds. That said, their technicians seem very competent, as far as I could determine without providing my credit card number.

The cost for a basic 25-user, Windows NT–based single firewall agent is about $2,000. The RealSecure VPN and remote authentication module is about as expensive, and costs for additional users hover around the $100-per-user point.

NetGuard Guardian NCC

NetGuard's Guardian NCC is a very popular policy-based stateful inspection firewall for Windows NT. Policy-based firewalls are configured based on lists of pass/block rule sets that are human readable, as opposed to IP addresses and protocol numbers.

Guardian does not contain proxy service applications, nor does it include protocol filters akin to those provided with Firewall-1. NetGuard seems easy to use, which is important considering that most firewall penetrations are allowed by firewalls that are improperly configured. Guardian is probably the easiest "strong" firewall to establish and configure.

Guardian's look, feel, and architecture are very similar to those of Firewall-1. Unlike Firewall-1, Guardian is available only for Windows NT and OS/2.

The Windows NT edition of Guardian NCC Requires:

- Windows NT 4 (Workstation or Server)
- Pentium 166 with 64MB RAM
- 170mb of free disk space
- Two or more network adapters

Since Guardian can run on Windows NT Workstation, you can save about $700 on the cost of the underlying operating system. Guardian performs the routing function itself, independent of Windows NT's built-in router.

Guardian uses a client/server management philosophy, using a server that runs as a Windows NT service called the Firewall Agent and a client application called the NCC Manager. This remote management feature allows you to manage the firewall remotely from any client that can authenticate with the firewall.

Annoyingly, the CD-ROM auto-run utility will only run with a color depth of 8 bits or better. This means you'll be forced to install a video adapter driver, which is otherwise not useful (and in some cases, a stability risk) on a firewall. You can avoid installing a video adapter driver by browsing on the CD to find the individual setup programs for the Agent and the Manager in the CD-ROM.

You can choose to install the firewall agent on any one specific adapter or on all NDIS (Network Driver Interface Specification) adapters. If you have more than two adapters, you must choose the "all NDIS adapters" setting to firewall more than one adapter. Since most firewalls are only connected to the Internet via a single adapter, it is not usually necessary to install the firewall agent on more than one adapter.

You must restart your firewall host after installing the Agent. You must also restart your firewall after installing the manager. To minimize restarting, you can install the agent, answer no when asked to restart, install the manager, and then restart the computer. Guardian installs on Windows NT Service Pack 0 (i.e., Windows NT with no service packs installed), but Service Pack 3 or above is required to make use of the encrypted tunnel functionality.

Like Firewall-1, Guardian uses a media-access control-layer driver located at the NDIS interface layer between the adapter driver and the network transport. This means that traditional attacks against Windows NT's TCP/IP implementation will not pass through the inspecting driver.

Major Feature Set

Guardian provides the following major features:

- Packet filtering Firewall
- Network Address Translation (NAT)
- Virtual Private Network (VPN) (requires Service Pack 3 or higher)
- User Authentication
- Bandwidth Control

Proxy applications are a glaring omission from this feature list.

Packet Filtering Firewall

As with most policy-based firewalls, you do not directly configure the packet filter. Rather, all protocols are considered blocked unless a rule in the currently applied policy (called a strategy in Guardian parlance) permits passage. Filtering can be based upon any combination of IP addresses and network masks by creating objects that represent the individual addresses and networks, and then creating policy rules that allow the passage of protocols to those addresses.

Network Address Translation (NAT)

Guardian's Network Address Translator is particularly easy to establish and provides the ability to perform both static port-based service assignments and IP pool sharing with a single public IP address. This translation capability is more capable than the Network Address Translator included with Checkpoint Firewall-1, which is not capable of providing both public address translation and pooled NAT for internal clients on the same public IP address. Guardian is also able to firewall demand-dialed RAS connections, so small installations that have only a dial-up connection to the Internet can still perform NAT using that connection.

Virtual Private Network (Requires SP3 or Higher)

VPN only functions between Guardian firewall agents—there is no software to allow remote access for individual client computers. The VPN product is included with the firewall at no additional cost, which is unusual in the high-end firewall market.

User Authentication

Guardian includes a user authentication feature, but that feature does not create an encrypted tunnel. User information is sent in the clear once the firewall has authenticated the client. Guardian recommends using PPTP if data encryption is required. Authentication modes include:

- Radius
- Windows NT Challenge/Response
- Proprietary One-time Password

Minor Feature Set

Guardian supports the following minor features:

- Bandwidth Control
- Transparent ARP support
- SYN flood protection
- Anti-spoofing control

Bandwidth Control

NetGuard includes a feature called Guidepost Bandwidth Control that allows you to assign a percentage of an interface's total bandwidth to specific service functions. This prevents the limited services from overwhelming your Internet connection and prevents the use of other services.

Transparent ARP Support

The firewall can be configured to ARP for devices behind it, which has the effect in a broadcast environment of making the firewall invisible. This mode would allow you to make public servers in your DMZ visible to the Internet without creating a routing table on the firewall. You would normally not enable this functionality for private hosts. ARP configuration is managed easily through the GUI interface.

After changing ARP entries, you have to stop and start the agent service in the services control panel and power cycle the router between the firewall and the Internet to clear its ARP tables. If your ISP owns the router, call their support team for information on how to properly clear the router's ARP table.

SYN Flood Protection

Guardian's MAC-layer inspector is capable of detecting and filtering out some types of SYN floods before they consume excessive resources on the server.

Commercial
Firewalls

PART 4

Anti-spoofing Control

Guardian has two features that help eliminate address-spoofing problems:

- IP addresses from internal adapters located inside your network are not accepted on external adapters connected to the Internet.
- Source-routed packets are dropped in the filter.

Most strong firewalls include some sort of similar anti-spoofing features.

Security

Using Guardian's Strategy Wizard, it's almost impossible to "blow" your security configuration by applying ill-conceived policy (unless you add bad rules after the Wizard has completed). It's easy to think you're more protected than you are, however. In our experience, it's rare to find stock security configurations that are completely appropriate across a wide range of users. Using a Wizard as the basis for a security policy is a good idea as long as the security administrator takes the time to study the resulting policy and to understand its susceptibilities.

Management security is controlled via a single, 15-character maximum password.

Interface

The Manager GUI interface for Guardian is reasonably easy to use. The interface paradigm is based upon the concept of strategies, which are containers for numerous elements of policy. Each agent can be loaded with a single strategy. Because a single manager can be used to monitor multiple agents, you can have various strategies assigned to various agents.

The interface itself is a multiple-document interface that performs well, even on small screens, although it is busy looking at first glance. The tree browser on the left side is capable of browsing all objects in the system, including strategies, agents, objects, logs, alerts, and histories. Oddly, it's not really hierarchical; it shows only first- and second-level objects. Tertiary objects are shown in another tree view inside the window that pops up when you double-click a secondary object. That second-level tree view suffers from the same odd constraint, but no quaternary objects have children, so the effect is at least not infinite. Figure 13.2 shows the Guardian firewall interface.

Figure 13.2   Guardian Firewall

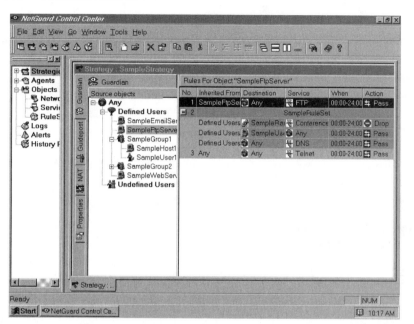

The bottom-level dialog for system objects is the same for all types of objects, which reveals a less than pure object-oriented design philosophy. Artifacts from this design strategy show up as paradoxical constructs like authentication assignments for the IP address provided by your ISP. The interface will happily accept and store these, and thereby convert that object into a user at least in the manager interface.

Strategies can be easily constructed for most common purposes using the Strategy Wizard. These strategies can then be modified for custom purposes using the manager interface.

TIP   We recommend using the Strategy Wizard as the basis of all your Guardian policies, and then modifying the Wizard's output. This guarantees that you've covered all the common bases without forgetting or misconfiguring anything.

The Wizard automatically creates network objects such as internal address pools, external address pools, service devices based on public IP addresses and specific ports, and so forth. Network objects are global: they are visible to all strategies.

Commercial Firewalls

PART 4

Documentation

Guardian's documentation is focused on installation and security policy setup. It contains almost no real detail on the methods used by the firewall and very little advanced configuration information. Experienced security administrators will find the lack of technical detail somewhat disconcerting because it makes it very difficult to analyze the firewall for potential security problems.

Cost and Support

Technical support is provided via e-mail only, which is not surprising, considering that NetGuard is located in Israel. The US distributor is LanOptics. U.S. Tech support is available through LanOptics at www.lanoptics.com and will provide telephone customer support.

You can request a free CD or download a 30-day evaluation of NetGuard Guardian NCC at www.netguard.com.

NAI Gauntlet

Network Associates, the new owners of Guantlet, is the result of the merge between McAffee (of virus-scanning fame) and Network General (makers of the Sniffer network protocol analyzer). The company then purchased PGP, Phil Zimmerman's encryption technology company, and Trusted Information Systems (TIS), the makers of Gauntlet. TIS developed the first security proxies under contract to the Department of Defense's Advanced Research Projects Agency (DARPA) when DARPA decided that stateless packet filters were not effective security devices. These original TIS security proxies are still available at no charge on the Internet and were covered in the previous chapter.

NAI has put Gauntlet in the PGP group and is in the process of merging all their security products together through a mechanism that they call "Active security." Active security is an event-driven publish/subscribe mechanism that allows the various software components of a security infrastructure to report exceptional events to other components in the security group. The security components are then able to make adjustments to their security policy to deal with the changed circumstance.

The level of conformance to this new active security infrastructure is low—most products can do little more than report events. But it does show that NAI is serious about integrating their security products and that they understand how it needs to be done. No other security product vendor has shown as much understanding of total security than NAI in this respect. How much of this talk becomes reality, and how useful it is when it does, remains to be seen.

Gauntlet is widely regarded in the security industry to be the most secure firewall on the market because it uses security proxies for all secured services rather than relying on stateful packet inspection. The new version (5.0) includes support for adaptive filtering, whereby connections are inspected at the application layer by a proxy server during initiation, and then dropped down to the network layer for stateful filtering once the connection is established and authenticated. This improves the performance of the firewall dramatically.

Gauntlet is available for Windows NT and UNIX. The firewall is multithreaded, which means it provides higher performance on multiprocessor machines.

System Requirements:

- Intel Pentium 133MHz
- 64MB RAM
- 1GB hard disk drive
- Two network adapters
- CD-ROM
- Windows NT Server SP3 or higher

Installation

The installation process is painless. You should install Gauntlet on Windows NT Server Service Pack 3 or 5. Avoid service pack 4, as a litany of patches and fixes must be installed to fix various problems with that service pack. Service pack 5 may also have issues, but none are known at the time of this writing.

The installation process will stop after a short automatic security survey if your machine fails to meet minimum requirements or some glaring security problem exists with the machine. You can examine the contents of the dialog box to determine what's wrong. The most common problems occur when Gauntlet is installed on Windows NT with service pack levels below 3 and when the administrator account has not been renamed.

Once the installation begins, Gauntlet will detect all network adapters in your machine and ask whether the adapters are inside or outside. Once each adapter is assigned, gauntlet will take its trusted network information from the IP addresses of the inside adapters. When the installation is complete, you will have to restart your computer.

As part of the installation process, Gauntlet configures its packet filter to block the ports of the simple TCP/IP services, the locator service on port 135, and the NetBIOS services on ports 137, 138, and 139. The installation program also disables the spooler service.

Very little information on the nature of the packet filter is provided by the documentation, and we were not able to discern what anti-spoofing measures were present.

Major Feature Set

Gauntlet provides the basic components required of a modern firewall:

- Packet filter
- Proxy Servers
- Network Address Translation, including illegal NAT
- Authentication
- VPN provided by separate PGP VPN product

Packet Filter

Gauntlet is now a combination of a security proxy and a stateful inspection filter. Each time a connection is established, the initial connection establishment packets are transmitted through the application proxy. Depending upon the security settings established by the security administrator, the proxy can continue to proxy all the data in the connection or determine that the connection is trustable and direct the packet filter to simply forward remaining packets in the connection without further inspection through the proxy. This approach lessens the rather serious performance and load problems from which security proxies suffer, but retains most of the security provided by an application proxy.

Proxy Services

Gauntlet provides support for an impressive range of both traditional Internet services and the newer multimedia and database services.

Standard Internet services include:

- FTP
- HTTP
- LDAP
- NNTP
- POP3
- PPTP
- SMTP
- SNMP
- SSL
- Telnet

H.323 Multimedia include:

- NetMeeting
- NetShow
- RealAudio
- RealVideo
- VDOLive

SQL, including:

- Microsoft
- Oracle
- Sybase

Network Address Translation (NAT)

Illegal Network Address Translation is NAT in an environment where valid IP addresses (those not in the 10, 192.168, or 176 domain) assigned to other owners are in use in your network and must be translated to legal addresses for proper operation on the Internet. Illegal network address translators can deal with the special problems posed by illegal addresses.

TIP Reconfigure your entire network to use the legal, non-routable 10 domain for internal addresses. There are illegal address problems that INAT translators can't solve. I've had customers who have tried for years to deal with their illegal address schemes rather than put in the few days of intense, IT organization-wide effort it would take to rebuild the address infrastructure using DHCP and legal addresses. If your network is so encrusted that you don't dare change IP addresses, it's a disaster waiting to happen anyway.

Authentication

Gauntlet provides support for the following authentication protocols:

- SecureID
- Radius
- S/KEY
- CryptoCard
- ActiveCard
- Microsoft Windows NT Challenge/Response

VPN

The separate PGP VPN suite provides VPN services for Gauntlet, as is common among high-end firewall services.

Minor Feature Set

Minor features of the firewall include:

- URL filtration
- CVP (Virus and content scanning)

URL Filtration

Gauntlet is capable of filtering URLs to block or log sites known to contain questionable or illegal content. URL filtration is only somewhat useful, however; illicit sites tend to move often, and search engines can find new ones you don't know about.

Much more useful would be a content filter that alarmed on certain types of textual content that could be configured by administrators, but we know of no firewall-integrated software that performs this function.

Content Vectoring Protocol

Content Vectoring Protocol allows firewall vendors and third party providers to create connectable content scanners through which certain types of content must pass before they clear the firewall. Gauntlet's virus protection and Java filtering are performed using CVP technology.

Security

Gauntlet secures the firewall with various policies that are actually accumulations OS service proxy rules. You are free to develop as many different policies as you need. These policies are then mapped to network interfaces for implementation. Two default policies are created when the product is installed:

- Trusted policies are mapped to network adapters that you identified as inside during the installation process
- Untrusted policies are mapped to interfaces you identified as outside during the installation process.

The trusted policy engages the following proxy services:

- FTP
- H.323
- HTTP

- LDAP
- Netshow
- NNTP
- PPTP
- RAP
- SMTP
- Streamworks
- Telnet
- VDOLive

The default trusted policy disallows the following proxy services:

- MS-SQL
- POP3
- SNMP
- SQL-GW
- Sybase-SQL

The effect of this policy is to allow most normal consumption content to pass through the firewall, but to block attempts by internal clients to interact directly with foreign untrusted e-mail servers or SQL servers.

The default untrusted policy allows the following services:

- FTP
- NNTP
- POP3
- SMTP
- Telnet

And disallows all others. This allows untrusted hosts to make FTP, NNTP, e-mail, and Telnet connections inside the network. Authentication is required for all of these services.

Interface

The interface is clean and simple—much less cartoonish than either Guardian or Firewall-1. The firewall manager application uses a tabbed view to switch between the various dialogs used to configure the firewall. As seems to be the standard among firewalls, the interface is not sizable and will not make use of a screen larger than 800 x 600.

Commercial Firewalls

PART 4

Documentation

All documentation included with the evaluation edition of Gauntlet comes in the form of the help file for the firewall manager. This makes the documentation somewhat difficult to read straight through, but easier to read in a digressionary click-through manner. HTML-based documentation would have combined the best of both worlds.

The documentation is light, focusing on simple explanations of broad security concepts and relying upon the administrator to figure out the technical nuances of firewall operation.

Cost and Support

Cost information about NAI Gauntlet can only be obtained on a per-configuration basis from a Gauntlet sales representative, which makes it very difficult to compare the firewall's price against the competition. I eventually found pricing on the Internet.

- 10 Node perpetual license: $1,750
- 25 Node perpetual license: $5,500
- 100 Node perpetual license: $17,500

Evaluation editions of Gauntlet firewall can be downloaded at www.nai.com.

Axent Raptor

Raptor firewall from Axent (formerly known as Eagle firewall from Raptor) is Gauntlet's strongest competitor in the area of security. Like Gauntlet, Raptor is a security proxy. Unlike Gauntlet, Raptor does not include the adaptive proxy filter technology that increases the speed of Gauntlet to near that of a stateful inspector. Raptor is among the fastest proxy firewalls, however, and is capable of handling dedicated circuits up to T3 (45Mbps).

Raptor runs on Windows NT, Sun Solaris (SPARC), and HP/UX (PARC), and is multi-threaded to take advantage of multiple processors. Raptor can be used with Windows NT Cluster Server to create high-availability firewall services.

Unlike most firewalls covered in this section, Raptor relies upon "best-fit" policies that are not order dependent. This means that the firewall applies the policy that most closely applies to each connection rather than filtering the connection down through a policy rule base until either a pass condition is met or the connection is dropped.

System requirements are:

- Windows NT 4.

- Intel Pentium II 300. Because Raptor is a proxy server, it is compute bound, so you should use the fastest available processor.
- 64MB RAM.
- 1GB Disk.
- Two network interfaces.

NOTE We did not have a running copy of Raptor in time to evaluate it for this book. The information contained in this section is based on Raptor's marketing documents and our evaluation of the information contained therein.

Major Feature Set

- Packet Security Filter for the gateway
- Network Address Translation
- Security Proxy
- Remote Authentication
- VPN support is provided through the add-on Raptor VPN and RaptorMobile VPN products.

Packet Filtering

Unlike other firewalls, Raptor does not allow network-level routing and therefore does not include a packet filter. All data, even low-level information like ICMP and TCP generic services, are routed through application-layer proxy services and regenerated on the firewall. This is the most secure method of passing information between interfaces, as it guarantees that no malformed packets can cross through the gateway.

In addition to performing no routing, the firewall automatically drops source-routed packets and packets containing internal addresses that appear on external interfaces. These packets are dropped before any connection proxying can be performed on them.

It is not entirely clear whether the firewall is capable of protecting the operating system's TCP/IP stack from denial-of-service attacks because it does not appear to include an NDIS-layer adapter driver. Considering that the installation requires service pack 3 and the addition of the teardrop patch (a patch specifically designed to eliminate a nasty denial of service attack in NT), it's likely that Raptor is indeed susceptible to network-level attacks directed at the operating system. None of these attacks provide access to the system, but they can deny Internet services.

Commercial Firewalls

PART 4

Network Address Translation (NAT)

Raptor relies primarily on its proxy service to perform the standard many-to-one address translation. But it also uses reverse address translation to support services on interior machines and true Network Address Translation through a feature Raptor calls Virtual Clients. The Virtual Clients facility also allows support for Illegal Network Address Translation.

Security Proxies

Raptor is primarily a security proxy that uses separate security proxies for every supported protocol. Third-party products must be used to perform virus scanning and Java filtration. Raptor includes security proxies for the following services:

- SMB/CIFS (Windows/LAN Manager network file and print sharing)
- SLQ*Net (Oracle SQL servers)
- Telnet
- FTP
- SMTP
- HTTP 1.1
- HTTP-FTP
- HTTP-Gopher and Gopher+
- HTTPs
- H.323
- Ping
- NNTP
- RealAudio and RealVideo
- NDS
- NTP (Network Time Protocol)

Authentication Support

Raptor can be configured to support the following authentication protocols:

- Security Dynamics ACE
- BellCore S/Key
- Defender (by Axent)
- CRYPTOCard

- Gateway password
- Windows NT Challenge/Response
- RADIUS
- TACACs+

Minor Feature Set

Raptor includes support for the following minor features:

MIMEsweeper virus scanning   This feature can be used to strip viruses out of downloads and attachments. Raptor is missing support for the standard CVP content vectoring protocol, however.

URL blocking   This feature is based on a client/server updated list of sites that have been categorized. There's no real way to keep up with the ever-changing world of the unseemly, however, so I doubt that any simple URL filter would actually keep people from accessing this sort of content.

Paging and audible alerts   This feature can be used if your firewall has a Hayes-compatible modem and/or a sound card. The paging alert is especially useful for administrators who want to maintain a real-time response capability.

Transparency   This feature is supported by Raptor, which is unusual for a relatively pure proxy. You won't have to configure client applications or rely upon clients that are proxy compatible to use Raptor.

Illegal NAT   This support feature, using the Virtual Clients facility, allows you to perform client address translation through the gateway for networks that use illegal IP addresses.

Dual DNS   This configuration feature allows different DNS names to be served to the public and private sides of the proxy.

Security

Raptor's gateway security architecture is extremely strong; it's highly unlikely that attacks through the firewall would succeed due to the proxy-only architecture. The application-layer support for Network Address Translation is also very strong and transparent.

Raptor's Achilles' heel is its reliance upon a stable operating system and TCP/IP stack. Telling requirements in the Raptor installation documents (like the necessity for the teardrop patch) show that everything in the firewall operates above the network layer. There appears to be no MAC-layer protection (such as a packet filter) for the operating system itself, so there's no support for things like anti-spoofing. This is a fairly common problem for pure proxies; Microsoft's Proxy Server suffers from the same problem. Ultimately, this means that hackers could be able to bring your firewall down and cause a denial of service, but they would not be able to penetrate the firewall to access your secured network.

Interface

Raptor version 6 uses the Microsoft management console to achieve a highly integrated and very useful user interface—it's the best user interface I've seen on a firewall. Raptor calls its MMC snap-in the Raptor Management Console, or RMC. The RMC is client/ server based and can support any number of firewalls. The interface is hierarchical following the architectural requirements of the MMC. Figure 13.3 shows the user interface for Axent Raptor firewall.

Figure 13.3   Axcent Raptor firewall user interface.

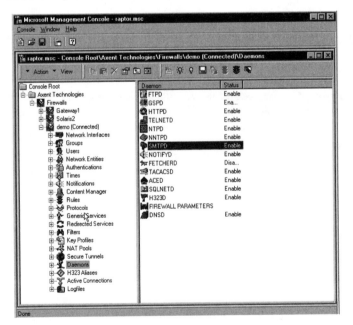

Management objects are completely hierarchical and very coherent, although the management interface is more complex than most firewalls. Network administrators familiar with the MMC should have no problems.

Documentation

Unfortunately, no evaluation edition of Raptor is available at Axent's Web site, which I consider to be a major flaw in their marketing. The Web site is driven by marketing rather than customer needs, so it's somewhat incoherent. The only significant documentation about the firewall available from the site is the downloadable firewall documentation.

The included documentation is very thorough and is task oriented rather than technology/training oriented, although solid coverage of basic topics is provided.

Cost and Support

Support is via the Web site or support agreement only.

Licensing costs for the firewall (no VPN):

- 1-100 users: $4,000
- 1-250 users: $8,500
- Unlimited users: $12,500

Standard support

- 25 users: $375
- 100 users: $600
- 250 users: $1,275

Unlimited: $1,875 per year

24×7 (no relation to this book) priority support is purchased as a single product rather than on a per-incident basis. Prices vary, depending upon which product modules you have. Prices without VPN support are:

- 100 users: $900
- 250 users: $2,000
- Unlimited: $2,800

Microsoft Proxy Server

Microsoft's solitary security product is MS-Proxy Server, now in its second release. MS-Proxy Server is a caching HTTP and SOCKS proxy that can be used to create a non-routing bastion host. In our opinion, MS-Proxy Server is the least secure product this book discusses, as it does not include transport-layer filtering or service-specific security proxies. It relies upon the operating system for filtering, authentication, and VPN services, and it does not provide Network Address Translation.

System requirements:

- Pentium 166
- Windows NT Server 4
- 2-24GB Hard disk, depending upon caching requirements
- 64MB RAM

These requirements are for medium- to large-sized businesses. Microsoft recommends one server for every 2,000 clients.

Major Feature Set

MS-Proxy Server supports only two proxy services: a Web proxy and a generic SOCKS proxy. MS-Proxy Server's compliance with the major firewall features is detailed below:

- Proxy services consist of a Web proxy and a SOCKS proxy; no other proxy services are provided, but the SOCKS proxy is capable of proxying a number of protocols such as Telnet, FTP, RealAudio, SMTP, etc. No protocol-specific filtering is performed on any service but HTTP.
- Packet filtration is not supported by MS-Proxy Server. Windows NT Server's built-in packet filtering must be used to protect the bastion host.
- Network Address Translation is not available in Windows NT 4. Windows 2000 supports NAT natively.
- Authentication is not provided by MS-Proxy Server, but is available via Windows NT's Challenge/Response architecture. This authentication is among the weakest authentication schemes in use.
- VPN support is not provided by MS-Proxy Server, available via Windows NT's PPTP encrypted tunnel. PPTP is not a particularly secure tunnel and is susceptible to numerous information leaks and denial-of-service attacks.

Minor Feature Set

Microsoft Proxy server supports the following minor features:

- Reverse proxying allows a single MS-Proxy Server to act as the single IP front end for a number of different servers by streaming HTTP to the various Web servers. This proxy function occurs at the application layer and does not involve IP address translation.
- Remote Management is provided by the Web administration tools for Windows NT and the Internet Service Manager (MMC snap-in).

- Third-party software interface for features like Anti-virus and Java blocking software is available via third party ISAPI filter plug-ins, as is URL filtration; proxy server does not support CVP.

- Strong logging features are provided, allowing two levels of logging: Standard and Verbose.

Security

MS-Proxy Server is not a firewall, despite Microsoft's assertions that it is. In our opinion, MS-Proxy Server cannot safely run in a production environment without at least a stateful packet filter in front of it (or running on the same machine) because Proxy Server does not include the basic mechanisms to protect itself from exploitation and denial-of-service attacks from the Internet.

Proxy server relies upon Windows NT Server's TCP/IP stack for network-layer security. This stack has been shown to be vulnerable to a number of different denial-of-service attacks and should not be considered secure without additional filtering at the NDIS level below TCP/IP.

MS-Proxy Server does not disable IP forwarding by default between the internal and external interface. Security is not provided with routing enabled because the bastion host will merely act as a router.

WARNING The MS-Proxy Server installation process does not disable IP forwarding or warn if it's enabled. This is a serious security flaw that you must check for and disable manually if you use MS-Proxy Server, since the software is only secure if IP forwarding is disabled.

The MS-Proxy Server does not disable or control Windows NT's built-in TCP/IP filters to protect the bastion host against denial-of-service attacks. If these ports are left open or surreptitiously opened, the bastion host is vulnerable to exploitation or denial of service.

WARNING The MS-Proxy Server installation process does not configure IP filters to block the default listening ports of 135 and 139, which can be used to perpetrate denial-of-service attacks or gain control of the server. You must configure Windows NT to filter these ports manually.

MS-Proxy Server is not capable of acting transparently; host applications must be configured to use the proxy. This puts considerable additional load on desktop support technicians. Only applications capable of being configured for a proxy can be used.

MS-Proxy Server does not support security proxies for anything but the HTTP protocol, and it's doubtful that the HTTP proxy provides significant security. The generic SOCKS proxy does not perform any protocol-specific blocking or filtration.

In sum, MS-Proxy Server is simply a caching Web server. It provides a modicum of security in that it is possible to disable network-layer routing to the Internet, but this does not represent much in the way of true security since so many attacks utilize the application layer exclusively.

The solitary security advantage of MS-Proxy Server is its ability to use the SOCKS proxy to allow internal IPX-based clients to connect to the proxy server, which will then issue TCP/IP requests on the public network. This allows administrators to connect existing IPX internal hosts to the Internet and provides a strong measure of internal security if TCP/IP is not routed or used internally. To penetrate inside the network, hackers would have to take control of the bastion host itself, not merely pass through it because a conversion from TCP/IP to IPX is necessary for penetration beyond the border. Trojan horses that open TCP/IP channels out through a firewall would not work because the clients upon which the Trojan horse must run would not have TCP/IP stacks. With a good stateful filter like Firewall-1 or Guardian running to protect the MS-Proxy Server, this scheme could provide a very strong measure of security.

Interface

MS-Proxy Server is administered through the Internet Service Manager, a snap-in to the Microsoft Management Console. The ISM is familiar to anyone who has run an Internet Information Server 4 Web site or installed the Option Pack for Windows NT Server 4.

The ISM presents a hierarchical view of the running Internet services on your bastion host, which could include Web, FTP, and NNTP services if you are running them on the same host. Administration and configuration is simple and easy. Remote administration is provided by connecting to the proxy server using the ISM on any other NT machine inside the network.

Cost and Support

MS-Proxy Server costs a mere $1,000. Unlike most Microsoft BackOffice products, no per-client license is necessary for the proxy server or for Windows NT Servers that act only as Internet or proxy servers. An evaluation edition of MS-Proxy Server 2.0 is available at www.microsoft.com/proxy.

Support is via Microsoft's standard support channels. Copious configuration information and a very strong knowledge base are available on the Web; anyone familiar with Windows NT Server should have no problem supporting MS-Proxy Server. Standard telephone technical support is included for free during installation and setup, and priority support can be purchased for $195 per call. Microsoft has a massive network of certified consultants in every locality in the U.S. if additional support is necessary; consulting prices vary greatly.

Buying a Firewall

Buying a firewall for Windows NT can be a frustrating experience for even the most patient network administrators. Because firewalls are not common enough to be retail products, you can't buy them at a store. This puts the software into the byzantine world of network software distribution that I first ran into as a fledgling network integrator years ago.

Two companies, Ingram Micro and Tech-Data, are the largest distributors of networking software in the U.S., and for most firewall products, they are the only top-level distributors. Essentially, software vendors sell the product to these two distributors, and they sell them to everyone else.

Both companies require very high levels of guaranteed annual sales from a company that wants to purchase software from them. So unless you work for the U.S. Government or a company as large as Johnson & Johnson, you can forget buying the software directly.

This means you have to purchase from the third tier: The Value-Added Reseller or VAR. VARs range from large integrators like EDS, SAIC, and the big accounting firms to small independent networking firms. VARs have very high margins because their volume is typically very low; you can expect to pay as much as 30% over cost for software you purchase from a VAR. Even large VARs that concentrate specifically on the firewall market will rarely sell more than 100 firewalls a year, so their volume is never high enough to warrant selling firewalls near their cost.

To their credit, VARs are generally very well trained to install firewall software—but that too will cost.

By the time you purchase software from a VAR, including their markup and consulting time to install the firewall, you can expect to pay 100% more than the actual cost of the software to get it installed.

While this is acceptable for companies that have no internal expertise, it's a vexing problem for those of us who are well qualified to install firewall software if we can just get our hands on it.

In the last two years, the Internet has sprung to our rescue—sort of. It is now possible to buy anything that Ingram Micro or TechData sells through Internet storefronts like hardwarestreet.com and buy.com. The low-price search engine, www.shopper.com, polls data from hundreds of online retailers on a daily basis. By searching for your product at shopper.com and sorting by price order, you can find the absolute lowest possible price for any software or networking hardware product.

Internet-based resellers apply a fixed low markup (typically 5%) to the prices charged by Ingram Micro, TechData, and their other suppliers, irrespective of how much volume they sell of a specific product. Because of their massive overall volume, they get the best possible pricing from top-level distributors, and they don't differentiate consumer products from corporate products when you purchase them. By purchasing directly over the Internet from vendors like these, you can save a tremendous amount of money and avoid the entire VAR market—if you're qualified to install the products yourself. You'll also have to have a credit card with a limit high enough to handle the entire order, since these resellers usually will accept no other form of payment.

The dark side of Internet purchasing comes when you have a problem. You can forget getting in touch with a qualified support technician, and since most software vendors push support down to their VARs, you'll be left out in the cold if you didn't purchase the product from a VAR. Internet resellers are not equipped to support anything. You can also expect trouble if you have a problem with your order, its shipment, or the product once it arrives. These resellers are optimized to sell over the Internet, not to deal with problems. If anything goes wrong, you can expect it to take days

merely to get in touch with a human being at the reseller's office and two to four weeks to resolve your problem.

You also have to be exceptionally careful that you're ordering the right product. There's no human to tell you that the item you've clicked is just a client license upgrade and not the full product; you have to infer from a line item like "FW-1 25 USER UG" that the product being referred to is an upgrade rather than a full edition. Always find the vendor's product number in the product description and compare it to the vendor's Web site to make sure you're purchasing the right piece of software.

Most of the firewall products in this chapter can be purchased directly over the Internet by searching through www.shopper.com.

24*seven* **CASE STUDY**

14

Unix Firewalls

A version of UNIX exists for every microprocessor being mass-produced today and for nearly every type of computer. UNIX is the closest thing to a universal operating system that has ever existed.

Most computer system manufacturers typically licensed UNIX from AT&T or Berkeley and quickly ported it to their new computers after writing a C compiler in Assembly Language for the new processor. This allowed them to get to market quickly with new advanced hardware without having to wait for the development of a custom operating system. Their development teams then typically used the UNIX that ran on the platform to develop a custom operating system specifically for the platform. As a result, many workstation class computers have "their own" operating system in addition to UNIX.

Examples of platforms that have proprietary operating systems as well as vendor-supported versions of UNIX include the Digital VAX (VMS and Digital UNIX) and Apple Macintosh (MacOS and A/UX). You may find that although a firewall may not exist for the custom operating system, you can run the vendor-supported UNIX (or a port of Linux) on the computer to use as a firewall.

Unfortunately, no two UNIX systems are exactly the same, and despite numerous half-hearted attempts at standardizing the myriad of operating system components and application interfaces among the various vendors, few UNIX systems are compatible enough with each other to run code compiled for a different variation. For example, a graphics manipulation application written for Silicon Graphics IRIX won't run under Solaris on a Sun workstation. This has hobbled the UNIX software market so badly that dark horse operating systems like Windows NT have been able to make serious inroads into the workstation and server market.

Most commercial versions of UNIX (and all the versions discussed in this chapter) are based on either original AT&T UNIX, whereas most open-source UNIXes are based on either the derivation developed somewhat independently by the University of California at Berkeley, or on Linux, a completely independent version of the UNIX operating system.

AltaVista Firewall 98

AltaVista Firewall is a high-end security proxy. Digital Equipment Corporation (now a part of Compaq), which makes the AltaVista software package, is one of the oldest firewall vendors. Their software runs on both Windows NT and Unix, presenting a similar interface to administrators of either system. AltaVista Firewall 98 is both a packet filter and a proxying firewall, securing your network against IP-level denial-of-service attacks on your Internet link and making sure data that travel through your firewall conform to protocol specifications.

Pros	Cons
Runs on Unix and NT	No stateful inspector
Easy to use	No Network Address Translator
Centralized management	
VPN	
Strong remote management	
OS hardening	
Transparent proxies	

Where the AltaVista firewall really shines (especially in comparison to just about any other complete firewall package) is in ease of use. The documentation is superb, the package is easy to install, and the setup and maintenance operations are straightforward. Digital has gone to a great deal of effort to demystify the process of securing your network against Internet attack.

NOTE   Installing AltaVista Firewall on Windows NT is a little unusual in that it installs as a service, but other than that, it's easy going.

System Requirements:

- Alpha or Intel processor running Windows NT; Alpha processor running DIGITAL UNIX.

- Two or three network adapters.

- CD-ROM reader.

- Disk space required for installation: 11MB for Windows NT; 25MB for DIGITAL UNIX.

- Disk space required for use: 2GB for Windows NT; 1GB for DIGITAL UNIX.

- Memory required: 48MB for Windows NT; 32MB for DIGITAL UNIX; 64MB is recommended.

- Windows NT Version 4.0 (Service Pack 3 or higher); DIGITAL UNIX Version 4.0B,C,D.

NOTE   AltaVista's SQL*Net proxy does not run on Alpha platforms running Windows NT.

Major Feature Set

AltaVista Firewall supports the following major features:

- Packet filter (Anti-spoofing, IP restriction)

- Application Proxies

- Authentication (Security Dynamics, Crypto Card, S/Key, RACAL, Watchword)

- AltaVista Tunnel VPN (separate product)

AltaVista's packet filter is not a stateful inspector; rather, AltaVista breaks the TCP/IP routing link on the host machine and forces traffic through the application proxy. Because no routing is performed through the firewall, there's no Network Address Translator. The proxy applications automatically hide IP addresses from the outside world. The AltaVista firewall itself is vulnerable to attacks that target the operating system's TCP/IP implementation.

AltaVista is based on a strong suite of security proxy applications for all of the common Internet services. In addition, a generic TCP and UDP SOCK proxy is provided (sometimes called a circuit level gateway) so you can create your own proxies for clients that support SOCKS.

The user authentication supports all the standard authentication types as well as one-time passwords. VPN and remote access is provided by the separate AltaVista Tunnel product.

Commercial
Firewalls

PART 4

Minor Feature Set

AltaVista Firewall provides the following minor features:

- Graphical interface
- Port redirection (virus scanning, Java blocking, URL blocking)
- CVP Support
- Split DNS
- Real-time monitoring and reporting
- Firewall modification logging
- OS hardening

AltaVista's user interface is very easy to use. The Web-based interface is especially easy to use and coherent; most administrators will choose it over the local management interface client. The Web-based administrator allows for strong remote administration.

The firewall supports the Content Vectoring Protocol, which allows you to connect to servers running virus-scanning and other content-scanning software. The firewall includes Java blocking and URL filtering services.

Split (or dual) DNS is provided to allow you to use internal names inside your network that are not accessible publicly.

AltaVista's real-time monitoring and reporting facilities are top notch; administrators can configure logging and alarming on any firewall events using e-mail or scripting to perform pager notification.

AltaVista Firewall performs very thorough OS hardening during the installation process. Known vulnerabilities in the operating system are scanned for and corrected, and all unnecessary services are shut down. This reduces the number of back doors available to hackers.

Interface

AltaVista Firewall's local and remote Web-based management console is complete and detailed, providing full information about the internal processes of the firewall, proxy services, logging, and report generation.

Security

AltaVista subscribes to the policy (endorsed by us as well) that real security means proxying the protocols and not just filtering packets between your network and the Internet. While AltaVista relies on the host operating system to fend off IP-level attacks, both NT and Solaris at the latest patch levels provide adequate protection from known IP exploits. AltaVista provides proxies for the most popular protocols, including:

- FTP—A standard FTP service proxy.
- Gopher—proxies the text-based hypertext protocol that (barely) predates the Web.
- HTTP—for basic port 80 proxying or for Web traffic on other ports, but using the HTTP protocol.
- S-HTTP—for secure Web proxying or for secure Web traffic on other ports, but using the S-HTTP protocol.
- SMTP—Stores and forwards email delivered to the firewall for delivery on your local network.
- NNTP—Forwards Usenet news through the firewall.
- POP—Provides a channel for internal clients to access external e-mail servers.
- Telnet—Proxies command-line control of remote computers.

The lack of a filter component below the TCP/IP stack is AltaVista's Achilles heel. Although exploitation isn't really possible, undiscovered denial-of-service attacks will probably continue to be a problem.

Documentation, Cost, and Support

AltaVista Firewall's documentation is lighter than most for firewall theory, but it is task driven and not difficult to read. Support for AltaVista firewall is provided via e-mail and the Web.

Pricing for AltaVista Firewall is as follows:

- 25 clients Windows NT: $2,495
- 50 clients Windows NT, DIGITAL UNIX: $3,995
- 200 clients Windows NT, DIGITAL UNIX: $7,995
- Unlimited number of clients Windows NT, DIGITAL UNIX: $14,995

TIP You can download an evaluation edition of AltaVista Firewall at `www.altavista.software.digital.com`.

Unicenter TNG Network Security Option

In really big networks containing hundreds or thousands of computers, the task of administering to all those clients and servers can be overwhelming. Computer Associates developed

Commercial Firewalls

PART 4

the Unicenter TNG suite of tools to help network administrators centrally administer to a large number of network devices, including client workstations, file servers, messaging servers, network devices, routers, and firewalls. The portion that implements a firewall for Unicenter-managed networks is the Network Security Option for Unicenter TNG.

The Network Security Option runs on various versions of Unix and on Windows NT. Unicenter provides for centralized management of multiple Network Security Option firewalls distributed throughout your enterprise, providing ease of configuration and use as well as a consistent security policy for your network. Because the Network Security Option ties into the rest of the Unicenter resource management tools, you can combine user authentication and resource access rules with the typical address and port restrictions of packet filtering.

The Network Security Option provides stateful packet inspection, Network Address Translation, packet inspection and rewriting for supported protocols, generic proxying for redirectable protocols, and centralized authentication. The sophisticated security event monitoring, logging, and response features of this firewall even allow for automatic reconfiguration of the security policy when suspicious or threatening activity is detected, which allows the system to lock itself down and gives you time to respond to the problem.

Pros	Cons
Runs on Unix and NT	Cost
Integrates with Unicenter	Requires Unicenter TNG
Centralized management	Long Learning Curve
Strong remote management	
Fast and flexible	

Platform requirements:

- Intel Pentium Microprocessor or Unix workstation of equivalent power
- 64MB RAM (128MB recommended)
- 500MB hard disk drive, additional for caching
- Unix or NT
- At least two network interfaces

Major Feature Set

Unicenter TNG Security Option provides the following major features:

- Stateful packet filter
- Secure Proxy for numerous protocols

- Network Address Translator
- Secure authentication

The included stateful inspection filter is very strong and comparable to the stateful inspection services provided by Checkpoint Firewall-1. Network Address Translation is built into the stateful inspector.

The proxy functionality of the Unicenter TNG Security Option doesn't really occur at the Application Layer; protocol payloads are rewritten directly by the stateful inspector rather than being handed off to a separate Application Layer service, which regenerates the connection in it's entirety. Rewriting provides much the same benefit; portions of the protocol that the firewall doesn't know about can't be rewritten, and such parameters as proper buffer length can be checked to prevent buffer overrun conditions.

Minor Feature Set

Unicenter TNG Security option provides the following minor features:

- Centralized administration
- Integration with overall enterprise management tools
- Databases logging, e-mail upon event detection, reconfiguration upon event detection

A central policy-based management application (Unicenter TNG) provides strong centralized management for the firewall. Policies can easily be created and applied across the enterprise from the Unicenter control application. Unicenter TNG also provides a platform for strong integration with the other IT management options available for the system and provides the foundation for the log, alert, event detection, and response features.

Interface

The Network Security Option provides a graphical interface for both Windows NT and for Unix. Firewalls appear as resources to be administered from the Unicenter administration suite. Because the Network Security Option uses the same framework as all of the other Unicenter options, administrators in a Unicenter shop will find the interface to be friendly and comfortable.

The graphical interface makes it easy to set up rules and enable or disable specific services for particular computers or users. The security objects are integrated with the other components of the Unicenter system (such as the Single Log On option), sparing you the effort of both establishing user account information and recording security restrictions in multiple locations.

Commercial Firewalls

PART 4

Security

The Network Security Option uses a stateful inspection packet filter, which keeps track of connection information across multiple packets. These include UDP packets, which do not retain session information. The packet filter checks all the typical IP packet features such as source and destination addresses, port numbers, options set, SYN bit, ICMP messages, and so on. In addition, the packet filter can integrate into its rule set additional information obtained from the rest of the Unicenter framework, including user identity, allowed access times, and network resource restrictions. The firewall checks every packet before the IP stack processes it, thereby blocking attacks against the firewall itself using malformed and maliciously constructed IP packets, such as the Ping of Death, teardrop attacks, and so on.

One performance advantage of the firewall is that it can perform the equivalent of protocol proxying for some protocols by directly manipulating the IP packets, rather than handing the packets off to a separate proxy server application. This provides for much faster proxying and therefore increased throughput and reduced latency between your network and the Internet. The firewall also provides for generic port redirection and integration with the Internet Web Management option to Unicenter TNG.

Documentation, Cost, and Support

Using the TNG Network Security Option requires a Unicenter TNG network infrastructure, which is designed for larger businesses. Because pricing varies widely and depends largely upon your Unicenter infrastructure, there's no meaningful way for us to provide pricing information. Contact a CA sales representative directly to obtain pricing information if you use or want to use UniCenter TNG.

TIP   You can get more information about Unicenter TNG at www.cai.com.

SecurIT Firewall

The SecurIT firewall from SLM (formerly MilkyWay) is available for both Unix and NT. This firewall, like the free TIS toolkit described in Chapter 12, does not perform any packet filtering. Instead it provides application-level proxies for each of the protocols that will pass from the internal network to the Internet. Also like TIS, the SecurIT firewall uses authentication to provide user-based as well as IP address based access control. Where SecurIT really shines, however, is in the wide variety of protocols it "scrubs" or provides proxy redirection for. In addition to the proxies, SecurIT has a strong VPN component that allows you to establish encrypted IP tunnels between your protected LANs over the Internet.

Pros	Cons
Runs on Unix and NT	No packet filtering
Supports a wide range of protocols	NT Version does not harden OS
VPN	Cost
Centralized authentication	Difficult to acquire
High speed application proxying	

Platform requirements:

- Sun Sparc 5 or any Ultra-SPARC, Intel Pentium
- 2GB hard disk drive
- 32MB RAM
- PCI Quad adapter
- 2 or more network cards
- CD-ROM drive

Major Feature Set

SecurIT provides the following major features:

- Proxy services for a wide variety of protocols
- VPN
- Secure authentication

SecurIT provides numerous security proxies for common Internet protocols, which makes its protocol security very strong.

SecurIT uses its generic TCP proxy functionality to perform client hiding, a function their documentation calls Network Address Translation. The functionality is not equivalent to true network-layer NAT.

Secure authentication is performed via Bellcore's (now Telcordia's) S/Key one-time-password algorithm.

Conspicuously missing from the major feature set is packet filtering and Network Address Translation. Neither function is necessary in a strong security proxy as long as the base operating system is sufficiently hardened. Neither Solaris nor NT is hardened in our opinion, and this considerably weakens the ability of firewalls that do not implement their own packet filtering accordingly. SecurIT ships with a version of Solaris that has apparently been hardened, but the NT version is susceptible to a wide range of denial-of-service attacks.

Minor Feature Set

SecurIT provides the following minor features:

- Logging to databases, e-mail upon event detection, reconfiguration upon event detection
- SQL proxying
- Remote administration

As with most true firewalls, SecurIT is capable of logging to databases and transmitting e-mail to alert on security events. A SQL security proxy is provided to support SQL*Net transactions through the firewall.

Security

SecurIT does not filter packets before they are delivered to the IP stack for processing. The firewall relies on the underlying operating system to be resistant to IP-level attacks. Both Solaris and Windows NT at their most current patch or service pack have finally been made highly resistant to known attacks, but undiscovered vulnerabilities almost certainly exist in both operating systems. SecurIT for Solaris ships with a hardened version of Solaris.

Instead, SecurIT is a proxy server, which examines the data portions of IP packets to ensure that the traffic traversing a particular port conforms to the protocol that for that port (that only HTTP requests and replies are going over port 80 for example).

SecurIT is designed with performance in mind. This highly optimized proxy server uses threads and shared memory to minimize the time required to filter the proxied protocols, allowing more traffic to pass through the firewall while still fully examining all of the data to ensure that it conforms to protocol specifications.

SecurIT comes with a number of application-specific firewall proxies. In addition to providing content filtering for the specific protocol (guaranteeing that the port is actually used by the appropriate protocol instead of some other program), each protocol can be configured to block certain IP addresses and Internet domains. SecurIT provides proxies for the following protocols:

- FTP—A standard FTP service proxy.
- Generic SOCKS—Allows the administrator to redirect easily proxied protocols by specifying the address and port to forward TCP and UDP packets to.

- Gopher—Proxies the text-based hypertext protocol that (barely) predates the Web.
- HTTP++—Allows basic Web traffic, but allows the administrator to block applets and URLs.
- HTTP—For basic port 80 proxying or for Web traffic on other ports, but using the HTTP protocol.
- LDAP—Allows network clients to access directory servers exterior to your firewall.
- Mail—Stores and forwards e-mail delivered to the firewall for delivery on your local network.
- NNTP—Forwards Usenet news through the firewall.
- POP—Provides a channel for internal clients to access external e-mail servers.
- Real Media—Channels audio and video conforming to the Real Media standard through the firewall.
- RPC—Provides for secure Remote Procedure Call through the firewall.
- SSL—Forwards secure socket communication through the firewall.
- Telnet—Proxies command-line control of remote computers.
- VDO Live—Mediates VDO multimedia from internal clients to external multimedia servers.

Documentation, Cost, and Support

The SecurIT firewall is sold by the number of open simultaneous connections (sessions) rather than the number of IP addresses inside the network. This means, for example, that a 15-user network could probably get away with a 10-session version of the firewall if only 66 percent of the users were using the Internet at any one time. Prices shown are for the Solaris edition with one year of included support. The U.S. distributor would not quote pricing for the NT version, as they considered Windows NT operating system to be nonsecure. The product is sold primarily to military and government channels since SLM has no significant marketing through commercial channels.

The product ships with a hardened version of Solaris so there's no need to purchase the operating system. Hardware costs for a Sun Ultra-5 run about $5,000.

- 10 sessions: $3,600
- 40 sessions: $7,200
- 100 sessions: $16,200
- Unlimited: $23,400
- VPN: +$1,200

Commercial
Firewalls

PART 4

TIP   You can browse SLM's Web site at www.milkyway.com. To purchase SecurIT, contact Neoteric at (212) 625-9300.

WatchGuard FireBox II

Most of the systems I've discussed so far require you to first install an operating system such as Unix or Windows NT and then install the firewall software. WatchGuard makes it easy by shipping you a completely preconfigured device with the operating system (Linux version 2.0) and their firewall (WatchGuard FireBox II) preinstalled and ready for you to customize and use. You don't need a monitor and keyboard for this firewall; you can install it in your equipment rack next to your hubs and routers like any other network device. To configure it, connect to it over the LAN using the remote management tools.

Pros	**Cons**
Integrated, preconfigured unit	Hardware not field upgradable
Compact	
VPN support	
Centralized authentication	
High-speed application proxying	
Cost includes unlimited users	

Device Configuration:

- 3 10/100Mbps Ethernet ports
- 2 serial ports
- 2 Cardbus slots
- Flash disk storage

Major Feature Set

Firebox II provides the following major features:

- Dynamic packet filtering
- application proxies
- NAT and port forwarding
- Authentication support for Firebox, NT server, Radius server, and cryptocard in separate authentication package
- VPN using IPsec or WatchGuard proprietary tunnel software in separate VPN package

Firebox provides dynamic packet filtering that, while not exactly connection oriented, is capable of preventing exploitations against the firewall itself. The firewall is primarily a security proxy and includes a strong set of proxy applications.

Network Address Translation is fully supported, providing port forwarding for internal servers as well as client hiding.

Authentication and VPN products are not included in the firewall.

Minor Feature Set

FireBox provides the following minor features:

- Logging, e-mail notification, execution of arbitrary programs
- Scan detection, spoofing detection, and automatic blocking
- Remote management from Windows desktop
- Web access control and network management tools available as separate packages

The firewall includes the standard set of e-mail notifications and allows the execution of arbitrary applications upon event detection.

The included Windows support and management tools are by far the best I've seen. Few firewalls include good support for real-time monitoring; Firebox provides excellent real-time monitoring tools.

Interface

The graphical Windows-based management tools make it easy to customize the Watch-Guard firewall devices for your network. Starting from one central computer you can remotely administer any number of firewalls and, using the centrally stored policy files, you can keep a uniform set of rules for all the firewalls on your LAN. The network management tools (available as a separate package) give you a visual indication of the condition of your network, including bandwidth used, traffic flow according to service type, sources and destinations of IP traffic, and other data link information.

The monitoring tools included with Firebox are superior to any other monitoring tools I've seen. Real-time views of all user connections are available, as are per-service and per-machine statistics. How useful real-time monitors for real security purposes are is debatable, but they sure are cool. Figure 14.1 shows the real-time user connection facility running from WatchGuard's demonstration software.

The other management tools included for the firewall exhibit the same level of software maturity, contrasting well with the plethora of clunky Windows managers and Web-based administration tools available for the majority of the firewalls I've surveyed.

Commercial Firewalls

PART 4

Figure 14.1   WatchGuard Firebox Real-Time Connection Monitoring

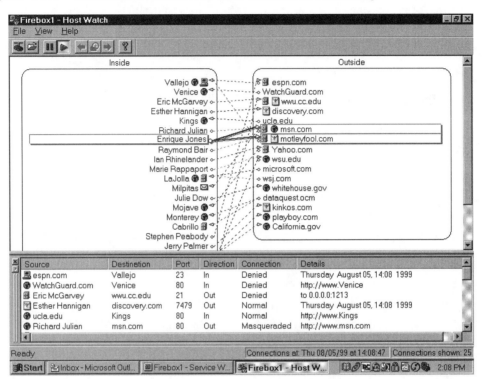

Security

The FireBox firewalls perform both packet filtering, Network Address Translation, and protocol proxying. Appropriate configuration of the packet filtering software will protect your firewall from IP-level denial-of-service attacks, while the application level proxies ensure that the ports allowed through your firewall aren't misused by back-door software to channel through data not supported by the appropriate protocol.

FireBox includes custom security proxies for the following protocols:

- HTTP
- SMTP
- FTP
- H.323
- RealAudio/Video

- VDO Live
- DCE RPC

Because FireBox is based on standard Linux and open source security tools, vulnerabilities for that operating system may affect the firewall. The advantage of using a pre-configured system rather than doing it yourself is that their standard configuration has been tested for various vulnerabilities and is configured by security experts.

Documentation, Cost, and Support

Documentation is provided in HTML format, but is somewhat context sensitive. The firewall management tools launch your Web browser and display the appropriate help page when you press the Help button. Documentation is clear and task driven; most administrators will have no problem with it. The firewall is sold with support for unlimited users.

Pricing for WatchGuard Firebox II is as follows:

- $3,200 for the product including 12 months of support
- $650 per Firebox Security subscription to Livesecurity for 12 months

---

TIP   WatchGuard's Web site is at www.watchguard.com.

NetWall

Digital isn't the only large corporation that has taken its internal network security expertise and packaged it as a firewall product. Group Bull, a major European manufacturer of electronics and software also has their firewall product called NetWall. This firewall runs on Sun's Solaris and IBM's AIX versions of UNIX as well as Windows NT. The secure remote control software for the firewall runs on Windows platforms as well as AIX.

NetWall gives you the full range of security options to work with—from stateful packet inspection to application level proxies for a wide variety of protocols, NAT, VPN, authentication, load balancing, remote control, and support for third-party content inspectors thrown in as well.

Pros	Cons
High speed	cost
High reliability	No content blocking
Centralized authentication	
Versatile proxying	

As with IBM's offering, NetWall suffers from a difficult setup and a lack of integration among software components. Configuring the firewall is not particularly easy compared to the majority of firewall offerings in this book.

Major Feature Set

NetWall offers the following major features:

- Stateful inspection filter
- Authentication
- NAT
- Proxies
- Optional VPN

NetWall includes a strong stateful inspection filter and Network Address Translator that supports both static and dynamic address mapping.

NetWall supports a broad range of authentication features, including low security options like ASCII plain text passwords and higher security options like Radius, MD/5 Challenge/Response, Bellcore S/Key one-time passwords, SecurID Cards, and smart cards. NetWall also includes a complete set of APIs to allow third-party vendors or organizations with programming support to create other authentication options.

The remote access VPN is different than the firewall-to-firewall VPN. The remote access VPN is somewhat unique in that it is based on a SOCKS proxy transmitted through an SSL tunnel, rather than IPSec. The remote access VPN supports standard 40, 56, and 128 bit key lengths. The firewall-firewall VPN is based on DES and triple-DES, and supports key lengths up to 192 bits.

Minor Feature Set

NetWall offers the following minor features:

- Load balancing and high availability
- Support for third-party content scanners
- Central management

Multiple NetWall firewalls can be used to balance the connection load between them and to continue operating in the event that one of them fails. This allows you to provide high availability of Internet services and protects you in the event of a denial-of-service attack.

NetWall supports content vectoring to third-party content scanning applications such as MimeSweeper or VirusWall.

Firewall management can be performed remotely from any Windows or AIX workstation. Communications between the firewall and the management workstation is encrypted.

Interface

NetWall's GUI interface is typical of policy-based firewall managers, providing a similar look and feel as Checkpoint Firewall-1's interface. As with Firewall-1, the interface can be run locally on the firewall or on a remote management workstation.

Security

NetWall's IP filter performs stateful packet inspection, keeping track of the state of TCP and UDP data streams (the state mechanism allows the firewall to keep track of UDP in spite of the fact that UDP doesn't keep session information in the packets). The NetWall packet-inspection engine can also inspect the data portion of some IP packets directly, which simplifies and improves the proxying performance of certain protocols. Protocol filters that the IP filter accelerates include HTTP, SMTP, FTP, Telnet, RPC, SQL* Net, and SAP.

While the IP filter accelerates the proxies and protects the firewall server from IP-level attacks, the application proxies make sure that only safe data traffic transits your firewall. NetWall comes with an impressive range of proxies, including the following:

- FTP—Filters FTP traffic.
- Generic—Allows the administrator to redirect easily proxied protocols by specifying the address and port to which TCP and UDP packets should be forwarded.
- Gopher—Proxies the non-multimedia hypertext protocol that (barely) predates the Web.
- HTTP—Proxies for basic port 80 or for Web traffic on other ports, but using the HTTP protocol.
- SHTTP/SSL—Proxies for encrypted Web traffic and for Secure Socket Layer communication.
- LDAP—Allows network clients to access directory servers exterior to your firewall.
- SMTP—Stores and forwards e-mail delivered to the firewall for delivery on your local network.
- IMAP4—Mediates mail delivery and mailbox checking through the firewall.
- NNTP—Forwards Usenet news through the firewall.
- POP3—Provides a channel for internal clients to access external e-mail servers.

- Real Audio/Video—Channels audio and video conforming to the Real Media standard through the firewall (AIX version only).

- H.323—Allows for videoconferencing through the firewall (AIX version only).

- SSL—Forwards secure socket communication through the firewall.

- Telnet—Proxies command-line control of remote computers.

- TN3270—Proxies TCP/IP access to mainframe and minicomputers.

- TNVIP—Allows TNVIP access across the firewall.

- SOCKSV5—Redirects protocols specifically designed to be redirected through the SOCKS proxy service.

Documentation, Cost, and Support

Bull's Web site directs you to NetScape to purchase the firewall in North America, but when I contacted NetScape, they had no idea they sold the firewall. They forwarded us to a distributor who'd never heard of it and who tried to sell us on the virtues of Firewall-1. I could not figure out how to purchase NetWall in the U.S., but European distribution is probably more firm. I could also not find pricing information about the firewall.

TIP   Group Bull's Web site is located at `www.bull.com`.

SunScreen EFS

All the big information technology companies have crafted their own firewall software, and Sun is no exception. They have a firewall called (cleverly enough) SunScreen, which runs on Sun SPARC workstations and is expertly designed for providing high-throughput protection for large networks.

Pros	Cons
High speed	High cost
High reliability	No Proxy support
VPN Support	
Centralized authentication	
Java-based administration	

Firewall Requirements:

- Sun SPARC workstation (SPARCstation 5, Ultra, or E450)
- 32MB of memory
- 1GB Hard drive space
- CD-ROM
- Networking adapter
- Solaris

Administration Requirements:

- Web browser with Java (1.1.8 or better) and SKIP (Secure Key-exchange for Internet protocol) installed.

One nice feature of the SunScreen firewall system is that you can tie two firewalls together so that a failure of one will not cause your Internet connection to go down. This is an important feature for Internet commerce companies for obvious reasons (just imagine how many people can buy things from your Web site if they can't get to it). High availability requires dedicated Ethernet or Fast Ethernet adapters and a direct non-switch connection (crossover Ethernet cable is ideal).

Major Feature Set

SunScreen provides the following major features:

- Stateful inspection packet filter
- Network Address Translation
- User authentication (passwords and SecureID)
- VPN

User authentication and VPN support is provided by the included SunScreen SKIP product, which implements the SKIP encryption algorithm.

Minor Feature Set

SunScreen provides the following minor features:

- Java GUI
- Remote control
- Audits and alerts
- Real-time statistical monitoring
- Load balancing/high availability

Commercial Firewalls

PART 4

Interface

Centralized management of multiple bastion hosts is performed via a Java applet running in Web browsers. This makes administration very flexible because you can administer the firewall from any Java-enabled browser with SKIP installed. It's no surprise that Sun would provide this option because Sun developed Java and is Java-enabling all their enterprise software.

The interface is clean, simple, and makes good use of Java technology. Management is policy based. Figure 14.2 shows the initial policy page.

Figure 14.2 The SunScreen Initial Policy Page

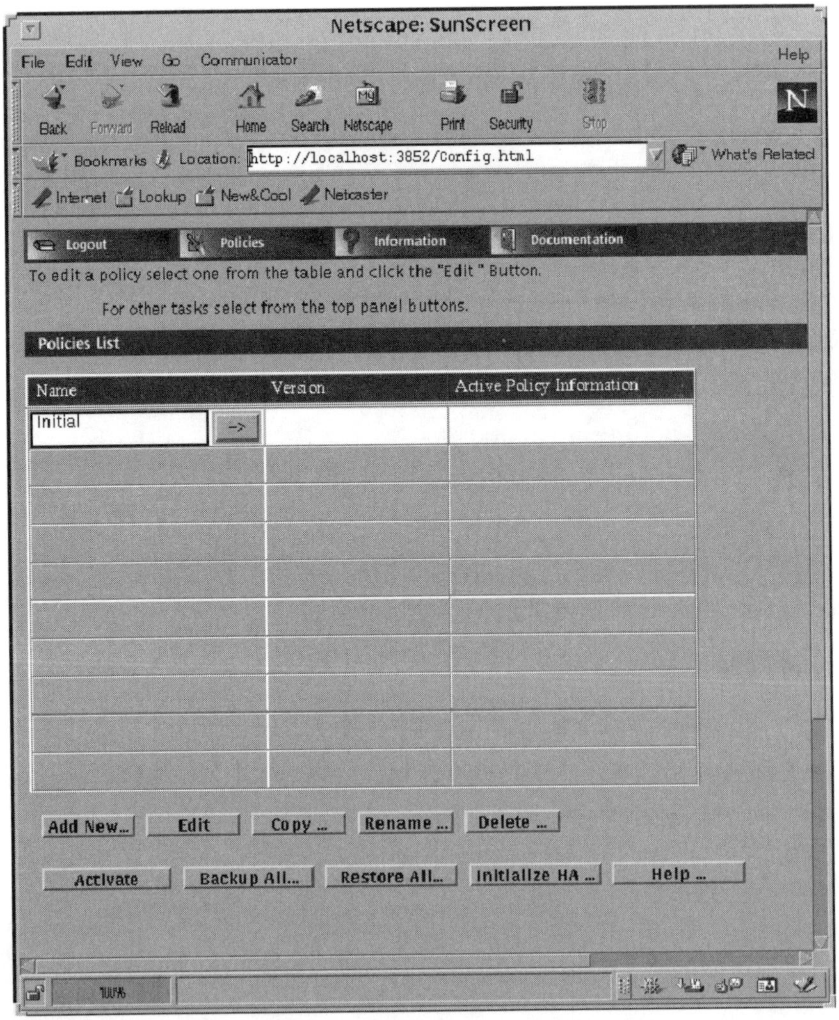

Security

SunScreen hardens a Sun SPARC workstation to perform as a packet filter and Network Address Translator. All packets are processed by the packet filter before being routed or translated. SunScreen provides the full range of packet filtering options, including the SYN bit, source and destination IP addresses, source and destination ports, packet type, and so on.

Because SunScreen does not inspect the data portions of the packets and locks down the operating system (so naïve administrators can't compromise security by running insecure services on the server), you will need a proxy server running on another computer to ensure that the traffic traversing a particular port conforms to the protocol for that port (that only HTTP requests and replies are going over port 80, for example). Many Web servers will also act as HTTP proxies, and you can use servers for store and forward protocols (such as SMTP and NNTP) unmodified as protocol proxies for their services. Ideally you should use address translation to redirect the appropriate traffic to and from these servers.

SunScreen evaluates every packet received by the network adapters in the firewall computer according to a set of rules you establish from the Java administration console. The rules are applied in order and one at a time until SunScreen finds a rule that matches the packet and specifies a terminal action, such as ACCEPT or DROP. Because the rules are applied in order, it is vitally important to craft the rules in the right order.

Documentation, Cost, and Support

SunScreen EFS is sold on a per-user basis, with VPN licensing as a separate cost.

- SunScreen EFS 3.0, unlimited users single server: $10,000
- 250 Client licenses for SunScreen SKIP: $10,000
- SSN 3.0 Competitive Upgrade: $3,000
- SSN 3.0 for Workgroups unlimited + 100 Clients for SKIP: $7,000
- SSN 3.0 Evaluation Kit: $100
- SSN 3.0/WG with 100 uses +100 SKIP: $3,000
- SSN 3.0 Site +250 SKIP Clients: $35,0000
- SSN 3.0/WG Unlimited use +250 SKIP Clients: $70,000
- SKIP client for Windows 9x/NT (1 server, 1 user): $150
- SKIP clients, 1000 pack: $41,000

Commercial Firewalls

PART 4

TIP   Visit Sun's Web site at www.sun.com/security.

Try to Buy

To provide cost and support information for the various firewalls in this book, I went through the same sales channels that any knowledgeable consultant would use. Primarily based on Web sites, I searched for sales channels for the product, contacted the contacts listed in vendors sites, and basically did whatever the company's Web site told me to do to acquire the firewall. I felt this approach would closely approximate the typical firewall buying experience.

Surprisingly, my survey yielded mixed results. Some firewalls were incredibly easy to buy—their Web sites went right through to an online store willing to take your credit card number and ship you the product the next day. Others went the more traditional route of listing numerous distributors.

I also had great success finding firewalls available from online distributors at www.shopper.com, for those firewalls in a traditional distribution channel.

Other firewalls were so difficult to obtain pricing information for that I would have given up had I not been doing research for a book. The companies that sell these firewalls have chosen to work exclusively through value-added reseller agreements, which leads customers down a Byzantine maze of voice mail in an attempt to find product sales information.

For one product, my phone calls to the numbers listed on their Web pages yielded numerous incorrect and out-of-date phone numbers. Calling their tech support reached a voicemail box, and leaving a message did not generate a return call. When I called the main number and asked for pricing information about the SecurIT Firewall, I was transferred six times until I reached a voice mailbox. I received a call back from a sales representative who directed me to their primary U.S. distributor, a company that appeared to be a very small operation—they had only one sales person who was qualified to provide pricing information about the firewall.

Another product from a major multinational vendor was simply impossible to obtain U.S. pricing information for. When I contacted the company that their Web site had listed as their U.S. distributor, that company had no idea that they carried the product. I was then transferred to another distributor that had no idea what I was talking about. I finally just gave up.

Firewall vendors who can't figure out how to sell their product are likely to be completely unable to support it. Although I hate to make recommendations based on non-technical criteria like sales and marketing, especially when the two firewalls that suffered from these problems are very strong security proxies, I just don't think it's worth the potential support problems you'll have with a completely non-responsive company.

15

Other Firewalls

Despite the hype, Windows NT and UNIX are not the only operating systems in existence. Firewalls for other operating systems abound and are, in many cases, more secure. This chapter covers those firewalls that run on standard computers (all PCs, actually) but do not use a standard UNIX distribution or Windows NT as their host operating system. Firewalls that ship with their own proprietary hardware (even if that hardware is just a PC masquerading as proprietary hardware) are covered in Chapter 16.

Because these firewalls are based on unusual operating systems, hackers have not yet created a trove of the various attacks against them, such as exploiting buffer overruns in the UNIX sendmail daemon or exploiting bugs in Internet Information Server on Windows NT platforms. Many of these operating systems were uniquely developed by their vendors to support a specific firewall product, so they are completely proprietary. This lends a strong measure of security through obscurity, and keeps the hordes of typical hackers (those that merely read and repeat known attacks rather than developing new ones) completely at bay.

Obscurity has its price, however. Almost all of these firewalls require unique adapter drivers and will only work with specific adapter models. Patches for these firewalls are rare, so if an exploit for one of them is developed, it usually takes until the next revision of the software before it's fixed. Some of these firewalls operate on platforms with arcane user interfaces that you may not be familiar with.

These firewalls also suffer from a lack of complete features. They are either based on generic SOCKS proxies or stateful inspection, and usually do not provide any support for the opposite type of firewall. The firewalls also suffer from a generational lag behind the firewalls developed for UNIX and NT because software is much harder to develop for smaller market operating systems.

NetWare is well entrenched in the server market, and thousands of "red" (Novell-only) networks exist. Managers in these environments rightly balk at the requirement to become an expert in a foreign operating system for the sole purpose of establishing a firewall. Novell markets a very strong firewall that runs on NetWare called BorderWare for these environments.

The mainframes of yesteryear have been converted to the application servers of today. VAX and AS/400 machines running VMS and OS-400 now serve as Web servers, e-mail hosts, and e-commerce engines. They also require protection, so there are firewalls available for them.

I've rolled these smaller market operating systems together into a chapter because of the limited fields they represent. In many cases, the firewalls I profile here are the only serious firewalls available for the platform shown.

Keep in mind that your choice of application or file server doesn't constrain your choice of firewall—you can use an NT firewall in a Novell network and a UNIX firewall to protect an AS/400. Because of the high cost of small market software, it's usually more economical to use a larger market platform for generic services like firewalling. To run an OS-400 firewall on the AS/400 will cost you tens of thousands of dollars, compared to the few thousand for a robust PC. These costs should be balanced against the cost of training administrators on an unfamiliar operating system and the security risk of operating a firewall in an environment that may not be completely familiar.

BorderManager

BorderManager is an ICSA certified suite of services that run on Novell NetWare servers that provide firewalling, Network Address Translation, proxying, authentication, and VPN services. These three packages are available separately or bundled together in the enterprise edition. BorderManager runs on NetWare 5 and NetWare 4.x platforms.

Pros	Cons
Runs on NetWare	No unlimited use license
Integrated with Novell NDS	Content filtering is proprietary and not well supported
SOCKS access for IPX clients	Clunky setup and interface
Strong remote management	Components not integrated

Because NetWare is highly optimized for speed, BorderManager's minimum requirements are lower than those of most full-spectrum firewalls. The platform requirements are:

- Intel i486 or higher microprocessor
- 32MB RAM (128MB recommended)
- 500MB Hard Disk Drive, additional for caching
- Novell NetWare 4.x or 5
- At least two network interfaces

Major Feature Set

BorderManager provides a full suite of high-end firewall features:

- Stateless packet filter
- Security proxies for numerous protocols
- Network Address Translator
- Secure authentication
- Virtual Private Network

The weak point is the stateless packet filter, but since all protocols run through security proxies, the packet filter need only filter for denial-of-service attacks, which are far less common on NetWare than NT or UNIX for lack of hacking effort against the platform.

BorderManager includes a very complete set of security proxies, including proxies for real-time multimedia services. Most proxies require SOCKS-enabled clients, however, bespeaking a lack of integration with the NAT component of the firewall, and reliance upon a basic SOCKS proxy as the source for many of the application proxies.

The Network Address Translator actually works at the Application Layer as something of a generic TCP proxy. Because it can be made transparent, it's something of a middle ground between a true NAT and a generic TCP or SOCKS proxy.

Secure authentication is provided by the BorderManager Authentication Services component, which is included in the enterprise edition of the firewall. BMAS is essentially an NDS plug-in for RADIUS authentication protocol.

VPN support is provided by the BorderManager VPN Services component, which is included in the enterprise edition of the firewall.

Minor Feature Set

BorderManager supports the following minor features:

- Java content filtering

- Logging to databases
- Reverse proxies for HTTP and FTP
- SOCKS support for IPX clients
- Dial-up service software

BorderManager's HTTP proxy supports Java content filtering, but strangely lacks support for Active-X filtering, an application protocol that is far more dangerous.

BorderManager's logging facility allows you to connect to ODBC compliant databases. If you've ever tried to export and import a massive firewall log to search for specific attacks) you'll really appreciate a direct database connector. As with all firewalls, you'll have to supply your own database software.

BorderManager supports a strange form of reverse proxying of external connections to internal (or DMZ) Web servers. Reverse proxy usually refers to the provision of multiple Web servers behind a single IP address, but Novell uses this term to refer to caching outbound Web pages on the proxy server itself, thus eliminating second and subsequent accesses to the Web server from public clients. This essentially makes the proxy server your Web server (unless you have an interactive Web site), which is rather pointless since the proxy server isn't any faster at serving Web pages than a good Web server. The server will store Web pages in its RAM cache for faster access, but UNIX and NT Web servers do that automatically as a file system function.

Like Microsoft Proxy Server, BorderManager is capable of proxying TCP/IP Application Layer protocols like HTTP and e-mail to internal clients that run on IPX. Using IPX as your interior network protocol makes network configuration faster, easier, and more secure since no direct route to clients exists, even if your firewall is compromised. The hacker would actually have to subvert the proxy functionality of the firewall to convert TCP/IP to TCP/IPX at the gateway in order to reach interior clients. This is practically impossible.

Novell Internet Access Server (NIAS) provides dial-up service akin to Windows NT's RAS service, and is included in the BorderManager Enterprise Edition. NT and UNIX both natively support dial-up, so this isn't a particularly compelling reason to choose this firewall over those based on more common operating systems.

Interface

BorderManager runs on NetWare 4.x and 5 and therefore uses the clunky text-based console interface of NetWare servers. ClearView, a Windows-based monitoring tool for BorderManager, is included; so once the software is set up and configured, you'll perform most of your administration from Windows-based workstations.

BorderManager integrates seamlessly into the NetWare's NDS directory, so you can select and manage firewalls and their options through the hierarchical browser NDS provides. NetWare administrators will find this compelling, but attempting to manage the firewall in non-NDS environments would not be compelling. For this reason, Border-Manager is a serious option only in NetWare environments.

BorderManager is a large package consisting of numerous components that are installed and configured separately. You should be at least a Novell CNE and be very familiar with the NetWare environment before attempting to install this software.

Security

Proxies are available for the following protocols:

- HTTP & SSL
- FTP
- DNS
- Gopher
- SMTP & POP3
- NNTP
- RealAudio & Real Video
- Real Time Streaming Protocol (RTSP)
- SOCKS 4 & 5
- Generic TCP/UDP
- Telnet

Most of these proxy applications are merely configurations for a generic SOCKS proxy, which means that the clients have to support connection to a proxy server. Only the HTTP proxy can operate in transparent mode so clients do not need to be configured for proxy operation.

Transparent proxy operation refers to the ability of a proxy to operate without being specifically configured on each client. Rather than being addressed on a certain port (usually 8080 for HTTP proxies) to which all Web browsers must be configured, transparent proxies (since they also act as network layer routers) inspect the routed traffic going from the internal to the external network and detect HTTP traffic on its way out. They then transfer these HTTP requests to the proxy service rather than forwarding them directly, and thereby insert the proxy functionality seamlessly and transparently. This makes it impossible for internal clients to bypass the proxy and eliminates the administrative burden of configuring the proxy.

Documentation, Cost, and Support

The documentation for BorderManager is clearly written although relatively shallow in concepts and theory. The various topics are given considerable detail and are task oriented, so firewall administrators should be able to establish and configure the firewall without problems.

Novell's posted comparison matrix on their Web site is laughable and filled with misleading information about their competitors' products. According to this bizarre document:

- Microsoft Proxy Server supports Network Address Translation. (In fact, it doesn't operate below the application layer.)
- Firewall-1 supports only static packet filtering. (In fact, Checkpoint was first to market with a stateful inspection firewall.)
- Firewall-1 supports content proxying. (In fact, only the SMTP service in Firewall-1 could be called a proxy. The other services are application layer content filters.)
- BorderManager supports stateful packet inspection. (In fact, BorderManager relies upon application layer proxies to maintain connection information.)
- Base price for BorderManager is listed as $995. (In fact, you also have to pay a per-user licensing fee that makes BorderManager very expensive indeed.) Novell compared this to MS-Proxy Server's all-inclusive price and Firewall-1's price for a 25 user version.

Fortunately, most of the rest of Novell's documentation appears to be written by people who knew what they were talking about.

Pricing is simple: $1,000 for the BorderManager Firewall Services, plus $30 per user, no volume discounts. License packs are available in 10, 25, 50, 100, 250, and 500 user increments. BorderManager includes a 2-user version of NetWare upon which the software is installed.

Technical support is available via Novell's extensive Web site at `www.support.novell.com`, which includes a very thorough searchable KnowledgeBase. You may also receive support from one of the hundreds of thousands of consulting Certified NetWare Engineers throughout the world.

Elron Firewall

Elron Firewall is available on its own proprietary operating system and was ported to Windows NT in its latest edition. I find the port to NT interesting in light of the fact that Elron considers their secure OS to be one of the primary features of their firewall.

Pros	Cons
Fast stateful inspector firewall	No proxy servers
Includes VPN	Adapters limited to 3c905 Ethernet
Supports IPX	Poor user interface design
Minimal hardware	

Elron employs multilayer stateful inspection rather than proxy servers for filtering in the Application Layer. This is somewhat similar to Firewall-1's support for HTTP and FTP filtering. Filtering in the Application Layer is capable of blocking numerous attacks, but filters may not recognize certain attacks that proxies would not forward because the attack would not be created. In other words, filtering still passes the originally formed packet, so undetected malformations can still be routed through. Multilayer filtering is considerably more secure than Network Layer filtering alone, but not as secure as security Application Layer proxies.

Elron Firewall running on its own operating system is not subject to standard operating system vulnerabilities. Although a proprietary operating system is not necessarily more secure than a standard operating system, few hackers attempt hacks against operating systems that are not widely deployed, so the firewall is not vulnerable to most of the exploits developed by hackers. Since superfluous firewalling services (like file and print sharing) are not provided, no holes exist in the operating system.

Elron software maintains that, because 32OS source code has not been released to the public, there is virtually no possibility that hackers will be familiar with it. While this may be true to some extent, good hackers can read machine language source code through a process called disassembly, where the binary image is turned back into human readable assembly language. While assembly language is not nearly as clear as the C programming language (relatively speaking), hackers who are familiar with the i386 microprocessor and its descendants could read it and thereby understand in detail the operation of a piece of proprietary software. I've done it, and so can any decent programmer. Though software based on a proprietary operating system will keep the masses at bay, security through obscurity should never be relied upon. Note also that 32OS uses MS-DOS as a boot loader, and could therefore be susceptible to certain types of RAM resident viruses.

Elron's documentation describes some alarming problems that can happen when the firewall runs out of memory, including losing Network Address Translation addresses, which would cause translated connections to be lost. While neither fatal nor a security

Commercial Firewalls

PART 4

risk, these sorts of problems are the result of using proprietary operating systems that aren't completely thought out.

Hardware requirements for the Elron Firewall are (SecureOS Version):

Connections <1.5Mb/sec (T1)

- 486DX-2/66
- 8MB RAM
- 200MB hard disk drive
- MS-DOS 6.22
- Two or Three 3C905 10/100 NICs
- Floppy drive

Connections >T1

- Fastest possible processor
- 16MB RAM

Requirements for the management station are:

- Windows 9x or NT
- 50MB available disk space
- 16MB RAM

Major Feature Set

Elron Firewall provides the following major features:

- Stateful inspection packet filter
- Network Address Translation
- Encrypted authentication
- Virtual Private Networking

Elron Firewall's stateful inspection filter is unique in that it is capable of filtering the application (payload) portion of a packet for known content. The firewall compares packets to bit-patterns of previously filtered packets before passing the packet into the protected network. This ensures that unknown deformations of packets will be filtered out.

Elron Firewall's NAT option supports IP address hiding only by using the Firewall's IP address. This provides an upper limit of about 64,000 outbound connections, but that's generally high enough that this limitation is not serious for most organizations.

User authentication clients are provided for Windows 9x and NT. Authentication is password-based and supports RADIUS and CHAP authentication. The user authentication software also supports periodic authentication.

The included VPN option provides IP in IP tunneling, which provides a measure of internal security by hiding the true source and destination addresses. IPSec is used to encrypt the encapsulated IP packet.

Elron makes two completely separate Application Layer filters called the InternetManager (HTTP) and the MessageInspector (e-mail, news, and FTP). These products run on their own Windows NT server and work with any firewall or security service. The Message-Inspector filter performs powerful keyword string matching and statistical analysis (for spam filtering) to block e-mail, newsgroups, FTP download.

Minor Feature Set

Elron supports the following noteworthy minor features:

- IP and IPX filtering
- VPN continuous key regeneration

Elron supports both IP and IPX filtering. IPX filtering is not usually a big concern unless you run a large IPX network where internal security between divisions is important. For most enterprises, IPX filtering is not a function required of bastion hosts. The firewall also supports IPX bridging (forwarding all IPX packets transparently and irrespective of their contents), which is not a security function and reduces the security posture of your network.

The continuous key regeneration feature provides a facility somewhat akin to Kerberos ticketing. After an established amount of VPN traffic has passed between two firewalls, the firewalls will both generate new keys and exchange them. This reduces the amount of useful time a brute-force-decrypted key would be useful, thus moving the probability domain for a brute-force attack from highly unlikely to practically impossible.

Interface

Elron firewall is configured remotely through a Windows-based policy manager. The firewall itself is initially configured using the firewall management software on a Windows computer and transmitted to the firewall located on the same Ethernet collision domain.

The user interface bespeaks an amateurish attempt at design, suffering from such problems as a non-sizeable main window that takes up the entire screen and the use of purely modal dialogs throughout the software, which prevents you from seeing two content windows at the same time. There seems to be an unwritten rule in the firewall industry that user interfaces aren't worthy of programming effort. Figure 15.1 shows the clunky management interface.

Figure 15.1   The Elron Firewall Management Interface

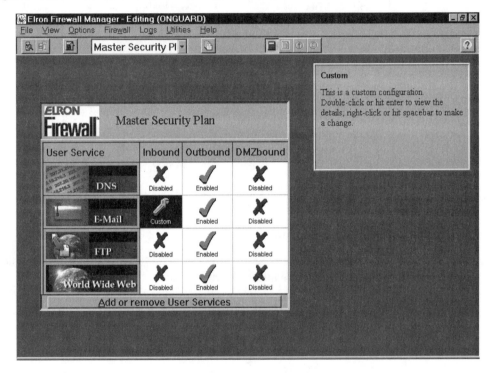

The interface is not particularly easy to use since it doesn't conform to any specific interface methodology. In some cases, you right-click to access features, while in others you double click. There's also no indication of which interface elements can be activated and which can't.

Security

Elron Firewall's multilayer inspection filter is the heart of the firewall. The multilayer filter is interesting because it can filter content in the Application Layer to reject unrecognized information. The level to which this functionality is actually used varies from protocol to protocol, but administrators can customize it on a per-protocol basis.

Customizing the firewall is not easy and requires a solid knowledge of TCP/IP and firewalling. If you've read through this book so far, you'll have no problems.

Elron Firewall running on 32OS should be considered hardened, since no OS specific exploits are known for the operating system. This makes it equivalent at least to a Windows NT installation with no extra services running, no extra user accounts, and in a state of complete lockdown where additional software (like Trojan horses) cannot be installed.

Hardened operating systems are operating systems in which no extraneous services or exploitable mechanisms exist because the operating system simply doesn't support them, or in which all software functions not directly related to supporting the firewall have been disabled. Hardening an OS reduces considerably the number of vectors a hacker can attempt to exploit, and thereby dramatically improves the security posture of the firewall system.

Documentation, Cost, and Support

Documentation is provided in PDF format and is very strong. It is highly task oriented, containing detailed procedures for performing most firewall administrative tasks, yet adequately covers the theory behind the features used. Most administrators will have no trouble getting the firewall up using the supplied documentation.

Elron has a small searchable knowledgebase online. Technical support is available via e-mail. Elron is a wholly owned U.S. subsidiary of the Israel-based Elron Electronic Industries.

Elron Firewall comes in various user levels and prices:

- 25 users: $1,000
- 50 users: $2,000
- 100 users: $3,250
- 255 users: $5,600
- Unlimited users: $9,000

Elron also sells annual maintenance contracts at about 25% of the initial purchase price.

GNAT Box

GNAT Box is an ICSA certified stateful inspection packet filter and Network Address Translator that runs on its own operating system, which it boots from a single floppy disk. GNAT Box also includes an SMTP proxy and a split DNS server. GNAT Box protects against IP spoofing and common denial-of-service attacks. Although GNAT Box does not provide a UNIX operating system environment, its kernel and TCP/IP stack are derived from BSD, which is an open source UNIX operating system. You can think of GNAT Box as a highly optimized firewall specific distribution of the BSD operating system.

Pros	Cons
Runs on cheap hardware	No VPN
No standard OS security holes	No user authentication
Fast	Cannot integrate with 3rd party tools
Inexpensive—less than $1000 for unlimited use	No content scanning or additional proxies

The complete system requirements are:

- 386 or higher Intel compatible microprocessor
- 8MB RAM, 16MB recommended for e-mail proxy, more than 32MB is not useful
- Floppy disk drive
- Two network adapters
- Display adapter
- Printer port (to attach a copy protection key circuit)

As you can see, the requirements are quite minimal—you won't even need a hard disk drive, and nearly any obsolete PC you have lying around will work fine. The big drawback to GNAT Box is its limited support for network adapters. Because the operating system is based on BSD, only network adapter drivers for that operating system are available. It appears that the vendor actively usurps open source adapter drivers for its firewall. So, many popular Ethernet models are available, but you can forget about using adapters that are even slightly esoteric. Support is provided for most adapters from:

- 3Com
- Compaq
- DEC
- SMC
- Intel (except ISA bus adapters)
- Various others based on similar chipsets.

A complete list is provided with the documentation. If you have a problem getting your adapters to work, you will need to purchase adapters from the supported list. This is usually not a problem, since most of the adapters are available for well under $100 each.

GNAT Box performs faster than most Internet connections. Performance is limited primarily by the speed of the network adapters, so the performance of GNAT Box is at least as good as the fastest PC-based firewalls. GNAT Box does not support VPN encrypted tunnels or remote user authentication.

TIP A downloadable evaluation edition of GNAT Box is available at www .gnatbox.com.

Major Feature Set

The following major features are included in GNAT Box:

- Stateful inspection packet filter
- Network Address Translator
- E-Mail Proxy

GNAT Box's stateful inspector is fairly sophisticated. By detecting "hard to firewall" protocols like FTP and real-time multimedia protocols on the way out of your network, the firewall will create virtual cracks, a term GNAT Box uses to describe temporary holes created for the return channels of these protocols. This makes GNAT Box compatible with these protocols without compromising security by simply opening up permanent holes.

The network translation facility supports static IP mapping to internal hosts. GNAT Box does not extend the IP mapping concept to ports however, so different services cannot appear to come from the same server, nor does GNAT Box does not support IP load balancing.

The e-mail proxy receives and regenerates e-mail messages. It includes light anti-spamming features, but does not include content filtering or attachment blocking.

Minor Feature Set

GNAT Box provides the following minor feature:

- Demand dialing of PPP connections

If configured to use a PPP connection as the External interface, GNAT Box will automatically dial the interface on demand whenever an internal client requests Internet data. The PPP interface can also be set to dedicated (dial on boot) or manual-enable mode (whenever the administrator enables the link).

Interface

The firewall itself has a text-based console interface, but you need never use that interface. System administration is performed on an administration computer that connects to the GNAT Box via a TCP port you define. Figure 15.2 shows the GBAdmin utility's interface.

Commercial
Firewalls

PART 4

Figure 15.2   The GNAT Box administration interface

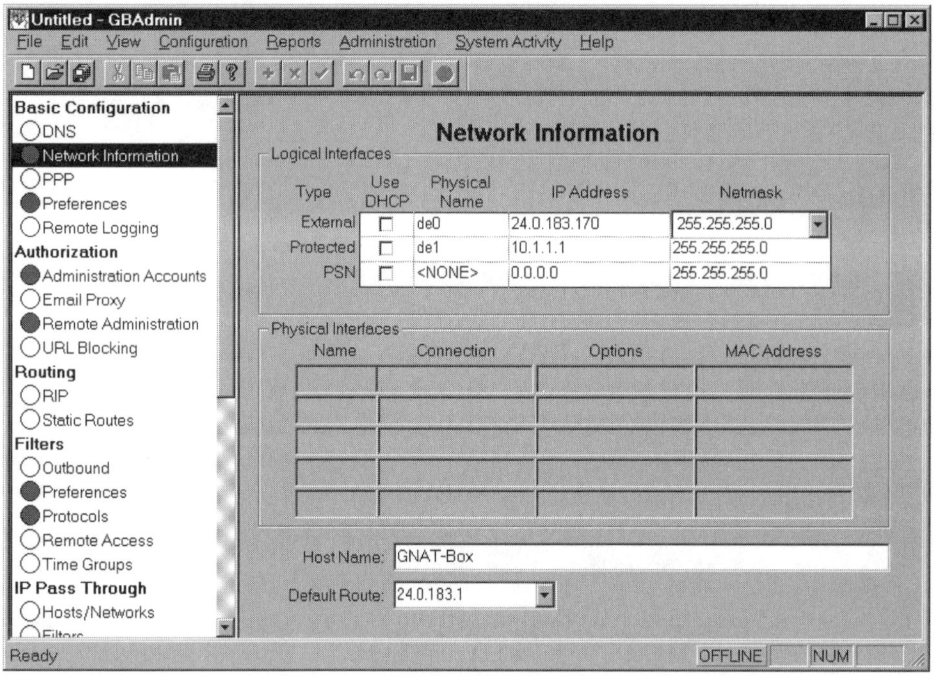

The GBAdmin utility requires Internet Explorer 3.0 or higher in order to operate correctly.

You can use the GBAdmin utility to configure an existing GNAT Box over your network, or to create a combined configuration and runtime floppy from which a fully configured GNAT Box will boot.

Security

Because GNAT Box is absolutely the only software running on the firewall platform, it should be considered more hardened than any firewall running on a standard operating system. There's no way to log into a GNAT Box firewall, so hackers cannot directly exploit it. There are no extraneous services to exploit and no extra information leaking services that a hacker might find useful. The same machine cannot be used to support mail, Web, or any other services. GNAT Box turns a PC into a firewall appliance and achieves a high degree of inherent security that way.

Documentation, Cost, and Support

Documentation consists of a PDF user's manual that is both extremely well written and very clear. Firewalling concepts are explained in detail.

GNAT Box is free for home and non-commercial use. The full version costs $800 for unlimited users. No other pricing is available. Technical support is available via the Web at www.gnatbox.com or via e-mail.

IBM Firewall for AS/400

IBM's family of firewalls is based on the firewall technology that IBM has been developing for 15 years. IBM has firewalls for AIX/6000 on RS/6000 microcomputers, Windows NT on Intel microcomputers, OS/400 on AS/400 minicomputers, and OS/390 on 390 series mainframe computers. Interestingly, IBM hasn't bothered to port its firewall to its own OS/2 operating system. This section discusses the latest version of IBM's Firewall for the AS/400.

Pros	Cons
Runs on esoteric IBM platforms	Expensive
Performs OS hardening	Poorly integrated
Firewall runs on embedded separate PC processor	Lacking true content filters or strong security proxies
	Stateless packet filter
	No support for DMZ

The AS/400 firewall actually runs on an integrated PC server embedded in the AS/400 computer. This provides system separation so that in the event that the firewall is compromised, no access to applications running on the AS/400 is achieved. The software runs from a read-only hard disk drive, so the firewall cannot be modified once it's installed.

IBM's firewall is something of an "also-ran" in the firewall field. It supports most of the major technologies, but it suffers from poor integration, the requirement for third party utilities for numerous security functions like alerting and scan detection, and a lackluster effort in the development of secure proxies for major TCP/IP protocols.

IBM Firewall for AS/400 requires:

- OS/400 version 4 release 1
- TCP/IP connectivity utilities for AS/400
- Integration services for FSIOP
- RISC AS/400 with integrated PC server

Commercial Firewalls

PART 4

Integrated PC server must have:

- 32MB RAM (64 recommended)
- 486 or higher microprocessor

Major Feature Set

The major feature set for the IBM Firewall for AS/400 includes:

- Packet Filter
- Network Address Translator
- Proxies for HTTP, SMTP
- SOCKS proxy

The packet filter is simple and stateless. It provides no functionality beyond the functionality provided by IP Chains or NT's built-in packet filtering. Services can either be passed or blocked based on their TCP port number, and the filter can use the ACK bit to deny inbound connection attempts.

The firewall is not normally configured to forward IP packets; rather, outbound connections are achieved via the circuit level gateway (i.e., SOCKS proxy) running at the Application Layer. This means that client software incompatible with SOCKS either cannot be used or relies upon the enabling of IP forwarding, which defeats many of the security features of the firewall. Support for real-time streaming multimedia protocols like RealAudio and H.323 also requires enabling of packet forwarding.

Security proxy services are provided for HTTP and SMTP. All other TCP services must be SOCKS compatible in order to work with the firewall as its remaining functionality is provided by a SOCKS circuit level gateway.

Minor Feature Set

IBM Firewall for AS/400 provides the following minor feature:

- Installs as standard AS/400 application

The IBM Firewall for AS/400 installs as a normal AS/400 application, so AS/400 operators will be familiar with its operation.

Interface

Firewall administration is performed through a Web browser using an HTML-based administration tool. The tool is simple, but it provides an adequate interface to the firewall. Very little policy abstraction exists, so a strong knowledge of TCP/IP is required. Figure 15.3 shows the configuration interface running in a Web browser.

Figure 15.3   The IBM Firewall for AS/400 Management Interface

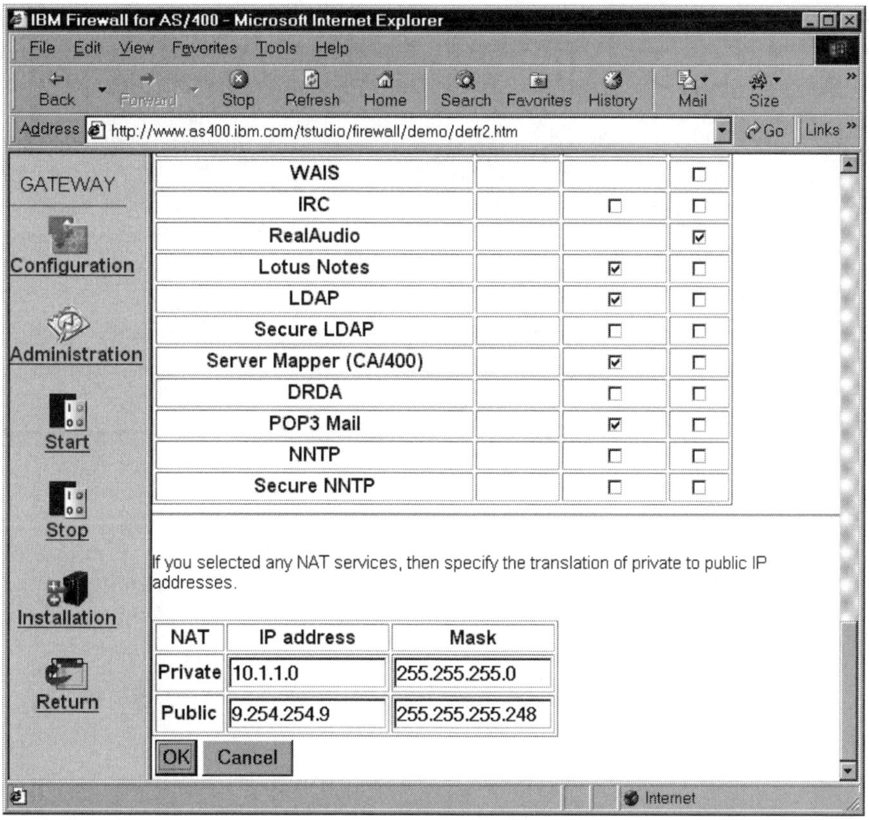

Security

The IBM Firewall for AS/400 relies primarily upon its SOCKS proxy for security. The filter is stateless and suitable primarily for protection against denial-of-service attacks. Network Address Translation is achieved via the SOCKS mechanism. True security proxies are available only for HTTP and SMTP.

The main AS/400 processor can disable the firewall if tampering is detected (the documentation does not specify what sort of tampering is detectable).

Firewall uses an implicit "deny all services" policy, so every service that is enabled must be explicitly enabled by the firewall policy. Remote administration is disabled by default, but can be enabled by the administrator.

In sum, the firewall is rather dated in its implementation and runs on esoteric expensive hardware. You will achieve better security at lower cost by using a non-integrated firewall.

Documentation, Cost, and Support

Documentation is available in hard copy or PDF format. The documentation is simplistic and lacking in real implementation detail, but is task oriented and will get you through the configuration.

Support is available via IBM's direct consulting services or through IBM consulting resellers. Pricing information for OS/400 was not available; prices for the AIX version are as follows:

- 25 users: $2,499
- 50 users: $4,499
- 250 users: $9,499
- Unlimited users: $16,500

Phantom Firewalls

It was difficult for me to come up with a useful case study about these firewalls for this chapter, having never been involved in the production deployment of a firewall that wasn't either dedicated to or ran on NT or UNIX. That's when it occurred to me: My lack of experience in the matter is a case study.

Having been a security consultant for some time, I've seen all sorts of firewall configurations and I've even had the rare privilege of being hired to attempt to hack through them. Yet in all my days, I've never seen any of these firewalls actually installed. This category makes up the smallest market segment for firewalls. Perhaps this explains why Elron software has ported their firewall to NT (and why the only job offering they have posted on their site is for a marketing manager).

Even my dyed-in-the-wool loyal IBM customers who use AS/400s opt for other firewalls: Cisco PIX in one installation I support, and Firewall-1 in another. All the NetWare installations I'm involved with use NT based firewalls—MS Proxy server is actually very popular in the NetWare market because it's cheap and it provides strong support for IPX to TCP/IP networking.

These firewalls do have their place in certain environments, especially innovative low cost, high functioning firewalls like GNAT Box, which are capable of putting small businesses on the Internet inexpensively.

But other firewalls like BorderManager and IBM Firewall for AS/400 exist more as a way to round out the vendors' product offerings and catch the business of the occasional corporate buyer than to provide cost-effective strong security. These offerings are sold to shops who have a fairly blind loyalty to their vendors or to consultants that have only a single operating system expertise support. These firewalls can't really compete when compared to the stronger and cheaper firewalls available for more common operating systems and to those used as firewall embedded devices. This explains why you don't see them around much. Since the future of any product offering is ensured by it's success, you'll probably find that these firewalls fade away as the more competitive UNIX, NT, and dedicated hardware firewalls carve up the market. Their vendors probably won't be able to justify the continual improvement necessary to remain competitive in the war against hacking.

16

Dedicated Firewalls

Many network administrators are faced with a shortage of talented staff, especially when it comes to complex problems like security and firewalling. In organizations where there's precious little time to keep up with existing work (much less the added demand of new security problems), implementing a firewall on a complex operating system like UNIX or Windows NT can be daunting indeed. Dedicated firewalls can solve this problem quickly and easily.

With dedicated firewalls, you don't need a firewall to run on the same operating system you use for file and application services, and there's no reason to learn a complex foreign operating system either. If you run a network that isn't based on UNIX or Windows NT, or if ease of installation is more important than constant monitoring and cost, dedicated firewalls are your solution.

Dedicated firewalls are computers dedicated to the task of firewalling that include a built-in operating system and firewall software. These devices usually have two or three network interfaces (external, internal, and possibly a DMZ), plenty of RAM, and a fast microprocessor.

From that configuration, dedicated firewalls diverge into two types. One is the solid state model that stores the operating system on Flash-EEPROM rather than on a hard disk drive. The second is a model that comprises standard computers that use hard drives and are pre-configured as firewalls. Functionally, there's very little difference between the two types, but the lack of a hard disk drive and (in well engineered models) a fan makes solid state firewalls highly reliable and unlikely to fail within your career. Some of these devices boot from a floppy drive. Because the floppy drive is only used when the device boots, it tends to last quite some time, although floppies are notoriously unreliable over time. Pre-configured standard computers are just as easy to use, but usually cost less because they're based on industry standard components. The trade-off between the two types is cost versus reliability.

Dedicated firewalls typically have a Web-based interface; you manage the firewall by pointing your Web browser to the firewall's IP address from inside the network and authenticating with it. An HTTP server built into the firewall serves up management pages you can use to configure the device. Typically, they ship from the factory with a default policy that's restrictive to the external interface but permissive to internal clients.

Older dedicated firewalls use a UNIX-like command line interface very similar to the command line interface used in routers. These firewalls aren't particularly easy to configure. In my opinion, if you have to get a consultant to configure your firewall, you might as well use a standard PC and an operating system you're familiar with.

The vast majority of dedicated firewalls are actually special purpose UNIX machines. Many of them are based on Linux or BSD because their vendors don't have to pay any licensing fees to use that operating system. The firewalls that aren't based on UNIX are usually derived from router operating systems like Cisco's IOS or Lucent's Inferno embedded network OS.

PIX Firewall

Cisco's Private Internet eXchange (PIX) firewall is one of the earliest dedicated firewalls available. Based on a Cisco's routing hardware with a custom real-time firewall operating system, PIX supports any TCP/IP-based network. PIX is probably the second best selling firewall after Checkpoint's Firewall-1, although it's difficult to determine how much market share free solutions like Linux with IPChains and the TIS (Trusted Information Systems) public domain security proxies comprise.

Pros	Cons
Fastest Firewall	Few content filters or proxy servers
Support for external security proxies and content filters	Interface support limited by proprietary network interfaces
Ethernet, Token Ring, and FDDI support	Weaker security than strong proxies

Because PIX is based on a high-speed custom hardware platform, filtering is performed with practically no throughput degradation. Performance is rated at up to 170Mbps, which is fast enough to filter an ATM-155 or OC-3 network connection without introducing latency. This is significantly faster than firewalls based on standard PC hardware because the PCI bus, even performing at its theoretical maximum speed, cannot compete with the speed of the PIX firewall.

Although performance isn't a requirement for most organizations, there are cases where an exceptionally high performing firewall is required, and in those cases, the PIX shines. Otherwise, it's an expensive firewall.

One problem with all proprietary OS firewalls is the lack of support for third-party security software like content filters and virus scanners. PIX supports URL filtration by connecting to another URL filter server, which requires another machine. Using standard operating systems and hardware for firewalling allows you to run all your security software on a single machine, albeit with slightly reduced security.

The Cisco PIX firewall runs its operating system from Flash memory, which makes the firewall nearly solid state (the product does contain fans, which are the component most likely to fail). This makes the firewall far more reliable than a hard disk based PC.

Major Feature Set

The Cisco PIX firewall supports the following major features:

- Stateful inspection filter
- Network Address Translator
- Authentication
- VPN

The heart of the PIX firewall is a connection oriented stateful inspection filter that Cisco calls the Adaptive Security Algorithm (ASA). From what we've been able to determine based on Cisco's white papers and marketing documents, ASA is just a fancy name for the same stateful inspection technology every other strong firewall uses. ASA also performs the Network Address Translation function.

The optional VPN is a hardware adapter that performs IPSec encryption using the Internet Key Exchange (IKE). This allows PIX firewalls to establish VPN tunnels to other PIX firewalls or Cisco routers running Cisco's IOS operating system, and third-party products that support IPSec and IKE.

Remote clients (or NT-based firewalls) can use Windows 9x/NT client software to connect securely to the firewall using the same VPN facility. The VPN technology was developed by RedCreek Communications, developers of the remote client software.

Minor Feature Set

The Cisco PIX firewall supports the following minor features:

- High availability
- Support for four security zones
- Java filter

High availability for failure situations is available by configuring two PIX systems in parallel (on the same internal and external networks with a proprietary HA (High Availability) cable running between them. If one firewall fails, the other will automatically assume its traffic without breaking connections.

External, Internal, DMZ, and a unique security zone all support servers like content filters and proxy servers. The security zone was established to provide some support for the firewall's missing proxy and content filter functions.

Recent releases of the PIX firewall include a Java blocking filter for HTTP. Although an e-mail filter is provided as well, it is not capable of stripping attachments or detecting most malformed e-mail, and the filters are not capable of blocking Active-X controls.

Interface

The PIX firewall is managed using a Java-based application that runs on any platform with a Java virtual machine. The application manages all PIX firewalls in an enterprise, providing a central point for security control. The interface provides functions for reporting and user-based accounting on such things as Web sites visited and file download volume. The management interface provides real-time attack alerting via pager notification or e-mail.

The firewall itself is nearly management free. The device boots automatically, and although a command-line interface is provided through a serial interface on the machine, there's no need to manage the device locally. Once the security policy is established, you can basically forget about the firewall. Be sure to get on a good security bulletin mailing list so you know how to modify the firewall for new threats.

Security

PIX is a strong stateful inspection filter and Network Address Translator, but it provides no content inspection, filtration, or regeneration (proxying). For these reasons, the firewall is appropriate in applications where high performance is required and content filtering is not necessary, such as in the primary bastion of a large corporation or that of an Internet Service Provider.

Despite downplay by Cisco's documentation, the lack of proxy services makes PIX incomplete on its own. Since the vast majority of security proxies also include strong stateful filters, there's little reason to buy both when one will do.

Cisco's VPN solution, based on IPSec and IKE Internet standards, is secure and compatible with a wide range of third-party products.

Documentation, Cost, and Support

Documentation provided by Cisco is light, but since the firewall is easy to manage, that's not much of an issue.

Support is provided by Cisco by telephone or e-mail, or is available from the growing number of Cisco certified support technicians.

The entry-level version of the PIX firewall, which supports up to 50,000 simultaneous connections and two Ethernet connections, costs about $7,000 through direct sales venues.

Lucent Managed Firewall

The Lucent Managed Firewall is based on Inferno, Lucent's communications equipment embedded operating system designed from the ground up as a secure network operating system and not even remotely related to existing operating systems.

Lucent developed Inferno to power everything from massive telephone switches to cellular telephones. In its current incarnation, Inferno is being used as the base operating system to support a number of embedded applications, like screen-phones for e-mail and messaging cellular phones. The operating system itself was not designed specifically to support firewalls, but it is an excellent fit. Since the operating system does not support user logons or a file system, it's extremely difficult to hack and has no known security holes. The firewall has no local console, so local attacks are not possible.

The Lucent Managed Firewall system is composed of two components: the firewall (referred to as a brick); and the security management server software, which runs on an administrative workstation. The security management server runs on Solaris and Windows NT.

The firewall is primarily a stateful inspection filter. For that reason, it performs reasonably well and operates without significant latency at speeds up to 45Mbps.

Lucent's marketing documents claim that the firewall is implemented as a bridge rather than as a router and that the router has no internal IP addresses of its own, so scanning does not report the existence of the firewall. While this would be intriguing and clever if true, it sadly is not. The firewall is actually a transparent router, and the device does indeed have an internal IP address that is used by the SMS server to establish connections. The firewall merely drops all other access. Many other firewalls are capable of performing transparently and performing firewall hiding through packet dropping, so this technology isn't nearly as innovative as Lucent would have you believe. Furthermore, unlike a bridge, the router is specific to TCP/IP and does not filter or forward other protocols. The fact that Lucent's marketing documents are misleading in no way impacts the effectiveness of the firewall and should not negatively affect your assessment of the firewall.

Platform requirements for the Security Management Server (the remote management client) are:

- Solaris-SPARC 2.5.1 with the following patches: 103566-08, 103600-03, and 103640-08 (or a later versions)
- Netscape Enterprise Server 3.5.1 (included)
- Netscape Communicator 4.05 (with the AWT 1.1 patch)
- Adobe Acrobat Reader 3.01 for online documentation (included)
- VeriSign Digital ID (included)
- 170 MHz processor (Sparc Ultra5 recommended)
- 4 GB Hard Drive (dependent upon logging needs)
- CD-ROM Drive
- 3.5 Floppy Drive Backup device

Major Feature Set

The Lucent Managed Firewall provides the following major features:

- Stateful inspection filter
- Network Address Translator
- User Authentication
- VPN

These features are all implemented by Inferno daemons, which are independent services that run on the firewall. The daemons are:

Administrative Daemon   Establishes authenticated management sessions with the Security Management Server to provide the management interface.

End-User Authentication Daemon   Performs the user authentication and encryption services. The VPN is included in the firewall. Lucent IPSec client for Windows 9x and NT is also included, allowing access to the firewall for remote users.

Logging Daemon   Receives messages from the other daemons and transmits them to the SMS computer.

Filter Daemons Perform the various filtering and Network Address Translation functions.

No other services run on the firewall, thus reducing the number of potential holes in the operating system.

Minor Feature Set

The Lucent Managed Firewall provides the following minor feature:

- High reliability

The brick loads its operating system and initial security policy from floppy disk, but then writes it to non-volatile flash memory for subsequent boots. Except for initial configuration and operating system updates, the floppy drive is not used. The only other moving parts are the processor fan and the power switch. This configuration provides extremely high reliability.

Interface

The firewall itself has no console and no interactivity mechanism. The firewall includes four 10/100 Ethernet interfaces and does not adapt to other network types; you must use routers to adapt other data link types to Ethernet.

Management software runs on a management workstation, which must run Windows NT or Solaris. Any Java-enabled Web browser can remotely access the management workstation. The management GUI is provided by a Java servlet, and (from the single blurry screenshot I've seen) looks fairly sophisticated and useful. Unfortunately, no evaluation editions of the firewall or its management interface are available, so we were not able to evaluate it for user interface functionality.

The firewall supports an unlimited number of security policy zones, which can be independently managed and accounted. This makes the firewall useful for ISPs or security application providers to implement security services for their customers down stream. Similarly, the firewall supports separate alarming and alerting configurations for each zone and varying levels of administrative privilege to configuration users. This allows a "super administrator" to tailor other administrative accounts to control their own security zones. The zoning feature allows ISPs to provide firewalling as a value-added service to their subscribers; obviously Lucent had the ISP market in mind when they developed the management interfaces.

Security

The Lucent firewall has the strong theoretical security of stateful inspection filters. Unfortunately, the firewall does not include content filters or proxies to manage the application layer, so content based exploits like Active-X controls in malicious Web sites will get right through. The lack of Application Layer filtering or proxying is the Achilles' heel of this firewall. Lucent recognizes this and commits to providing true security proxies in future editions of the firewall.

The firewall itself is completely transparent to network information flowing through it and does not require much in the way of configuration.

Documentation, Cost, and Support

Lucent provides 24/7 customer support via telephone and the Internet.

A firewall system requires at least one copy of the Lucent Managed Firewall Security Management Server software and one or more "bricks" or actual firewall hardware components (one for each connection to the Internet).

Direct from Lucent, the firewall costs:

- Firewall software + firewall + documentation: $16,000.
- Software only: $9,000
- Hardware only: $9,000

TIP   You can read what sparse documentation for the firewall exists (and purchase it) at www.lucent.com/security.

SonicWALL

The SonicWALL firewall appliance is a secure stateful inspeciton filter and Network Address Translator. No proxy applications are included. SonicWALL's target market is small businesses (fewer than 100 users) and satellite offices of larger businesses.

Pros	Cons
Small footprint	No security proxies
Quick setup	Low security user authentication
High reliability	No support for external content filtering
Application Layer filtering	
VPN compatible with Firewall-1	
Very low cost	

Default security is fairly strong; sessions initiated from the inside are allowed to pass, but all other traffic is blocked. The firewall is completely transparent to network applications and can simply be inserted behind the Internet connection and powered up to begin providing default security to the network. We know of no easier firewall to install.

SonicWALL is based on a proprietary real-time operating system that does not expose unnecessary services. For this reason, the OS should be considered hardened. The firewall is also completely solid state—there are no hard disk drives or fans. This makes the firewall extremely reliable.

SonicWALL comes in 10, 50, unlimited, DMZ (3rd interface), and Pro (Fast Ethernet) models.

The various models are differentiated primarily by price. SonicWALL hardware is appropriate for connection speeds up to T1, except the Pro model, which includes fast Ethernet ports and can be accelerated to handle T3 connections.

Major Feature Set

SonicWALL supports the following major features:

- Stateful inspection filter
- Network Address Translator
- User authentication
- IPSec VPN (Included in Pro, otherwise optional)

The stateful inspection filter is hardened against denial-of-service attacks such as Ping of Death, Land Attack, SYN Floods, IP spoofing, and other packet deformation based attacks. Network Address Translation supports interior IP masquerade, but does not support port redirection to internal servers.

Conspicuously absent from the feature list is security proxies. SonicWALL does include an HTTP filter application, but the firewall has no ability to prevent e-mail attacks or attacks on using other high-level services.

User authentication is performed via user logon with an account name and MD5 encrypted password (somewhat similar to Windows NT Challenge/Response logons). Account-based security is easy to hack and should not be considered for highly secure facilities.

SonicWALL supports IPSec encryption on the firewall that is compatible with numerous other IPSec implementations including Firewall-1. Client software is available for Windows. The firewall supports a tunnel-only IP within IP mode that is not encrypted, but

Commercial Firewalls

PART 4

flows between two sites only after performing an IPSec authentication. This improves performance because the SonicWALL device is more CPU limited than most standard PCs.

Minor Feature Set

SonicWALL supports the following minor features:

- Content filtering with numerous options
- Strong logging and reporting
- DHCP Server
- Application Layer HTTP filtering

SonicWALL supports URL filtering based on custom lists you create and weekly updates from the CyberNOT list. Alternatively, the firewall can be configured to allow no access except to sites on an approved list. For administrators of highly secure environments or sites with high liability risks (such as schools), this sort of filtering (with careful site selection) can provide complete control over which portions of the Internet users are able to access. The firewall allows a password bypass to allow users unrestricted access to the Internet. The filter also allows blocking by keywords in the site, so sites that haven't yet appeared on block lists can still be detected by the presence of keywords contained in them. Finally, you can configure the filter to allow and log the access if you prefer a hands-off approach to management.

Logs can be viewed via the Web management interface, or the firewall can be configured to periodically e-mail the log to any address. The log can also be transmitted automatically to a syslog daemon running on any UNIX platform. Alerting is performed via e-mail, so paging functions would have to go through an e-mail-to-pager gateway.

The Application Layer HTTP filtering allows the firewall to block embedded Java applets, Active-X controls, and cookies. SonicWALL can also block attachment to external proxy servers.

Interface

SonicWALL is managed via a Java applet-based management application served by the firewall to the internal interface. Any Java-enabled Web browser can be used to perform firewall management.

The interface is clean and well organized—it's actually better than most of the Windows-based managers for similar firewalls. The initial screen shown in Figure 16.1 provides a plain English description of your current security posture.

The firewall is exceptionally easy to administer, but it is rather limited in its application; if you have unusual security requirements or use non-standard TCP/IP applications, this firewall may not work well for you. For example, there's very little support for real-time multimedia streaming or SQL access through the firewall.

Figure 16.1   SonicWALL Web management interface

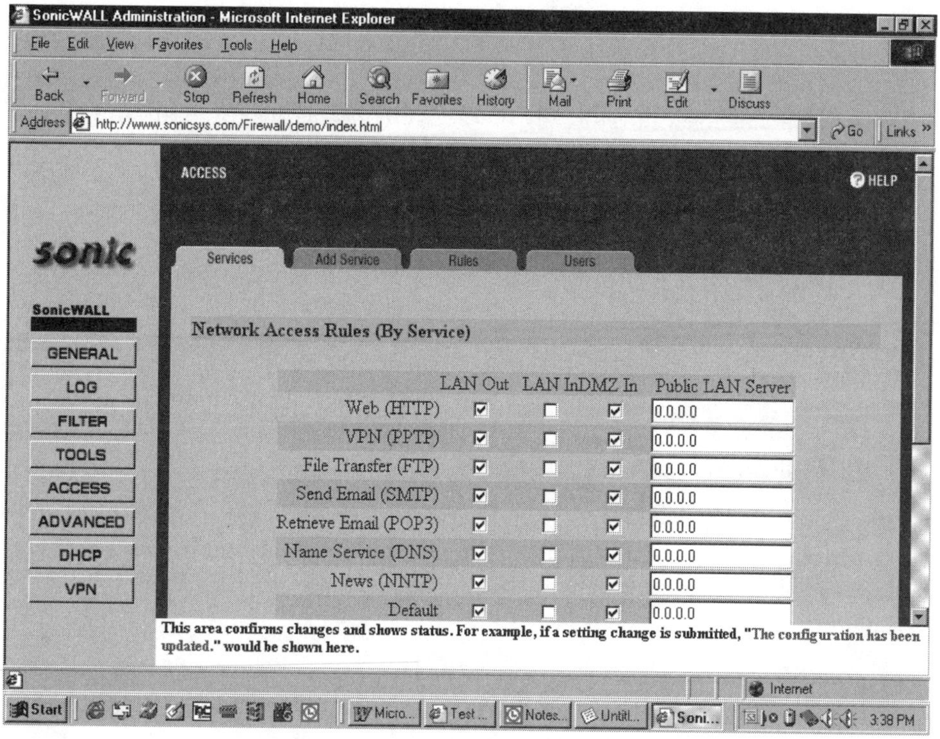

Security

SonicWALL is essentially equivalent to Checkpoint Firewall-1 in its security implementation; it is a stateful inspector with Network Address Translation and an HTTP security filter. Speed is limited by the interfaces and the comparatively slow microprocessor.

Although the firewall does not include security proxies, it does include an HTTP filter capable of blocking Java applets and Active-X controls. The filtering is capable of detecting Web servers that run on non-standard TCP ports.

The lack of security proxies prevents SonicWALL from performing content filtering on protocols, like e-mail, which are often exploited to push Trojan horses into organizations. Assuming a successful Trojan horse attack, the firewall's default security policy would not prevent the Trojan horse from connecting to the Internet, but the firewall can be configured to restrict all unknown protocols.

Documentation, Cost, and Support

The documentation for the SonicWALL firewall is built into the firewall as a Web site. Although this may, at first glance, seem like a security risk (hackers could use the documentation once they've gained access to an internal site), complete documentation of just about every major firewall is already on the Web in other locations anyway.

Perhaps the best feature of the SonicWALL is its extremely low cost. For less money than firewall software, you get a complete solution including hardware.

SonicWALL 10 Users: $400

SonicWALL 50 Users: $800

SonicWALL DMZ: $1,500

SonicWALL Pro: $2,500

VPN Option: $400

VPN Client: $75 each

Support subscriptions are also reasonably priced—between $100 and $200 for most options annually. The firewall is so easy to use you'll probably never need technical support. Content filter subscriptions are also available, as are upgrades from 10 to 50 and 50 to unlimited users.

> **TIP**   Sonic's Web site is at www.sonicsys.com, (or www.sonicwall.com) and you can buy SonicWALL by searching www.shopper.com.

NetScreen 10 & 100

NetScreen 10 & 100 are hybrid (stateful inspection and SOCK proxy) dedicated firewall appliances based on a custom application-specific integrated circuit.

Pros	Cons
High performing	No security proxies
Built in VPN	No content filtering
DMZ support	
Small form factor	

Basing the firewall engine on a microchip designed for firewalling makes the firewall considerably faster than competing firewall appliances and most computers. For example, NetScreen claims 84 Mbps throughput for 64 clients, which makes the firewall capable of firewalling a 100Mbps Ethernet connection with no noticeable latency (but no performance information is provided under connection saturation conditions). The NetScreen firewall is only slightly slower than Cisco's PIX firewall, is considerably less expensive, and provides a higher degree of inherent security through its Application Layer packet regeneration.

The device is one-rack unit (1 3/4 inches) high and 19 inches wide, so it mounts directly in a standard TIA 19-inch rack. Three network ports (internal, external, and DMZ) are provided along with a serial port for optional command line interface management. Two versions of the device are available:

- Ethernet 10Mbps (4,000 simultaneous connections)
- Fast Ethernet 100Mbps (34,000 simultaneous connections)

Like most true network translators, the firewall supports transparent operation so internal hosts and routers do not need to be reconfigured when you install the firewall.

Both versions of the firewall include VPN support, and a reasonably priced remote access client is available.

Major Feature Set

NetScreen provides the following major features:

- Stateful inspection filter
- Network Address Translation
- SOCKS proxy
- Authentication
- Virtual Private Network

The firewall is a combination of a stateful inspection filter and a generic TCP proxy, and therefore qualifies as a hybrid technology firewall, although no security-specific proxies are provided. Sophisticated NAT is provided, making available such features as single IP hosting and port redirection.

Unlike most firewall appliances, this firewall includes support for a generic SOCKS proxy. Although the proxy cannot filter content and is therefore not a security proxy, it is capable of completely breaking the routed link in the firewall and thus providing a higher degree of immunity to undiscovered network and session layer attacks.

Commercial Firewalls

PART 4

VPN supports IPSec for interoperability with other vendors' firewall solutions (check with vendors first), Internet Key Exchange (IKE), and uses DES or triple-DES for payload encryption. Two shared-secret algorithms provide user authentication: MD-5 or SHA.

Minor Feature Set

NetScreen firewalls provide the following minor features:

- Traffic management
- Load balancing
- Virtual IP
- Real-time logging to syslog systems
- E-mail alerting

The traffic management feature allows you to prioritize available bandwidth per service. For example, if you use real-time streaming multimedia services, you can allocate a specific amount of bandwidth to dedicate to those services, assuring the quality of service necessary to make them work.

The load-balancing feature allows you to put multiple servers behind a single IP address to share the client load. Connections can be assigned on a round-robin basis, a manually weighted round-robin basis, a lowest number of connections basis, and a weighted lowest number of connections basis. These methods do not require communication with the servers, so no monitoring software is required. The weighting options allow you to lighten the load manually for machines with lower capability in the server group.

The virtual IP function allows you to translate specific ports on a single external address to various hosts in the DMZ, so that a single IP address can provide multiple services on multiple machines. This feature can be used in combination with the load-balancing feature to provide large scale Web services via a single IP address.

The firewall supports logging to syslog daemons on UNIX platforms, so any syslog compatible logging and alerting systems can integrate the firewall into your logging infrastructure. E-mail alerting is the only alert mechanism available from the firewall, so paging systems would have to operate through an e-mail-to-pager gateway.

Interface

The Web interface for NetScreen is clean, simple, and efficient. It allows considerably more customization than the interfaces of simpler devices like the SonicWALL firewall, and provides a policy-based rule set interface rather than a simple on/off service selector.

The firewall is SNMP manageable, and can also be configured via a command-line interface by a terminal or terminal emulator through the serial port. Figure 16.2 shows the Web-based interface for NetScreen firewalls.

Figure 16.2   The NetScreen Web management interface

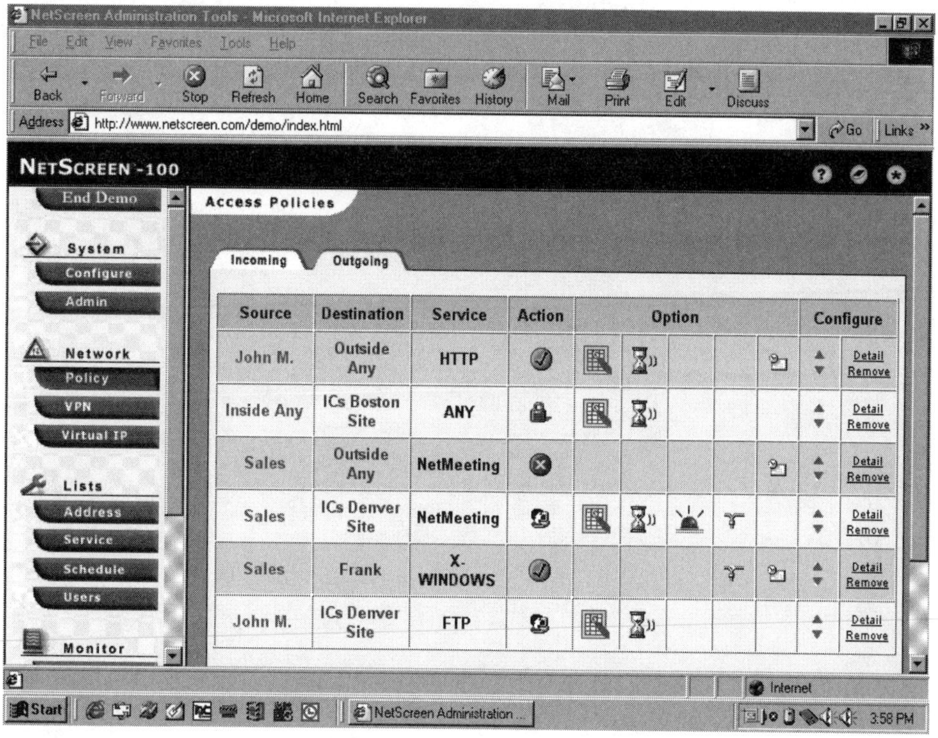

Security

NetScreen provides both stateful packet inspection and a SOCKS proxy, which technically makes a hybrid firewall. Client hiding is performed through Network Address Translation, so internal machines are protected from the network. It is the only firewall appliance we know of which includes a SOCKS proxy. Because the firewall runs on a dedicated device, it should be considered OS hardened.

Although a SOCKS proxy improves the firewall's security posture, no generic proxy can provide content security. Features like Java and Active-X blocking, URL screening, and e-mail attachment security are not available.

Commercial
Firewalls

PART 4

Documentation, Cost, and Support

Unfortunately, the documentation provided with the product was not available for review. However, the management interface is simple and clear, so anyone familiar with TCP/IP and Internet security will be able to configure the device without any documentation at all.

Support is available via telephone or e-mail, but NetScreen prefers to push support to the VAR that provided the hardware. NetScreen is available only through regional value-added resellers, which makes it both more expensive and more difficult to purchase than products available through standard distribution channels. Most value-added resellers will not deviate much from the list prices shown here.

NetScreen 10: $3,995

NetScreen 100: $4,995

NetScreen Remote Client (1): $95

TIP   NetScreen's Web site is located at www.netscreen.com.

Home Security

One of my clients researches ways to safely dispose of hazardous waste. To date, the company has not really made its existence public; it is privately capitalized and has no products except the results of its research. The Internet security posture was routine: A single Firewall-1 firewall provided security and passed mail to an internal e-mail server. No other services were provided.

Remote users are a necessary problem with this network since some scientists involved in the company cannot make the daily commute to work. For these scientists, Firewall-1's IPSec based remote software is used. They run Windows NT, and NT's packet filtering is used to rebuff simple threats from the Internet.

The company has recently identified a serious security threat. It will soon makes its existence known, through an industrial conference, to a foreign multinational competitor that is widely known to use any and all means at its disposal to acquire trade secret information. For this reason, the security posture of the company must be able to resist serious directed attacks.

The plan is to create a new security zone for public servers. Essentially, the e-mail server will run Firewall-1 to harden its OS, and a new high security hybrid server (Gauntlet) will secure the internal network. No inbound connections will be allowed to pass through the interior bastion host. The e-mail server will sit outside, protected by its Firewall-1 hardening. Confidential e-mail will be encrypted in the event that the external e-mail server is exploited.

The new security posture is a problem for remote clients, however; the easiest way to attack a secure network is to exploit an improperly secured remote PC and then use it to enter the network.

To enhance security for remote users, we will be using SonicWALL firewalls between the cable-modem and the home PC. This puts a strong stateful inspection firewall between the home computer and the Internet without costing too much. The SonicWALLs will be configured to receive an IPSec based tunnel coming from the primary server inside the company. The connection is established in this direction because the interior firewall is configured not to receive connections of any sort, and so that the company retains easy local control of who can connect and when. The SonicWALL is further configured to limit access to the Internet for the home PC by forcing access through the corporate proxy server; in other words, a Web connection from home to the Internet must travel through the IPSec tunnel to the interior of the local network and then be routed back out through the security proxy. This ensures that the strong interior host's security filters are used to filter all connections going to the home PC. Although significant latency is added, security is extremely strong.

The availability of high security, low cost devices like the SonicWALL makes this sort of remote user security possible. I'll be getting one for my own home network.

Part 5

Additional Security Tools

Topics Covered:

- Small security tools you should know about
- How hackers attack networks
- Tools hackers use
- How to detect network intrusions
- Tools to detect network intrusions
- Tools to search for network vulnerabilities
- Tools to mislead hackers
- How to perform strong monitoring with standard PCs and firewalls
- How to respond to an intrusion
- How to find hacker Web sites

17

Security Utilities

There are a number of important security functions that firewalls do not fulfill, such as vulnerability analysis and disk encryption. Furthermore, the network administrators of small networks may not have a budget allocated for Internet security, so they may have to do as well as they can without a real firewall. This chapter covers the software utilities we've found to be especially useful and a good value in our security practice.

You have to be cautious when using multiple small scale tools to provide security; they are not integrated, they are usually not robust, and they invariably rely upon the strength of the operating system's TCP/IP stack, which could be vulnerable to denial-of-service attacks and other problems.

The lack of integration among numerous security utilities causes the "Swiss cheese" effect where a combination of separated tools leave holes through your bastion host. Multiple tools can't prevent problems that integrated solutions can. For example, using a separate NAT and proxy is an either/or solution: you can either proxy a protocol or you can use NAT to pass it to the Internet. Good firewalls can both proxy and perform Network Address Translation on connections flowing through, thus providing stronger security.

Some security is always better than no security (as long as you aren't lulled into complacency by thinking your solution is stronger than it is). Given the budget realities in many small organizations, we think it's better to do what you can within the limits of your resources.

NOTE The security tools presented in this chapter are not replacements for firewalls, and they should not be used instead of firewalls except when budget conditions absolutely prevent the use of strong security.

This chapter presents security utilities for Windows NT or UNIX; they hold by far the most market share among bastion hosts. This chapter should not be considered an exhaustive review of small security utilities—rather, it's a mixed tool bag of software we know works well over the long term.

Software You Already Have

You should be aware of what the operating system utilities you already have can do for you. Windows NT and UNIX come with a wide range of security related tools that you can use to monitor your network. Other operating systems like NetWare and the Macintosh OS are considerably more limited in this respect.

NT Event Viewer

The NT Event Viewer utility displays system logs and allows you to filter the display to show certain types of events. The security log includes security violations, such as account lockouts. Any auditing you turn on with User Manager's Audit Policy dialog box also causes events to be written to these logs. You have to enable security logging in the User Manager for anything to happen since all auditing is disabled by default.

Event Viewer is located in the Administrative Tools menu under the Start menu. When you first run the Event Viewer utility, a list of events in the system log is displayed. An icon indicating its significance precedes each entry. Figure 17.1 shows the NT Event Viewer.

Figure 17.1   The Windows NT Event Viewer showing the security log.

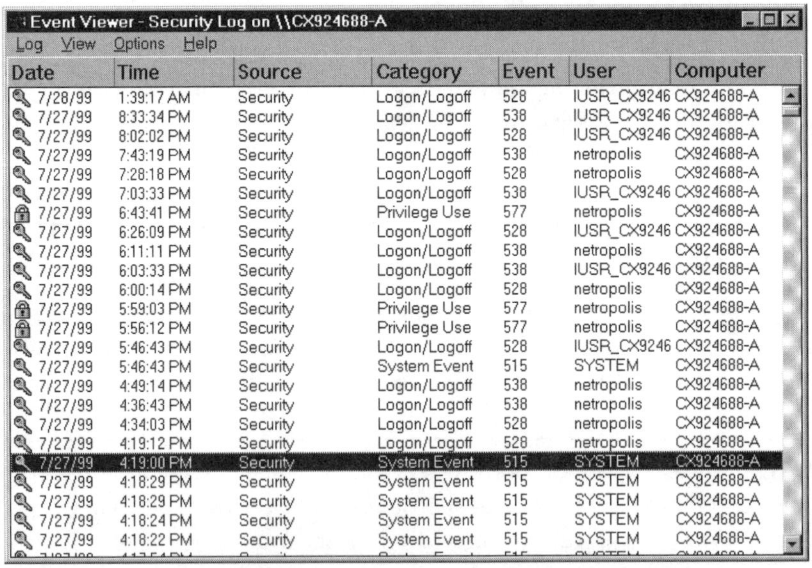

NT Network Monitor

NT's Network Monitor allows you to capture network packets and display information about them in extremely detailed form and with the protocols clarified. This can be a useful tool for monitoring the usage of the network, as well as searching for specific packets to track down security problems.

Before Network Monitor can be used, you must install the Network Monitor Agent on one or more computers and the Network Monitor Tools and Agent service on the computer from which you will do the monitoring.

To install these services under Windows NT, open the Network control panel. Select the Services tab, then click Add to add a service. Select the appropriate service (either Network Monitor Agent or Network Monitor Tools and Agent) and click OK. You must then restart the computer. Figure 17.2 shows the Windows NT Network Monitor performing a packet analysis.

Figure 17.2 The Windows NT Network Monitor

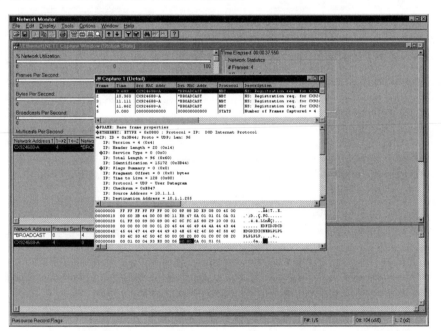

The version of Network Monitor included with Windows NT can only capture packets coming from and going to the current workstation, which limits its use as a packet sniffer. This should be sufficient for a bastion host because all Internet traffic must go through the machine. A version included with Microsoft SMS (Systems Management Server) can capture all packets. This version may be more useful to perform diagnostics or just get an idea of the type of information a hacker could obtain by packet sniffing.

Performance Monitor

The Performance Monitor utility is one of Windows NT's most useful utilities for optimizing and monitoring performance and also has a few uses relating to security. To run this utility, select Performance Monitor from the Administrative Tools menu.

Performance Monitor deals with individual parameters, called *counters*, that relate to the system. You can use the View menu to switch between four methods of monitoring these counters:

Chart Displays a running graph of selected counters.

Alert Allows you to set minimum and maximum values for one or more parameters. You are alerted when a counter crosses one of these values.

Log Creates a log of specified counters to a disk file.

Report Allows you to create a customized report based on counter information.

There are a wide variety of counter categories available in Performance Monitor, each of which includes several counters. The Server category includes several counters dealing with security:

Errors Access Permissions The number of times users have attempted to access files without proper access. A high number might indicate that a hacker is searching for accessible files.

Errors Logon The number of invalid logon attempts. A dramatic increase in this counter may indicate that a hacker is attempting to guess a password, or running a program to try passwords in succession.

Logon/sec The number of logons per second. A change in this value may indicate that an intruder is repeatedly logging in and out, perhaps trying different default accounts.

Depending on your needs, other counters may be useful. For example, you can monitor network use and errors for the TCP/IP protocol using the TCP counter. Figure 17.3 shows the IP counter being examined for the number of datagrams received per second.

Figure 17.3   The Performance Monitor

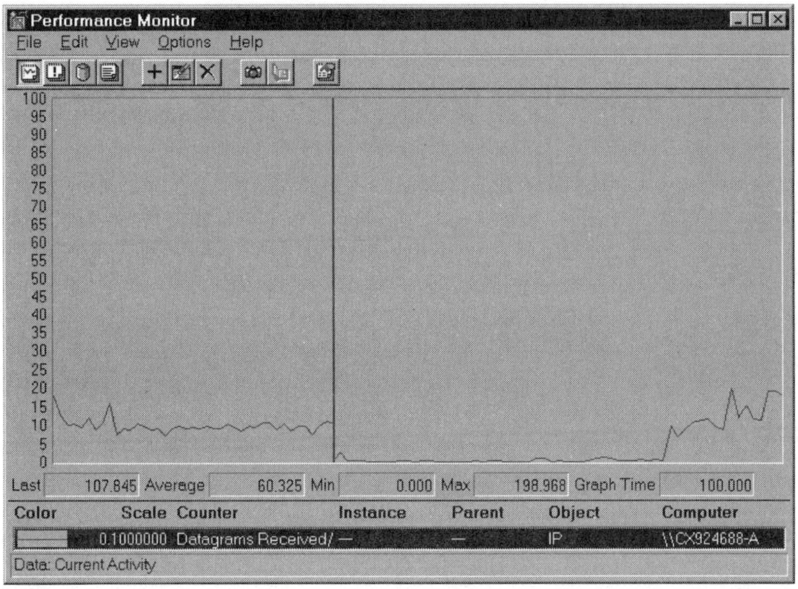

AT

The AT command allows you to schedule tasks to be performed at a certain time or periodicity, for example, at midnight every Thursday night. The AT command allows you to add, remove, and view entries in the scheduler service's execution list. The AT command could be used to run nightly intrusion scanning services, to periodically send a "heartbeat" e-mail to indicate that the host is running correctly, to scan for new open service ports, or for any other periodic security purpose. Be sure your NT installation is secure, however, as the schedule service could be exploited to gain administrative control of the computer if someone were able to modify a batch file that it runs.

When you type in AT with the help (/?) switch at the command prompt, you'll see instructions on its use. Figure 17.4 shows the AT command help listing. If you type AT with no parameters, the scheduler service only lists scheduled jobs.

Figure 17.4   The AT Command

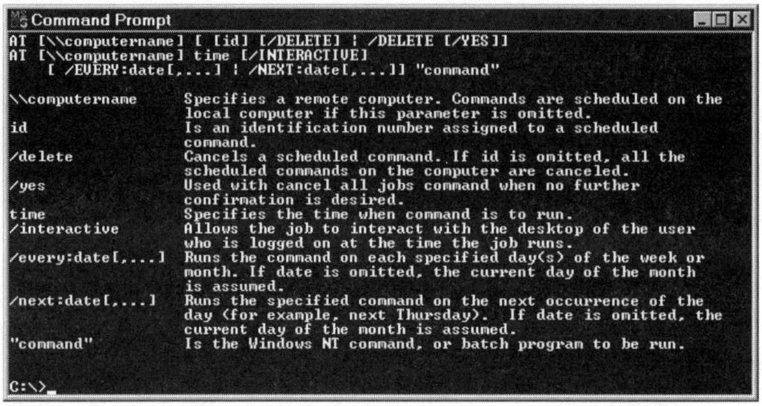

Schedule entries have the following parameters:

- Computer that should run the job (defaults to local computer if not specified)
- ID number used to refer to the job (defaults to next number for added jobs; required for deletion)
- Time at which the command should be run
- Dates or days of the week when the command should be run (optional)

The AT command uses the following switches to control job entries:

/delete Deletes the specified job. If no job is specified, all jobs are deleted.

/delete /yes Deletes all jobs without individual confirmation.

/interactive Specifies that the program should interact with the logged on user. If you do not specify that you want interactive control, you will not be able to answer alerts or dialogs that the executing program may raise.

/every Specifies that the command should be executed every date or day of the week specified.

/next Specifies that the command should be executed on the next date or day of the week specified, but not thereafter.

NOTE You must specify the full path and command name, including extension, to any command you specify. The Scheduler service cannot use path information to find a command.

The AT command is most commonly used to schedule tape backup sessions using the NTBACKUP utility. To schedule NTBACKUP to back up the entire contents of the C: and D: drives every weekday night, use the following command:

```
C:\>at 01:00 /EVERY:T,W,TH,F,SA "c:\winnt\system32\ntbackup.exe
backup c:\ d:\ /v /r /b /hc:on /t copy
```

Of course, you'll have to modify the path to your `ntbackup.exe` command to match your computer and change the parameters specified to match the way you want backups performed. If you don't include the /interactive switch, a logged on user will have no indication on the screen that a command is running in the background and will not be able to interact with the command. In the case of NTBACKUP, this means that if an error occurs that causes NTBACKUP to raise an error window, the NTBACKUP command will hang. You won't be able to use the task manager to shut down the command even if you are logged in as the administrator.

WARNING Avoid the temptation to use the AT command to schedule the execution of a batch file. If the file system security on that file is somehow compromised, an unauthorized user could change the contents of the batch file with a text editor to gain access to your computer as the system.

The Adminstrative user in Windows NT does not have ultimate authority to perform any action. For example, if you pull up the task manager and attempt to end a system service, the system will deny even the administrator permission to do that. Only the system, a special purpose user account used only by Windows NT, has permission to shut down system services. If you need to act as the system to shut down a malfunctioning process, you can schedule an interactive task manager session. When the task manager appears, it will have the permissions of the system so you won't get any access denied messages. Watch out though—if you shut down system critical processes, your server may crash. You can schedule an interactive task manager session like this:

```
C:\>at 12:05 /interactive "c:\winnt\system32\taskman.exe
```

Of course, you'll have to change the time specified to a minute or so after you type the line, and you'll have to change the path to match your Windows NT installation.

CACLS

CACLS (Command-line Access Control Lists) is an NT command line utility that provides fine control over the assignment of permissions to files and directories. Since CACLS is a command line utility, you can use it in batch files to perform mass changes to the permission structure of your drives.

WARNING   Be careful of the order in which you perform permission changes so that you don't deny yourself access before you can grant it! Always add new access permissions first, then delete inappropriate permissions.

When you type in CACLS with no command line parameters, you'll see the instructions on how to use it, as shown in Figure 17.5.

Figure 17.5   The CACLS Permissions Tool

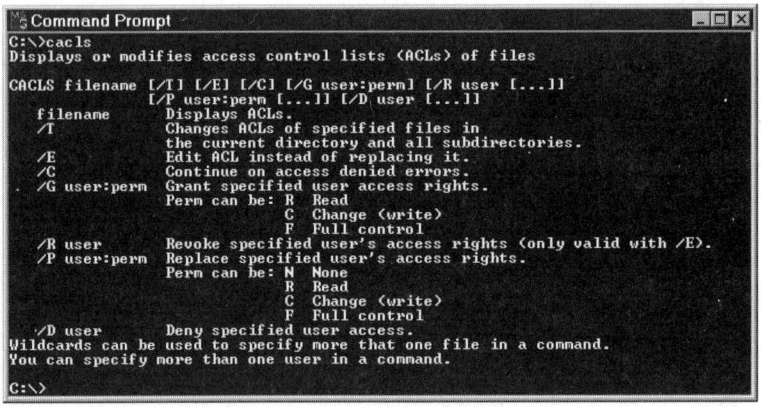

Most of the functionality of CACLS is described by the above commands, but there are a few things you should be aware of that are not immediately apparent:

- If you type CACLS with the name of a file or directory, the permissions for that file or directory are displayed. This is useful for showing exactly who has permission to what before you change anything. You can also save this information as a text file and later use a command interpreter like qbasic.exe to rebuild permissions.

- If you don't include the /E (edit) switch, the access control list is completely replaced. The access control list for an object is then created anew. You should usually include the /E switch.

- Accounts (user or group) with spaces in their identifiers (like "Domain Users") must be preceded by a single " character, as below. Accounts without spaces do not require a quote.

      CACLS . /E /R "NETROPOLIS\Domain Users

- You can use a period to specify the current directory. Wildcards will show all files in the current directory.

- Use the /T operator to show or change permissions from the current location and in all subdirectories thereafter. The command below will record permissions for every file on your hard disk to a text file:

```
CACLS C:\*.* /T >C:\PERMIT.TXT
```

You can use batch files to control the functionality of CACLS; otherwise, there is little advantage to using it instead of the desktop explorer to change permissions on an NTFS volume.

Finger

Finger is used to access directory information such as the e-mail address, username, and telephone number for users of remote network systems. Most new network systems no longer support the finger protocol due to its usefulness to hackers.

To get information about a user, enter the following command:

```
C:\>Finger user@host.com
```

To get information about all users on a host, enter this:

```
C:\>Finger @host.com
```

NOTE   Very few computers actually still serve finger requests. Usually, you'll get a connection refused error or a connection timed out error.

NSLOOKUP

NSLOOKUP (Name Server Lookup) is used to resolve Internet names to IP addresses. When you type in NSLOOKUP with no command line parameters, and then type "?" at the greater-than prompt, you'll see instructions on how to use the command (this is true for most versions).

Typically, you'd use NSLOOKUP to resolve an IP address given a name, as in:

```
C:\>Nslookup www.ibm.com
```

This command will return the IP address of IBM's Web server. Unlike most command line utilities, NSLOOKUP has two modes of operation. If you type NSLOOKUP [name] and press return, NSLOOKUP will resolve the address using your default name server, return the results, and exit back to the command prompt. If you provide no parameters when you launch NSLOOKUP, it will run as a UNIX style command line program, complete with its own prompt and list of commands. You can then use these various commands to perform all sorts of name server related functions such as changing your default name

Additional Security Tools

PART 5

server. The use of most of these commands is esoteric and usually not necessary except for troubleshooting purposes.

PING

Ping is used to send ICMP echo messages (pings) to a remote host to determine if the host is available for further TCP/IP traffic. Ping is so often used to test for the existence of hosts and for the proper operation of network clients that it is commonly used as a verb among TCP/IP network integrators, as in "did you ping the server?"

Ping is especially useful as a remote link status monitor. Using the –t (ping continuous) option, you can open a command shell and use the text output as a running second-by-second indicator of the connection status between the monitoring host and the monitored host. In Windows NT and X-Windows, you can open as many command shells as you want in order to monitor numerous hosts constantly. You can also use a scripting language to e-mail or page you when the link status changes.

You can control the various ICMP message parameters of the generated ping packet using the available parameters. Most of these options are used only during esoteric trouble-shooting sessions.

TIP The success of a simple ping request can be used to determine exactly how a malfunctioning client is operating. If a ping to another computer succeeds, you know that the physical layer, data link layer, and network layer are all functioning correctly and that any communications problems you may be experiencing must be occurring in higher layers.

Hackers also use ping for various detrimental purposes. For instance, you can generate a ping of death from Windows 95 machines by typing the following:

```
C:\>Ping 10.1.1.1 -l 65510 -n 1000
```

The ping of death generates exceptionally large (>64K) and malformed ICMP echo requests that are transmitted to hosts with delicate TCP/IP stacks. Many TCP/IP implementations will crash when they can't decipher an ICMP message correctly, so these ping-of-death attacks can be used to crash some TCP/IP servers remotely. Windows NT was susceptible to various ping-of-death attacks prior to Service Pack 3, and may remain susceptible to some undiscovered attacks.

Telnet

Telnet is used to establish console user sessions with multi-user computers. Windows NT does not support multiple simultaneous users interactively, so it does not have a Telnet server. The Telnet client included with Windows NT is useful for establishing user console sessions on UNIX and mainframe computers.

Telnet is especially useful to probe the presence and functionality of various Internet services. Since most classic UNIX services provide plain-text responses, you can telnet to hosts and specify the service port to determine whether or not the service is running correctly. You can use Telnet to attach to the following services:

- Simple TCP/IP services like Echo, Daytime, Chargen, etc.
- Content services like HTTP and FTP
- POP3, SMTP, and NNTP

More advanced session layer services like CIFS/SMB and NFS don't provide human readable responses and may not connect to a Telnet client.

TRACERT

TRACERT (Trace Route) is used to display the routers between two communicating Internet hosts. Figure 17.6 shows the command line parameters of the TRACERT command and a sample route traced between two Internet hosts.

Figure 17.6   TRACERT command sample trace

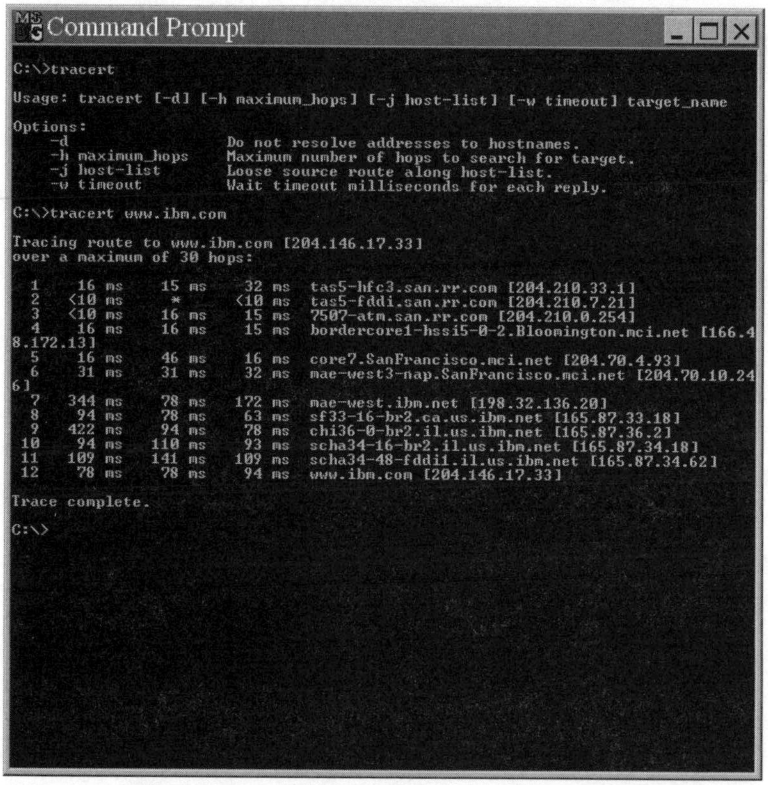

Since most Internet Service Providers use meaningful names on their router interfaces, you can often determine quite a bit about the route taken between two hosts. From the example shown in Figure 17.6, we can determine the following:

1. The first router interface is listed as `tas5-hfc3.san.rr.com`. Since we know from other hops on this service provider that they usually include the protocol for the interface, we can assume that hfc3 is some sort of physical port technology. It may stand for "High Frequency Cablemodem channel 3," which would indicate that the end user is using cable modem technology to connect to the Internet. This line also indicates that the router is probably located in a city beginning with the letters "SAN"—or following the common router practice of identifying a city by its three letter airport designator, which in this case would be San Diego, CA.

2. The next line is another interface on the same router—this time using fiber distributed data interface (FDDI), a 100Mbps token ring over optical fiber technology.

3. The next line indicates that the next higher router is using Asynchronous Transfer Mode (ATM) technology. This technology operates at bit rates varying from 25Mbps to 2200Mbps. As routers get closer to the Internet backbone, they should use increasingly faster data link technologies. This probably means that the ATM link is either 155, 622, or 2200Mbps.

4. The next line indicates that the next higher router uses High Speed Serial Interface (HSSI) technology, that it is located in Bloomingdale, and that it is operated by MCI.

5. The next line indicates that we've reached the Mae West Network Access Point (NAP) in San Francisco. This network access point is one of four commercial Internet exchanges in the country that forms the backbone of the Internet. So far, the route includes only very high-speed protocols and is relatively close to the Internet backbone—lucky user!

6. The next line indicates a switch from MCI's network to IBM's. This indicates that IBM has a presence on the Internet backbone directly, and would be a good candidate for consideration as an Internet Service Provider, as would MCI.

7. The next router is still in San Francisco and still on IBM's network.

8. The next router appears to be in Chicago (another NAP location).

9. The next router is in some city abbreviated "SCHA"—perhaps Schenectady, NY?

10. The next router indicates a shift down to FDDI.

11. The final hop is the destination server.

With practice and a strong knowledge of data link technologies, you can determine quite a bit about the identity of remote hosts on the Internet.

Security Analysis Tools

Security analysis tools scan target hosts for various known security vulnerabilities from another machine on the Internet. In essence, these tools provide one-stop-shopping to determine which known bugs or vulnerabilities your machines are susceptible to. Until you're completely familiar with Internet and operating system security, you should use these tools to discern where you need to shore up your host security.

Unfortunately, these tools operate from databases with a known problem—the databases can't find vulnerabilities that hackers don't already know about. This makes them more suitable for catch-up than strong security scanning. Exploits developed after the tool has been updated will be open. The only solution to that problem is to subscribe to e-mail vulnerability reports like SANS (www.sans.com) and Microsoft Security Advisor (www.microsoft.com/security), and then do what they tell you to do.

SATAN

The Security Administrator's Tool for Analyzing Networks is an open-source UNIX based network security analysis tool that probes hosts on TCP/IP networks for security vulnerabilities. Although SATAN is primarily designed to find flaws in UNIX hosts, it can point out problems in other operating systems as well.

SATAN's original release caused a considerable stir because hackers immediately used it to probe and break into numerous public hosts. Since that time however, its ubiquitous availability has made many an Internet host safe from intrusion.

SATAN can be downloaded at http://www.fish.com/~zen/satan/satan.html. Other versions of SATAN (with cute names like SAINT and SANTA) also exist as separately maintained offshoots of the original tool.

WS-Ping

WS-Ping is the "best of breed" TCP/IP administration tool. It provides a number of other TCP/IP client services to help you administer your network. The very services that make WS-Ping useful to administrators also make it useful to hackers, so it's likely you'll run into hackers using it if you have monitoring software installed on your public serves.

Installing WS-Ping is simple—just run the included install program and the rest is done for you. You then launch it using the Start menu. WS-Ping provides the following services, which you can select by clicking the appropriately named tab:

Ping Allows you to ping a host automatically with any sized packet for any duration.

TraceRoute Performs a TCP/IP trace route.

Lookup Performs normal or reverse DNS name lookups.

Finger Performs the finger function to get user details from Internet hosts.

Whois Attaches to servers running the Whois services to resolve e-mail names.

LDAP Allows you to attach to servers running the Lightweight Directory Access Protocol to glean account information.

Quote Provides a Quote of the Day.

Scan Allows you to automatically ping across a range of IP addresses to find responding hosts. It also allows you to scan TCP ports to determine which ports are accepting connections; this indicates the services running on a server and often allows you to identify the operating system running on the host.

SNMP (an SNMP MIB browser) Allows you to get low-level SNMP information from managed network devices and hosts.

WinNet (a NetBios probe) Returns Windows Networking information about hosts on the local network.

About Provides information about your local host's TCP/IP configuration.

The Scan tab is the most useful for hackers as it identifies targets of opportunity within a specific IP address range. You can use port scanning to see quite clearly what your firewall vulnerabilities are from the Internet, and therefore protect yourself in advance. Figure 17.7 shows the results of a scan against a wide variety of computers.

Figure 17.7 Results of a scan against a network

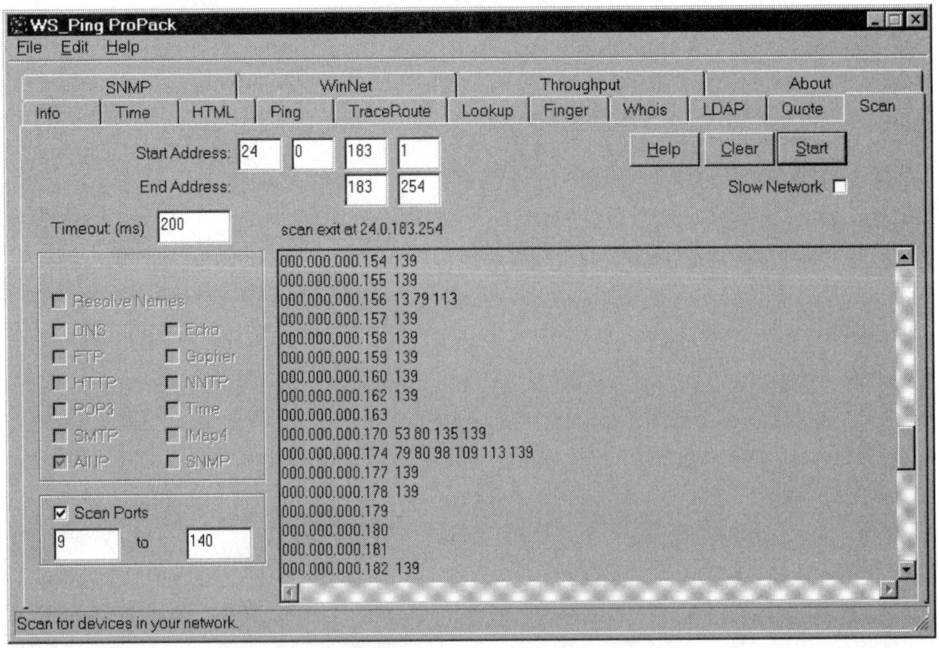

Internet Scanner

Internet Security System's Internet Scanner is the most comprehensive security checking utility we've found for Windows NT, Linux, and Solaris. It checks a vast array of common security problems and ranks them according to the level of risk they present. The security scanner is client/server based, so you can scan systems remotely. Figure 17.8 shows the ISS Internet Scanner in action.

Figure 17.8   The ISS Internet Scanner

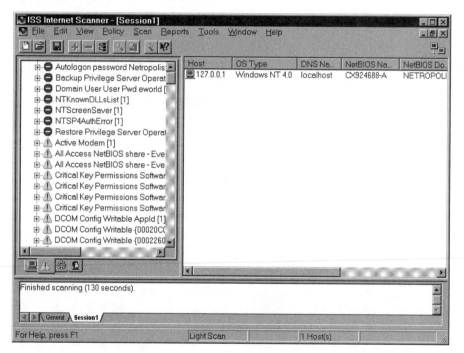

Installing IIS Internet Scanner is straightforward, but you will have to install a raw packet driver manually and reboot your system. Once installed, you simply launch the application and select whether you want a light, medium, or heavy scan. These various grades indicate the depth (and time) Internet Scanner will devote to uncovering security problems in your system.

When finished, you'll see each problem listed in a display window. The Internet scanner can generate a report in HTML or text format that delineates each problem found and its effects. This report is very useful in determining what measures you'll take (if any) to correct the problems found.

Additional Security Tools

PART 5

A number of the problems turned up by the scanner (especially in the low risk category) can't be avoided because they are inherent risks in providing service to clients. You should concern yourself mostly with correcting those problems shown as high or medium risk.

WARNING Never rely too heavily upon a single tool for security administration. Tools cannot check for problems their creators weren't aware of, so they go out of date quickly. Update security analyzers often.

Kane Security Analyst

The Kane Security Analyst scans through the registry to determine which security related settings are weaker than they should be. As an analytical tool, KSA is not capable of determining security vulnerabilities other than those listed in its database.

Installing and running KSA is straightforward, but you will have to contact Security Dynamics through their Web site at www.securitydynamics.com for a free evaluation key. Once you've got KSA up and running, you can scan your system for vulnerabilities. KSA will grade your system, pointing out specific areas where security is especially weak.

KSA's interface is rather cheesy, bespeaking an obvious visual basic background. But KSA is a fast way to check security on a system for which you've become responsible to quickly point out where you need to make immediate changes.

Protocol Analyzers

Protocol analyzers are the test equipment of networks. They receive and decode the low-level packet information for every frame that travels across the link they're attached to. Protocol analyzers are heavily used by hackers to ferret out network information from connections, look for bugs or vulnerabilities in protocols, and sniff for passwords or other improperly encrypted high value data.

Sniffer Basic (Formerly NetXRay)

Sniffer Basic is a protocol analyzer (commonly known as a packet sniffer) that runs under Windows NT and provides a very user friendly graphical interface. Like all modern packet sniffers, Sniffer Basic provides features for packet capture and decoding. But unlike many others, it can provide graphical charts pinpointing exactly where in your network heavy traffic congestion is occurring.

Sniffer Basic shows data link layer frames and the data contained within them. The top window is the frame buffer, which shows each captured frame. Selecting a frame in the frame buffer allows you to view the frame's contents in the two content viewers below. The content viewers show you the raw (bottom) data and the decoded (top) information represented by that data. Reading from top to bottom in the decode button is like reading up the OSI stack, from the Data link Layer (Ethernet) to the Network Layer (IP) to the Transport Layer (UDP) and finally the Session Layer (DNS). Since this packet doesn't actually carry user data, it stops at the Session Layer. The user interface for Sniffer Basic is very similar to the interface for the Windows NT Network Monitor.

Sniffer Basic is far too complex to detail its use here, but we can browse through a list of its major features:

- Client/server architecture allows you to attach to other copies on other machines for remote monitoring.
- Triggers alert you to conditions that you specify based on errors, utilization, or any other network characteristic.
- Packet Generator allows you to put your network under very specific load so you can test its ability to deal with heavy conditions. You can also use the packet generator to transmitted custom (or forged) packets.

Microsoft Network Monitor

The Microsoft Network Monitor is the protocol analyzer included with Systems Management Server (SMS), which is a BackOffice network administration utility. Network Monitor is the same software that ships with Windows NT as the NT Network Monitor, but it includes a special promiscuous mode NDIS driver that allows the software to monitor all the traffic on the connected network, not just traffic going to or from the server. This makes the software generally equivalent to robust protocol analyzers like Sniffer.

Light Proxies

Light proxy servers are smaller proxy servers designed primarily for Web sharing and caching. They do not include any specific security services, but can be useful security tools due to the inherent security advantages proxies provide.

WinGate

WinGate (www.wingate.net) is the granddaddy of low cost proxy servers. WinGate was originally developed to provide Web sharing in peer-to-peer networks. It is not a security proxy because it does not check the consistency of incoming data, nor does it sniff for suspicious content. But as with any proxy server, WinGate can provide the following important security functions:

Internet Host Hiding Because all internal connections come from a single source, information about your internal hosts is protected.

Route Breaking Packets aren't forwarded between the public and private networks, so internal hosts are protected from Network and Session Layer attacks.

These two functions alone can provide all the security many networks require. To use WinGate securely, you must ensure that the public interface will not accept inbound connections; otherwise, hackers could exploit the proxy in reverse to enter your network with certain protocols, or use your proxy to launder connections. WinGate 2.0 is the favorite "laundromat" for hackers due to its lax default installation and widespread use. Version 3.0 has much stronger default security. You must also be certain your base operating system is secure—run WinGate only on Windows NT machines, and be certain that access to the NetBIOS ports (135 through 139) are blocked. Your bastion host will still be subject to denial-of-service attacks, of course, as is the case with any software that relies upon the host operating system for security. Figure 17.9 shows the WinGate Gate-Keeper administrative utility.

Figure 17.9   WinGate GateKeeper administration utility

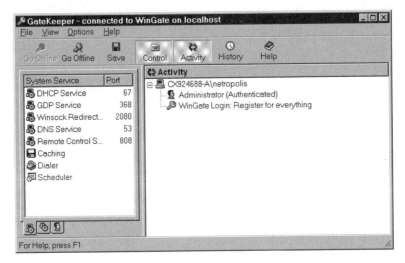

Virtual Private Networks (VPNs)

Virtual Private Networks allow you to connect networks or remote users securely over the public Internet by encrypting the communications between both hosts. Most firewalls have the additional cost of add-on VPN products, but you can use freely available software for NT or UNIX to secure your Internet communications.

PPTP

Microsoft's Point-to-Point Tunneling Protocol comes with all versions of Windows and allows users to establish shared-secret Virtual Private Networks over the Internet. PPTP's level of security is fairly weak because of some implementation flaws, especially if you use the 40-bit version. Despite these weaknesses, the 128-bit version remains fiendishly difficult to crack by brute force, so unless your company is a direct target for espionage, it should be sufficient.

The biggest problem with PPTP is that it allows anyone with a copy of PPTP (a free download if they don't already have it) to access your network by providing a valid account name and password. Unless you're certain you can control both the quality of passwords and the distribution of accounts on your network, you should not consider using PPTP.

VPND

VPND is an open-source transparent TCP/IP tunnel for Linux that uses the Blowfish cryptographic algorithm to establish fixed VPN tunnels between hosts using keys of between 0 and 576 bits. Blowfish with large keys is extremely secure. Best of all, VPND was developed in Germany and is maintained on Danish download servers, so U.S. export restrictions have no control over it. This makes it perfect for securing international tunnels with an end point in the U.S. VPND does not rely on licensed cryptography engines as do many other Linux VPN solutions.

VPND can be found at `http://sunsite.auc.dk/vpnd/`.

Encryption Tools

Encryption tools help you store and transmit your data securely. Two varieties are covered in this section: e-mail cryptography and disk encryption.

Transparent Cryptographic File System

TCFS is an open-source file-level encryption system for Linux based on NFS that is very transparent to clients. The encryption and decryption of files take place on the client machine, not the server. This puts the compute load on the client, ensures that only encrypted data travels over the network, and ensures that encryption keys are stored only on the client; they do not travel over the network. TCFS is available at `http://tcfs.dia.unisa.it`.

PGP

Pretty Good Privacy (PGP) is strong e-mail and disk encryption software written by Phil Zimmerman and released for free to provide strong encryption for everyone. Phil's company (also called PGP) has merged with Network Associates (NAI), but a freeware version of PGP is still available at `www.nai.com`. PGP will automatically install support for file encryption and e-mail encryption on Win32 platforms, and has plug-ins for Eudora, Outlook, and Outlook express on Win32 platforms. It also has strong Macintosh support, and many variations for UNIX.

PGP provides the strongest cryptography that is publicly available, and uses your choice of algorithms with key lengths up to 4096 bits. (Every bit takes twice as long to crack; compare that to the standard 128-bit security to get a feel for how much stronger PGP is than standard cryptography.) Perhaps the coolest thing about PGP is the fact that NAI and MIT maintain public key servers upon which you can store your public key for others to encrypt messages to you when they don't already have your key. That service makes PGP highly useful and is the reason why it's the ubiquitous encryption solution.

Thawte Certificates

Thawte Consulting (`www.thawte.com`) is the second largest root certification authority in the world, and unlike all other root-CA's, they don't charge for personal encryption certificates to encrypt individual e-mail. This allows you to use compatible e-mail software like Microsoft Outlook or Netscape's integrated e-mail software to automatically transmit your public key to others, add their keys to an encryption keyring, encrypt mail using the recipient's key (if you have it), and decrypt your encrypted mail. Best of all, the encryption and decryption processes are nearly transparent (Outlook does feel compelled to issue lots of modal dialog boxes like "Encrypting Message Using Public Key!" that are annoying). Get your free certificate today!

Password Strength Checkers

Password strength checkers read the encrypted passwords stored on your server (when run locally) and run brute-force decryption against them. The longer it takes to decrypt the passwords, the stronger they are. Network based strength checkers perform remote logon attempts automatically at a high rate, but are far slower than locally executed password strength checkers.

L0phtCrack

L0phtCrack is a password strength checking utility that will allow administrators (and hackers, on improperly secured systems) to view the passwords that users select. L0phtCrack was developed by a hacking group to expose the security risks inherent in Windows NT.

Profile

Name   L0phtCrack

Vendor   L0pht Heavy Industries

Cost $0 (Freely distributed)

Use   Decrypts Windows NT passwords from Windows NT's security accounts manager (SAM) using brute force methods.

Issues   None

By providing backward compatibility with LANManager clients, Microsoft has drastically reduced the password strength of Windows NT. Valid LAnManager passwords are far less secure because they allow a restricted set of characters and because they are limited to 14 characters in length. In addition, they are grouped into two 7-character passwords, which makes computing the password far easier because it takes large orders less computing power to decrypt two 7-character passwords than one 14-character password. Figure 17.10 shows passwords being decrypted on a Windows NT Server.

Figure 17.10 L0phtCrack decrypts passwords on an NT Server.

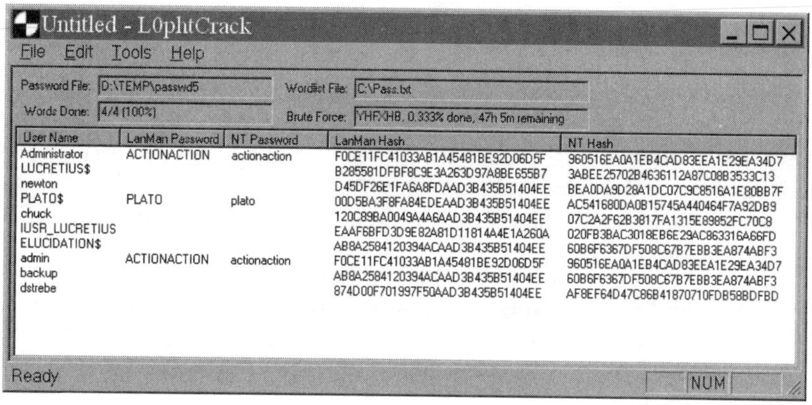

An Administrator can run L0phtCrack on a server to dump password hashes directly from the registry and then run a brute-force decryption to expose the plain text passwords chosen by users. This allows you to determine if users are using strong passwords or passwords that can be easily deciphered.

NetBIOS Auditing Tool

The NetBIOS Auditing Tool is technically a NetBIOS security auditing tool. Its purpose is to expose security flaws in NetBIOS networks, but there tools better suited to that task.

Profile

Name	NetBIOS Auditing Tool
Vendor	Microsoft
Cost	$0 (Subject to the GNU CopyLeft)
Use	Command Line Utility used to show the mapping between physical adapter addresses and IP addresses.
Issues	Command Line Interface.

The NetBIOS Auditing Tool's automated password checking feature makes it a favorite of hackers. Using the NetBIOS Auditing Tool, a hacker can launch an automated attack against an NT Server from over a network and attempt to attach via NetBIOS (which allows the remote user to map a drive, for instance) by repeatedly trying passwords against accounts. The NetBIOS Auditing Tool accepts a list of accounts and passwords and then tries each password against each account in the order presented.

The NetBIOS Auditing Tool accepts three command line parameters:

```
usage: nat [-o filename] [-u userlist] [-p passlist] <address>
```

- -o specifies a log file to which output redirects.
- -u specifies a text file of account names, one per line, to attack
- -p specifies a text file of passwords to attempt against each account.

A few normal security measures can prevent NetBIOS Auditing Tool attacks. If user accounts are to time out after a few password attempts, these sorts of hacks will never work against them. But the NT Administrators account cannot be locked out. Since this is the account hackers are after, The NetBIOS Auditing Tool is still an excellent tool.

Foiling NetBIOS Auditing Tool attacks can be accomplished by renaming the administrator account and by restricting administrator account logons from the network. You can then create another administrative account (that can be locked out) and use that for network administration.

TIP You can create a simple intrusion detector by renaming the administrative account and then creating a normal user account called Administrator that has no permissions to access anything and a complex password. Then, establish auditing on logon attempts for that account. Any time anyone tries to use it, you are under attack.

Hacking @Home

While preparing some of the security tools for this chapter on my home machine (which is connected by cable modem through @Home's service), I naturally ran a port scan against the class-C IP range that my computer is a member of. Nearly 70% of the available IP addresses responded, and about 80% of those machines had the Net-BIOS port (139) open, indicating that they were either Windows with file sharing turned on, Windows NT, or Linux computers running Samba.

Purely for the purpose of gathering statistics for this book, I attempted to map drives on the computers that were listed using a command like:

```
C:\>net use z: \\10.0.0.138\c
```

A shocking 30% of NetBIOS clients allowed this mapping (or the related c$ mapping for NT machines) without providing a password (or in the case of NT, a blank password).

Of course, I disconnected the mapped drives after taking the statistics.

If you use a high-speed constantly connected service like xDSL or cable modems, you need to be especially alert to the possibility of intrusion because you don't have a firewall between your personal computer and the Internet.

I suggest using an old computer with software like IPROUTE or GNAT Box to create a simple firewall between your home computer and the Internet. If you can't do that, at least disable the binding between port 139 and the network adapter you use to connect to the Internet. If you have to have file sharing among computers, consider using IPX or NetBEUI so you don't have to allow Net-BIOS bindings to IP.

24seven **CASE STUDY**

18

Attack Profiles

This book discusses a number of potential attacks without necessarily defining them. This section profiles all of the common attacks hackers use to localize, identify, and attack your systems. Given the information about how these attacks work, you can configure sophisticated firewall logging and alerting mechanisms to detect them. This chapter is broken down into the following broad categories:

- Denial-of-service attacks
- Exploitation attacks
- Information gathering attacks
- Disinformation attacks

These broad categories describe the purposes of nearly all hacking attacks.

Denial-of-Service Attacks

Denial-of-service attacks attempt to prevent you from providing a service by crashing or overwhelming your service computers. Denial-of-service attacks are the easiest hacks to attempt, so they are quite common. This section lists the most common attacks:

- Ping of Death
- Teardrop

- UDP floods
- SYN floods
- Land
- Smurf
- Fraggle
- E-mail bombs
- Malformed Messages

Ping of Death

The Ping of Death is the granddaddy of all denial-of-service attacks. It exploits the fact that many TCP/IP implementations trust ICMP packets to be correctly formed and perform too little error checking.

> **WARNING**   Attack Status: The original Ping of Death is Obsolete; undiscovered effective malformations of the ICMP echo request may exist, however.

Profile

In order to test the throughput capabilities and packet size restrictions, ICMP packets can be created having anywhere up to 64KB. This allows you to determine the actual maximum packet size between you and a target system on the Internet. In the early days of the Internet, this functionality was important because many routers had maximum packet size restrictions. In large ping packets, the payload portion of the packet is filled with meaningless data. The maximum payload size is 2^{16} (packet data overhead).

Ping-of-Death attacks are propagated by creating a malformed ICMP echo request packet in which the claimed packet size exceeds the maximum possible size. Because the payload size indicator is 16 bits yielding a maximum possible packet size of 65,535 bytes (the actual limit is around 65,500 bytes due to packet header data overhead), packets that claim to be larger than 65,500 bytes can cause TCP/IP errors in the receiving system.

In a typical TCP/IP implementation, when a packet header is read, the information contained in the header is relied upon to create a buffer for the payload. When the claimed size of the packet header plus payload exceeds the 64KB maximum defined by the TCP/IP specification, the TCP/IP implementation may crash due to memory allocation errors.

Defense

All standard TCP/IP implementations have been hardened against oversize packets, and most firewalls automatically filter these attacks. Windows versions since Windows 98,

Windows NT since Service Pack 3, Linux, Solaris, and the Mac OS are all immune to standard variations of the Ping of Death. Configuring firewalls to block ICMP and any unknown protocols will prevent this attack. For this reason, this attack in its current form is already obsolete and has no real future.

Teardrop

Teardrop attacks exploit a potential weakness in the fragment reassembly process of some TCP/IP implementations.

> **WARNING** TCP/IP implementations can easily be hardened against Teardrop, but many operating systems are still vulnerable to it.

Profile

Teardrop exploits implementations that trust information in the packet headers of IP fragments. IP fragments contain fields that indicate which portions of the original packet the fragment contains. Some TCP/IP implementations (including Windows NT until Service Pack 4) will crash when presented with forged fragments that have overlapping offsets.

Defense

Apply the latest service pack. If you run Windows NT and must remain on Service Pack 3, apply the teardrop hotfix. For other operating systems, check with your vendor for a patch to this problem. Configure firewalls to reassemble fragments rather than forwarding them; most firewall TCP/IP implementations should be hardened against this attack.

UDP Floods

Various spoofing attacks exploit simple TCP/IP services like Chargen and Echo to transmit useless bandwidth wasting data.

> **WARNING** Attack Status: These attacks are most easily defended against by not running the unnecessary services they exploit.

Profile

UDP floods are extremely simple: By forging a UDP connection to the Chargen service running on one host that has the reply address of a host running the Echo service, a hacker can create a useless stream of data flowing between the two hosts. Creating enough of these streams causes a bandwidth denial of service.

Defense

Configure hosts to disable simple TCP/IP services that are not necessary. Configure routers to block UDP requests from the Internet to these services.

SYN Floods

SYN floods are simple attacks that exploit the connection mechanism of TCP.

> **WARNING**   Attack Status: SYN Floods are easily defended against, but watch out for future variants.

Profile

The requesting client transmits a SYN message to the host service requesting service, and the receiving server responds with a SYN-ACK message accepting the connection. The client then responds with an ACK message, after which traffic can flow over the established bi-directional TCP connection.

When a server receives the initial SYN message, it typically creates a new process thread to handle the client connection requests. This process thread creation requires CPU compute time and allocates a certain amount of memory. When the TCP session is closed or after a fairly long time-out period, the server closes the TCP session which releases the memory used. The amount of memory and compute time therefore determines the number of simultaneous sessions a server can support.

SYN floods are bogus SYN messages sent to servers. How a SYN flood affects a victim computer depends upon its implementation of TCP/IP.

Some TCP/IP stack implementations are only capable of waiting for ACK messages from a limited number of computers because they have a limited memory buffer for connection establishments. If this buffer is filled with bogus connection initiations, the server will cease responding to further connection attempts until the attempts in the buffer time out.

In implementations that are not connection establishment limited, SYN floods have a similar effect. Since the server doesn't know a legitimate SYN message from a bogus message, it allocates compute and memory resources to establishing a connection. By flooding the server with a large volume of requests, the server's maximum capacity can be used by these bogus and useless connection attempts.

Defense

The only defense against SYN floods is a good firewall that can recognize the characteristics of a SYN flood—numerous identical connection attempts coming from the same IP address. These firewalls can filter subsequent connections from the same host, thus eliminating these SYN floods.

There's a scary future for SYN flood attacks. Since the SYN flood source machine isn't looking for a response, there's no reason why the SYN flood attack software can't simply use randomly generated IP addresses in the source field. This sort of SYN flood could not be discerned from a simple high volume of traffic and would be able to get past SYN flood filters. We expect to see attack generators of this sort appearing very soon.

Land Attack

The Land attack is a variation of the SYN flood that can cause unhardened TCP/IP implementations to "chase their tails" in a never-ending connection-establishment loop.

WARNING Attack Status: Land attack is already obsolete and easily defended against.

Profile

In the Land attack, a specially crafted SYN packet is transmitted to a server host. Both the source and destination addresses of the SYN packet are set to the server's IP address. This causes the recipient server to SYN-ACK to its own address, which it subsequently ACKs and establishes an empty connection. Each connection will remain until the server operating system times out the connection due to inactivity. Various operating systems respond to the Land attack differently—Windows NT becomes extremely slow for about five minutes. Many UNIX implementations crash. Most vendors have supplied a fix for the Land Attack.

Defense

Apply Land attack patches, hotfixes, or the latest service packs. Configure firewalls to drop any packets that have an internal source address inbound on the external interface. This always indicates a spoofed address and dropping these packets should be default policy in every firewall.

The following IP addresses are illegal on the Internet and should always be filtered:

- 10 domain
- 127 domain
- 192.168 domain
- 172.16 through 172.31 domain

In addition, you should filter your own assigned IP addresses.

Smurf Attack

The Smurf attack is an extremely effective denial-of-service attack based on the direct broadcast addressing feature of IP that allows a host to transmit data to all hosts in its subnet.

> **WARNING**   Attack Status: Smurf attacks can be filtered by firewalls, but they may still waste the bandwidth of your Internet connection because Smurf attacks outside your network can affect you.

Profile

A simple Smurf attack proceeds by flooding a victim host with ICMP echo request (ping) packets that have the reply address set to the broadcast address of the victim's network. This causes all the hosts in the network to reply to the ICMP echo request, thereby generating even more traffic—typically one to two orders of magnitude more traffic than the initial ping flood.

A more complex Smurf attack proceeds as above but with the source of the echo request set to a third-party victim, which will receive of all the echo requests generated by the targeted subnet of hosts. This attack is useful to hackers because they can use a relatively slow link like a modem to cause an avalanche of ping traffic to be sent to any location on the Internet. In this way, a hacker with a slower link than his ultimate victim can still flood the ultimate victim's pipe by smurfing a higher speed network than that of the ultimate victim.

Defense

To prevent hackers from exploiting your network to attack others, shut off the broadcast addressing feature of your external router or firewall. To prevent being the ultimate victim of a Smurf attack, configure your firewall to drop ICMP ping messages. If a high-speed provider (like your ISP) has been successfully smurfed and your network is the victim, there's nothing you can do about relieving the congestion that the ICMP traffic will cause even if you filter it out on your end. Contact your ISP about their firewall policy if this is a concern.

> **NOTE**   Check out www.powertech.no/smurf/ to determine if your ISP is vulnerable to Smurf attacks.

Fraggle Attack

The Fraggle attack is a simple modification of the Smurf attack, which uses UDP echo messages rather than ICMP.

> ***WARNING*** Attack Status: Like its sibling, the Fraggle attack can be filtered but may still consume network bandwidth in areas outside your control.

Profile

Fraggle is a simple rewrite of the Smurf attack that uses UDP rather than ICMP. This allows the attack to pass through firewalls that only filter ICMP.

Defense

Filter out UDP Echo messages at the firewall.

E-mail Bombs

Hackers can flood an e-mail server by repeatedly sending the same large e-mail file to your e-mail server.

> ***WARNING*** Attack Status: E-mail bombing and its relative, spamming, are fairly easy to filter, but they waste bandwidth outside your zone of control.

Profile

E-mail bombs are one of the oldest annoyance attacks around. By setting up a machine to constantly transmit e-mail to the same address, the attacker can use up bandwidth on the receiver's network.

This attack isn't all that serious, considering the fact that it requires nearly as much bandwidth on the transmitter's end as it does on the receiver's, which makes true denial of service difficult. E-mail bombs are also easy to trace, unless they've been transmitted through a mail host that strips headers.

Defense

Configure mail hosts to automatically delete excessive or duplicate messages from the same host.

Malformed Message Attacks

Many services on various operating systems will crash if they receive malformed messages because the services do not adequately check for errors in messages before processing them.

> **WARNING**   Attack Status: Malformed message attacks will always be around. The number and variety of them makes it impossible to make general statements about vulnerability.

Profile

All operating systems have susceptibilities (known or unknown) to various message malformation problems. Variations include:

- E-mail buffer overruns from malformed e-mail messages
- Web services that can be exploited by providing exceptionally long URLs

Defense

Stay up-to-date on the latest vulnerabilities reported by your software vendor. Apply patches and hotfixes to production machines as soon as you're certain that they are stable.

Exploitation Attacks

Exploitation attacks are those attacks that attempt to take direct control of a machine. The three most common are:

- Password Guessing
- Trojan horses
- Buffer overruns

Password Guessing

Once a hacker has identified a host and found exploitable user account based services like NetBIOS, Telnet or NFS, a successful password guess will provide control of the machine.

> **WARNING**   Attack Profile: Password guessing attacks are quite common, but are easily defended against.

Profile

Most services are protected with account name and password combinations as their last line of defense. When a hacker finds an exploitable service running on a target machine, the hacker must still provide a valid account name and password in order to log in. Automated password guessing software uses lists of common passwords, names, and words from the dictionary to attempt to guess high-profile or important account names, such as the root user password on UNIX systems or the Administrator account in NT systems. The software typically takes a list of account names to try and a list of possible passwords and simply tries each account name with each password.

Defense

Use passwords that are difficult to guess, such as combinations of words and punctuation. Make sure exploitable services like NFS, NetBIOS, and Telnet are not exposed to the public. Establish lockout policies if the service supports it.

Trojan Horses

Hackers install software on exploited computers to further gain control of a system.

> **WARNING**   Attack Status: Trojan horses remain an extremely dangerous, though difficult to accomplish, form of attack.

Profile

Trojan horses are programs that are surreptitiously installed on a target system either directly by a hacker or by an unsuspecting user. Once installed, the Trojan horse either returns information to the hacker or provides direct access to the computer.

The most useful sorts of Trojan horses are called backdoors. These programs provide a mechanism whereby the hacker can control the machine directly. Examples include maliciously designed programs like NetBus, BackOrifice, and BO2K, as well as benign programs that can be exploited to give control of a system like netcat, VNC, and pcAnywhere. Ideal backdoors are small and quickly installable, and they run transparently.

Defense

Strip executable attachments from e-mail and avoid downloading untrusted software. Use network scanning software to constantly monitor listening TCP services on interior hosts—this will expose many known Trojan horses. Use proxy filters that block unknown protocols at the border.

Buffer Overruns

Buffer overruns are a class of attacks that exploit a specific weakness common in software.

> **WARNING** Attack Status: New buffer-overrun attacks are found all the time.

Profile

Buffer overruns exploit the fact that most software allocates blocks of memory in fixed-size chunks to create a scratchpad area called a buffer within which it processes inbound network information. Often these buffers are programmed to a fixed maximum size, or they are programmed to trust the message to correctly indicate its size.

Buffer overruns are caused when a message lies about its size or is deliberately longer than the allowed maximum length. For example, if a message says it's 240 bytes long, but it's actually 256 bytes long, the receiving service may allocate a buffer only 240 bytes long but then copy 256 bytes of information into that buffer. The 16 bytes of memory beyond the end of the buffer will be overwritten with whatever the last 16 bytes of the message contains. Hackers exploit these problems by including machine language code in the section of the message that is past the buffer end. Even more disturbing is the fact that software is often written in such a way that code execution begins after the end of the buffer location, thus allowing hackers to execute code in the security context of the running service.

By writing a short exploit to open a further security hole and postfixing that code to the buffer payload, hackers can gain control of the system.

Defense

Buffer overrun attacks are common and crop up all the time. The only defense against them on public servers is to stay up-to-date on the latest security bulletins for your operating system.

Information Gathering Attacks

Information gathering attacks are not exploits or denial-of-service attacks; they themselves do nothing harmful to the target. These attacks are used to provide information for further intrusion into a system. Hackers routinely employ these methods to obtain and identify targets. This section covers the following information gathering attacks:

- Various scanning techniques
- Architecture probes
- Exploiting information services

Address Scanning

Hackers use automated software to transmit ICMP echo messages to a range of target IP addresses. Those that respond indicate that they exist.

> **WARNING** Attack Status: Address scanning is a common first sign of attack. Hackers often use address scanning and related scanning techniques to find hosts. Fortunately, address scanning is easy to filter.

Profile

By using automated software, hackers transmit ICMP echo messages across a very wide range of IP addresses (usually entire subnets). Those computers that respond become targets for further information-gathering attempts.

Defense

Filter out ICMP echo messages at the firewall.

Port Scanning

Hackers use automated software to establish TCP connections to various important ports on servers to determine if hosts exist and which exploitable services they run.

> **WARNING** Attack Status: Port scanning is widely used by hackers to identify targets, but is easy to detect.

Profile

By using an automated tool, hackers connect to a sequence of TCP ports across a wide range of hosts. The scanning software reports those hosts with which it successfully established connections. Port scanning is the usual first step in an attack.

Defense

Software that can detect numerous connection attempts from the same host can be used to detect scanning. You can also use seduction servers (such as Suck server) operating on ports normally used by standard TCP/IP services to detect scanning. Many firewalls detect scanning and can be configured to automatically block scanning attempts.

Inverse Mapping

Scanning is becoming worthless for hackers since firewalls can filter ICMP echo messages, and scan detectors, or deception services, can detect scanning activity. Hackers have figured out how to use packet types that cannot be filtered to infer information about the interior of a network.

WARNING Attack Status: Inverse mapping attacks are easy to filter out.

Profile

Inverse mapping works by inferring information from ICMP router replies. Hackers can infer which hosts exist by the lack of an ICMP "host unreachable" message when they transmit bogus response messages to hosts. These responses generate no reply from the host, but they also generate no error from the forwarding router. Those hosts for which no "host unreachable" messages are returned obviously exist. This information attack is a response to scan detectors.

Since normal scanning activity is easily detected by firewalls, hackers use common message types that firewalls cannot be configured to trigger on. These message types include:

- RESET messages.
- SYN-ACK messages, which would come from legitimate connection attempts to public servers from internal clients and are, therefore, extremely common.
- DNS response packets, which are replies to messages generated internally.

Defense

Stateful inspectors and true Network Address Translators automatically protect against this exploit, as do non-routing proxy servers. To be certain, filter ICMP host unreachable replies.

Slow Scanning

Port scanning detectors can detect a high rate of similar connections going to numerous ports. Solution: slow down the scanning rate.

WARNING Attack Status: This attack is a modification of the port-scanning technique. Its utility is dubious considering the time delay it causes.

Profile

Slow scanning methods rely upon the fact that firewalls and scan-detection software expect to see a high rate of connections from a single address to determine whether or not a scan is occurring. Scan detectors detect high rates by keeping track of the number of connections a specific host requests in a certain time frame (10 per second, for example).

By scanning slower than the time out rate of scan detectors (one attempt per second, for example), slow scanners avoid detection.

Unfortunately for hackers, the slow scan inherently takes a long time, so these attacks are only used when specific systems are attacked for a purpose.

Defense

Slow scans are very difficult for scan detectors to find. Seduction services are a more appropriate detector since they shouldn't be hit at all for legitimate traffic.

Architecture Probes

Hackers transmit garbled packets to host computers. By examining the responses, hackers may be able to determine the operating system running on the target machine.

> **WARNING**   Attack Status: Currently rare, these attacks will become increasingly common.

Profile

Hackers examine the responses to bad packet transmissions from a target host using an automated tool that contains a database of known response types. Because no typical response definition exists, each operating system responds in a unique manner. By comparing unique responses to a database of known responses, hackers can often determine which operating system the target host is running.

Defense

Assume hackers can determine which operating systems your public hosts run. Plan your defenses such that they do not rely upon security through obscurity. For example, you shouldn't assume a hacker can't tell you're running Windows NT Server on your machine because you've blocked identifying ports. You should still take all security measures to secure an operating system even if you don't think a hacker knows which operating system it is.

DNS Zone Transfers

Hackers can transfer name information from your DNS server to identify internal hosts.

> **WARNING**   Attack Status: This attack does not constitute a denial of service or exploitation itself and is easily defended against.

Profile

The DNS protocol does not perform authentication for transfers or informative updates. This makes the protocol exploitable in a number of different ways. Hackers can perform a zone transfer to get the names and internal IP addresses of all your hosts in a single operation if you maintain a public DNS server.

Defense

Smaller organizations should not run their own DNS servers. Use firewalls that support split DNS to ensure internal names and addresses remain private. Filter zone transfer requests at the firewall.

Finger

The finger protocol can provide enough information about users to allow hackers to guess usernames or passwords. Finger was commonly employed in the early days of the Internet as a way to lookup e-mail addresses.

Profile

Hackers use the finger command to probe a finger server for information about the users of a system. Often, account names and even clues that yield passwords can be obtained.

Defense

This common attack made the finger protocol obsolete. Nobody expects to get useful information from it anymore, so simply disable it. Block and log finger connection attempts at your firewall.

LDAP

The Lightweight Directory Access Protocol is yet another information leaking service. By providing LDAP information to the public, which might include valuable clues into the nature of your network and its users, you provide a wealth of information to hackers.

Profile

Hackers use the LDAP protocol to glean information about systems inside networks and their users.

Defense

Block and log LDAP probes into your inside network. If you provide LDAP services on public machines, allow LDAP into your DMZ. Consider a "split LDAP" policy where you provide full LDAP services inside your network but only a limited set of information publicly.

Disinformation Attacks

Disinformation deceives the attack target to plant incorrect information. This information paves the way for future attacks. This section identifies three disinformation attacks:

- DNS cache pollution
- Registrar usurpation
- Forged e-mail

DNS Cache Pollution

Hackers can provide bogus updates to DNS servers with incorrect IP addresses.

> **WARNING** Attack Status: DNS cache pollution is becoming increasingly difficult for hackers to accomplish due to strong security by major ISPs, but it is still not impossible.

Profile

Because DNS servers do not perform authentication when exchanging information with other name servers, hackers can insert incorrect information that would divert users to the hacker's own hosts.

Defense

Filter inbound DNS updates at your firewall; no external name server should update your internal server's knowledge of interior machines. Firewalls that support split DNS already support this line of defense.

Registrar Usurpation

Internet registries (also called Internet Network Information Centers) form the root of the DNS name system. Some registries have reported successfully forged update messages that have allowed hackers to redirect site traffic from the legitimate owners.

> **WARNING** Attack Status: Most registrars have changed their update policies to more carefully guard against these attacks.

Profile

Some Internet name registrars rely on e-mail messages for updates. They compare the e-mail address of the registered owner to incoming e-mail addresses containing update messages, and, if they match, the registrar performs the update. Because e-mail can be forged, these updates may be illegitimate.

Defense

It is not possible for end users to defend against these attacks. Most registrars have enacted more stringent update confirmation mechanisms, including reply-to e-mail and telephone confirmation.

Forged E-mail

Hackers can create e-mail that appears to be coming from anyone and requires a reply. In a variation of the attack, they can spoof the reply-to address as well, making the forgery undetectable.

WARNING Attack Status: E-mail forgery is probably the most serious form of attack against your network, and it's extremely difficult to defend against.

Profile

Using techniques as simple as configuring an e-mail client with incorrect information, hackers can forge e-mail to your internal clients. By claiming to be from someone the client knows and trusts, this e-mail uses a psychological attack to induce the reader to return useful information or includes an installable Trojan horse or a link to a malicious Web site.

SMTP does not authenticate the identity of an e-mail sender, and many versions of e-mail programs do not log enough information to properly track the source of an e-mail message.

E-mail servers normally include a chain of transmission headers in their e-mail messages, but numerous e-mail servers are known to strip these headers. Since hackers know which servers strip e-mail headers, they use them to make their attacks anonymous. Laundering IP addresses through a poorly configured proxy server can also make e-mail untraceable.

TIP Reading a list of servers known to strip e-mail headers (called "anonymizers" by hackers) is like reading a who's who of the .gov (government) domain. Why does the government run so many servers that strip headers? So it can keep track of all the machines from which requests to send striped-header e-mail originate.

Defense

The only true defense against e-mail forgery is user awareness; make sure your users understand that e-mail forgery is possible and constitutes a likely attack mechanism in well-defended networks.

You can use S/MIME enabled e-mail clients and install personal encryption certificates to sign e-mail from all internal users. Unsigned e-mail should be considered potentially suspect. Filter executable attachments out of e-mail at the firewall.

24seven Case Study: As You Sow, So Shall You Reap

About a year ago, I visited an old high school friend who had recently become very adept at hacking in his spare time. Eager to show off the spoils of his newfound pastime, he pulled up movies, music, and software he'd gotten for free from the Internet.

Reluctant to moralize, I sat back and took the opportunity to immerse myself in the psyche of an active hacker. While we talked and watched the random gyrations of WinAmp (an MP3 music player that creates random psychedelic patterns on the screen that are synchronized to the music), a command-prompt window suddenly popped up.

We both leaned forward and watched incredulously as the following letters appeared one at a time, as if typed by unseen hands:

C:\>**Format c:**

The cursor paused at the end of the command line. My friend rushed to his machine and immediately closed the command prompt. We expressed shock at what we both knew was a Trojan horse attack, and then I immediately set about to defend and respond. Having never actually been present during an attack, the opportunity excited me tremendously.

My first step was to issue the "netstat –a" command. We quickly identified an unknown listening service on port 12345.

Since I recognized the common listening ports for a Windows computer, I knew this one was unusual. I recorded the remote IP address of the computer attached to it.

The mysterious command window appeared again, so I immediately shut it again. I then pulled up a port scanner and scanned the IP address of the remote computer. The results of the port scan revealed a listening service on port 135—the sure sign of a Windows NT computer. The computer wasn't running other proxy services, so I was comfortable that the hacker hadn't laundered his (I'm assuming the hacker was male) IP address.

To end the attack, I took a chance that the hacker hadn't updated to the latest service pack and telneted to his RPC port. Typing random data into this port caused a blue-screen denial-of-service attack in early Windows NT 4 service releases. Sure enough, a subsequent port scan revealed that the attacker's machine was no longer responding.

We then set about searching for the Trojan horse program on my friend's computer. After some research and looking, we found a copy of the NetBus Trojan horse. It had been installed by one of the pieces of pirated software my friend had downloaded from a hacker's Web site.

19

Intrusion Detection

If someone broke into your network, how would you know? There wouldn't be any muddy footprints. If you had a strong firewall that has good logging capabilities, you might find evidence of an attack in your logs, but a smart hacker can even get around that.

To make the case for rigorous intrusion detection beyond that provided by firewalls and their logs, consider the case of a classic Internet worm: A worker receives e-mail from a coworker's home account saying that he's found a copy of a file that's been missing for a few months. The worker clicks on the executable attachment that says it's a zip file, which installs a Trojan horse that lies in wait until it detects a period of keyboard and mouse inactivity for long enough to assume that the worker isn't looking at the computer. The Trojan horse then opens a connection to a hacker's computer. Even if your firewall is designed to block outbound connections on unusual ports (the vast majority are not), nothing prevents the hacker from serving his attack software on a common port like 80 (HTTP). Your firewall will merely see what looks like an HTTP connection flowing out of the network to a Web server, a type of connection it sees thousands of times a month.

This sort of attack will get right past even a strongly secured stateful inspection firewall like Firewall-1 or Guardian. Only proxy-based firewalls like Gauntlet and Raptor can be relied upon to reject improper protocol data on standard ports.

Even in that case, a clever hacker will simply use a binary data port like FTP that can only be filtered for initial connection data; the true binary file data cannot be filtered because there's no way to predict what the file should contain. The hacker designs the Trojan horse and attack server to transmit fake session establishment data, while the client appears to be merely uploading a file, but is in fact uploading screen images and accepting mouse and keyboard input. A well-designed Trojan horse could even work through an FTP proxy. Any other binary protocol could also be exploited.

If you rely upon firewall logs to tell you when an intrusion has occurred, you'll never find this sort of attack because it will appear to the firewall as if it were a regular client-initiated FTP upload session. Nothing about it will set off any triggers or alarms.

So we've established that even the strongest firewalls cannot prevent certain attacks. Any useful connection to the Internet is a potential vector for attack.

This chapter covers how to secure your network against those attacks your firewall can't prevent, how to determine when you've been (or more importantly, when you're being) attacked, and how to assess the scope of the damage should an intrusion succeed. This chapter covers many intrusion detection techniques that you can use without spending additional money on specialized software, as well as some of the major software packages available for intrusion detection.

Unusual Intrusion Problems

This chapter is concerned primarily with detecting intrusion into your network from the Internet. But before we discuss TCP/IP and Application Layer intrusion detection, it's important to understand that intrusion takes many forms at many other layers in your network.

Hackers are notoriously nonchalant, and have simply walked into businesses to get data directly or install software to propagate a further penetration into the network.

If your company has secrets worth stealing, foreign espionage agencies are known to go to extraordinary lengths to acquire information in their national interest. Many foreign governments also ask their agents to acquire information in the economic interest of the country's large businesses.

The measures in this section are exceedingly rare; most companies need not worry seriously about physical security. But if your company performs any research and development activity, then you should use more stringent security policy to protect the product of your research.

Real intrusion prevention begins with premises security, Physical Layer security, and Data Link Layer security. If your network is so fortified against Internet attack that a dedicated enemy cannot breach your defenses, they will simply change tactics and intrude more directly.

Possible vectors for attack include:

- Impersonating an employee
- Impersonating service personnel
- Wiretapping public data links
- Adding devices to the network
- Outright theft

Do you know everyone who works at your company? You don't unless you work at a small business. Does your company issue ID badges that everyone wears? They probably do not if you work at a small business. Employee impersonation is particularly risky, especially in medium-sized businesses.

Impersonating service personnel is the easiest way to gain trusted access to a company. If a phone repairman walked in and told your receptionist or security guard that they were experiencing telephone problems in the building, would that receptionist or security guard call to verify their story or would they simply escort them to the wiring closet? Would they know the difference between the attachment of a legitimate bit error rate tester (BERT) to a T1 line or an illegitimate wireless bridge?

If a salesman showed up and offered and demonstrated a new laptop, and said his company would be willing to let your staff evaluate the device for a month at no charge, would you accept? Heck, I would.

If you hired a security expert to evaluate your network, would you bother checking her credentials? I've won a number of contracts to evaluate network security based on my experience and the fact that I've written a number of security related books—but I've never had a customer check my driver's license to see if I was actually who I said I was. For some reason, companies go to reasonable effort to check out employees, but they let contractors and consultants parade around the company without so much as a look at their personal identification.

Any of these examples of lax facility security could lead to a network intrusion. A minute alone with a firewall is long enough to modify the policy to allow a surreptitious service port entrance for further exploits, or to change the policy for an existing service. The policy abstraction allowed by modern firewalls is nice, but nothing prevents a hacker from creating a service called SMTP on port 5900 that actually accepts VNC (remote control software) connections. All you'd see in your rule base is that SMTP allows inbound connections; you'd have to dig to find out that that SMTP wasn't SMTP at all.

Intrusion Tools and Techniques

Hackers use a variety of tools and techniques to attack networks. A typical intrusion takes the following form assuming that the intruder begins with no information about your site other than its address:

1. Address scans
2. Port scans
3. Services evaluation
4. Target selection
5. Vulnerability probes
6. Automated password attacks
7. Esoteric attacks

Each of these attacks is detailed in the following sections:

Address Scans   Scan across the network range, if any, to find service hosts. Hackers usually scan at least the entire class-C range of IP addresses around your host and may use reverse DNS lookup to determine if those other hosts are registered to your company. For this reason, you should assume they'll find any public hosts you have on the Internet even if you don't publicize its address.

Port Scans   Scan across responding hosts to find running services. This information tells the hacker what services are running on each publicly reachable host. Port scans typically work through firewalls as long as a host can be reached, especially if the scan is limited to service ports like 21 and 80 rather than scanning across all ports (which some firewalls are capable of detecting immediately and blocking on).

Services Evaluation   Determines the operating system type of each host. After probing common service ports like Echo, Chargen, FTP, Telnet, SMTP, DNS, HTTP, POP, NNTP, RPC locator service, NetBIOS, NFS, etc., the hacker will determine what operating system each host appears to be running. Windows based hosts typically respond on NetBIOS ports but do not respond on Telnet, whereas UNIX hosts respond on Telnet but not on the RPC Locator service used by Windows NT. Linux hosts in their default configurations respond on a wide array of services and are easy to spot for that reason.

Target Selection   Selects the weakest found host. Hackers will usually target the host with the most running services in the assumption that little to no work has gone into securing that host's default configuration. Windows hosts that respond on port 139 (NetBIOS) are certain to be attacked, since exploiting that service can lead to full control of the machine.

Service Specific Probes Use vulnerability analysis tools like SATAN against UNIX systems or the Internet Scanner from Internet Security Systems for Windows hosts. These probes check for a wide range of known service vulnerabilities that are easy to exploit, so they're checked first.

Automated Password Attacks Used against services like FTP, HTTP, NetBIOS, or others that allow access to the file system. Hackers employ software specifically written to perform a high rate of logon attempts (like the NetBIOS auditing tool) using dictionaries of common passwords. Failing this attack, most hackers will concede defeat or resort to simple denial-of-service attacks if they hold a grudge against you.

If a hacker ever gains console access to a machine, they're certain to run a high-speed local automated password cracker like Crack or NT Crack against your host to exploit other accounts.

Hackers have also been known to set up seductive Web sites offering free utilities to browse for account names and passwords. They've got your IP address when you visit. If you enter an account name and password, the software can associate the account and the IP address—so they know where you are and what identification you're likely to use. Do you ever use the same password and account name you use at work on Web sites? Like Microsoft's Technet? Or the thousands of support sites for network software? Most people do. I do. This makes it easier for hackers to access your preferred account name and password.

Esoteric Attacks Comprise the remaining range of attacks a hacker might employ, and include the unusual, uncommon, or difficult tactics hackers might use if they really want to exploit your Internet servers and no previous techniques have worked. These attacks include source-routed attacks, hijacking attempts, network sniffing for passwords, or seductive e-mail to install a Trojan horse. These attacks are exceptionally rare.

Hackers employ a wide body of software tools in their trade. Tools meant for administrators, like the SATAN and the Internet Security Scanner, become potent weapons in the hands of a hacker.

Hackers also exploit the specific software tools you use in your network. For example, enterprise firewalls have remote management applications, most of which are based on a fairly short shared secret password. Many firewalls have "hidden rules" that allow the attachment of their remote management client software in the mistaken perception that you'll always want to be able to remotely manage your firewall. Nearly every firewall we've covered in this book can be downloaded for free from the Net. While the firewall engine might time out after 60 days, the management interface works forever. This means that every hacker on the planet has the remote tools to manage your firewall—all they need is your password.

Intrusion Detection Systems

Intrusion detection systems (IDS), also known as intrusion detectors, are software systems that detect intrusions to your network based on a number of telltale signs. Active response systems attempt to either block attacks, respond with countermeasures, or at least alert administrators while the attack progresses. Passive IDS systems merely log the intrusion or create audit trails that are apparent after the attack has succeeded.

While passive systems may seem lackluster and somewhat useless, there are a number of intrusion indicators that are only apparent after an intrusion has taken place. For example, if a disgruntled network administrator for your network decided to attack, he'd have all the keys and passwords necessary to log right in. No active response system would alert on anything. Passive IDS systems can still detect the changes that administrator makes to system files, deletions, or whatever mischief has been caused.

Inspection Based Intrusion Detectors

Inspection based intrusion detectors are the most common type. These intrusion detectors observe the activity on a host or network and make judgements about whether an intrusion is occurring or has occurred based either on programmed rules or on historical indications of normal use. The intrusion detectors built into firewalls and operating systems, as well as most commercially available independent intrusion detectors are inspection based.

Intrusion detectors rely upon indications of inappropriate use. These indicators include:

- Network traffic, like ICMP scans, port scans, or attachment to unauthorized ports.
- Resource utilization, such as CPU, RAM, or Network I/O surges at unexpected times. This can indicate an automated attack against the network.
- File activity, including newly created files, modifications to system files, changes to user files, or modification of user accounts or security permissions.

Intrusion detectors monitor various combinations of those telltale signs and create log entries. The body of these log entries is called an audit trail, which consists of the sum of observed parameters for a given access object like a user account or a source IP address. Intrusion detection systems can monitor the audit trails to determine when intrusions occur.

Intrusion detection systems include:

Rule Based Intrusion detectors that detect intrusion based on sequences of user activities (called rules) that are known to indicate intrusion attempts, such as port scans, system file modifications, or connections to certain ports. The majority of intrusion detection systems are rule based.

Statistical Intrusion detectors that detect intrusion by comparing the existing base of valid audit trails to each new audit trail. Audit trails that differ substantially from the norm are flagged as probable intrusion attempts. Systems like these have the potential to detect hitherto unknown intrusion methods, but may miss rather obvious intrusions that might appear to be normal usage.

Hybrid Intrusion detection systems that provide the best of both worlds by combining statistical and rule based detection systems. Some of these systems are capable of creating new permanent rules from detected intrusions to prevent the intrusion from happening again without the overhead of statistical analysis.

IDS systems always require system resources to operate. Network IDS systems usually run on firewalls or dedicated computers; this usually isn't a problem because resources are available. Host based IDS systems designed to protect servers can be a serious impediment, however.

Rule based IDS systems can only detect known intrusion vectors, so all intrusions cannot be detected. Statistical intrusion detectors stand a better chance of detecting unknown intrusion vectors, but they cannot be proven to detect them until after the fact.

Because of these limitations, IDS systems generally require monitoring by human security administrators to be effective. Countermeasure technology and response systems that temporarily increase the host's security posture during attacks are all in the theoretical research stage. Current IDS systems rely upon alerting human administrators to the presence of an attack, which makes human administrators an active part of the intrusion detection system.

Decoy Intrusion Detectors

Decoy intrusion detectors operate by mimicking the expressive behavior of a target system, but rather than providing an intrusion vector for the attacker, they alarm on any use at all. Decoys look just like a real target that hasn't been properly secured.

When a hacker attacks a network, they perform a fairly methodical series of well known attacks like address range scans and port scans to determine which hosts are available and which services those hosts provide. By providing decoy hosts or services, you can seduce the hacker into attacking a host or service that isn't important to you and which is designed to alert on any use at all.

Decoys may operate as a single decoy service on an operative host, a range of decoy services on an operative host, a decoy host, or an entire decoy network. Decoy networks are very rare. Most decoy software runs on an operative host.

Software systems like Suck Server (written by yours truly) are decoy intrusion detectors. Suck Server works by creating TCP/IP service on ports that are otherwise unused on your machine. When hackers perform a port scan, the attachment to these unused ports is logged and can be used to trigger an alert. Simple systems like Suck Server won't do much for you beyond detecting port scans because they don't emulate the full functionality of a true host. In the case of Suck Server, the hacker would get timeout errors when attempting to connect with an FTP client or a Web browser, so they would either go on to another host or try some additional attacks on responsive ports that service actual services.

Much more effective is the establishment of a decoy host. You can establish an effective decoy host by installing a real running copy of the operating system of your choice on a computer with all normal services active. Using your firewall's Network Address Translation, send all access to your public domain name to the decoy machine by default. Then add rules to move specific ports to your other service computers; for example, translate port 80 only to your actual Web server.

When a hacker scans your site, he'll see all the services provided by your decoy host plus the services you actually provide on your Internet servers as if they all came from the same machine. Because the services running on the decoy host include services that are easy to attack, like the NetBIOS or NFS ports, the hacker will be immediately attracted to them. You can then set up alerts to alarm on any access to those services using the operating system's built-in tools. You'll be secure in the knowledge that if the hacker intrudes into the system, he'll be on a system that contains no proprietary information. You can then let the attack progress to identify the methods the attacker uses to intrude into your system. I suggest installing a network monitor (like the one that comes with Windows NT) on the decoy host so you can keep logs of specific packet based attacks as well.

Decoy hosts are highly secure because they shunt actual attacks away from your service hosts and to hosts that will satisfy the hacker's thirst for conquest, giving you plenty of time to respond to the attack. The hacker will be thrilled that he was able to break into a system, and will be completely unaware of the fact that he's not on your real Internet server until he browses around for a while. You might even consider creating a bogus "cleaned" copy of your Web site on the decoy server to maintain the illusion in the hacker's mind that the actual site has been penetrated. Any desecration performed on the decoy site won't show up on your actual site.

Best of all, decoy intrusion detection costs only as much as a copy of the operating system (NT Workstation can be used to decoy for NT Server, Linux can mimic any professional UNIX server), target hardware, and your existing firewall. You won't have to pay for esoteric software.

Available IDS Systems

Few reliable intrusion detection systems really exist. Firewalls with logging and alerting mechanisms are by far the most widely deployed, and the majority of those have no way to respond to an attack in any automated fashion.

Both Windows NT and UNIX have strong logging and auditing features embedded in their file systems. Windows NT also has an exceptionally strong performance monitoring subsystem that can be used to generate real-time alerts to sudden increases in various activities. This allows you to create simple and effective IDS systems for your servers without adding much in the way of hardware.

Windows NT System

Windows NT has strong operating system support for reporting object use. This support manifests in the performance monitoring and auditing capabilities of the operating system, and in the fact that the file system can be updated with date-time stamps each time certain types of access occur. These capabilities make strong inherent security easy to perform.

File System and Security Auditing

Windows NT has exceptionally strong support for file system and security auditing. You can configure Windows NT using the User Manager's Policies Audit menu to create log entries in the security log each time any one of the following events succeeds or fails:

- Logon attempts
- File or object access, like copying or opening a file
- Use of special rights, like backing up the system
- User or group management activities like adding a user account
- Changes to the security policy
- System restart or shutdown
- Process tracking, like each time a certain program is run

Additional Security Tools

PART 5

What all this means is that you can create your own intrusion detection software simply by configuring Windows NT to audit any sort of behavior that could indicate an intrusion attempt.

Pervasive audit policy can slow down an NT server dramatically, so you have to be careful of how wide ranging your audits are in systems that are already under load. Audit on unusual events like use of user rights, logon and logoff, security policy changes, and restarts.

File and object access is a special case in auditing. You have to enable file and object auditing and then use the security tab of each file or folder's property panel to enable auditing for specific files. This allows you to limit the files that you audit. For system files, you should audit for writes, changes, and deletes. For proprietary or secret information you store, you should audit for read access.

File and object access occurs constantly, so if you audit a large number of commonly used files, you'll increase the amount of chaff (useless information) in your log files and slow down your computer. Audit only those files that are real intrusion targets, like the system files and your proprietary information.

There is a problem with NT's audit policy: If a hacker actually gains administrative control of your system, the hacker is free to erase your security policy after it has been changed. To detect changes even in that event, see the next section.

Tripwire for NT

You can use the built-in functionality of Windows NT to test for changes to your system file in cases where you can't or don't want to use NT's built-in file auditing system. The command prompt directory command can be used to display the last written-to time for a file by including the /TW (display last write time) switch, as in:

```
C:\>dir c:\winnt\*.* /TW
```

By redirecting the console output of that command to a file and storing that file on a removable media cartridge or over the network to another machine, you can compare it to the directory at a later date by reissuing the command and creating a new file. You can then use the file compare command line utility to automatically compare the two files and point out changes between the initial write times of your system files and their current write times.

Many system files are written to frequently, while others never should be changed except after system updates or service pack installations. By recognizing which ones change routinely and which never change on your system, you can use this functionality to automatically detect unauthorized file system changes that have occurred on your system in much the way that Tripwire detects these changes in a UNIX system.

In Windows NT, you should be particularly concerned about the following directories and their subdirectories (assuming your system drive is C: and that you've installed to \winnt; otherwise, replace the example with your system root):

```
C:\
C:\winnt
C:\winnt\system
C:\winnt\system32
```

To implement this system, type in the following batch file and use it to create your initial difference file for each protected machine:

```
@echo off
REM baseline.bat
REM Use this batch file to create a baseline
REM for for file system changes.
Echo Creating Baseline...
Dir c:\*.* /TW >base1.txt
Dir c:\winnt\*.* /TW >base2.txt
Dir c:\winnt\system\*.* /S /TW >base3.txt
Dir c:\winnt\system32\*.* /S /TW >base4.txt
Echo Baseline created. Store baseline files
Echo In a secure location.
```

Whenever you suspect an intrusion, use the following batch file to create a comparison file that you can inspect with notepad or any text editor:

```
@echo off
REM compare.bat
REM Use this batch file to create comparison
REM files for file system changes and to generate
REM the compared output
Echo Checking for system changes...
Dir c:\*.* /TW >comp1.txt
```

```
Dir c:\winnt\*.* /TW >comp2.txt
Dir c:\winnt\system\*.* /S /TW >comp3.txt
Dir c:\winnt\system32\*.* /S /TW >comp4.txt
FC base1.txt comp1.txt >root.txt
FC base2.txt comp2.txt >winnt.txt
FC base3.txt comp3.txt >system.txt
FC base4.txt comp4.txt >system32.txt
Del comp?.txt
Echo Finished finding changes. Changes are
Echo stored in the following files:
Echo root.txt stores changes to c:\
Echo winnt.txt stores changes to c:\winnt
Echo system.txt stores changes to c:\winnt\system
Echo system32.txt stores changes to c:\winnt\system32
```

Using this procedure, I deleted temp files in my winnt directory and added a comment line to the wintab.ini file. This resulted in the following output, which show the lines above and below each change as well as the change itself:

```
***** start.txt
01/05/99  01:06p                    7,023 WINNT32.LOG
03/03/99  07:21p                    1,799 WINTAB.INI
01/25/99  03:06a                  162,576 wjview.exe
***** FINAL.TXT
01/05/99  01:06p                    7,023 WINNT32.LOG
07/11/99  09:08p                    1,815 WINTAB.INI
01/25/99  03:06a                  162,576 wjview.exe
*****

***** start.txt
06/28/99  11:53p                      164 _delis32.ini
```

```
06/10/99   11:57a                          0 ~DF23BD.tmp
06/10/99   11:49a                          0 ~DF2544.tmp
06/10/99   11:43a                          0 ~DF29B9.tmp
07/01/99   09:32a                          0 ~DF2BF4.tmp
06/10/99   11:02a                          0 ~DF3240.tmp
07/11/99   06:17p                          0 ~DF3421.tmp
06/29/99   07:08a                          0 ~DF3B0E.tmp
06/23/99   11:07p                          0 ~DF3F97.tmp
06/24/99   06:44p                          0 ~DF4670.tmp
06/23/99   10:57p                          0 ~DF4B0E.tmp
11/05/98   06:33p        <DIR>               ~offfilt
***** FINAL.TXT
06/28/99   11:53p                        164 _delis32.ini
07/11/99   06:17p                          0 ~DF3421.tmp
11/05/98   06:33p        <DIR>               ~offfilt
*****


***** start.txt
06/11/99   04:45p                         50 ?
              296 File(s)     119,295,337 bytes
                            1,031,680,000 bytes free
***** FINAL.TXT
06/11/99   04:45p                         50 ?
              287 File(s)     119,295,353 bytes
                            1,031,700,480 bytes free
*****
```

Ignoring the first and last line of each block, the output clearly shows changes to the wintab.ini file's size and write time, the missing temporary files, and the difference in directory size.

Extremely clever hackers know how to change access times back to their original times, and can be certain to make sure files are exactly the same size. So this method is not as theoretically pure as the method used by Tripwire, which relies on comparing cryptographic hashes made of each file. Hackers this careful are very rare though, so this method can be used to find the vast majority of file system changes.

You can also use the FC command to find changes in the system registry using a similar method that cannot be batch scripted:

1. Using the registry editor Regedit.exe, browse to the system key you wish to check for changes. You should be primarily concerned about the following keys:

   HKLM\SYSTEM\CurrentControlSet

   HKLM\SOFTWARE\Microsoft\Windows NT\CurrentVersion

2. With the key selected, select Registry ➤ Export Registry file.

3. Enter a filename on a removable media or network drive.

When you need to compare the files, repeat the process and use the following command to find changes to registry settings:

   C:\>**FC baseline.txt current.txt**

The resulting text file will contain the changed registry settings.

Comparing file systems is sometimes the only method you can use to detect intrusion if the intruder has gained administrative access to your system in a manner that your intrusion detection systems can't track. If they've made any useful modification to your system at all, you'll be able to detect it with this procedure.

Unfortunately, you can't use this procedure to detect information that has simply been copied off your system. But Windows NT also maintains a "last read time" that can be output by the directory command, so if your security policy requires it, you can modify this procedure to look for changes in the last access time of any file. Be prepared to dig though—most system files are accessed very frequently. For that reason, you should define very narrowly the set of files you're interested in tracking and use this system to track only them.

Performance Monitor

The Windows NT performance monitor can be used to alert on sudden changes in resource utilization and on such attack indicators as a high number of logon attempts per second. The performance monitor can be configured to run programs to send e-mail, network alerts, or pages when any thresholds are reached.

Unfortunately the performance monitor is a user-level program that doesn't run as a service and only works while you are logged on. This makes it somewhat fragile. You can monitor machines remotely, however, so a single alerting workstation could be set up to monitor all your servers.

NAI CyberCop

Network Associates' CyberCop is a suite of four tools you can use for intrusion protection outside of simple firewalling. These tools are available for Windows NT and UNIX, and can be downloaded for evaluation from NAI's Web site at www.nai.com. The tools are:

- CyberCop Scanner works much like Intrusion Detection System's Internet Security Scanner or SATAN to probe for known vulnerabilities.

- CyberCop Monitor is a true hybrid intrusion detection system that can alert on real-time packet analysis and perform monitoring of system events and logs.

- CyberCop Sting is a decoy intrusion detector that can be used to mislead hackers away from your actual machines and to a protected host where the hacker's techniques can be studied safely and where information on the hacker can be observed.

- CyberCop CASL is a scripting language that can be used to script automated attacks against your network to prove its invulnerability. CASL is available for download at no cost, but any attacks you discover using CASL become the property of NAI.

By integrating these tools with NAI's gauntlet firewall using their active security infrastructure, you can create a network security posture capable of automatically responding to threats and defending itself.

Tripwire

Tripwire scans files and directories on UNIX systems to create a snapshot record of their size, date, and signature hash. If you suspect an intrusion in the future, Tripwire will re-scan your server and report any changed files by comparing the file signatures to the stored record. Tripwire was an open-source project of Purdue University, but it continues development as a licensed package of Tripwire Security Systems, at www.tripwiresecurity.com. The original open-source version is at ftp://coast.cs.purdue.edu/pub/COAST/Tripwire.

Suck Server

Suck Server lets you establish port suckers on unused TCP/IP ports on your public Internet servers. Port suckers are server programs that simply record all the data sent to a specific port along with the IP address of the client that sent it.

Additional Security Tools

PART 5

This tells you when hackers are attempting to attach to your computer for services it does not provide, and tells you when your server has been port scanned by tools like Ping Pro. For instance, if you had a Web server that only allows connections on ports 21 (ftp) and 80 (web), you could run port suckers on otherwise unused ports that invite attack—like the NetBIOS session port (139) that hackers use to gain access to Windows computers. Suck Server will log the connection attempt and the data sent to these ports, so you can tell exactly what the hacker is trying to do by the data recorded in the log (Suck Server is available at www.24sevenbooks.com).

Suck Server is also capable of launching an external application each time a new hacking connection is established. This facility can alert you over the network using the net send command or run a program capable of paging you. Suck Server sends both the port being attacked and the IP address of the attacker to the external application. This facility alerts you to attacks when they first commence, so you can respond to them as they happen. It's the best chance you'll have of actually catching someone in the act.

WARNING 79% of all companies that have been hacked never find out that anything happened. Using a tool like Suck Server is often the only way to find out when your server is under siege.

To a hacker, ports with established port suckers appear as normal services when they perform a port scan. Then, when they attempt to establish a connection (with, for instance, the NetBIOS Auditing Tool or with a Telnet client), the service simply doesn't respond—it looks like a slow connection or a connection with broken routing. Nothing gives away the fact that it's actually a countermeasure tool.

Suck Server automatically drops connections (freeing up the memory and compute resources those particular connections use) after 60 seconds to keep hackers (who may realize what's happening) from flooding your server with connection attempts. Suck normally requires about 5MB of RAM, and we've been unable to allocate more than 20MB under very serious automated attacks.

Serious Intrusion

A friend of mine runs a network for a fairly large insurance firm, and they employ a number of sophisticated computers for both internal and external services. Being a cautious soul, he installed a number of intrusion detection and alerting systems on their public servers, but left the internal servers mostly alone, secure in the knowledge that their firewall would be able to block intruders from them.

One night at about 2:00 A.M., his pager went off and woke him up. He checked it; sure enough, it indicated an alert from the intrusion and service monitoring workstation that he used to monitor the servers and to collect intrusion data. Rather than indicating an intrusion attempt (his usual 2:00 a.m. wakeup), it indicated that one of the servers had gone down. Moments later, another page indicated that a second server had gone down.

He immediately booted his home computer and did a ping against his company's public Web server. Sure enough, it gave no response. He assumed that a power outage had occurred that was long enough to cause the uninterruptible power supplies to force a shutdown. They would come back online as soon as power was restored, so there was no point in his traveling to work to sit in the dark and wait for that to happen when he could just as easily sleep.

Then it occurred to him that the monitoring workstation wasn't on the UPS because he considered it expendable. The monitoring station should have gone down first because it's in the same room and runs from the same source circuit as the rest of the servers, but had no battery backup.

This panicked him. It meant that some serious environmental problem, perhaps a broken water main or even an earthquake had caused some of his servers to fail. He immediately got dressed and drove the 20 minutes to work.

As he pulled up, he noticed a large van pull out of the parking structure and drive right past him through the empty parking lot. As it went by, he noted that it had no rear license plate mounted, but had the name of a common carpet cleaning company on the side.

He immediately called the police from his cellular phone and reported the van. When he entered the parking complex and went up the stairs, he saw that the outside doors had been forced open and could hear the alarm system inside the building going off. However, he'd had no response from the facility alarm people.

Fearing the worst, he entered the server room. The place was completely destroyed. Servers, hubs, routers, and switches had all been stolen out of their racks. Some computers lay broken on the floor, having been dropped in the vandals' haste. The vandals hadn't even bothered to unplug network cords; they pulled the power cords out and used a hedge trimmer to cut the masses of network cables going to the expensive switches and hubs they used.

The only computer that remained untouched was the fairly cheap workstation he used to perform ping testing and alerting for all the other servers. Even the firewall had been stolen.

He immediately called the alarm company to ask them why nobody had been called about the alarm intrusion. The alarm company operator told him that a number of alarms in that area had been set off that night, so they were checking for a system failure. Disgusted, he called his boss to explain the situation and then left to go back home to bed.

On his way back to the freeway, he saw two police cars ahead on the side of the road with the carpet cleaning van pulled over. He pulled over in front of the police cars, and when the officer approached, he went back with him to the van and identified his equipment as the vandals sat in the back seats of the police cruisers.

Amazingly, the van was stuffed with far more expensive equipment than they owned. Servers were stacked on top of each other like so many boxes of fruit. The police were surprised when my friend told them that although some of the equipment was his, it certainly hadn't all come from his company. After making his statement and going through the necessary procedures for actually getting his equipment returned

(after it was entered into evidence), he went back home.

To make a long story short, it turned out that this van full of vandals had broken into nearly every company on that block, breaking open doors, going directly to equipment rooms, and then stealing network equipment. The numerous alarms that the alarm company had decided were spurious turned out to be real.

During the trial, in which my friend was a witness, it came out that one of the burglars worked for a janitorial service employed by the property management company that managed the entire block, which is how he'd identified which businesses had high value equipment and where it was located. Another vandal worked at a used computer store that would have acted as a fence for the equipment.

Despite all the destruction and time lost, all the recovered equipment actually worked when they got it back. Apparently, the bandits had wrapped each computer in eggcrate foam before stacking them to protect their resale value.

Though the alarm company completely failed in their obligation to alert the company, my friend's intrusion detection software actually came through in a most unexpected way.

Appendix

On-line Resources

Firewalls aren't necessarily easy to find; many administrators actually choose from the firewalls that they've discovered themselves rather than from a broad base of choices that represents the market. This list profiles the tools and vendors we've found to be useful in our security practice. The list is by no means exhaustive, but you can find solutions to most security problems by starting here.

The appendix is broken down into the following sections:

- Firewall software
- Intrusion detection software
- Security analysis software
- Encryption and authentication software
- Security organizations
- Hackers

Firewalls

Every firewall vendor profiled in this book maintains a Web site. Some change nearly daily—others have been static for over a year. Most provide downloadable demonstration software and technical support through their Web sites.

www.nai.com

Network Associates has a vast array of network security and intrusion detection software, including CyberCop intrusion detection, Gauntlet firewall, Sniffer, McAfee Virus Defense, and PGP VPN. This is the most highly integrated line of security tools available. The free PGP personal e-mail and disk encryption software is also available at this Web site.

www.cisco.com/security

Cisco's security products, including the PIX firewall and the IOS firewall modules for Cisco's routers, are profiled at this site. Cisco offers a Secure VPN client, the NetRanger intrusion detection system, the NetSonar security scanner, and links to consulting services.

www.lucent.com/security

Lucent's Web site discusses the Lucent VPN Gateway and the Lucent Managed firewall. The site has very nice graphics, but lacks any useful information.

www.sonicwall.com

Sonic Systems profiles their SonicWALL family of firewall appliances at this site, as well as their other small business Internet connectivity offerings. Though Sonic focuses primarily on marketing, the site does provide technical support.

www.netscreen.com

Netscreen's site describes the NetScreen 10 and 100 models of their firewall device. Technical support and contact information is easy to find here.

www.elronsoftware.com

Elron Software's Web site is the place to go if you subscribe to the philosophy that employee use of the Internet should be strongly monitored. Their CommandView product family, which includes the Elron firewall, offers two potent content policy enforcement and inspection applications: the Internet Manager content policy manager and Message Inspector e-mail filtering software. Elron Software also provides bandwidth optimization, Y2K solutions, and software metering applications.

www.gnatbox.com

Global Technology Associates provides downloadable demos and single-user licensed downloads of their inexpensive Gnat Box firewall at this Web site. The site is marketing oriented, and no non-firewall products are available here.

www.altavista.software.digital.com

AltaVista software, now a division of Compaq, offers their firewall, encrypted tunnel, and network search solutions through this Web site. Downloadable demos of all their software is available here, as is technical support.

www.milkyway.com

SLM Software has recently acquired Milkyway networks, but other than the banner graphic on the home page, the site hasn't changed much. This can be slightly annoying because numerous phone numbers don't work correctly on the contacts page. You can download an evaluation copy of their SecurIT firewall for Windows NT here. Solaris users are out of luck though—no demo is available for that platform.

www.watchguard.com

Watchguard offers their very compelling Firebox II firewall appliance, as well as a full suite of Internet security solutions called the LiveSecurity System. You can download a demo of their system from this site.

They have a bizarre "Call Me Now" link, in which you can enter your phone number to be immediately called back. It's somewhat disconcerting how quickly it calls, but you're immediately placed on hold anyway, so its advantage over a regular toll-free line is unfathomable. It's a great way to annoy unsuspecting people whose phone number you know, however.

www.checkpoint.com

Checkpoint, vendor of the best-selling Firewall-1 firewall, provides their marketing, sales, and technical support through this site. Downloadable demos are available, as are their VPN products and a number of security packages they re-label, such as ISS RealSecure.

www.netguard.com

You can download an evaluation copy of NetGuard's Guardian Firewall, now called the NetGuard Control Center because it includes a bandwidth metering application. Although NetGuard claims to provide technical support at this site, all they really provide in that venue is an e-mail link to support@ntguard.com.

www.axent.com

Axent has a broad line of network security and administration tools profiled on this site, in addition to their primary firewall product: Raptor. NetRecon provides security analysis. NetProwler and Intruder Alert provide intrusion detection and response. Raptor-Mobile is a firewall product for individual computers that don't have the benefit of perimeter defense. PowerVPN is Axent's encrypted tunnel solution, and Defender is their authentication solution, which is based on one-time passwords.

www.sun.com/security

Part of Sun's massive Web site, the security section contains links to their SunScreen firewall and VPN products. You can download copious amounts of documentation here, and although you can't download a demo, you can purchase their products directly from this site.

www.microsoft.com/proxy

Microsoft advertises its proxy server product at this location, which consists mostly of product comparisons and links to vendors who provide add-ons for proxy servers. You can download a 90-day evaluation edition here as well.

www.fwtk.org

This cool site is the main location for the open-source TIS FWTK suite of firewall proxy servers and related security applications. Although it's not for the faint of heart or the UNIX novice, you can literally "roll-your-own" strong firewall based on nearly any version of UNIX, including Linux or FreeBSD, with these tools. It's worth a look just for the documentation and tutorials.

drawbridge.tamu.edu

Drawbridge is a scriptable packet filter for FreeBSD developed at Texas A&M University, and is available at no charge. You can download it and all previous versions (2.0 ran on MS-DOS) from the linked FTP sites.

www.wingate.net

WinGate, a pure proxy that isn't a security filter, can be downloaded for evaluation at this site. You can also get support and purchase the product here as well.

Intrusion Detection

About half of the firewall vendors listed in the section above have intrusion detection offerings. These sites offer intrusion detection independent of these firewalls.

www.tripwiresecurity.com

Tripwire Security Systems, Inc. has taken the original open source Tripwire code and improved upon it to create a commercial package. Tripwire detects intrusions by comparing cryptographic hashes of system files on production systems against stored hashes made when the system files were known to be in a good state. This positively detects changes made by hackers in their attempts to reconfigure your system or introduce Trojan horses.

The original open-source version of Tripwire is located at: `ftp://coast.cs.purdue.edu/pub/COAST/Tripwire`

www.iss.net

Internet Security Systems was an early leader in the Windows NT intrusion detection market. Their flagship product, RealSecure, is re-labeled by a number of the firewall vendors listed in the first section including Checkpoint and Lucent. RealSecure provides client/server intrusion detection capability by running a detection agent on numerous machines. These agents report their status to a centralized management machine.

In addition to RealSecure, ISS offers the Internet Scanner, System Scanner, and Database Scanner security analysis tools. They also sell SAFEsuite Decisions, which is a cross platform security analysis tool that helps you identify security trends across different firewall platforms.

Security Analysis

Most firewall and intrusion detection vendors also have security analysis solutions. These vendors compete primarily in security analysis, or provide tools or services, which can be used to perform security analysis.

`www.powertech.no/smurf/`

The utility at this location will send a broadcast packet to the network you specify to determine whether or not it's vulnerable to the Smurf attack. It's important to test your ISP's network because a firewall cannot defend against this denial-of-service attack since the attack occurs outside your network. If the site reports that the network you've scanned exhibits the vulnerability that the Smurf attack exploits, you can inform your ISP so they can fix the problem.

`www.fish.com/~zen/satan/satan.html`

The Security Administrator Tool for Analyzing Networks (SATAN) was the original Internet security analysis tool. At its home page, you can download the original software and documentation. The site is a little out of date these days, but its historical importance is undeniable—hackers used it to perpetrate numerous security breaches, thus spurring the firewall industry and security software industries into high gear.

`www.ipswitch.com`

IPSwitch, makers of numerous useful TCP/IP applications, have an IP scanning tool called WS Ping ProPack that makes it easy to find extraneous services running inside your networks. Best of all, it's very inexpensive. You can download a demo from their site.

Encryption and Authentication

Encryption and authentication resources on the Internet are rather hard to find, due mostly to U.S. Government restrictions on encryption export. Since it's difficult to control geographical distribution of a Web site, most encryption technologies offered by U.S. vendors can't be provided over the Internet. That's a big reason why most VPN products aren't integrated into firewalls, and why most of the operations listed below either operate entirely outside the U.S. or maintain their headquarters outside the U.S.

www.securitydynamics.com

SecurityDynamics is the product end of the RSA Data Security consulting company created by the developers of the RSA public key encryption algorithm. SecurityDynamics provides the SecurID line of security authentication products, which works with the ACE/Server product to provide strong encrypted authentication for network access. Security-Dynamics has also purchased the formerly independent Kane Security Analyst, which provides security analysis for Windows NT.

www.thawte.com

Thawte is the second largest Root Certificate Authority (behind VeriSign) in the world. Root Certificate Authorities certify the identity of those who use certificates they've issued, so you can trust the contents of a certified Internet transaction if you trust the Root CA. Certificates are currently required to establish SSL connections, to use the S/MIME based encryption functions of Outlook and Netscape Mail, and to digitally sign Active-X controls.

Unlike VeriSign, Thawte provides personal-use S/MIME certificates for encrypted e-mail at no cost. Having a trusted certificate makes it possible for you to sign and encrypt e-mail easily. Thawte performs this survey through a Web site interview, which although not entirely secure, is adequate for most routine security requirements.

PGP provides a different (incompatible) "grass roots" method (pardon the pun) of proving identity: You create your key and post it on their Web server, allowing others who presumably know you to sign it with their own keys, thus attesting to your identity.

sunsite.auc.dk/vpnd/

VPND is the maintenance site for the Virtual Private Network Daemon, a public domain open source VPN implementation for Linux that relies on the Blowfish algorithm for strong security.

www.xs4all.nl/~freeswan/

FreeS/WAN is an implementation of the IPSec and IKE (Internet Key Exchange) protocols for Linux. You can download the latest releases from this site. The encryption algorithms used for all S/WAN implementations are Triple-DES, RSA, and Diffie-Hellman. Although full interoperability with other vendors is in the works, FreeS/WAN currently operates only with other manually configured Linux FreeS/WAN implementations.

tcfs.dia.unisa.it

TCFS, the Transparent Cryptographic File System, is a client/server encrypted file system for Linux based on selectable CBC-DES, IDEA, or RC5. TCFS was developed by the Dipartimento di Informatica ed Applicazioni of the Universita di Salerno. The Transparent Cryptographic File System allows keys to be exchanged transparently to end-users.

Security Organizations

Security organizations provide neither tools nor firewalls—they provide information about security. Most of these organizations provide mailing lists that can inform you of important new security problems shortly after they become public. This is considerably easier than trying to browse thousands of hacker Web sites looking for trouble. Some are non-provide collaborations of security professionals, others are for-profit organizations that provide informative security services as a marketing tool.

www.sans.org

SANS (System Administration, Networking, and Security) Institute is a security training organization that maintains a Web site and mailing list dedicated to security.

www.cert.org

The Computer Emergency Response Team (CERT) Coordination Center studies Internet-based security problems and assists victims of new types of Internet attacks in order to study the effects of the attack. They then issue advisories on the nature of the attack and what measures can be taken to prevent it. The primary purpose of CERT (an operation of Carnegie-Mellon University's Software Engineering Institute) is to rapidly investigate new security breaches and disseminate corrective information in order to stem the tide of broad-based automated attacks like worms, viruses, and Trojan horses. It was created in response to the infamous Internet Worm of 1988. All serious security administrators should be on the CERT mailing list (and should validate their PGP signature—forged CERT advisories have been circulated).

www.icsa.net

ICSA, a commercial entity derived from the National Computer Security Association, certifies the security and the claims of various security products like firewalls, virus scanners, and intrusion detection software. ICSA is a commercial enterprise; vendors pay to be certified, so you wouldn't find certification of open-source systems even if they were secure. ICSA certification is also not an indicator of total security—it's merely an indicator that the product passed ICSA's test suite for that product type. Their certified products page makes a good starting point to explore the various commercial options in security software.

www.ntsecurity.net

NTSecurity's Web site is probably the best place to go to stay on top of current Windows NT hacks and security risks. The site is easy to navigate and targeted to keeping NT security administrators on top of hacking activity as it pertains to Windows NT. If you use NT, you should check this site weekly!

www.microsoft.com/security

Microsoft releases its advisories, patches, refutations, and excuses at this site. If you use Microsoft software, you need to stay on top of security issues at this site.

www.trustedsystems.com

Trusted Systems Services has grown out of one man's security consulting practice. TSS evaluates and reports on Windows NT security for numerous organizations (including Microsoft). They have a suite of security tools that perform Windows NT Security analysis, administration, and maintenance.

Hackers

Most hacking cabals maintain a Web site somewhere, but because of their illegal trade in pirated software and copyrighted material, these sites are not publicized outside the hacking community and must be found with search engines. To find these sites, search on the words "hackz," "warez," and "crackz," but beware that Trojan horses and viruses abound in executable software available at these sites.

Legitimate hackers (those that do not break the law) maintain permanent Web sites and act as something of an information intermediary between the media and the hacking realm.

www.10pht.com

L0pht Heavy Industries is the media's favorite hacking cabal. Vaulted into hacking stardom with their NT Crack software, which decrypts encrypted passwords stored in the Windows NT Registry, these guys have shown up on television and in the media as advocates for security, privacy, and the rights of the common hacker. And they have a pretty cool Web site.

www.thecodex.com

A very interesting security and privacy advocacy site which has (at www.thecodex.com/hacking.html) a very good index into the hacking netherworlds. It makes an excellent portal for both understanding the motivations of serious hackers and for exploring the "netherweb."

www.2600.com

2600 was the original hacker 'zine (fan magazine) back when the only effective way to distribute information to the masses was on paper. Currently 2600 maintains a "recently hacked" list and acts as an advocate of hackers' rights. There's nothing but news and a few FAQs at this site however, so actual hackers rarely visit it.

Index

Note to the Reader: Throughout this index **boldfaced** page numbers indicate primary discussions of a topic. *Italicized* page numbers indicate illustrations.

Index

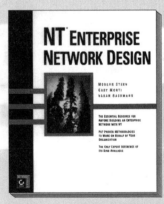

Become an Expert in Microsoft BackOffice

with 24seven books from Network Press

- This new series offers the advanced information you need to keep your systems and networks running 24 hours a day, seven days a week.
- On-the-job case studies provide solutions to real-world problems.
- Maximize your system's uptime—and go home at 5!
- $34.99; 7½" x 9"; 544–704 pages; softcover

How to...